A Matter of Perspective

Sarasha sighed. "You deal with horses all the time, right?"

"My whole life." Kendra raised her eyebrows. "Why?"

"Did it ever occur to you that horses are huge and powerful, yet you have to be so careful with them because one little thing can ruin them, make them completely ineffective, or even kill them?"

"I noticed."

"I find people very much the same."

Until the peals of laughter rang out, Sarasha didn't realize that she had said anything funny.

OCEAN OF GRASS

PETRELLAN SAGA 1

Gordon A. Long

AIRBORN PRESS
Delta, B. C.

Ocean of Grass

Gordon A. Long

Published by
Airborn Press
4958 10A Ave, Delta, B. C.
V4M 1X8
Canada

ISBN: 978-1-988898-09-4
Printed by CreateSpace

Cover Design by Mihaela Voicu

More from Gordon A. Long

Other Titles Available at Smashwords, Amazon and other outlets

"Zoysana's Choice" Petrellan Saga Book 4
"The Innkeeper's Husband" Petrellan Saga Book 5

"Out of Mischief" World of Change Book 1
"Into Trouble" World of Change Book 2
"Mountains of Mischief" World of Change Book 3
"The Trouble with Tents" World of Change Book 4
"Queen of Mischief" World of Change Book 5

"A Sword Called...Kitten?" Cat with Many Claws Book 1
"The Cat with Many Claws" Book 2
"Cloud Cat" A Cat with Many Claws Tale
"Sword Called Kitten: The Early Years" Short Stories

"Storm over Savournon"
A novel of the French Revolution

"Why Are People So Stupid?" Social Humour with a Point

Look for Gordon's books, selected reviews, poetry and short stories at <airbornpress.ca>

Gordon's opinions on humanity are at the
"Are People Really That Stupid?" blog

Find his weekly reviews and his ideas on writing at
"Renaissance Writer"

CONTENTS

"Doing your duty for your Family and Crew brings the greatest fulfillment."

"Can I quote you on that?" Leide reached for a pen.

"Don't you dare."

– From "The Teachings of Sarasha the Lame" by Kendie Palawan

1. Suicide

Sarasha dragged the bowstring back and loosed another shaft, cursing when a gust of wind wafted the arrow aside from its intended victim to drive harmlessly into the deck of the approaching Mastership. Tugging her bandana down to dry the sweat from her forehead, she glanced at her dwindling supply of ammunition as she nocked the next one, then peered down, searching for another target.

There were plenty to choose from. The bowcastle of the approaching Mastership bristled with archers, sailors, and the surging throng of its boarding party, screaming and stamping, preparing themselves to swarm over the rail and down onto the deck of the *Sea Eagle* when the hooked ram pierced her hull.

"Come on, stand still a moment. It's just a little battle. You look like idiots, jumping up and down like that. I just want to stick an itty-bitty arrow...right...there!" Her remaining three arrows hit their marks, but the boarding party closed over the injured as if her efforts meant nothing.

As she retied her bandana over her unruly hair, Sarasha allowed herself a brief glance aft to where her father stood at the *Eagle*'s helm, swinging the big wheel over. From her high vantage in the foremast crow's-nest, she could see there was no chance. In the crush of battling Ships there was scarce room to maneuver, and the *Sea Eagle* responded sluggishly, despite the spread of battle canvas surging her through the water.

Slowly, painfully slowly, the *Eagle*'s bow edged away, but the metal-sheathed battle ram of the huge Mastership tracked her. Four cables of choppy water between the two Ships became three, then two. Fascinated, Sarasha let her useless bow sag in her hands as she watched her Familyship's doom run down upon her. *What's wrong? Why doesn't the* Eagle *respond?* She turned to Priest-Captain Tourn again, standing stock-still at the wheel, his eyes roaming from the sea to the

1

sails, but always returning to the death bearing down on his Ship. She pounded the rail of the crow's-nest in frustration. *What is he doing? He doesn't even have the helm all the way over!*

Then her father made his move, and it all became clear.

Just when the collision was imminent, when the bolder Raiders of the boarding party balanced precariously on the rail of the *Wolverine*'s high bowcastle, eager to swoop down on their prey, her father shouted a command and spun the wheel to port.

The foresails below Sarasha flapped, and the Ship, released from their pressure, spun far faster than any Captain had a right to expect. Instead of presenting her side to her attacker, she spun her bow into the collision so the rams of the two boats met at an angle. As they slid across each other, the bowsprits tangled, tearing rigging and spars from both Ships and sending splinters and flailing canvas in all directions, but mostly down onto the boarding parties.

After that, Sarasha had no time to watch. The jar of the collision whipped the *Eagle*'s mast forward and she clung to the rail, her right arm wrapped through a rope-end. Then a sharp crack sounded behind her. Horrified, she glanced back to see the maintopmast toppling forward. She threw herself frantically away, but the crows-nest gave her no room. The huge spar leaned into the foretop on her side, slithering down upon her. There was a rending crash, and fiery pain shot through her right leg.

For a stunned moment, Sarasha stood there. Somehow, she was still on her feet. Her bow was gone, but it was useless now. She scrabbled away the tangle of ropes and torn canvas and started to climb clear, but was stopped by agonizing pain in her ankle.

She looked down. The maintopmast had missed her, but her foot was pinned under its bulk. She carefully tried again, but the pain returned. Gritting her teeth, she took hold of her leg below the knee and pulled. Nothing moved, but a stab of agony dropped her to the planks.

This made the pain worse, and she struggled back up. Placing her weight on her good foot, she stared around. Crashes continued to shake the Ship as spars and pieces of rigging showered down to the deck far below. The foretopmast still stood, held up by one inner forestay that had miraculously escaped the ravaging prow of the larger warship.

The two vessels remained locked together, and far below, the boarding parties clawed towards each other with single-minded purpose. More attackers scrambled down from the other Ship. It was only a matter of time before Sarasha's people, fighting in the tangle of the bowcastle, would be outnumbered and overrun. After that, the Ship was done.

Then, through the crashes and screams and the howl of the wind, came a familiar voice:

"Foretop!"

She twisted to peer back and down to her father, still at the wheel, his face tilted up to her.

"Back the foretops'ls."

She understood. The wreckage had cut control of the yards from the deck, but if she could back the sails, the wind would push the bow of the *Eagle* away from the other Ship. The weight of men jumping from the *Wolverine* onto the *Eagle*, plus the rush of the *Eagle*'s own party forward, had lowered the smaller Ship's bow, and the huge Mastership had risen enough that the *Eagle*'s ram could slide out from under the downward hook of the other Ship's beak. Sarasha struggled again to free herself, but was again decked by the pain.

"I'm stuck! My foot!"

Her father's head came up, and she screamed her message down to him again, pointing at her foot, making a futile pushing motion against the spar that held it trapped.

He left the wheel, staring upward, oblivious to the chaos around him, scanning the rigging for other crewmembers. There was no one near. Then he held up his hands and tilted his body to the right, the signal for "heel to starboard." She returned him an enthusiastic positive.

3

He raised a hand to her, "message received," and returned to the wheel, calling instructions to the handful of sailors aft who still stood to their posts. They hauled in on the sheets; the spars on the upper mizzenmast, uninjured by the collision, creaked around. The huge mizzen boom inched to windward. One by one, the sails caught the wind, and the Ship heeled ever so slightly to starboard. There was a brief, sharp pain in her ankle, and then she was free.

She tossed a "thank you" gesture to the Priest-Captain and scrabbled her way into the rigging. Once her feet left the planks, her hands took over and she moved out smoothly, swinging from rope to rope, her practiced eye surveying the wreckage, tracing intact lines, assessing broken spars. It took longer than she wanted, with her people dying down on the deck and more enemy boarding each moment, but finally she had a network of sheets snagged together. Swinging out to the end of the tops'l yard, she signalled to the deck below.

"Haul away the upper sta'b'd sheets!"

The deck crew responded with desperate strength, and she watched anxiously as the belaboured foremast pivoted, its spars dragging the detritus of the maintop with them.

But all held, and then the wind caught. The Ship heeled as the high sails took the strain. There was more grinding and ripping, and then the injured *Eagle* began tearing herself free.

Sarasha saw the problem before her father's shout could reach her. Grabbing that last remaining forestay, she slung herself below it, her useless leg dragging beneath her, and slid forward and down to where a twisted web of rope held the *Eagle* tangled in the rigging of the larger Ship. Her knife was hacking the moment she reached the first line, and she clove her way downward, leaving a widening gap in the jumble above her.

As she worked, a new danger threatened. She was sliding down towards the struggling mass of soldiers on deck, and an archer from the *Wolverine* had spotted her plan. She kept moving, aided by the swing of the Ship, but his arrows buzzed uncomfortably near. As long as they kept missing...

4

Then a lurch, and the *Eagle* was free. A wild cry of despair went up from the *Wolverine*'s boarding party, drowned by a wave of cheering from the Eagles who stormed forward, pinning their trapped enemy against the forward rails, hewing them down.

Sarasha pried her gaze away from the slaughter, scanning for danger upwind, but the *Wolverine* had problems of her own. Her forestays were down, and she was forced to bear off the wind to keep the pressure from her masts. This left the *Eagle* room to maneuver. Sarasha clambered painfully back aloft, scanning the thinning pack of Ships around them.

The battle was not going well for the rebels. The superior tonnage of the Priest-Admiral's fleet had taken its toll. She looked below, to where her father snapped orders to the Signals page. Soon the flag she had hoped never to see crawled up the mizzen signal halyard. It was black, unrelieved by any other emblem.

"*Beach the Fleet.*"

Horrified, she gazed around the battle again and understood. She had sat with the rebel Priest-Captains at their final Conclave, scribing their grim words. This was their last stand. If they could not break through the Priest-Admiral's blockade, they would take the only freedom available: the land. The unthinkable solidity of rock.

Tears blurring her vision, she began to cobble together whatever canvas she found, cannibalizing the lines from the torn sails, patching what she could. She knew they needed all the power they could scrape up. Her father had reconnoitered the shoreline in the preceding days, and he knew the exact point to run aground, where the receding tide would leave them with access to land. She remembered his bitter laugh the day before.

"That's one place they won't dare follow us, one order the Priest-Admiral won't dare give. There'd be Fleet-wide mutiny!"

A younger Priest-Captain, Tory of the *Osprey*, nodded. "Especially to follow some of their own people."

5

Priest-Captain Tourn shook his head sadly. "We aren't their own people any more, Tory. We're heretics."

There was glum silence at that, broken by her father's hand slapping the table. "No matter which way it goes, we'll be free of the Masterships and their tyranny."

There were brightening nods, and the meeting broke up on a lifting note.

Now, the moment had come. The wounded *Sea Eagle* heeled under the force of the increased sail, straining towards the threatening, rocky coastline. Two of the lumbering Masterships of the Priest-Admiral turned to cut her off, but Priest-Captain Tourn had an answer for them. Four funeral lanterns - huge, fragile pots of volatile fluid - were brought on deck, their oiled wicks lighted. With straining muscles, the sailors hoisted them aloft to hang out to either side on the longest spars fore and aft. The *Eagle* had made her intentions clear. If any Ship grappled with her, the torches would drop, immolating both vessels in a suicidal inferno.

Sure enough, the Masterships sheered away, and an open lane appeared.

Sarasha stood as straight as she could, tears streaming as she watched her father preside over the death of his beloved *Eagle*. Standing stiffly, his the only hand on the helm, he steered her, perfectly straight as ever, towards her doom. The dying Ship responded as she always had, cleaving the water cleanly, riding smoothly, as proud in her final moment of defeat as she had been in all her victories.

Once they were clear of the battle, however, her father handed the wheel to Chan, his Chief Helmsman. Issuing orders in his calm voice, he strode the deck. The funeral lanterns were hauled down, their oil poured into leather bags. The *Eagle's* crew was going ashore, and nothing would be wasted. Plans, long prepared in the apprehension of disaster, now swung into action. The elderly and the young filed on deck clutching their personal belongings and mustered silently to their stations. Sarasha watched as if from a dream, her high vantage giving it all a surreal aspect.

She lifted her gaze. Seven other rebel Ships were breaking free, arrowing for the rocky beach. A huge cloud of black smoke rose to the south, where the Masterships had called the old *Condor*'s bluff. The ancient warship had taken two of the enemy with her to her grave. Sarasha watched numbly, unable to find sadness in the midst of this upheaval.

Her lower right leg had become a mass of hot throbbing. Without another task, she had to look at it. The shoe had been torn off, ripping the skin, but she could see no bone sticking through and there was blood, but not much . *I suppose that's a good sign. The Surgeon will tell me the rest, but I have faint hope. It feels really mashed.*

A grinding noise beside her drew her sharp glance. The broken maintop had started to move with the rhythm of the waves. Now, it was imperative that nothing should change the delicate balance that kept the dying Ship on her course. Sarasha gathered broken line and lashed the fragment as securely as she could to the foremast. The grinding slowed, then stopped, as she wrapped rope after rope around the two spars.

When she had finished, she glanced down again. The deck was returning to its usual order, save for the chaos of the broken bowsprit.

"Mast'n to the deck!" The Priest-Captain's voice cut through the bustle as it always did. Sarasha began her painful scramble down, seeing only four figures in the rigging: herself on the foremast, one on the main, and two on the undamaged mizzen. It had been a long, hard-fought battle, starting at dawn when the rebel fleet had broken from shelter and tried to force a way through the encircling blockade. Enemy archers and battle damage had taken the rest of the high rigging crew. She hoped some of them were on the deck already.

She also hoped they had good reason to be there. No sailor deserted his post in battle and lived to celebrate with the Ship.

She reached the rail and stood, weight on her good foot, balanced by a hand on the ratlines. Instead of that last, graceful leap to the deck, she had to climb down carefully. Then she stood still again, leaning on the rail, wondering what to do now.

"Mast'n to the helm."

She eyed the rods of bare deck between her and her father. Hop? Crawl? Her dignity seemed the only thing she had left. Then a hand gripped her elbow.

"Need a lean?"

She glanced over her shoulder. "Yong! Where were you?"

The boy grinned down at her from his considerable height. "The maintop almost got me. I was out on the end of a yard that broke. I had no choice but to ride her down. Dropped me in the middle of the battle on the bowcastle."

She tried to check him over. "How did you get through that?"

"Luck." He tossed his mop of black hair aside. "I landed right on top of one of them, flattened him, grabbed his sword and got in the fight. Next thing I knew, a bunch of canvas swept across the deck right on top of me. By the time I got untangled we were swinging clear, so I helped mop up the boarders and tried to get some order on the bowsprit." He held out a hand. "Coming?"

"As long as you're not expecting a hornpipe."

They reached the Priest-Captain and stood in a broken row. His quick glance assayed their condition. "There's no hurry now, but I want to run her in as far as I can. That means we take time to prepare, then pile on the sail at the last moment. She'll hit hard, with the waves lifting her. I want no one in the rigging at that time, in case another mast goes down. Sarasha, are you fit? Can you go aloft?"

"Slowly, sir."

"Then you take the mid on the foremast, and Yong can do the foretop. Firm it up, bend on all the canvas that still works. You two," he indicated the next sailors in the line, "get as many of the lower mains'ls ready to unfurl as you can. Pers, you could splice that crack in the mizzen boom if you can find a piece of spar long enough. All of you keep an eye out for weak spots. There'll be the gods' own crash no matter what, and we have a lot of people on deck. Keep in mind that the pressure will be forward, but there might be a whiplash back. Bosun!"

"Aye, sir!"

"You heard their orders. Two men on deck for each one aloft. You supervise the main and keep an eye on the mizzen. Sarasha will call the fore. Carry on."

There was a ragged chorus of "Aye, sir," and the sailors sprinted for the ratlines. Yong helped Sarasha forward to the rail, where she pushed him ahead.

"You get up there. Start by doubling the lower aft stay; the upper aft went with the maintopmast. Replace the upper stay if you can. I want to check it over from down here first." She turned to the two deckmen. "Yong needs you to watch the halyards. Any that aren't working sails, he'll be using to stay the mast. Figure them out while he climbs. I'll call you when I need you."

They nodded and spun to their tasks, and she turned to regard her mast.

The foremast was a sorry jumble. The foretop was cleaned off on the port side where the other spar had scraped down. All the rope and canvas from that collision lay atop her crow's-nest, along with the splinters of the yards. Cleaning those up would be Yong's next task. She worked herself up into the forward rigging, her eye tracking the lines she would need. Most of the jib halyards were still in place, and if she could tie them off on what was left of the bowsprit...

"Twenty cables to shore. Spread all sail!"

She looked up from her work, muttering a curse. The rocks seemed much closer than that.

"Mark ten fathoms!" A leadsman had found a clear space on the bow to swing his sounding line.

The bosun strode into sight below her, with two deckmen. "We're done aft, Foremaster Tourn. We're to help you."

I've been promoted. That won't last long. Not if the Surgeon's word is against me. She pushed that thought aside and started giving orders. Soon, every possible piece of canvas

9

she could carry plunged the *Eagle* towards the unforgiving shore.

At three cables from the rocks and in four fathoms of water, the Priest-Captain ordered all hands out of the rigging. The Crew stood on deck, clinging fast to whatever they could, mesmerized by the shoreline approaching closer and closer.

A rugged skirting of rocks fronted a sloping beach of sand dunes. Beyond them, a smooth green expanse stretched towards the horizon, the grass rippling in the gusts of wind. The Great Prairie. Their new home.

With a dull scraping sound, the graceful forward motion of the Ship hesitated, then continued. Lifted by the next wave, she sailed calmly on towards her doom.

The next one wasn't so easy; the wave dropped out from under her, and she crashed into an underwater reef. A shudder ran from the keel upwards, and debris rained to the deck. There were a few sharp cries from the children, but no other sound. Another wave, and she was lifted onward. A splintering from aft told the destruction of the rudder, and the wheel spun in the Priest-Captain's hands.

"Sheet trimmers stand by."

Steering the Ship by sails alone was a skill in which her father had some pride. It was perhaps fitting that the *Eagle* should end her life so. Under the Priest-Captain's quiet orders, the sailors trimmed their lines: now tightening, now slacking, and the crippled bow again pointed towards the rocks.

When the end came, every soul on board felt it. A larger wave lifted the *Eagle*, but instead of falling, she continued to climb out of the water in a long, slow slide that rose and rose until the bow pointed far above the horizon. The screech and grind of protesting timbers intensified, then died away.

"Haul in the mizzen. Loose all foresails. Harden the mainsheets to port." The change in pressure slewed the stern around, and the Ship settled sideways to the shore, listing towards the rocks she had spent her lifetime cheating.

Sarasha was thrown, her injured foot striking the deck, and hot fire raced up her leg. She found herself doubled over the rail, staring down at white surf boiling around the hull. A grinding, crunching sound arose from deep inside the Ship, the planks twisting beneath her feet. The bow began to drop, but the stern stayed fixed on the rocks. A jagged line splintered across the deck, beams punching up like bones through skin. With a grinding roar, the foremast tore free of its stays and toppled, descending in a mass of flaying lines, ribbonned canvas and broken spars.

There was a sudden, awful, stillness, disturbed only by the rumble of the receding waves and the cry of a gull. Sarasha stared at her mast, the mainstay of her life, lying across the bowcastle. Her topmast, with the maintop still lashed beside it, rested...

...on the rocks! Cursing her injury, she hauled herself forward along the rail. "Mast'n forward. Lash her down!"

Generations of training paid off; nobody questioned her order. Everyone leaped to do her bidding. They hacked off the twined rigging and shards of the crow'snest, lashing the fallen masts firmly in place. She sent a party out along their length to clear away loose ends and splinters. When she was satisfied, she turned to the Helm with the traditional call.

"Gangplank secure, sir. Ready for lading."

The Priest-Captain's mouth twisted in irony, but his only response was a nod to the bosun. The officer strode forward, his voice ringing out. "Abandon Ship routine. Portside Families forward will begin!"

With quiet precision, the crew of the *Eagle* filed out along the masts, carrying their assigned possessions. They moved surely, showing little emotion as they trekked down the slope to the rocks. There, the orderly line scattered as they continued inland, clambering over the ridges that lined the shore.

A shout from ahead signalled a better path, and soon the speed of the evacuation picked up. Sarasha leaned against the rail, wondering what she could do. A familiar voice caught her ear.

"Permission to adjust procedure, sir."

What is Yong doing?

11

"Is your assigned task covered?"

"Aye, sir."

She craned her head around. Her father and her friend regarded her.

"Permission granted, Yong." The Captain nodded to the bosun. "One deck hand."

The bosun pointed to a man about Yong's height, and the two sailors stepped toward her.

"Let's go, 'Rasha. Time for shore leave." Yong grinned at her, but his lips curled down.

She slid her arms over their shoulders, and they easily boosted her wiry frame across the deck. It was no difficult matter for the sailors to walk as wide a path as two masts with so light a burden, and they made quick work of it.

Soon they were on a sandy path winding inland. They had not even set her down for a breather when they reached the first refuge. Deep in the tangle of rocks and sand that fronted the beach, in an easily-defended swale, the Crew-Families were setting up temporary shelters of sailcloth organized into specific areas: supplies, families, injured, cooking. Yong and the other sailor, a Shipwright's helper that Sarasha did not know well, deposited her in the line of wounded outside the Surgeon's tent and returned to the Ship to continue the final off-loading. With a pang, Sarasha knew she would never sail in the *Eagle* again. She would certainly never walk her deck.

The Surgeon's Assistant checked her over briefly and determined that her injury was not lifethreatening. He gave her a potion to ease the pain and moved on. She wriggled herself a hollow in the sand, lay back and drowsed.

Screaming pain awoke her.

The Surgeon, a gruff, clean-shaven man who had never spoken to her before, observed her face as he manipulated her ankle. "Hurts?"

She gritted her teeth, not trusting her voice, and merely nodded. Cold sweat broke out on her brow, and nausea churned her stomach. His fingers prodded, producing a lesser pain overlying the background throbbing caused by the original movement. She could not bear to see the swollen, bleeding, mangled mass at the end of her leg, so she watched the Surgeon's face closely. The next word he said might be the one that sealed her fate. She also watched his right hand. If he reached for his scalpel, it would be even sooner.

To her relief and dismay he shook his head, but he did not speak to her. He gave thorough instructions to his Assistant, and was gone before Sarasha got up the courage to ask the question.

The Assistant immediately got to work, binding her ankle firmly in a wide cloth bandage. When he had finished, he propped her leg up on a rolled blanket, nodded to her and went about his business.

She regarded this new development. At least it was better than before. It was a neat, white bundle, with only her bruised big toe sticking out the end. She could bring herself to regard it in a drowsy way. Gradually, the pain faded as the drug reasserted its hold on her.

She was just waking when her mother stumbled, disheveled, dirty and exhausted, into the refuge. "How goes it, daughter?"

Sarasha slowly raised her eyelids, then her head. Verlene's dark hair stood out in coils and a smudge of oil covered her cheek. "Mother. You look like a rough day of fishing, and you were the bait."

The older woman dragged out a smile and reached out to pat Sarasha's own dark curls into place. "Well, at least you sound normal. How is the foot? Your father told me."

Sarasha shook her head. "The Surgeon wasn't too happy, Mother. He frowned and shook his head."

Verlene winced, then smoothed her face. "He has a lot to deal with right now, none of it happy."

"Happy or not, it still isn't good, Mother." Sarasha shrugged. "I don't see myself running any races soon. Or ever."

"Is it that bad?"

"You didn't see it when it was unwrapped. Like last year's salt cod."

Her mother slid down beside her, a strong arm around her shoulders. "Don't worry, dear. There won't be any decisions made in a hurry. Not about an injury like this, and not in this situation."

Sarasha frowned. "I was just thinking. If we have to move in a hurry, I'm definitely excess tonnage."

Verlene gave her daughter a small shake. "Don't think like that. We won't be moving in a hurry."

"Won't the Priest-Admiral send a shore party?"

"So far, he hasn't. We gave the Fleet quite a tearing. The *Condor* took two Masterships down with her."

Tears prickled behind Sarasha's eyelids. "She was a fine old Ship."

"One of the best in the Fleet. They were fools to divide us. They've lost a great deal."

"Not as much as we have." She peered down at her foot, then out at the orderly camp, the tired, dejected people.

"Sarasha, we all agreed. It was a life we could not bear. We knew there was a chance we would lose the good as well, but it couldn't be helped. The tyranny afloat was worse than being ashore."

"We went over that often enough." A brief memory flashed through her mind: her pride at the brave array of their little fleet as they sailed into the uneven battle this morning.

Her mother's back straightened. "Standing up against tyranny was the best thing we've ever done. No matter where it ended us."

Sarasha studied her bandaged lump. "You may be ashore, but I may be Beached."

Again, her mother shook her. "Don't borrow trouble before it happens. You just lie there and think getting-well thoughts. I have some things to do."

"Haven't you done enough for a while?"

Her mother smiled wearily. "When the watches are set, and the Families are in their Cab-... their tents asleep, then I rest."

Sarasha reached up and squeezed her mother's hand. "Priest-Captain's wife as always."

"I know it's been hard on you, Sara."

"Never regretted it a moment. Not since I was old enough to understand what it meant."

"Thank you, Sarasha." Her mother gave her a final squeeze, then turned away and clambered slowly to her feet. Not before Sarasha noticed the tears glistening on her cheek in the rays of the dying sun.

2. BEACHED

The following days were a blur to Sarasha. The Surgeon's Assistant continued the doses of potion, which deadened the pain but also killed all her feelings and her interest in what was happening around her. He sounded pleased that there was no more swelling. She clung to that small solace in her waking moments. Someone moved her to a bunk in her Family tent: not a bunk, but blankets on the soft sand, which became hard if she lay in one position for any length of time.

Yong and Pers visited often, telling her what was going on, but she couldn't remember what they told her. She did recall the alarms and shouts when a probing landing party from the Fleet was repelled. She woke up fully for that one, grasping her dagger and sitting up in bed. Then the shouts faded, as did her awareness. All the rest was lost in a hazy dream where her leg took on huge, throbbing dimensions, dominating her whole being. Somehow, it became a separate entity, and she was Beached: alone with no one but this massive, painful companion.

She awoke one morning aware that she felt different. The Surgeon's Assistant was there, unwrapping her foot. He glanced up from his task to see that she was awake, and nodded to her. "We'll just have another look at this. The pain seems to be better."

"It does?"

A wan smile. "I've been reducing your pain-killing dose the last two days. Haven't you noticed?"

"I feel like I slept properly, now that you mention it." She stretched her arms, dismayed at how weak they felt.

The Assistant unwrapped the binding, gently tugging where the ends had stuck to the healing flesh. It took a soaking in warm water, but finally the last bandage came free, and her injury emerged into the daylight.

It wasn't good.

Her foot was mottled blue, yellow and green from above her ankle to the tips of her toenails, with especial darkness between the toes and under the anklebone. She grimaced.

"Don't worry. That's only the bruising. It will go away. No infection. Can you move your toes?"

Sarasha had a vague memory of him asking that before, but couldn't recall the result. She clenched her toes and was rewarded by a spike of pain and a small tremor in her foot. Gritting her teeth, she tried again, slower this time. Her big toe definitely moved: once, twice, then again, until the tears streamed down her face.

His hand on her shoulder brought the trial to an abrupt stop. "Don't try too hard. It works. That's a good sign." Then he grasped her whole foot in both hands. "Can you move the ankle? Push against my hand."

This time the pain was worse, with less result. Once again, he stopped her when the tears flowed. He moved the ankle himself, watching her face.

"Let me know when it hurts. Otherwise I can't judge your progress."

She felt her lip curl. "It always hurts. There's only less and more."

He smiled again, that tired lifting of one corner of his mouth. "Then let me know when it hurts more."

"It hurts more when you move it side to side. Up and down is painful, but not so bad."

His nod brought a stab of hope to her heart. "I'll just wrap it up again, not so tight this time, now that there's less worry of swelling." He suited actions to his words, then shot her a piercing glance. "Do not put any weight on it at this time. That is an Order."

Hearing the authority in his voice, she searched for a witty retort, but her mind failed her. "Aye, sir."

He nodded, finished his job and left. She leaned back in her bed, aware now of her surroundings. The sun shone through the canvas, making the tent a bright, airy place, like lying in the crow's-nest. Fresh stitching on faded canvas showed that the

17

Sailmakers had been working hard to create new accommodation. Now that she was aware, the old outlines of a hatch cover showed in the ceiling of her shelter.

Another stab of reality pierced her. She had ordered the wreckage of her crow's-nest cleared from the fallen mast so the Families could leave the dying Ship. A grin twisted her lips. She had been promoted to Foremaster, then watched her mast fall, along with her promotion, less than a glass later.

She grieved the loss of her mast. The foremast crow's-nest had been her sanctuary, away from the closeness of the Families, the careful coldness of other children, the delicate course she had to sail: always the Priest-Captain's daughter; never accepted, ever feared.

She had loved the new forward rake of the mast, which had moved her refuge out closer to the bow. Many hours she had spent staring straight down at the sea frothing around the forefoot, the dolphins splashing and squirming ahead. The rake had been her father's idea. He had shortened the bowsprit as well, and while the Ship had lost its former long, racy lines, it moved the whole rigging forward and straightened up the luff of the foresails, giving them better draw to windward. The Priest-Admiral had not liked the idea that a mere Familyship could sail closer to the wind than his Mastership. Her father and the other captains who had followed his lead were ordered, upon threat of Beaching, to put their Ships back into "Traditional Form." When they refused, they were branded heretics, and the power of the whole Fleet was turned against them.

So here we are, Beached after all.

And that was the lesser of her problems. She glared down at the bundled foot in front of her. If the foot did not heal enough for her to perform her function in the Crew, she would be Beached with a week's supply of food and water and left to her own fate.

She snorted in derision. That was one of the reasons her whole Family was on the beach. The desires of the Fates had seemed too often to coincide with the fortunes of the Priest-

Admiral and his cronies on their huge, luxurious Masterships. The smaller Familyships, like *Eagle* and poor old *Condor*, who made their living by fishing, raiding, trading and carrying cargo for the Landbound, seemed to be always paying, always obeying, yet receiving little in return.

And now, even that was finished. They were branded heretic by the Priest-Admiral's Conclave. The *Eagle* lay on the rocks, her back broken, her single intact mast reaching forlornly back towards her home: the great, cold Southern Ocean.

And Sarasha's foot hurt.

* * *

"Father, I have to be there."

"Is that wise, 'Rasha? Do you want to show everyone your condition?"

"I want to show them I am alive, alert, and ready to stand up for myself!" She tossed her hands up. "Even if I can't Scribe for the Conclave while I'm under threat of Beaching. Or stand up on my own."

Her mother nodded. "I believe she's right, Arlijn. The truth is stronger than gossip. Word is going around the Lower Decks that she is incapacitated."

Her father copied Sarasha's gesture, exaggerated by the size of his hands. "I am overwhelmed by superior numbers. How will you get there?"

"I have friends."

His face cleared. "That is also a good idea. Display your forces."

"Father, trust you to find a political slant. I wasn't considering it that way."

"You should be. Politics becomes doubly important when the fabric of the Crew is strained."

"I bow to your superior knowledge, my Priest-Captain."

To her dismay, this lighthearted gibe brought a cloud to her father's face.

19

"No longer a Priest, no longer a Captain."

"Father, that's not so!"

"Yes, it is, Sarasha. Our Families have no use for Priests any more. Neither do I, as you well know. And since there is no Ship, there is no Captain." He spread his hands in a gesture of finality.

"But the Families still need leadership." Her mother placed a hand over his. "More so than ever."

"Perhaps. But the form that leadership takes will be different. It must be. We are trying to break away from the old forms that were destroying us."

Verlene smiled calmly. "Wait and see, my dear. The more things change, the more people cling to the forms with which they are familiar. Priest or Captain or whatever the name, you have been a good commander, strong, intelligent and fair. There will be few who would seek new leadership."

"That is probable. We shall have to see."

Yong showed up to take Sarasha to the Conclave. She had expected him to bring someone to help carry her, maybe one or two more, but he showed up with a small crowd of the younger Crew: twenty at least; men and women. She watched them from her couch under the sailcloth awning as they approached. The presence of the Priest-Captain's tent caused them to settle somewhat, but there was still an aggressive swagger to their step. When her father stepped out to speak to them, they positively swelled.

He looked them over for a brief, silent moment, then greeted them more formally than Sarasha had expected. "Good day, Crew members and Family."

Yong was equal to the occasion. "My greetings, and those of my friends, to you, Priest-Captain Tourn. We have come to take our friend to the Conclave."

Her father gave each member of the group a moment of personal regard. Then he turned to Yong again. "I am pleased to welcome my daughter's friends."

Yong's head dropped in a slight formal bow. "We believe there will be changes, Priest-Captain."

"There have been grave changes already. More must follow."

"Be aware, Priest-Captain Tourn, that your daughter's friends will give good heed to her counsel."

"My daughter is a thoughtful Crew member."

"Then it is important that her counsel be heard."

Her father nodded. "I understand. It has been good to speak with you, Crew members and Family." He bowed and faded back into the tent as the young Crew gathered around her.

Yong and Pers made a chair with their hands and scooped her up. As they walked across the swale to the Conclave, she twisted to get a straight look at their faces. "Yong, what was that all about?"

"Do you know what an election is?" Yong tossed her his usual grin.

"Of course I know what an election is, you idiot! What has that got to do with me?"

"What it has to do with you, my dear idiot, is that we all got together and had an election."

"And what were you electing?"

"We were electing our spokesperson."

"Elections? Spokesperson? Where did you learn words like that?"

He stared ahead smugly. "Your father."

"What?" She also looked forward and saw how close they were to the assembled Families. "Wait a moment. Yong, Pers, you just put me down right here. We are going to talk about this."

"Why?"

"Because you have some kind of plan, and I'm some part of it and I'm not going into the most important Conclave of our lives with no idea of what's going on!"

Yong stopped and grinned over her head at Pers. "Should we put her down?"

Pers pretended to consider, his blond mop of hair tossing. "If she gets real mad, I don't want to be this close to her with my hands occupied."

"All right, you two comics. Stop fiddling around and put me down on that piece of driftwood over there."

They complied, and the group knelt and sat around her.

"Now, I will ask you one more time. What is going on?"

"Doesn't she sound like her father when she gets mad?"

"My father doesn't get mad. Don't change the topic."

Yong's handsome face sobered. "We got together, Sarasha, because this is a very important Conclave. Our whole way of life is changing. Look around you. Our friends are the offspring of the most important people on the Ship: Officers, Rigging, Auxiliary and Belowdecks. Sooner or later, we will be the leaders. We want to have our say now, because whatever the Crew decides, we will be the ones who have to live with it."

"Fair enough. And where did you hear all those heretical ideas? My father doesn't talk like that."

"He does in Captains' Conclaves."

"But those are always secret. I was only there because I'm his Scribe."

Pers grinned, but his pale blue eyes did not lose their sharp regard. "But they often took place on the *Eagle*."

"Oh." *That explains several things.* "You took some serious risks, you realize. If you'd been caught in that old companionway that everybody thought was boarded up..."

"We weren't caught. And we've had our own conclave, and our own election for our spokesperson. And you're it. I mean, it's you."

"Me!" She stared at her bandaged foot. "I may not even be around a half-moon from now."

"You will if we have anything to say about it."

A warm glow suffused her chest. "Well, thank you. I didn't really think...well, ...thank you."

"Some spokesperson," Pers sniffed. "Can't even find anything to say."

"All right. I'm your spokesperson." She shot him a withering glance. "What do you want me to say?"

"We don't know."

"You have nothing to say and you have me all primed to say it. Great. Are you setting me up to look stupid? That'll be really useful in the Conclave."

Yong's face lost its humour. "That's the problem, Sarasha. We don't know enough about what's going on. Nobody does. Not until the Conclave. You think fast. You've had more information than we have for a longer time, and you've been considering it. We trust you. Speak for us."

She considered a moment, running through all the ideas her father had spoken of. "Very well, but you realize the danger. That kind of attitude is what allows people like the Priest-Admiral to take over. If the Crew gives the right to talk to one person, and lets that person say what will happen, then that person is very dangerous."

Instead of making them reconsider, this brought smiles to their faces. "See? I told you. She's always coming up with things like that." Yong leaned forward. "That's why we want you to speak for us. You can try to let us know what you plan to say ahead of time, but you say what you have to, when you have to. We'll back you."

She nodded. "Fine. But if I say something you don't like, you haul me down quick and straighten me out. Deal?"

A glance passed through the group. "Deal."

"Fine. Now that we have created enough suspicion by having a strategy meeting where everyone can see us, we might as well go in as a group. We'd be fooling no one if we tried anything else."

They picked her up again and moved at a confident pace toward the large, dished curve in the lee of a dune where the Crew was formed up. She couldn't help but note that as her supporters started forward, they fell into raiding party formation: scouts, main body, flankers, rearguard. Her group contained some of the finest of the young Raiders in the Crew:

23

those left after two months of running skirmishes and that final, destructive battle.

She pointed to a position that was just right: an open area they could command without disturbing anyone already seated, just close enough to the Chart Table to be noticed and far enough to the side for a view of the Crew. As Yong and Pers set her down, two others brought a piece of driftwood, and there she sat, head and shoulders above the rest.

This exposure made her uneasy, but she had no choice. *No point in trying to conceal my infirmity. If I sit on the sand, I'll have an awkward struggle to get up. Better to have it out in the open, but no reason to make it obvious.* She used her position to advantage and gazed around.

Hers wasn't the only group that entered and sat together. The next thing she noticed was that the Captain's Scribe was her younger cousin, Leide. The girl entered behind the Priest-Captain and Captain's Wife, looking self-conscious and a little afraid, although her Scribe's tabard was sharp and spotless as usual, her auburn hair slicked down under a formal kerchief. Sarasha sympathized. If things went badly for the Priest-Captain, his Scribe would find it difficult to distance herself from him. Also, any mistake she made at this important Conclave could haunt her all her life.

Priest-Captain Tourn sat at the Chart Table, a huge, carved monolith that must have taken a great deal of trouble to get out of his cabin and across the beach. As he sat, silence descended, until only the sighing of the wind in the sea-grass, the rumble of the breakers and the odd seagull cry could be heard.

He sat there, gazing out at his Crew, his craggy, weathered face calm.

"My people. There is no sense in trying to cushion the blow. I have never lied to you, and I will not start. The *Eagle* is no more. Her back is broken, and she will never sail again. We are Beached. We knew this might happen, and it has. No one need apologize. We all did our best, but we were throwing against loaded dice, and we lost.

"Now, there are decisions to be made. Many of what seem to be decisions are really not. In many cases, we have no choice. For example, it has been suggested that we stay here, use the timbers from the *Eagle* to build a town, and start a trading port.

"I cannot think of a worse choice."

A mutter arose from a group to the left of the Table. Sure enough, it was the Quartermaster and his brothers. Trust them to want to become merchants.

Her father ignored the interruption. "Don't think the Priest-Admiral has forgotten us. We dared to defy him, and we still live. We did him enough damage in the final battle that he is unwilling to risk an immediate foray against us. His confidence in his control of the Fleet has also been shaken. How many others might be disaffected? For the moment, he does not know. He does not dare give an unpopular order in case it brings him down."

He paused, staring around.

"Do not fool yourselves into thinking it will take him long to reaffirm his grasp of the Fleet now that his main detractors are crushed. Do not dream he will not come searching for us, the first moment he is able. When he comes, we must not be here."

Again, he scanned the crowd, waiting for dispute that did not come.

"Ask him where we're going."

Sarasha leaned down to return the whisper. "I can't do that, Pers. I don't want to seem like his stooge in the crowd, asking the obvious questions so he can answer them. Don't worry, I won't have to."

"Where are we going?"

They grinned at each other as the question, from a woman on the other side, was taken up by several voices.

The Priest-Captain held up a hand for silence. "That is a point where we have choices. Of course, we must go inland. However, there are three routes."

He gestured with one hand. "To the west of us lies a fair land, well-watered, with good soil. It is peopled by a race of Farmers, not fierce, but stubborn in the defense of their homes. We should know; we have raided them often enough."

A grim chuckle ran through the crowd.

"There is no room for us there. We would have to push them out and fight a continuous battle to keep them out. They are many, and we are few at the moment.

"The next choice is to the north. In that direction lies open prairie: dry grassland, rising slowly to a huge mountain range many leagues inland that cuts off all congress with the more civilized peoples to the north, around the Inner Sea."

Another murmur. To hear the fabled Inner Sea mentioned so casually, as if it were reality!

"The third choice lies to the east, where the mountains approach the ocean, and high valleys might afford a sparse living. Our scouts have found a narrow inlet we could fortify without too much effort, to give us limited access to the sea. There, if all the Families from all the Ships that died here put their boarding parties together, we could probably fight off any attack the Priest-Admiral is likely to mount.

"Those are the three choices we have discovered. I would like to invoke a quarter-glass recess, so you may discuss them among yourselves. In a quarter of a glass we will reconvene, and you may have your say on these options or on any other ideas you may have."

He rose and turned over the small sandglass, placing it in the middle of the Chart Table where everyone could see.

3. CONCLAVE

In the buzz of conversation that followed, Sarasha turned to her group. "Well?"

"What do you say, Sarasha?"

She considered. "You are some of the best young Raiders in our boarding parties. As the Priest-Captain said, with help from the other Ships, we could thumb our noses at the Priest-Admiral for years to come."

"But..."

"What do you mean, 'but', Yong? I didn't say 'but'."

"I could hear it in your voice. What is the other side, the one you didn't say?"

"We have always lived a precarious life. There are storms and riptides, and the young men go raiding. The chances of death and life are about even. Our advantage is that we are in control. When a storm comes, we can ride it out or run for shelter. We raid when we wish, and we can retreat at any time.

"If we pen ourselves up in a fortress, we will put our lives under the control of the Priest-Admiral again."

"How? You just said we could thumb our noses at him."

"Yes, but it would always be his choice when he would attack. We would forever live in fear of the next foray. That is the life of the Landbound."

She flipped a hand to the east. "It would be the same if we ran the Farmers out. We would create a neighbour who was our enemy. We would always be awaiting the next attack. Shipfolk have always lived on the offensive. You wouldn't like defensive warfare."

They nodded. Yong looked over his shoulder and pulled his faded canvas smock tighter. "So you think we should go north, into the plains."

"I do. So does my father, you can tell. It would be very different from our lives now. If we hit a few bad years, we could starve. But we would control our own lives. We are strong, and we are together. I'm sure we would do well."

Yong laughed. "And there's one other thing. Have you ever seen a horse?"

For a moment, Sarasha glared at him. "What do you mean, 'Have I ever seen a horse?' I'm not a complete sea-slosh. Of course I've seen a horse."

Yong smiled again. "Not those awkward creatures the Farmers use. Real horses. I was on one of the scouting parties. We walked for two days out into the plains. There was a herd of wild horses out there. Not too big, but shaggy and tough. They live out in the plains, winter and summer. They know the water holes and the sheltered spots for weathering storms. We shot one for meat. It seemed a shame, it was so beautiful."

"All right, so there are horses. What does that have to do with us?"

"Horses are for riding on, Sarasha. Have you seen one run?"

She nodded. "I see. You figure we can net some of these horses and use them to ride on as our transportation, instead of a Ship."

He nodded enthusiastically, flexing his big, work-scarred knuckles. "That's right. We met a man out on the plains who told us all about it. He's sort of a hermit: lives all alone, but he was riding a horse. Taller than the wild ones, but kin to them. He said it was crossbred, mating a domestic horse with a wild one, and had the qualities of both: the length of leg of a carthorse, the lean speed of a plains pony. It ran like a rain-squall across the face of the ocean."

She looked around the group. "So we are all agreed? We support the northern plains? Horses or not?"

Enthusiastic nods all round. She turned back, scanning the crowd to see if she could read anything. There were tight clumps, big and small, but many sitting in pairs or threes, as well. *Good. Those are the undecided. They could be swayed by reason.*

Or else they were already decided, in which case there was nothing you could do about them. She looked at her father, sitting relaxed behind the massive Chart Table, in casual

28

conversation with her mother and Leide. *How does he tell? How does he read the wishes and needs of his Crew? He's always one step ahead. Where is he now? He always has a plan. Many plans. I'll have to watch him more closely, learn more from him, if I'm going to be a leader in this new Crew.*

As the sands trickled down, the Conclave quieted. She could understand what that meant. Within the groups, the discussion was already over. Concurrence. The opposing factions were ready to bring their opinions before the Crew.

As the last grain of sand dropped, the Priest-Captain rose, and the silence was complete. "Is it the desire of the Conclave that the Deck be clear for all to speak?"

There was a brief murmur of assent.

"Is there any discussion or call for a vote?"

There was silence.

"I then declare the Deck clear."

Several men jumped to their feet. The Priest-Captain considered each one before he spoke. "Precedence to Family Heads. Armourer Kyso of the Yonghal, will you speak?"

The others sat, and Kyso, a burly man of about forty-five, moved forward. "The Family Yonghal and the Armourers concur. We will follow the majority. These are our reasons. If we stay and fight, or go either east or west, the armourers will have occupation. However, our arms are in sore condition, and we question our own ability to comply with the demands of another battle. Thus, while it will mean great change in our occupation, we are willing to go north. If we stay and fight, we will do our best, as we always have. That is all. May the Lo..." He cut off the usual final blessing, bowed to the Table and sat.

"None question the commitment of the Armourers to the Ship and its Crew. Thank you, Family Yonghal. Precedence to Family Heads. Quartermaster Baetor of the Huin, will you speak?"

The portly Quartermaster stood and paced forward slowly, as if his movement would give weight to his words. "The Quartermasters concur. We would prefer to stay near the Ocean. Our lives have always been here, and now that our way of life is in jeopardy, we feel it unwise to move into uncharted territory. We could all be dead from starvation before the next winter is over. We do not presume to tell those in command who to fight, and we will, as always, expend our utmost effort and abilities to support those who fight."

"After filling your own belly with the first profits."

The quiet comment from somewhere in the seated Crew carried perhaps farther than the anonymous speaker intended, and brought a trickle of laughter from those seated nearby, as well as a few angry shushings. A flush of red rose to the merchant's face, and he turned in the direction of the comment.

The Priest-Captain's voice rode over Baetor's rejoinder. "Thank you, Family Huin. Please remember that we could have all been dead, thanks to the tender mercy of the Priest-Admiral and his lust for control, any time in the past six months, and if we stay near the Ocean, we still could satisfy him.

"Precedence now to Officers. First Officer Dwayo Kaya, will you speak?"

The greying head of the First Officer rose above the crowd. His hands twisted in his belt, and his head moved from side to side. "The Deck Officers concur. The lifetime of knowledge that gave us our positions will be useless if we leave the Ocean. However, we all understand that this was the course set for us last year when we decided to defy the Priest-Admiral. Our way of life died the moment we made that decision. It only took half a year of running and the final battle, with the *Eagle* broken on the beach, to make the choice real for us. We must leave the sea, no matter the personal cost. If my children and their children must become rovers of the plains instead of the Ocean, and if it means the loss of my position and status, then so be it." He stared around at the Crew and then sat, radiating dignity.

"Officers are chosen first for their leadership ability and second for their knowledge. Thank you for your insight, Officer Kaya. Precedence to Heads of Crafts. Shipwright Papan, will you speak?"

"The Shipwrights do not concur. Some would rather move to the east, despite the necessity of fighting. However, there are forests to the west, with much wood for our craft. Others feel that, with such difficult times, we need the close support of the whole Crew, and a fortress to the east would make a better basis for this new enterprise. Another group wishes for relief from this unceasing warfare, and time to practice our trade, no matter where we go, whether there be wood or not. However, we will go where the Crew decides, as is our tradition."

"Thank you, Shipwright Papan. You bring up a point that needs to be spoken. There is one major change in our situation that may make this decision easier.

"For all our lives we have lived on a Ship. Where one went, all went. Now we are on the land." He swung his hand to the north. "Any person may go where he wants, at any time. There is nothing to stop you."

A dismayed buzz percolated through the Crew, and faces turned towards the towering clouds that scudded across the sky to the north. It seemed that few had considered the idea. The Priest-Captain waited until the conversation died. "Of course, the windward side of that shelter is that every group that leaves the Crew weakens the Crew. If we all divide up and go our separate ways, we will be easy pickings for any enemy we meet.

"Have no illusions. The Fleet has raided up and down this coast for centuries. We will have no friends among the Landbound here. Who wishes to speak?"

No one rose.

Sarasha stood, trying to make the move as graceful as possible. She held her face still against the shot of pain that lanced her leg. It was difficult to balance, with land unyielding under her foot, so she leaned the back of her leg against the driftwood to steady herself.

"Sarasha Tourn of the Crew Aloft, do you wish to speak?"

"I am no longer of the Crew Aloft, Priest-Captain. My foremast lies as broken as the *Eagle*. I speak only for myself and my friends. We have no choice to suggest. We have a prediction. This prediction is important, because it is not where we go, but when we go that matters.

31

"Yes, many of you think we can go where we wish. We are the Sea People, and we have always been free to roam where our desire took us. But we are no longer a people of the Ocean. We have become a people of the land, and on land, a different wind blows. We can move west and attack those who live there, driving them from their lands. Or we can move east and set up a fortress in the rocks.

"But there is one main difference. When we were on the Ocean, we fought when we chose. When the fight was over, we were gone like the ebbing tide. If we find a place to stay on land, we will fight when others choose. We will always be there, in that one place, if anyone wants to attack us.

"And we are not a large group. Even if all the Crews of eight Ships band together, we may not be strong enough to hold a large enough piece of land to support our Families. So if we stay here, west or east, sooner or later someone more powerful will come and drive us away because there is not enough room for us here. When we are driven out, there will only be one place to go: the prairie to the north where there is room. Many leagues of room. Perhaps we can treat the Great Prairie as if it were the Great Ocean. Perhaps we can range the land as we did the sea: moving where we will, raiding if we choose, leaving if we choose not to fight.

"So the question is not if we move, but when we move. If we go to the grasslands now, in summer when we are strong and have supplies and equipment to use or trade, we have a chance of learning the life of the Great Prairie on our own terms. If we wait to be driven out in winter, beaten and with nothing but what our backs can carry, our chances of survival are much reduced.

"That is the thought of my friends, Families and Crew. My group of friends, with no official name, concurs."

"And what will you use for Ships, you and your friends, to sail this new Ocean of yours?" The voice was anonymous, but it came from the direction of the Quartermaster's Family.

Sarasha raised her hands, shoulders and eyebrows in a dramatic shrug. "Have you never seen a horse?"

She looked around, waited, then continued. "Oh, not those big, plodding things the Farmers use to pull their plows. Imagine a tall, slim, long-legged horse, bred for the love of running. A horse that moves through the swaying Prairie grass like a dolphin through the bow wave of a Ship. Yes, there are such horses. My friends have seen them, out there." She swept her arm to the north. "With such horses, we can become the masters of the Great Prairie, Families and Crew, and live a life of freedom such as we never lived in the Fleet under the lash of the Priest-Admiral."

She stood a moment longer, then bowed towards the Chart Table and sat. Her friends murmured congratulations and clapped her on the knees, waiting in silence for the response.

A hum of conversation rose, and the Priest-Captain waited it out. Then he rose. "Thank you, Sarasha, for the opinion of your friends. It is inevitable that new groups, new occupations, and even new Families will arise in this new land."

"How can you give this girl precedence, Priest-Captain Tourn? Why should we listen to her? She is a cripple. She cannot man her station any more. When we leave here, she will be Beached. Her opinion means nothing."

Sarasha shot erect before her father could speak, facing the Quartermaster squarely and laughing out loud. "Look at yourself, Quartermaster Huin. Look around you. Where do you stand? You are Beached, as are we all. The rules are changing, Quartermaster. We are in a very difficult position. Perhaps the new rules will have to become even harsher than before. Perhaps we will have to leave behind anyone who cannot walk fast enough. Then both you and I will be left on this beach, to await what the Fates have in store for us together."

Then she smiled. "Perhaps we would do better learning to be friends, Baetor Huin. We may have to depend upon each other much more in the future."

The Priest-Captain's voice cut through the rising noise of the Crew. "I gave precedence to neither Sarasha Tourn nor Baetor Huin. We will keep the order of this meeting. Both of you, please be seated until the Table invites you." He stood eyeing them until they complied.

"But your discussion brings up good points. The first point is this. We are in a new situation where new rules will soon apply. All of our old traditions come from a different life. The reasons for many of them are gone.

"So, before we apply any of the old traditions, we must first decide whether it is still a useful practice. If it is, we will continue to follow it. If it is not, we will change it." He smiled. "There is no Priest-Admiral watching us through his lens, sending his signals, demanding that we do what he says.

"So, at some future time, when the decision must be made as to whether Sarasha and the other wounded go with us or stay behind, we will be discussing the reasons for that tradition before we make any decisions."

There was a murmur in the Crew: a sigh of relief. Sarasha had been so caught up in her own troubles that she had forgotten how many wounded there were, and how many Families were going through the same agony she was.

"The other point is more general. We are on the beach together, all of us, and we had better look to each other for friendship, since we will certainly depend upon each other even more in the near future."

Sarasha felt a burst of pride to hear her father using her arguments. Since her outburst had been in response to an antagonist's charge, no one would accuse her of an orchestrated parroting of her father's policies. *The Quartermaster played into our hands perfectly.*

The Priest-Captain did not offer precedence to anyone else, but continued. "On that subject, I have sent to the other Captains to see how they would like to proceed. Most have responded that they would like to meet, and I have offered our encampment as the meeting place, since it is central. Five Captains have accepted. There is no reason the other two would refuse, so that meeting is called for two days from now.

"We will continue this discussion, as many wish their opinions known. For those of you who are used to short

Conclaves, where the Heads of Family and Craft speak and it is done, you will have to get used to a new tradition. It is important that everyone speak his or her mind. If we are to survive together, all must agree on what we do. Who desires to speak?"

He gave precedence to a woman from the Sailmakers, who had a question about new sources of canvas. The Quartermaster answered, eager to regain his status by a show of competence, and the Conclave continued.

It was a full two glasses later when the Priest-Captain finally stood. "We have heard the thoughts of most of our people. I am starting to hear the same opinions repeated, several times each. I am also getting hungry." That brought a chuckle from the Crew.

"We will close this Conclave on a result of No Concurrence, as expected. I will take our thoughts to the Meeting of Captains in two days. I doubt if any of them will have Concurrence either. Unless circumstances force us otherwise, it would be foolish to make any sudden decisions, especially those that go against the wishes of many Crewmembers.

"We will talk about this for as long as it takes to gain a firm resolve from the whole Crew and the Crews from the other seven Ships." He scanned the Conclave. "That is how decisions are made when there is no one person with the authority to make them."

He picked up the Log Book in both hands – pausing a moment where he should have said the ritual prayer – closed it, then turned and strode towards his tent. Leide picked up the sandglass, pen and ink, and followed.

Sarasha turned to her friends. "Well, what do you say?"

They jumped to their feet, and she rose as smoothly as she could. Yong was grinning. "It went very well. I was watching them when you talked about horses."

Pers nodded sagely. "That's the first time I have heard anyone suggest a positive solution to our situation. It has all been, 'Go and fight,' or, 'Stay and fight,' or, 'Wander into the plains and die.' You showed us a way of life we might look forward to."

"I loved that part about moving like a dolphin!" That was one of the younger lads.

"You don't think I laid on a bit too much wind?"

Yong clapped her on the back, then caught her when she staggered. "Of course not. It was beautiful! How do you come up with things like that?"

"I read the Sagas and the Poets. Some of the Holy Works are quite poetic, too."

Tonu, the Sailmaker's first daughter, regarded her. "You have read the Holy Works?"

Sarasha grinned ruefully. "There's a lot of reading to be done if you're going to be the Priest-Captain's Scribe. Not all of it is poetry, believe me!"

"Too bad all that's wasted, now."

"How do you mean, wasted?"

The girl's broad face reddened. "I didn't mean any slight, Sarasha, I just meant...well, now that we aren't following the Priest-Admiral any more, and we aren't using all the old rituals and rules, all that reading will pretty well go to waste, won't it? I couldn't help but notice that your father doesn't call himself Priest-Captain any more, just Captain."

Sarasha nodded. "I see what you mean, and I agree. Partially." She gazed around. "Are we all going to stand here talking about this? Because if we are, I need something to eat."

Yong reached down, caught her behind the knees and swung her up in his work-hardened arms. "In that case, let's go somewhere cool and comfortable. My Family tent."

She did not protest because her foot was starting to throb, and she knew she needed to sit and put it up. She relaxed against the corded muscles of his chest, secure in his grasp.

"You are very light, Sarasha." After carrying her at a quick stride across the encampment, he was not even breathing hard.

"I've lost weight."

"They're sending out hunting parties tomorrow. I'll shoot you a nice, fat pony to chew on."

36

"Don't shoot a horse, Yong. Shoot a deer or something else. If you find a horse, bring him back to camp alive."

He laughed. "That's a tall order, 'Rasha. Do you know how fast they run?"

"It was just a thought."

His glance followed hers down to her bandaged foot. "Don't worry, Sarasha. We'll get you a horse."

When they were all established in the shade at the front of the Han Family tent, and Yong and his older sister were bustling about bringing everyone food and drink, Tonu sat down beside Sarasha, her broad, friendly face puzzled. "What did you mean, you agree with me partially?"

"I agree with the part about not using all the old rituals and rules. No one who has lived through what we have will ever be ruled by a Priest again. However, I wouldn't scrub that deck completely clean when you're talking about the Holy Works."

"No? Why not? Aren't they the source of the rules the Priest-Admiral used to keep us in chains?"

"No, they aren't."

There was an exclamation of surprise among her friends.

"Truth. The Holy Works are simply a collection of writings by famous holy men and scholars from the far past. In some cases, they were written even before we took to the Oceans. That means that in places, they have no relevance to what life is like today. Therefore, the Priest-Admiral and his cohorts could interpret them whatever way they liked and make up rules that kept them in power.

"But that doesn't mean the Works are all wrong. Those were intelligent men, the Ancient Ones who wrote those Works. They had important things to say about life. What we have to do is go through the Works again and see if they have anything to say that will help us survive in our present situation."

Pers handed her a glass of ship's beer and sat beside her, nodding. "You're right. In fact, if there are some Writings that predate our move onto the Ocean, maybe those will be the ones that could help us the most, since we are leaving the Ocean."

"What a good thought. Let's talk to the Helmsmen about getting hold of a copy."

"I can do that." The small voice came from the lad who had spoken before: Cheynou Chan of the Helmsman's Craft. He was slighter than most, about 16, although his calm, dark face made him seem younger.

They all turned, and he reddened under their regard.

"How can you do that, CheyChan?"

He grinned impishly. "I am studying my Navigation skills and I must know all the Great Writings, including the Holy Works. I have a copy of my own, given to me on my Naming Day, when I became an Apprentice to the Family Craft."

"Good. Bring it to my tent tomorrow afternoon, and let's have a peek at it."

The boy reddened again and bowed. She returned the bow from her seated position and turned again to Yong and the others. "That's a good start. What else?"

Yong grinned. "Horses."

"What about them?"

"I was just thinking about what you said on the way over here. You aren't the only one who needs a horse, Sarasha. Many game animals live in this area right now, but after a few weeks of feeding eight Crews, the available prey will get farther and farther away. We'll need horses to get out and hunt, bring back the meat."

One of the other lads nodded. "How much better would it be, should we discover an enemy, if we had messengers on horses to warn the other Crews?"

Pers leaned forward. "There are lots of good reasons to want horses. How do we get some?"

"There are plenty of them, you said."

"Oh, there are plenty, Cheynou. But those are the wild ones. They run a lot faster than we do."

"So we net them?"

"Net them? You can't drag a fishing net across the Prairie."

Cheynou shook his head. "I don't mean with a real net. What do the Landbound use to keep their stock close by?"

"They use a fence like a ship's rail. Spars lashed to other spars, driven into the ground like trees."

"So we have to build a fence and chase the horses into it."

"Sounds like a good idea." Pers viewed the group. "Shall we try?"

Everyone nodded enthusiastically.

"Fine. We'll be hunting for meat tomorrow, but we'll find a good place for a horse fence. The following day, we'll go catch us some horses. Won't the Families be surprised when we all come riding into the camp?"

Sarasha had a feeling it wasn't going to be quite that easy, but she held her tongue. This was Pers' idea, and he was the one to lead it. She bit her lip. *I'll have to sit at home and do nothing while they have all the fun.*

No, wait a minute. I remember one of the Writings, about Farmers and how they worked. Maybe in that scripture...

"Yong, I'm tired. I want to go back to my tent. I've got a lot of reading to do."

As Yong and Pers made her a chair, she realized how tired she was. *I wonder if I'll have the energy to lift a book.* With a wave over her shoulder to young CheyChan, she allowed them to cart her off like a coil of old anchor line.

4. HOLY WORKS

"So, Cheynou, what do the Helmsmen think about this move? Your father and uncle didn't say anything at the Conclave."

The boy stretched out on the sand beside her, his lithe body relaxed, and she regarded him with curiosity. Rather a loner, he had only attached himself to their group since the battles started, but he had already shown a confidence and self-sufficiency to match the older youths.

Now he shook his head. "The Navigators don't take sides. We only provide information. It's up to the Pr... up to the Captain to choose where to go."

Sarasha nodded. The Helmsmen were a separate group, not mixing with the other Crew much because a lot of their work needed stars, and most of their studying took place at night. "But...?" She grinned at Cheynou. She knew he couldn't keep from talking.

His head tossed, side to side, and he matched her smile. "Well, if you think about it..."

Oh. So I have to guess. "Well, if I was a Helmsman and Chartmaker then I'd say being on the beach in a farming town or fortress would render my skills pretty useless. Out on the trackless Prairie, on the other hand..."

"Good thinking, Sarasha."

She nodded. "Let's have a go at that book, then." She turned it over in her hands. "This cover is beautiful work."

He nodded with enthusiasm. "Yes. It is very important to a Navigator that his References are of the best quality in every detail. The work on the cover shows what care has been taken with the important part: the information inside."

"Have you been reading it since we talked?"

"Oh, I checked in a couple of places. I didn't really see anything that might apply to what you were saying. Of course, the parts I studied have more to do with Navigating." He looked at her guiltily. "The other stuff is pretty boring."

"I remember thinking the same thing. I guess we'll have to study it from a new perspective."

"Fair enough."

They regarded the List of Works. Some were named with their authors, some without.

"The titles don't help much, do they? What about this: 'On the Occurrence of Heavenly Phenomena' by Tsalstan?" She raised an open palm.

"That is one I worked on. You have to study it pretty hard, but Tsalstan knew his Astronomy. He makes good points about the movement of the planets counter to the stars. Of course, he says that movement is caused by the basic antagonism between stars and planets, and concludes that when certain planets are approaching certain stars, then the people who look to those planets have to be very careful around the people who look to those stars, in case there is trouble."

Sarasha nodded. "And let me guess. The Priest-Admiral and his Fleet Captains all look to the biggest stars."

"That's right, and us lower types always get planets."

"Great." Sarasha pulled a piece of parchment towards her. She stopped as Pers stuck his head through the door.

"Started already?"

"Sort of. Say, Pers, would you do me a favour? Leide is supposed to be coming, but I didn't know when Cheynou would show up. Could you pop over and tell her we're meeting now?"

"Sure. Back in a bit."

She squared the parchment away. "All right. Point one. Tsalstan knows about stars and planets, but not people. Where next?"

She studied the List again. "What's this about 'The Principles of Natural Precedence'?"

"We don't have much about that one. It's so old that no one knows who wrote it. Something about the reasons one person has power over another."

"That sounds interesting. Let's start reading."

41

By the time Pers and Leide showed up, panting, Sarasha and Cheynou were deep in discussion. They brought the other two on course and continued.

Finally, Pers threw up his hands. "This is just flotsam. All he's saying is that some people are naturally better than others. That was exactly the sort of stuff the Priest-Admiral used to put himself over everyone else. I think we can safely disregard this Writing."

"Oh no, we can't."

"Why not?"

Sarasha pointed to the page. "See what he says there."

Pers leaned forward. "Um...'Some people, through their heritage, are naturally larger, stronger, and more intelligent than others.' Oh. I guess there's nothing wrong with that."

"That's right. Some people are better, some are worse. They are born that way. I don't think anyone would argue with that. Now, listen to this. 'Those fortunate enough to be born into a superior family, and given a superior education and training, will have advantages over their weaker brethren.' What do you think of that?"

"That's the jetsam the Admiral used to support his Superior Families. They were the ones who lived on the Masterships and got all the luxuries."

"Yes, but that's a perfect example of the problem. This Work isn't talking about some class of Superior Family, like on the Masterships. He's talking about good families. The kind who feed their children properly, protect them, teach them, and treat them well. And down here he talks about the 'loving aers of the home.' He's talking about loving families, not some sort of privileged elite."

"You're right. I've been reading with a blind side. If I don't take it from the Priest-Admiral's position, it all makes sense. The important thing is, what does this writer say we're supposed to do about it?"

"That's the problem. He doesn't."

"What?"

She turned the page. "This is one of the Fragmentary Works."

"I can guess what happened to the end part."

They all turned to Leide, who blushed but nodded earnestly. "It's easy. He probably said the superior people were supposed to help and support the inferior ones, and give them a chance to do their best for the good of everyone, and things like that. So one of the old Priest-Admirals got rid of those pages."

They all nodded. Leide continued, her slim fingers sweeping the paper. "I think this is one of the most important Works. If we can figure out what the end was, we'll have an idea of how we should live our lives."

"Some chance."

Sarasha grinned. "Not so difficult, Cheynou. We don't have to figure out what he said. It doesn't matter what people thought a thousand years ago. He has given us a good idea of where to start. Now, we have to figure out what *we* think. We have to find a philosophy that matches our ideas, today."

"So what do we think today?"

Pers reached out and took the Works. "We won't solve that in an afternoon. We can come back to this one. Let's examine some others."

Their heads came together over the small book, and the ideas flew.

Several glasses later, Pers leaned back. "This is all very interesting, but I notice something. Do you realize how few of the actual laws, rules, and traditions we live by are written down in these Works?"

They stared at each other.

"I think you're right. So where did they come from? They didn't appear out of nowhere." Sarasha thought a moment. "I learned something about that when I was studying to be a Scribe. Leide, what was that stuff in the Traditional Law section about the origin of law?"

"Oh, I was just reading that last month. Laws grow up through usage. At least, that's how our laws have developed. I should have mentioned that when we started this study. People think somebody sat down one day and wrote a bunch of laws. Maybe you thought they would be in the Holy Works."

Pers regarded her and frowned. "Sort of. You mean they aren't all written down somewhere?"

She shook her head. "No. The only writing is in the Records of Judgement."

"And what are those?"

"They are the notes taken by the Scribe at each trial. At the end of the trial, the Scribe condenses the case and states the judgement of the Captain or Tribunal, and then keeps them all. The next time a similar case comes up, the Captain can use the old cases to guide him in his judgment."

"You mean he only uses them as a guide? He can really make up his own mind and do whatever he likes?"

"Well, yes, but it isn't that simple. If he goes way off course, the Denounced can demand a Tribunal with one Captain designated by the Denounced. Then, believe me, the Scribes do an incredible amount of pawing through the books, trying to find anything that applies in any way. Then the Tribunal has to go through all those cases and decide what applies in the case in question.

"And in the last fifty years, as a matter of record, the Captain's decision has been supported in almost every case."

Pers looked at Sarasha and raised his eyebrows. "So they undermined the appeal system until it was ineffective."

Leide nodded. "Thus creating each Captain as dictator of his Ship. Any Captain who lays a different course will find himself up on charges, with the same chance of obtaining justice. So the power flows up to the top, with the Priest-Admiral the ultimate dispenser of justice."

"Just as he is the ultimate dispenser of Holy Grace."

"You begin to understand why our Captains decided to rebel."

"That's disgusting."

There was silence for a moment. Then Sarasha shook herself.

"All right. So now we have a better understanding of why our Captains acted as they did. How does that help us in our present situation?"

Pers reached out and closed the Holy Works. "We don't need this as much as we need other information. We need to find out what all these judgements were. How do we do that? What are you two grinning about?"

Sarasha shrugged. "If you want the Scribes' records, you ask the Scribes."

"Well, why are you sitting there with silly grins? Go get them!"

"I don't think so." Sarasha held up her hand. "We have made good progress today, and we all have other things to do. Why don't we meet again tomorrow? Leide and I can pull out some appropriate volumes to examine. It's a lot of information to go through if you don't know where to start."

The group filed out, and Sarasha realized how tired she was. She had been able to ignore the increasing ache in her foot, but now that the excitement of discovery was over, all she wanted to do was lie down and try to sleep.

5. HORSE HUNT

Two days later, Sarasha sprawled in her hammock in the shade of the tent awning, the Holy Works lying ignored on her stomach. She clenched her fists weakly and stared at the canvas above her. *I want to be useful. I hate doing nothing. I can't even get up enough energy to read. I can't clench my fists for any length of time before they begin to ache.*

She forced herself to pick up the book, but the words said nothing. Nothing about helplessness, about not being able to do what you had to. Nothing about your body letting you down when you needed it the most. About never being able to climb, to run, even to walk gracefully.

She squeezed a tear from the corner of her eye, but wiped it away. *No sense letting my problems fall on anyone else. After all, there are plenty of people who would be glad to be in my situation. I'm alive, my father and mother are alive, my friends are still alive—most of them.*

An uproar burst from the other end of the camp. She swung gingerly out of the hammock and hopped to where she could lean on a tent pole and see what was going on.

All she could make out was a cloud of dust rising from a crowd of people, a lot of shouting and, it seemed, laughter. She strained to see more, but could not. At least it was heading her way. She waited, her sorrow and weakness forgotten for the moment.

The crowd jumbled forward, some sort of action in the middle of it. Then the head and front legs of a horse reared up above them all. The crowd cheered and laughed again. The horse disappeared, and the dust cloud roiled up even thicker.

A gust of wind blew the cloud away, and she could make out what was happening. The horse was throwing itself from side to side, held by two ropes around its neck. It wasn't a big horse, but when it hit the end of the portside line, the three young men hauling desperately on that rope were jerked until their feet skidded through the sand. Then the horse threw itself the other way, and one of the men on the starboard line tripped and splayed on his stomach, knocking the feet out from under his mates. The horse surged forward, dragging them, until the weight on the first rope hauled it to a stop directly in front of Sarasha.

It stood there, its flanks heaving, its brown coat darkened by sweat and dirt. Yong hauled himself to his feet and grabbed for the rope again, but she raised a hand. "Don't."

He froze. The cheers of the crowd faded, stopped.

She kept regarding the horse, its head hanging in weariness, but its eyes still open wide in fear.

"Go away." Her voice was low, but in a tone meant to be obeyed. "All of you. Leave in silence. Now."

A general shuffling, and the crowd began to disperse. Yong raised his eyebrows, gently reaching for the rope. She nodded. He took it but did not pull, just held it.

Sarasha surveyed the horse. It was a poor specimen as far as she could judge. Its hair was long and shaggy, falling off in patches. Its hooves were ragged and chipped. She tried to remember farm horses she had seen, whether their backs sagged so much in the middle. Parallel white lines scored its sides, like scars from a battle. High on one shoulder lay another patch of white hair the size of her hand. The animal stood, head low, and regarded her.

After a while, its sides stopped heaving and its eyes lost their wild stare. Sarasha began speaking, low and even, as if to a fearful youngster or a ship's ratter you were trying to tame. She did not move, but continued to talk. Yong and the other lads held their positions, hands on the ropes.

As she talked, the tension faded out of the poor animal. Its head sank lower, but it still eyed her suspiciously.

She continued the even tone of her voice, but directed it at her friends. "Cheynou, go in and ask my mother for some of the breakfast grains. A double handful on a plate. Slowly." She continued her soothing words as she waited. Soon he slipped up beside her and handed her the plate. She held it out to the animal, kept still and waited.

Just as I held out the piece of meat to that scruffy ratter I tamed from the bilges so many years ago. Patience and calm: that's the trick with animals. All that shouting and noise must have driven the poor creature mad.

The nostrils snuffled, and the head rose. The ears swivelled forward, flicked back, then came forward again.

Again, she directed her speech to her silent audience. "Look at its ears, how they move around. It can direct them wherever it wants to listen."

"I think it's a she."

"Thank you, Cheynou. We'll call her 'she' then. She's relaxing, now. She smells the grain. Come on, girl, come get the candy."

The horse stretched out her neck, her nose wrinkling. Then she moved one step forward. Sarasha moved the plate a bit, letting the horse hear the sound of the grains scraping together.

"Move upwind of her."

"Good idea, Pers, but I can't without hopping, and that will scare her. She'll just have to figure it out."

Slowly, one hesitant step at a time, the horse came to her. When it was close enough, Sarasha considered. *Should I put the plate down?* Horses were more used to eating on the ground, but this one might not want to put her head down with enemies all around. *Better to stay still. Let her make up her own mind.*

The horse stretched her neck out, and her nose reached the plate. Then the long upper lip stretched out even farther, twisted around a few grains and withdrew. There was a quiet chuckle from the group.

"She almost had you jumping, Sarasha."

Sarasha spoke quietly. "That's for sure. Did you see how long her lip is? Watch. There she goes again."

Having tasted the rich grain, the horse moved a full step forward, reaching for more. Soon the plate was empty. After a moment she began to search the ground for fallen remains. When she got too much sand in her mouth, she snorted loudly.

48

This time, Sarasha did jump and almost fell. Her windmilling arms startled the horse back a few steps.

"Drat. Stop your laughing, Cheychan, and get me some more grain. Now I have to start all over."

The horse knew what was coming, so it didn't take as long. This time Sarasha held the plate close to her body so the horse had to smell her as well. Once the grain was gone, she let the plate slowly fall to her side. The horse nosed in for more. Sarasha did not move until the velvety nose actually touched her. Then she gently placed her hand on its cheek, stroking lightly. The horse did not shy away, so she stroked some more. When there was no reaction, she reached slowly along the horse's neck to the first rope. She took it in her hand and pulled it forward until it caught under the jaw and behind the ears. Then she pulled, ever so lightly. The horse pulled back.

She took a very small hop backwards. The horse did not move. She pulled again, harder. The horse refused to move.

Again, her audience chuckled. "What happens when the powerful wave meets the rocky headland, Sarasha?"

"One of them has to break, and it won't be me. Get me some more grain."

This time, she pulled on the rope and held out the plate. The horse stepped forward and took a bite. She pulled on the rope again and moved the plate ahead. Once more, the horse stepped forward. Pulling and feeding, she had the horse perform a full circle around her before she ran out of grain. Still she kept pulling, holding out the plate, and the horse followed, reaching ahead with her upper lip. The third circle, Sarasha hid the plate behind her and kept the horse moving by gentle pressure of the rope alone, her friends scrambling to keep the long tails of the lines from getting mixed up in the horse's feet or around Sarasha's legs, still trying to move gently so as not to disturb the training.

"Now who gets to laugh?"

Yong shook his head. "That only took you half a glass. We've been trying to get the dratted thing to follow all the way in from the prairie."

"You didn't have any grain."

"What do we do now?"

"If I had just lost a line-hauling match against six of you in the hot sun, I'd be thirsty. Let's get a water keg and a big bowl."

These quickly appeared, but when Yong put the bowl at her feet, Sarasha shook her head. "No, not here. Put the bowl over there and fill it. Then one of you come and lead her. Pull very gently and firmly. Don't jerk, and don't let up. Keep the other rope clear, but be ready to hold on if she jibes around on you. If she pulls back hard, let her pull, but keep the pressure on. That's it. There you go."

Reaching out for Yong's shoulder, she hopped over to where the horse was slurping noisily from the bowl. When it was empty, they filled it again and again.

"She sure drinks a lot."

"I would imagine they don't get near water very often. She can probably store a day or more inside her. If you caught her before she drank, she'd be really thirsty."

They stood in a circle and gazed in awe as the horse continued guzzling water.

"What will you call her?"

Sarasha shrugged. "Why is it up to me?"

"She's yours."

"Mine?"

Yong laughed. "Of course. You asked for a horse, we brought you one."

"What? I ask for a horse, and you bring me the first mangy, spindly little thing you lay eyes on?"

They stopped laughing and exchanged sheepish glances. "Well, actually there were quite a few."

"Yes, but those things run really fast!"

"This was the only one that didn't start up and take off like a squall was chasing it the moment we appeared."

"Oh. So you also brought me the slowest one."

Yong pretended to be hurt. "At least she pulls well."

"You would know." Then Sarasha forgot the joking. "She does pull well, doesn't she? She could almost pull as much as six strong men, and with the nooses tight on her throat. If we put some sort of stiff padding so the weight came on her shoulders and not her neck, she could pull even more."

Pers rubbed a shoulder. "As long as I'm not on the other end of the rope."

They all laughed at that, but stopped quickly. Sarasha turned to see her father standing in the shadowed doorway of the tent. He stepped forward.

"So, friends of my daughter, what is all this uproar about?" His mode of speech put them on a personal note, so Yong bowed 'youth to elder' before he answered.

"We have brought your daughter a horse, Tourn Uncle."

"So I see." Her father strolled slowly up to the horse, where it stood, comfortable now. He held out his fist, and the horse took a sniff, snorted loudly, and turned her head away. His grin signalled them that they could give way to laughter.

He placed a hand on the horse's shoulder, ran it down her back. "Well, she seems healthy enough for an old mare."

"Old? Is she old?"

"I think so, from the look of her."

Sarasha turned a glare of mock anger on her friends. "So you brought me a horse that is old as well as slow, skinny, and mangy. Father, what do I do with friends like that?"

He shrugged. "I don't know either. Thank them, probably."

She turned back to her friends, her face serious. "He's right. This is wonderful. She's my very first horse, and I will never forget her. Thank you all very much."

She felt a tightness in her throat and a stinging in her eyes as they crowded around to slap her back and grasp her arm. When they let her go, her father was still checking over the horse, running his hands across her back.

"I wonder if she's broken?"

"Broken? Is that why her back is so bent?"

It was the Captain's turn to laugh. "No, Sarasha. 'Broken' is the expression the Landlocked use for subduing a horse so that it will let you ride it. See this scar here?" He pointed to the white patch. "That's from a gall. Someone has left an unpadded saddle on her and it rubbed the skin raw. She was once owned by a man."

Yong considered this. "So she didn't run away so fast because she wasn't that frightened of humans."

"Probably. It took Sarasha a very short time to get her to lead."

Pers shook his head. "Huh! All that trouble, and we caught a horse that was already tame? If we'd treated it like Sarasha did, we could have led it easily all the way back to the camp."

Her father smiled. "Don't set yourselves down. You have caught our first horse. She is a tough little beast who has had a taste of freedom, and she might never be easy to handle. I would like to add my thanks to Sarasha's," he bowed more formally, "because I think this horse is something very important. Both for her and for all of us."

They all nodded sagely.

"Besides," the Captain raised his dark eyebrows, "if you'd have led her in tame as a rabbit, you wouldn't have put on such a great show for the whole Crew."

Everyone laughed at that, and the Captain returned to his tent.

"So, what will her name be, this old mare of yours?"

Sarasha tilted her nose up. "I will give it due consideration and consult the Holy Works to find exactly the right name to make her dignified, cooperative and able to run like the wind."

Her nose wrinkled. "Now, please find a place to moor her, preferably close enough that I can get to her, yet far away enough downwind that nobody smells her." She eyed the steaming pile. "And somebody please clean that up."

"You get the horse, and we have to clean up after it?"

Sarasha shrugged. "There has to be some advantage to being a poor, helpless, cripple."

6. LOOK AHEAD

"I suppose you're going to argue this one, too."

She grinned at her father. "So, why don't you save yourself the effort of breasting those crosscurrents and go with the ebb? You know all my arguments, and you agreed with them last time."

"Yes, but that was within our Crew. This is…"

"…the whole Fleet, such as it is. Doesn't change a thing."

"You think that interrupting the Priest-Captain in the middle of a sentence is…"

"…neither Priest nor Captain. Heard it from his very mouth."

He shook his head, but out of the corner of her eye she could see a quirk to his lips. "Insubordination. From my own Family. Life has come to a pretty pass."

She turned back to him seriously. "Never in public, Father. Not even in jest. Your leadership is too important to the Crew."

His eyebrows rose, and he glanced at his wife. She merely smiled, and Sarasha knew the argument that hadn't started was over.

"It's good that the Conclave is on our deck. I mean, in our camp. That means I can be sitting when they come, and I can stay there until they leave. They might not even notice."

"Until I need someone to run an errand."

She put up her nose. "The Priest-Captain's Scribe runs no errands."

"I'll have Leide standing by for you." He rolled his eyes. "She would enjoy that."

"She might as well. She has no choice, now."

Verlene's brow wrinkled. "What do you mean?"

"She sat at the Table at the Conclave. She can hardly go against Father after that. No one would believe her. She's with us now, no matter what."

"Do you think she realizes that?"

Sarasha chuckled. "She seemed pretty nervous up there."

"Perhaps we should ask her, in any case. She still isn't bound."

"I'll ask her if you like. She's coming by this afternoon to help me with Ebb Tide."

"Is that what you named your horse? Why ebbing?"

"Because the ebbing tide takes you somewhere new."

"Good choice. You ask Leide, then. I don't want her to feel forced, despite the circumstances."

Sarasha waited until they had finished grooming Ebb Tide, feeding her, and watering her. Then she motioned to a nearby log. "I have something I need to talk to you about, Leide."

"I thought you might." The girl knitted her long, slim fingers together under her chin. "Strategy?"

"Strategy?"

"Yes. We have to get together, the whole Family, to plan our strategy to back the Captain."

Sarasha grinned. "So I don't have to ask you."

"Ask me?"

Sarasha became serious. "I suppose you realized that when you Scribed for the Captain at the Conclave you were declaring your allegiance."

"Of course I was."

Sarasha shook her head. "Do you realize that declaration limited your choices?"

"I was proud to."

"You were?"

"Of course." The girl's head rose. "He is my uncle, my Family Head, and my Captain. I have followed him this far, and I am proud to follow him further, wherever he leads. I am also proud to be your cousin, and to be allowed to learn Scribing from you."

Sarasha winced. "That's all very well, Leide, but this might get serious. There could be a cleavage of the Crew if we don't achieve Concurrence."

"And who else would I go with but my Family? Don't worry, Sarasha. The Family Tourn is fully behind the Captain. I

54

heard my father and Uncle Sten say it. I'm sure they have told your father."

"Well, it's good to hear, and I'm glad you're so happy."

"I'm not happy, Sara. This is too serious to be happy. But I am proud, and ready to serve in any way I can."

"All right. This is what we have to do…"

She explained the situation at the Captains' Conclave and what she was trying to achieve. Leide nodded several times, but did not interrupt until Sarasha finished.

"You want me to be available to run errands so you don't have to move. Fine. If the Captain needs me, he'll call. If you need me, use Mast'n signals. I'll be keeping an eye on you."

"Good idea. I'll have plenty of ink, pens and parchment, but you never know. There isn't a signal for most of that, so…"

They discussed changing the signals to suit their needs for a while. Then they heard a slithering footstep in the sand behind them.

"What kind of plotting is going on here, and in the presence of a stranger in camp?"

They looked up to see Yong and several of the others approaching. Sarasha grinned. "Scribe business, Sailor. Sorry, but we can't tell you."

"What about her?" He indicated the horse. "I doubt if she's a Scribe. Hasn't got the coordination."

"Oh, she's very important to us. She's contemplating becoming parchment some time not too long from now."

Pers frowned comically. "Sarasha! How heartless. Your faithful steed?"

Sarasha shrugged. "Don't worry. She has a stoic attitude towards life and death. We could all take a lesson."

"It'll be a rough quartering sea when I start taking lessons from a horse."

"On that topic, Yong, don't you think it's time we tried riding her? She's getting very tame."

"Tell that to CheyChan."

"Father says that doesn't count. Many horses kick if you stand behind them where they can't see you. They think it's a threat. Father says Cheynou is lucky. A horse can break bones or even kill you with a kick."

"I doubt if Cheynou feels very lucky every time he tries to breathe."

She shrugged. "The Surgeon said no ribs broken. He'll be fine." Then she glanced slyly at her friend. "I guess he sort of learned a lesson from a horse, didn't he?"

"Point taken, Sarasha. Do you think someone ought to try to ride her?"

"I'd like to try myself, but that would be too dangerous. If she threw me off and I landed on my sore foot, I could damage it even more than the first time."

"All right. I guess I'm elected. How should we do this?"

"Let's take it in easy stages." She turned to Leide, who had not spoken a word. "Want to help?"

To her surprise, the girl went signal red. "I...I guess so."

Sarasha was about to ask what the problem was when she realized where Leide wasn't looking: Pers. That explained a lot.

"All right, Yong. Untie her and lead her out into the centre of that clear spot of sand. We don't want you thrown on anything hard."

"Thanks."

Sarasha soon had her crew all lined up the way she wanted. "Remember, everyone, the last thing we want to do is startle her, so stay quiet. Those of you holding her head, keep holding on. If she can't rear up, she can't throw him off, and it's harder to kick you with her front feet."

"She kicks with her front feet too?"

"Wouldn't you?" She turned to Yong. "I think you should do it gradually. First, press on her back. Then lean on her. Watch her ears. She flattens them back when she's angry. That's to keep them from getting injured in a fight, I suppose. Once you're sure, lean over her back, a bit for'ard of centre, right behind her shoulders. Once she's used to that, the others can give you a boost up, and you can lie right across her. That way, if she rears, you can slip off.

"Then stop, no matter what. I want her to get a rest at that point."

They all nodded and circled around the horse, flexing their hands as if for a battle. The subject of their attention stood relaxed, her head in a normal pose, her ears twitching forward and to the side.

The two men assigned to her head took a firm grip on the halter Tonu had braided to fit her head.

"Go up and introduce yourself again."

Yong approached the horse, holding his fist under her nose for a sniff. She flicked her ears towards him and lipped his fist briefly.

"She wants grain."

They all chuckled.

Yong glanced at Sarasha, then moved to the horse's shoulder. The animal ignored him. He placed his hands on her back and pushed down. No response. He pressed harder. She shifted her weight and everyone froze.

They watched the horse's ears, but she seemed only mildly interested in the whole proceeding. Sarasha nodded encouragement, and Yong laid his weight across the horse's shoulders.

Getting no response, he glanced at Pers, who bent over to take his ankle.

Sarasha hid a grin at the sight of Leide gazing at this action with rapt eyes. She peered around. *How funny we all look: as tense as before a battle.*

Pers straightened slowly, and Yong laid his weight over the horse. Still, she did not move.

He lay there, then raised his head to look back at Sarasha. "This is very uncomfortable. I think I'll stop."

He slid down to the sand and moved forward to the horse's head, rubbing her ears and under her jawline.

"Give her some grain."

Leide broke from her trance to scurry over to the keg.

"Easy now..."

The girl slowed and returned with exaggerated care, carrying the plate of grain. "Give it to Yong."

Yong held the plate under the horse's nose, talking to her as Sarasha had. Ebb Tide snorted to take in the rich smell, then gobbled up the grain while they all watched, fascinated.

When she was finished, the tableau broke.

"What do you think, 'Rasha?"

"She seemed pretty bored to me. I'm almost sure now that she's been ridden before. Are you willing to try the real thing?"

Yong flexed his muscles. "The hero is ready any time to do battle with the ferocious beast."

She punched his arm. "Don't you even consider making this a battle. If she gets upset, you get off as quickly as you can. I don't want her to think this is worth a fight. If she won't let you mount, we'll do it more gradually."

"Aye, ma'am." He grinned and strode back to the horse. "All right, boys. Hold her fast. Pers, give me a leg up."

They complied. Yong swung his long leg over the horse's back, and then he was sitting astride.

There was a frozen moment of silence. No one moved, not even the horse. The men holding the horse's head looked to Sarasha. She motioned them back. One passed the end of the halter rope to Yong, and everyone stood away.

Again, nothing happened. Ebb Tide turned her head around and snuffed at the rider's knee, then faced forward again. They all laughed, quietly though.

"What do I do now?"

"You can probably get off now."

"Get off?"

"Yes. We've proved what we wanted to, today."

He seemed about to argue, but then he glanced at Sarasha, noted her stance, and nodded. Leaning back, he kicked his foot over the horse's neck and started to slide to the ground. She tossed her head and shifted sideways. He almost fell, grabbing her shoulder to steady himself. She shifted away again and he stumbled, then caught his balance. He stood, panting, and the horse turned her head again to regard him with disdain.

This time, everyone laughed louder.

"I would guess that's not the proper way to get off a horse."

Sarasha grinned. "First lesson learned, Yong."

"Shall I try again?"

Shearasha shook her head. "No, that's enough for today."

"But we were just getting started."

"Right. And I don't want to spoil everything. Come back tomorrow after you get in from scouting, and we'll try again."

He nodded and led the horse back to the cleat where she was tethered. Unbidden, Leide brought a bit more grain, and Pers refilled the canvas bucket with water.

Once they were away from the horse, their voices got louder, as did their laughter, when they recounted the great anti-climax of their attempts.

"You looked pretty silly there, Yong, sitting so tall and worried on that poor little horse." Pers chuckled. "Your feet almost touched the ground."

Yong tossed his head. "I didn't notice any of the rest of you stumbling over each other to volunteer."

There was a chorus of offers, but he shook his head. "After I take all the risks, you want all the glory. Give up on that."

The conversation broke up into other topics, and Yong turned to Sarasha. "Want a lift?"

She shook her head. "I've got to learn to use this crutch. It works all right, but it keeps sinking into soft spots in the sand."

Pers watched her struggle for a moment. "You need a bigger end on it, so it doesn't sink."

"And I bet it hurts under your arm." Leide immediately looked down, as if abashed to have spoken.

Sarasha turned to her cousin. "That it does. Do you have any ideas?"

"Well..."

"Go ahead. Right about now, I'm ready to listen to anything."

The girl moved her fingers in a helpless gesture. "Well, I've watched you in the rigging. You have very strong arms. With the crutch, you aren't using them. You're putting all your weight on your armpit, which is a tender spot."

Pers stepped forward. "That's right. You should have some kind of crossbar, here," he indicated where her right hand grasped the shaft, "so you can push down on it."

"But not across. It has to be..." Again, Leide stopped. "Oh, I'm sorry. You go ahead, Pers."

"No, no, you're right. It can't be across, because then she can't put her palm on it, because the shaft is in the way."

"It has to stick out on one side."

"That's right. We could drill a hole through..."

"...but that would weaken the main shaft. How could we...?"

"Maybe a bolt all the way through?"

"Right. Then we could wrap the handle tightly in cloth for padding..."

"...and cover it with sharkskin like a cutlass hilt for good grip..."

They both stopped, puzzled when they heard the chuckle.

"What's wrong?"

Sarasha laughed harder. "That was so funny. It was like two parts of the same head talking to itself!"

The two glanced at each other. Leide blushed.

Pers didn't notice. "But what's so funny? Isn't it a good idea?"

Sarasha laughed again. "Yes, Pers. It sounds like a wonderful idea. Why don't the two of you go over to the Shipwrights' cabin...tent, and see if they will make that for me?"

Pers' face cleared. He glanced at the younger girl. "Come on, Leide. Let's do that."

"Um...shouldn't we measure the old crutch?"

Pers pulled a piece of string out of his pocket, laid it against the crutch and began tying knots in it.

"Maybe Sarasha as well."

He didn't answer, merely started with the other end of the string, measuring the length of her arm and the distance from

60

the ground to her armpit. When he finished, he turned to Leide. "Anything else you can think of?"

She shook her head.

He nodded sharply, turned and strode away.

Leide, with an apologetic glance at her cousin, scurried after him.

Sarasha shook her head and continued her stumbling progress back to her tent, where Yong watched the pair's departure with a bemused expression.

"Is she really smart or something?"

"You saw for yourself. Anybody who can keep up with Pers when he gets one of his thinking jags on..."

He nodded. "She seemed uncomfortable, though."

"A bit."

He stopped and regarded her. "What do you mean?" When she didn't answer, he thought a moment. "Oh...she likes him."

"You're so perceptive."

"Only when I'm hit over the head with it."

Sarasha struggled on, exhausted with the effort of making reasonable speed back to her tent. She swung into her hammock, and Yong wordlessly disappeared inside, coming back with a cup of water.

She gulped it gratefully, then lay back. "We've got a good bunch there. They were great while you were working with Ebb Tide. Not a sound, everybody held his or her place. Pers and Leide aren't the only ones with brains, either."

"Is there any way we can put that intelligence to work?"

"I can't help but think that the Captains will meet in their Conclave and make up their minds like they always do, and then we will all do what they decide."

He shrugged. "What's wrong with that? They are all good Captains. I trust every one of them to do what is best for his Crew."

"That's not the point. If we let them make all the decisions, even good ones, it will be just like it was back in the Fleet. One leader making the choices for everyone."

"That's pretty revolutionary, Sarasha."

61

"I keep saying. It isn't any more revolutionary than what the Captains did. But we have to make sure they stay revolutionary."

"I see." He was grinning. "And how will you do that?"

"Yong, be serious. I mean it."

"I am serious."

"Then if you had been listening to what I said, you wouldn't be asking me to solve the problem either. That would only transfer the responsibility to someone else."

He held up his hands in surrender. "All right, all right. How do *we* make sure the Captains stay revolutionary?"

"Hmm." She fixed him with a stare to make sure he wasn't laughing. "When a group is used to following a strong leader, they stop thinking ahead. They wait to see what the leader will do. Then they may complain or argue, but they don't have a plan of their own. They merely react. The plan is still his."

"I see. So the power rests with him, because even if they argue, the argument is based on what he has decided."

"Exactly."

"So how do you...pardon me, how do we break out of that pattern?"

She grinned. "That part is simple."

"Of course. Come up with a plan of our own. That's easy. The tough part is coming up with a good plan."

"Right on tack again. But we already have a plan."

"We do?"

"Yes. It's what came out at the Crew Conclave. We have to come up with positive things that will get people enthused about our new life. We have to forget about weeping and wailing over our problems."

Yong nodded. "You're right. There's a different atmosphere when the scouting parties go out. There's a sense of adventure, of excitement in finding new places. Then we come back to the Crew, and everybody is so down and worried I sometimes feel guilty about how much fun I've been having."

"Wait." She held up her hand, then raised her voice. "Father, are you in there?"

Her father's voice came faintly from inside the tent. "Your servant awaits your orders, my Lady."

"Stop being silly, Father. Are you busy? Could you come out here a moment?"

Her father's head appeared through the tent flap. "Oh. You already have one of your loyal servants here. Why do you need a mere father as well?"

She gave an exasperated sigh. "Stop trying to cheer me up. I'm happy. See? I'm smiling."

Her father seated himself on a nearby log. "All right. I'm sorry. I can tell by the way you're trying to sit up in that hammock that you have something serious to discuss."

"We do, Father. Yong, tell him what you said about the scouting expeditions."

Yong repeated his observation, and the Captain nodded. "It's a good thing you brought this to my attention. You and your friends seemed to be dealing with the situation much better than anyone else, and I had wondered about it. I thought they were just being cheerful to keep your spirits up, Sarasha. I should have realized it was more than that."

Yong grinned. "I have to admit that was part of it, sir. It was a good excuse to show high spirits in camp when we might have felt guilty about it."

The Captain mulled that over. "So you're suggesting people need a task that looks forward, thinking ahead to what our lives will be like in the future."

He glanced at Sarasha and smiled wryly. "You know, I need some of the same medicine. I was sitting in there, feeling sorry for myself, wondering if I'd done the right thing for my Family and Crew and worrying about what might happen now. I need to be planning what we will do, not what will be done to us.

"Yes, it's time for a Conclave of Family Heads. Sarasha, call one... oh sorry, you can't. Yong, will you make the call? Family Heads, Officers and Heads of Crafts. Make it the tenth bell. That will give everyone a chance to have supper and hear the complaints of their families. They'll be ready for anything we come up with."

"Who are these 'we' you're talking about?"

"What do you mean?"

Sarasha wove her head back and forth. "Father, that's another thing you've been telling me. If you do everything yourself, then people depend on you too much. If you come to this Conclave with a plan, then it will be your plan, and nothing else will be discussed."

"And that was the downfall of the Fleet. Thank you, Sarasha. I count on you to keep me on my best behaviour. You are suggesting I should prepare the other Heads and Officers before the meeting, so they can come up with their own plans."

"I wasn't suggesting anything, Father." She smiled sweetly. "I think that's a good idea."

Her father gave her a "don't play those games with me" stare, and turned to Yong. "You understand what I'm trying to do. This is your idea, after all."

"It is?"

"With a little nudge from us, yes it is. So don't just deliver the message like a cabin boy. Stop and talk with the Heads. Tell them what you told me. Say I'm searching for ideas... no, say we need ideas, and to bring any thoughts they have to the Conclave."

Sarasha could see Yong's back straighten. "I understand, Captain Tourn. I will do my best."

He didn't quite salute as he left. Sarasha shared a chuckle with her father.

"He'll be a good officer some day."

She shrugged. "Or whatever we have instead of officers."

"True." He regarded his daughter for a moment. "You young people are dealing with this change better than the older folks. You should be making yourselves ready to take on more responsibility much sooner than you might have expected."

She nodded soberly. "I've already been thinking about that."

"Good." He regarded her sideways. "Does that mean I don't have to be cheerful to keep your spirits up any more?"

"Oh no, you can carry on as you were. You have no idea how good I feel every chance I get to tell you that you've made a mistake."

Her father rose to go into the tent and stood peering down at her. "I'll make you a deal. If I don't go looking for an excuse to have you Beached for fear of my position, will you promise not to Beach me when I'm no use to you any more?"

She lurched upright and threw her arms around him. "Father! Don't make jokes about things like that!"

He patted her shoulder. "Don't worry, Daughter. I'll never have you Beached."

She pulled back, staring up at him. "I was just about to say the same thing to you!"

They both roared with laughter. Hearing the disturbance, Verlene put her head out of the tent. "What are you two up to?"

Her husband shook his head, spreading his hands in a Storyteller's gesture. "You have heard tales of the dreadful stillness, when the Kraken has been aroused, and the whole Ship waits to see where it will erupt from the deeps?"

Verlene nodded, puzzled.

The Captain hooked a thumb at his daughter. "Her. I'm just waiting for what she's going to do next."

In the laughter that followed, Sarasha could almost ignore the pain in her foot.

7. CAPTAINS' CONCLAVE

"... a people without laws is not a people. I foresee nothing but trouble if we were to follow such a dangerous course."

Sarasha suppressed a sigh and wondered, as she scribbled away, if it might be permissible to edit the Log. In the past glass, Captain Kletsh of the *Raptor* had said the same thing, in different words, five times. At length. *If we wait a breath, one of the younger Captains, probably Lukin Frey of the* Falcon, *will restate Father's position. Ah, yes, there he goes.*

"I must repeat, Honoured Captains. The old laws are a recipe for failure. If we follow them, we will end up in the same predicament as exists in the Fleet. We will only have a new tyrant. It may be one of us here or one of our offspring, but a tyrant we will have. Those laws are what allowed the Priest-Admiral to dominate us. We must not follow them, or we will not survive."

Sarasha looked around the table in the brief silence that followed. No one seemed anxious to add to the discussion. Several of the Captains had turned to their neighbours and were muttering together. She took a deep breath and addressed her father.

"Honoured Captain Tourn, may I speak?"

As she had hoped, her quiet voice surprised them to attention. Her father regarded her, his brow furrowing. He glanced around the table, then nodded. "No one can be denied the right to speak. That is one of the main reasons we broke with the Priest-Admiral and his rules. What do you have to say, Captain's Scribe, that might aid us in our deliberations?"

Sarasha stood, keeping her good leg against the chair to steady herself. "It seems to me that Captain Kletsh is right." She noted her father's surprised expression. "And so are you, Captain Tourn."

She nodded, accepting their incredulity. "My friends and I have been discussing this very problem. We have come to the conclusion that a society of any sort is not possible without a set of rules. However, we also concur that the set of rules we once lived under were out of date, impractical, and often misused to the detriment of the Fleet."

Hamon Kletsh snorted a bark of unhumorous laughter. "And who are you and these friends of yours? It sounds to me like the usual carping of the young, who can't discipline themselves to follow the proper rules."

She swung to face the Captain squarely, ignoring the pain it caused her. "I speak for a group of the sons and daughters of the leaders of our Families, some of the strongest Raiders and the best Craftspeople. Not simply a clutch of disaffected young rebels, any more than you, our Captains, are. We follow you, not only because you are our Captains, but because we believe you have acted honourably and properly."

The older man stared at her a moment, then nodded. "Well, speak on, then, Voice of the Young. You have a sly tongue. What wisdom do you have to impart to us?"

"Hmm." She eyed him so he understood that she had caught his sarcasm, and it did not affect her.

"What we have been doing, Honoured Captains, is studying the Holy Works, the Log books and the Scribe's Records of the *Eagle*."

"You have been sharing the Logs of your Ship with all and sundry?"

"There is nothing secret in any of those books. Everything that has happened occurred in front of the whole Crew. That was another reason we broke from the Priest-Admiral, was it not? Secrecy and the control of information."

There were several nods around the table. A quiet voice slid through. "Let her speak. We need this."

It was not a voice she had heard much today, but she silently thanked the speaker, Captain Bren, for his reasonable tone.

"We have been examining all the rules we live by. We have also been studying the records of how those rules have been applied over the years."

"And what is your intention?" Kletsh raised his hands. "What do you hope to find in this search?"

"It came from an observation Captain Tourn made about this new situation. We must regard each rule and try to decide whether it is a good rule for our present situation."

"So every law is open to interpretation? Every man may choose to obey, or not obey, depending on his whim? You are charting a course to anarchy, I suggest."

She tried to keep the careful patience out of her voice. "Which is only one step above the chaos we would have if we obeyed no rules at all. What we think should happen is that we, as a Fleet, or a Group, or whatever we decide to call ourselves, should decide as a group which rules we should follow, which we should adapt, which we should reject. It must be decided by some carefully selected procedure upon which everyone agrees. Once it has been decided, then the law becomes a law, and so all must live by it.

"There are two reasons to obey a law, Captains. The first is because it is a law, and so you must follow it. This is the law of the Priest-Admiral. Notice the word 'must' in that statement. If there is force written into a law, then there has to be someone to enforce that law. Until now, the Priest-Admiral had the strength to enforce his laws, no matter how unjust.

"The second reason to obey a law is because you believe it is a good law. There is no force needed. If all feel the law is right, then all will obey it."

She raised her hand to forestall the outbursts. "Oh, we're not naïve enough to believe there really is such a system. Some laws need to be enforced. There will always be those who, for reasons of passion, greed or principle, will want to disobey, and the Crew must have the means of enforcing compliance in those cases. But the less force required, the easier the law is to administer. That is our contention, Captains.

"What the Fleet lives by is the wisdom of the ages, petrified by time, then mismanaged for the benefit of tyrannical leaders. What we want is the wisdom of the ages tempered by the thoughtfulness of understanding people of our time. That is the kind of law my friends and I want to live under in our new lives."

To her surprise, the greying head in front of her bobbed in agreement, and a deep chuckle arose from Captain Kletsh's barrel chest. "Young lady, you bring a fresh breeze to these becalmed proceedings. It is a pleasure to hear someone young and idealistic, no matter if a bit naïve. If we Captains assembled here had not been so idealistic, we would not have set our Ships on this destructive course."

He sat back, his glance around the table offering Precedence to the others.

"An interesting concept." Again that calm voice arose, and she turned to face him: Orrick Bren, Captain of the *Storm Petrel*. She knew him only by reputation. He was the youngest Rebel Captain by many years, yet his little Ship had done more damage to the Fleet than several of his larger allies. "Captain's Scribe, can you give us an example of a law you have discussed with this formidable group of friends of yours?"

"Certainly, Captain Bren. We have discussed the laws that govern the Beaching of the unclean, the unfit, and the unwelcome. I have some personal interest in that practice."

"And I suppose you have decided that this is one of the laws that should be scrapped."

She spun to face this new attack, but the *Petrel*'s Captain raised a gentle hand and smiled. "Perhaps you do the lady an injustice, Captain Cawbur. Let her finish."

"If you think about it, Captains, Beaching may be one practice we may be forced to apply with more rigour in our new life."

There was a mutter of surprise around the table.

"Yes, when you consider the reasons for that law, its value is clear. The use of Beaching probably developed for practical reasons. Infectious disease or the inability to cooperate with the Crew could be very destructive to the Families, and in some cases, removal from the Ship might be the best solution. What we cannot conceive is how a Crew would allow the rules to develop into what they became: an excuse for the Priest-

69

Admiral and his cronies to get rid of anyone who disagreed with them.

"In our new situation, the currents run in other directions. There would be no practical need, on a Ship, to remove someone such as myself. Even if I couldn't work the rigging, I can still be a Scribe, still do innumerable tasks on a Ship, and the Ship would suffer little from having me aboard.

"Off the Ship, however, this changes. If I cannot move myself, then someone else must be taken from his task to carry me. If that someone is a Raider, then keeping me with the Crew weakens the Crew. One might argue that the rules should be changed so that those who cannot move themselves must be left behind."

They all regarded her a moment, and she wished someone would speak.

"Oh, don't think I'm being so altruistic as to doom myself as a matter of principle. I don't plan on being one of those left behind."

Old Kletsh let out another bark of laughter. "No, I don't imagine you do, young lady."

He turned to the other Captains. "What do you say, my friends? Is this the temporary, partial solution we have all been searching for? Is this the compromise that will keep us together as a people until we have learned to exist on this wild shore where we have all been Beached?"

There was no argument.

"Fair enough." The old head swivelled, the pale brown eyes pinning her. "And has this group of brilliant young minds come up with a solution to our other problem?"

She met his gaze and raised her opinion of the old Captain. The usual sarcasm was there, but also a glint of interest. *He really hopes we have something.* She decided to use this to her advantage.

"Captain Kletsh, if you were a Farmer over there, and eight Ships of the infamous Horde who had raided you for years suddenly beached themselves down the shore from you, what would you do?"

"I can't tell what a Farmer would do, but if it was me, I'd get together everyone I could and attack as quick as I could: hit 'em before they knew it."

"Which is why we have been keeping our scouts moving all over that area. Correct?" She nodded. "Now, does anybody have any doubt what the Priest-Admiral will do the moment he has reknotted his hand firmly on the helm of the Fleet?" She looked around the table.

"Exactly. No matter what anyone would like to think, we will soon find ourselves moving to the only place where there is room for us: north into the Great Prairie. If we go now, when we are strong, we might survive. If we wait until we are driven in defeat, we will die. That is the harsh reality, Honoured Captains. While my friends and I understand the need for discussion, we are aware of why you are spending all this time talking. You made this decision long ago. You only have to discuss it in order to work the idea around in your heads until you can accept the consequences of your decision."

"You presume to challenge us at our own Conclave?" She could hear suppressed anger quivering in this Captain's voice. "Do you have the temerity to question our decisions?"

"Not at all, Captain Cawbur." She met his eyes. "We realize that this procedure must be followed. Some of us have stated the wish that we move through it as quickly as possible: before we are attacked and while summer is still high on the Prairie, giving us time to settle in somewhere and prepare for winter. The gathering of sufficient fuel may, in itself, be the difference between life and death. I believe the Holy Works tell us that refusing to make a decision is a decision in itself, and often the worst one."

Kletsh's battered hand cracked down on the table. "Fair enough. I asked, and I have an answer to my question, whether I like it or not." Again, his eye seemed to pin Sarasha in place. "So, my young Scribe. You are a straight talker, but you don't seem to be doing your assigned task. Who will write this conversation?"

71

Sarasha shot a glance at her father, at the other Captains. "I have most of it written for you already, Captain Kletsh, and my assistant has been keeping track of what was said here today."

The sharp laugh rang out once more. "Once again I must concede defeat, young lady." He turned to Arlijn. "Don't worry about your daughter, Captain of the *Eagle*. If there were any attempt to Beach her, I suspect most of your Crew would choose to stay alongside her."

Sarasha straightened to her full height, ignoring the pain this caused her foot. "I would not be a source of disharmony in the Crew, Captain Kletsh. If it were necessary, I would Beach myself and make sure no one followed."

He regarded her for a moment, all humour gone from his face. "I believe you would, young lady. I believe you would."

Then he turned to the other Captains. "I tire of this conversation on impractical matters. The topic has gone around the circle long enough for us to understand each other's positions. I have plenty to think about, plenty to discuss with my Families and Crew, and I have been sitting still for too long. Did you manage to salvage any decent food off the *Eagle*, Captain Tourn?"

There was a general chuckle at that, and the Captains rose and filed out of the tent. Kletsh paused beside Sarasha. "Young lady, if you would accept a piece of advice from a slow-moving old man..."

She grinned at him.

"...most of us have heard enough Scripture quoted at us, usually to support unpopular arguments."

She nodded. "Force of habit, sir. I have much to learn."

He barked his laugh again. "Glad you know it, young lady."

He turned and followed the other Captains. Captain Tourn waited until last. He turned for a glance at his daughter, shook his head, then followed the others.

Leide frowned. "I wonder what that meant?"

Sarasha shrugged. "He doesn't sound angry. It worked, after all. Did you get it all down?"

Leide's nod seemed worried.

"What's wrong? Did you miss something?"

"No, it's just that some of the things you said aren't quite what you had written."

Sarasha laughed. "I'm sure they aren't. That's what happens when a plan hits reality. Keep both sets of ideas. Somewhere in the middle is what we'll end up with."

* * *

Sarasha did not attend the meal, but a report of the discussion that took place reached her before suppertime. She stormed off to confront her father and found him perched on a rock overlooking the ocean and the wreckage of his Ship. The look on his face almost drained her anger. Almost.

"Father, I have to talk to you."

He took a moment to regard her. "I'm not sure I want to talk to you. Not when you have that look on your face."

She swept aside his humour. "Did you really say what I heard you said?"

"And what was that?"

"You know."

"You mean about the mast?"

"Yes, I mean about the mast. The story's all over the camp. Apparently, while you were eating, one of the other Captains asked you how you dealt with such a strong-minded daughter. Apparently, you said you liked it better when you could keep me up the foremast!"

"That sounds about right."

"How could you, Father? Everyone is laughing at me, now."

"Are they?"

"Of course they are!"

"I'm not so sure. Maybe they're laughing at me." He patted the rock beside him. "Is your foot bothering you?"

"My foot is always bothering me. Don't change the subject."

"I'm not. If your foot wasn't bothering you, you would see what I did."

"What was that?"

"You tell me."

She stared at him. He always played this game with her, and sometimes she hated it. "All right. What did you do? You made fun of me."

"No, I didn't."

She thought a moment. "You made fun of our relationship."

"That's more accurate. Why?"

"That's what I can't understand. I thought I made some good points at that meeting, and now you undermine my credibility."

He shook his head. "You know I wouldn't do that."

"That's what I thought. So why...? Right. I'm supposed to figure out why."

He waited, so she thought it over. "All right. I had just given the Captains a bitter potion. They knew it was the right medicine, but it tasted bad."

"Exactly. Cawbur was starting to get angry."

"And he was getting angry at me. Then Captain Kletsh cut him off."

"A good move on his part. I couldn't do it, because you are my daughter."

"So it would make it harder to accept the distasteful medicine if they were angry at the person doling it out."

"Exactly."

"So by making a joke, you remove me as a danger, so make it easier for them to accept the medicine."

"And by making the joke about me rather than you, I minimize the damage to you."

"But what about damage to you?"

He smiled. "I receive no slight. Every man there wishes he had offspring who could face down a Captains' Conclave, tell them what they didn't want to hear and get away with it."

A smile dragged across her face. "I did, didn't I?"

"That's right. Don't let it go to your head."

"Don't worry. It wasn't all me. It was my friends who gave me the ideas and the strength to present them."

74

"Fine. But this is a delicate time. It's not a time for those in charge to fear another new power arising."

"I suppose."

"I more than suppose. Have you read any of those History scrolls we kept in the Ship's Archives?"

"I glanced through them. Most of them weren't anything to do with the Fleet."

"Well, we aren't anything to do with the Fleet either, now. As it happens, it's a pattern that has occurred more than once in history. A tyrannical regime is overthrown by a group of reasonable men who have taken all they can stomach. A more radical group, usually younger, takes advantage of the breakdown of law and order to take over from the original rebels and install an even more tyrannical regime of their own.

"After a while, the populace gets tired of this new tyranny and overthrows the radicals in their turn, but not until many good people have been killed."

"I see."

"Right. We can't afford to have anything like that happen. It would destroy us."

"Father, we will do nothing of the sort! We still follow you Captains and are loyal to you!"

"As long as we keep making decisions you approve of. What if you thought that our lack of a decision would put the Crew in serious danger? What would you do then?"

"Father, that is an impossible question, and you know it."

"Nonetheless. You keep those young rebels of yours on a short anchor rode."

She regarded him for a breath. "I can't do that, Father."

"You can't?"

"No. That's the whole point of what you did, what we all did. We don't let one person take charge of us, ever again. I won't do that to my friends, and I've told them never to let me do it to them."

"You told them. So you really are in charge."

"No, I'm not. I refuse to be."

"You aren't in charge. Let's call it very influential."

"All right, Father. If you say so. I'm influential with my friends. I will use what influence I can to make sure we cause no revolutions. All right?"

He smiled and shook his head. "Sometimes it is so hard to persuade you to do what you're already doing."

She gave him her most withering 'don't play those games with me' stare.

8. FLIGHT

The meetings went on and on. First, there was another Heads of Families. Once the information from the Captains' Conclave was given to everybody, there had to be another Crew Conclave, one that took all evening. Captain Tourn came away from that one rubbing his hands.

"That was much better."

His wife nodded. "The whole tone was much more positive."

"Sarasha?"

"I could feel the same thing. This was a planning meeting, with everyone reporting their progress on their projects, and everyone being impressed at how much we had all achieved. We will be ready to move out soon."

"Yes. They don't know where they're going, but they're getting ready to go."

Verlene frowned. "Is there any question of where we're going?"

"None at all." Arlijn laughed. "If Sarasha says we're going to the Great Prairie, then that's where we're going."

"Father! I keep telling you not to joke about that sort of thing."

"And I keep telling you, dear, that it's the best way to deal with it." He sat down, reached for the drink his wife put in front of him. "The Captains are pretty well agreed. They were happy to have something they could show concurrence on because they're divided on the greater problem of what to do for laws. Despite Sarasha and her friends' ideas, they still haven't lashed their minds to that one."

He took a long drink and sat back. "Now we have to start our own plans for the move. What do we take, what do we leave behind."

Sarasha cocked her head to one side, regarding her father. "I would have thought there was no question on the last one."

"In what way?"

"I didn't think we'd leave anything behind. Anything at all."

"Oh, I take your meaning. Yes, I agree with that. We're not leaving the good old *Eagle of the Sea* to be picked over by scavengers. There's plenty of tar that we don't need and we can't carry." A shadow fell across his face. "I'm sure it will burn very well."

On that sombre note, they went to bed.

Sarasha tossed and turned, trying to find the position in which her foot hurt the least. She had refused the Surgeon's potions because they made her drowsy, and she needed her mind at its best for these deliberations.

Of course, if I don't sleep, my mind won't be at its best. She stared at the dim canvas above her, trying to let the reflected flicker of the low fire send her mind drifting. After a long while, she slept, but restlessly, half the time flying across the plains on her horse, the other half dragging a huge, ungainly weight attached to her leg: a weight that was her leg.

In the morning she was not completely rested, but she threw herself into as much activity as she could manage. By mid-afternoon she was tired and feverish again. She took the bandage off her foot to see if there was anything wrong, but it lay there, inert and swollen, the same as always. When she tried to move her toes and ankle, she had limited success. Wrapping it away, she grabbed her new crutch. It was short, ending at her elbow. The tightly wrapped sharkskin handle fitted into her hand, and a strap fastened the top of the pole to her forearm, making it like an extension to her arm. She liked the feel of it. It was solid and made use of her main strength, her arm. She hoped that when they moved inland where the ground was more solid, she could travel better. The small plate screwed to the bottom of the crutch helped some, but the whole contraption still dragged in soft sand.

She was swinging across to check on Ebb Tide, which always cheered her up, when she heard her name called. Turning, she saw Yong jogging into camp at that slow, distance-covering pace the scouts had developed. Perhaps a bit faster than usual. A frisson of fear went up her spine.

78

"Why are you back so early?"

He was panting more than usual. "Get over there and learn to ride that horse, 'Rasha. You'll be needing it."

"Who's coming?"

"The Farmers. They've hired a bunch of mercenaries. They're about two days west of the port, which means three days from the *Osprey*'s camp. I just got word, and I'm headed over to tell your father. I mean it. Get on that horse."

She nodded and hurried on, her crutch scattering sand in all directions.

When she reached the horse's enclosure, she calmed herself. This was no task to be done in haste. She called and held out her hand. Ebb Tide came over, snuffling for the grain or small vegetable Sarasha always gave her. While she was chewing, Sarasha slipped the halter over her nose. She had attached another rope under the chin so she could pull in either direction, the way her father had told her that Farmers steered their horses.

There was no putting it off. Yong had walked the horse around the enclosure, and Sarasha knew the mare obeyed in a docile fashion. Of course, no one had tried to make her do anything she didn't want to do. For the moment, Sarasha had no intention of changing this. She was searching around for a way to get aboard when Pers came panting up.

"Yong said you needed me. What's up?"

"The Farmers have raised an army. We'll be moving in the next couple of days. I have to be able to ride."

"All right. Have you got your steering lines? I've put Yong aboard several times. You bend your knee, I hold your lower leg, and up you go."

He heaved and she floated up. Sitting astride the horse seemed comfortable. She shifted around to find the best position. When she felt ready, she lifted the lines and kicked the horse lightly in the ribs. Ebb Tide snorted and stepped forward.

Sarasha pulled the starboard line, and the horse turned obediently. She let the line slack, and the horse straightened her course. She tried a turn to port. Then she hauled back on both lines and brought them to a standing stop. She turned to look back at Pers.

"So far, so good."

He nodded. "You just have to keep practicing."

"Right. Drop that log, will you?"

"Are you going out?"

"No time to mess around, Pers. I have to be able to ride her in less than two days. If she tosses me off, they'll have to carry me or Beach me."

Shrugging at the inevitable, he lowered the bar that closed off the fence.

She nudged Ebb Tide forward and steered her out through the gap, chosing a path down by the beach because the sand below the tide line would be firmer under the horse's feet. They paced around, turning port and starboard, stopping, then continuing. Pers easily kept pace with Ebb Tide's slow steps.

"I wonder how it feels when she goes faster?"

"Be careful!"

"Don't worry." She kicked the horse more firmly.

Immediately, she was bouncing up and down. Every step the horse took jarred her to the top of her spine. She tried to haul back on the lines but that only pulled her forward, up on the hump of the horse's shoulders. Her sore foot flopped painfully against Ebb Tide's leg. Finally, she fisted one hand in the horse's mane, grabbed the lines in the other hand and hauled back. Ebb Tide slowed to her usual walk.

"Are you all right?" Pers jogged up beside her. "I was afraid to come alongside in case I frightened her into running faster."

"I'm not sure."

"That must have been painful. I was worried you'd fall off."

"You were afraid I'd fall off? I was afraid I'd be split in half!"

Pers shook his head. "There has to be some way to do it. The rich men who ride horses have metal loops attached to a seat across the horse's back. They can stand up in the loops so they don't bounce."

80

"There's no time to build one of those."

"And I don't think the Farmers are likely to sell us one."

She rounded on him. "Don't you dare try to steal one! We can't waste people or time on that sort of thing. If I can't figure out the trot, I'll be riding her at a walk anyway, and if there's an emergency, I can hold on to her mane and suffer."

They turned around and started back. She kicked the horse into a trot again, and did a little better by grasping the mane. She slowed to a walk again.

"Holding on works a bit. I don't flop my sore foot against her leg all the time. But I can't steer with only one hand, and I still bounce around."

She worked at it several times on the way back, and had some success, but by the time they returned to the fence, her backside was sore.

"Help me down, Pers. That's something else I have to figure out. How do I get up and down?"

He grinned. "For a mast'n, getting up should be no problem."

"You mean grab her mane? Won't that hurt her?"

"How much pulling were you doing when you were bouncing around?"

"Quite a bit, I guess. It didn't seem to bother her. Here, let me try."

She took a double handful of the horse's mane and pulled herself up. When her head was clear of the shoulders, she pushed herself upright, then swung her right leg over. "That works, all right, but it's awkward."

"Could you do it the opposite of what Yong does when he gets off?"

"You mean swing my right leg up?"

"Yes. It seems to me you could use the weight of the leg to swing yourself over. You do that all the time, up in the rigging."

She got off again, stood facing the horse.

"You probably need to face the stern."

"She's not a boat, Pers."

"All right, the back. We have to find out what everything is called."

"Right. When we have time, we must find someone to show us how to do this whole thing properly. Right now, I'd settle for being able to get on easily by myself."

She faced the rear of the horse, grabbed its mane, and swung her right foot a few times. Yes, the momentum would help. Swinging her foot back farther, she kicked herself up...

...and screamed in pain as her ankle collided with the horse's back. Ebb Tide shifted away nervously, and Pers grabbed Sarasha before she could fall.

"Are you all right?"

"What do you think?"

"I think, no."

She stood a moment, her teeth ground together, as waves of pain rolled up her leg. "I think I have to sit down."

He did not answer, simply gathered her up in his arms and carried her to the fence. She sat in the sand with her foot propped up on the lower rail. He checked her once more, then went to Ebb Tide and picked up the lines, which had been trailing on the sand.

"So much for that idea. I'm sorry, 'Rasha."

"Don't be sorry. It was a good idea, but I did it wrong. I'll try again in a moment."

"No, you won't!"

"Yes, I will."

"You're hurt!"

"I've been hurt for a month. It's worse at the moment and it's getting better."

He shook his head. "All right. But maybe I'll try the idea a few times first."

She managed to grin. "Good idea. It is yours after all."

The frustrating thing was how easily he did it. The second try, he swung neatly aboard the horse, and there he sat, erect and ready to ride. He tried it again a few times to get it right.

"All right. I've got it. Are you sure you want to try?"

"With you making it look so easy? I should say!"

He brought the horse over to her and gave her a few instructions. She listened, watched as he demonstrated.

Then she took the two lines in her left hand, grabbed the mane, made sure of the path of her foot, and swung up.

"Ouch!"

"What? What happened?"

"I hit my foot on her other side. But I made it! I got aboard by myself!"

"Great. Are you going to practice now?"

She leaned forward and slid off. "No, I've done enough for one day. We'll give her some grain and water, and then I suspect we all have packing to do.

9. BOOKS AND HORSES

The next two days were filled with the organized chaos of a disciplined people attempting the impossible. Sarasha spent her time packing delicate items into chests. The Shipwrights had outdone themselves in creating ways for people to carry things. They had even taken the handspokes off the helm and attached two long poles to the shaft. Two men could push and steady it with a lot of weight hung on the poles on either side of the wheel. Others were using two poles to carry a heavy trunk like a stretcher between them.

A lead group of Stevedores had gone out the first morning, carrying extra tents and sailcloth as far as they thought the Crew could go in a day. They had then turned around and walked back, arriving late in the evening, exhausted. The second day they left again with supplies and other essentials.

That morning Sarasha realized Yong was missing. She was feeling useless, so she went looking, but she couldn't see him. Now that she thought about it, Pers and two of their other friends were nowhere around, either. There could be no thought of them running away, so she wondered what they were up to. She began thinking.

"We have to leave so much behind!" She turned to see her mother, for once looking forlorn. Her capable hands hung at her sides, and her shoulders had a new stoop. "We should have gone earlier when we had time."

"We have time, Mother. The men have taken two full trips already. See how bare the camp is? We'll be able to carry a lot, ourselves."

Verlene shook her head. "I know, but I would like to take so much. What about all your books?"

A pang shot through Sarasha. "I've been trying not to think about them. They may be so important, but then again, if we run out of food…"

"Well, select three piles. The most important ones we'll take for sure. The next pile goes in if there's room. The others will stay unless there's a miracle."

"Aye, ma'am!"

Her mother found energy for a smile at that, then returned to her work.

Sarasha was just finishing her selection when Tonu found her. "Sarasha! I have a present for you."

She turned to her friend, dragging out a smile. "If it's something I have to carry, could you give it to me in a day or so?"

The Sailmaker's daughter laughed. "Oh no. You want this now!" She was carrying a concoction of canvas and straps. "Let's take this out to Ebb Tide."

Intrigued, Sarasha grabbed her crutch and scrabbled behind the other girl. When they reached the pen, Tonu draped the canvas over the fence and went to get Ebb Tide.

"You hold her head here, and I'll put it on."

"Careful, Tonu. Strange things scare horses."

Tonu laughed again. "This isn't strange. I've fitted it on her several times."

"You what?"

"I couldn't very well make the lady a gown and not have a fitting, could I?"

As she spoke, she had tossed the canvas over the horse's back, and she was now under the belly, fastening a strap around Ebb Tide's chest. Then she brought another strap around the front of the horse's chest, passed it through a loop that came between the front legs, then tied it to the other side of the canvas.

The result was like a short skirt, going all the way over the horse's back, with a strap around her chest and another horizontal line passing under her tail. Sewn into the skirt were several huge, baggy pockets with ties at their tops. There was room for Sarasha to sit, with padding in the right places.

"That's wonderful! How long have you been working on this?"

85

"Since the day you got her. I didn't start hurrying until the news of the move came. It's pretty rough."

"Let's go see how much we can put in it."

"Are you going to ride?"

"I guess so, if you'll carry my crutch."

"I don't carry your crutch. It goes here." Tonu slipped the crutch into a long pocket that ran down the edge of the skirt in front of the rider's right knee. The handle kept it from slipping, and it rested there comfortably. "Up you go."

Sarasha was more practiced at swinging aboard now, although she had to be careful not to hit her foot on the bulging pouches. She wriggled herself around. "This is perfect!"

"Cheynou tried it out for us. He's about your weight, if a bit shorter."

"Thank you so much. You don't know what this means to me." She pulled a pouch open. It was huge.

"Oh, I think I do. You're already counting the books, aren't you?"

They walked over to the Captain's tent, or where the tent had been. All that was left was the frame, with their hammocks hanging rather forlornly over empty sand. The big table would be left behind with the planks that had been used for counters and benches.

They loaded books into the pouches, and both of her important piles fitted easily. Tonu fended off more thanks and returned to her duties, leaving her friend happily choosing books from the discard pile.

Then Sarasha had an idea. Emptying the pouches, she started again, but this time she took out her rigging knife and began slashing the books' bindings.

"Sarasha! What are you doing?"

She glanced up. "I'm following through with something Cheynou and I discussed, Mother. The worth of the information in a book has nothing to do with the cover. I can get about twice as many books in if they don't have covers. If I take the centre sticks out of these scrolls, I can roll them all up together and take about twice as many of those as well." As she spoke, the keen knife was slashing.

She came to Cheynou's beautiful little Holy Works and paused, knife in one had, book in the other. She regarded her mother. "There is something to be said for workmanship."

Verlene smiled as her daughter reverently placed the undamaged book in the pouch.

By the time she was finished, there were only a few books and scrolls left. Sarasha put them in a crate, one of those which would be taken on the last day, when the stevedore crew came back to see if they could snatch anything else before the Farmers' army showed up. It all depended on how fast the mercenaries moved.

It was past midnight on the second night, and everyone was beginning to stumble wearily towards their beds when the Stevedores staggered back into camp, their eyes black holes in their heads, their shoulders slumped. Immediately, there was a bustle of hot drinks and soft places to lie. Sarasha was tending a pot over a fire when she heard a strange noise out to the north.

A gradual silence descended on the camp as everyone stopped what they were doing to listen. It was a jingling, combined with the thudding of heavy feet.

"Soldiers!"

The whisper spread through the camp, but Sarasha knew better. "Not soldiers. Horses!"

Surprised faces turned to her. She grabbed up her crutch and hobbled towards the edge of camp. Soon, the jingling and thudding came closer, and a pair of huge horses burst into the firelight, snorting and shaking their heads. Yong shouted and hauled on the lines behind them. He was balancing on the deck of a flat, wheeled thing, and once he got the horses stopped, Sarasha recognized a wagon, the kind Farmers used to haul large loads of hay.

"Nice team, Yong, where did you get them?"

"Oh, they were wandering around in a field. We didn't think the Farmer would need them for a while."

She moved forward, taking the halter of the nearest horse to steady it down. "This harness is all twisted."

"Complaints! I've never put harness on a horse before, and we did it in the dark. We had to stop twice when parts started falling off."

The Captain strode up, his eyes sweeping the team. "You've picked a couple of good ones, lads. Let's get them unhooked from the wagon and over in Ebb Tide's pasture for the night. We had better keep them tied up. We wouldn't want to lose these beauties."

He undid buckles as he spoke. Soon the horses were gone, and the huge wagon stood, bare and alone, in the middle of the camp.

Sarasha grinned. *There go the rest of my books.*

The Captain roused the camp two glasses before sunup the next morning. He stood in the light of the big central bonfire and spoke. "The soldiers are a day away. Our scouts have been discouraging reconnaissance, so that means they'll head straight for our camps. By the time they get here, we'll be a day's walk inland.

"That leaves us a full day ahead of them, but soldiers walk faster than heavily laden people, so we must move as quickly as we can. We hope they won't be keen to chase us once they see we're leaving. So load up and get on the trail as soon as you can. Unfortunately, some of us can't stay to carry anything. We have other tasks."

There was a grim mutter. Everyone knew what he meant. Their first task would be the *Eagle* and everything in her. They would leave nothing for the Landbound to scavenge.

The second would be to harry the approaching army, to slow it down so the rest of the Crew could escape. These were experienced Raiders, top fighters, but even so, some would not join their Crew tonight in the new camp.

Sarasha loaded Ebb Tide with everything she could. She had no idea how much the little horse could carry, but she planned to move slowly and hope. Taking one last gaze around, she mounted and started out.

She had almost reached the edge of camp when she detected moving dots coming towards her along the trail ahead. Dots too large and swift to be men, even running men. As they got closer, she counted ten of them. They were moving fast, and soon she could see that they were horses, two with men on them, the rest without.

Before she could figure out any more, they swept past her with Pers whooping a greeting as he went. The other man, the one riding the tall lead horse, nodded to her and kept going. The horses strung out behind were galloping freely, with no lines to tie them, and they all had contraptions on their backs similar to the one Tonu had made for Ebb Tide.

Sarasha smiled and slapped her pony's shoulder. "You've got company, little horse. Pers went and found us some horses that carry things. I wonder what he had to promise that man to pay for his services?"

She rode on, trying to adjust herself to the rhythm of the horse's movement. After a while, she found that if she moved each knee forward at the same time as Ebb Tide's leg went forward, she flowed along with the horse and it felt smoother, somehow. She wondered if that would help with the jarring when the horse ran.

As she rode, concentrating on her own problems, she noticed that the people near her had stopped and were gazing back, their packs sliding to the ground, stunned expressions twisting their faces. She swung her horse around.

There, billowing up from the distance behind them, soared a wide black pillar of smoke. They were still close enough to see the tiny, licking flames shooting up from the skyline. Tears stung her eyes, and through their blur she could see others collapsing in the path, slumped over their packs in grief. A burning rage welled up inside her. She raised her head and stared at the death of her Ship. It was hard to see the end of the *Eagle*, but harder to see the effect it had on her people. Somebody had to do something.

She raised her fist and her voice, shouting to all who could hear her. "There dies the *Sea Eagle*. She fought her best to the end. When my time comes, I hope whatever gods that exist will help me fight like the Sea People and die like the *Eagle!*"

Several voices nearby took up the shout. "May I die like the *Eagle!*"

"Die like the *Eagle!*" She could hear the sound echo up and down the trail. Soon, people were picking up their burdens, turning their backs on the funeral pyre and trekking inland through the rolling prairie grass.

10. Solen

Despite her steady pace, the horse did not seem to need rest, and by noon they were out in front of the Crew who had left camp the earliest that morning. The trail was well marked by the feet of the lading crew, but Sarasha slowed to keep the leaders in sight. There was no sense in setting off on her own. This was unknown territory with an enemy army near.

The trail led up a small creek valley, and she was wondering if she should stop to give Ebb Tide some water when she rounded a corner and found herself in the noon mess. Soup pots hung on tripods over campfires, and somehow a few tables had been carried and set up for the cooks to work at. She watered her horse, tied her where she could graze on the tough grass nearby, and went to help prepare lunch. The cook gave her a pot to tend, and she doled out stew to everyone who approached, pleased to be of service, no matter how simple the task. As soon as the last bowl was served, the cooks cleaned up and left for the evening camp to prepare supper.

While they were stopped, she heard the sound she had come to know as the thudding of horses' hooves. Hauling herself to her feet, she peered back down the trail to where a cloud of dust resolved itself into the little fleet of carrying horses, with the tall stranger riding in the lead and Pers at the back, a bandana over his mouth and nose to keep out the dust.

The horseman pulled up short of the camp and merely dropped the lines of his horse. It stood still while he strode around among the loose horses, checking packs, pulling at straps. Pers followed him, asking questions and mimicking his every move. Sarasha grinned as she hobbled over to them. By the time three days were over, Pers would be an expert at lading horses. In two weeks, he would be an expert at everything else.

"May I bring my horse close?"

The man took in Sarasha's crutch and her little horse. He grinned slowly.

"Sure. Unless you figger she's gonna have a fight with my stallion."

She shrugged. "Long as he doesn't start anything, he's safe."

The man shot her a harder glance, then laughed out loud. "Hey, Pers, is this the one you told me about?"

Pers glanced over and grinned.

The man stepped forward, holding out his right hand. It was large and rough, but the calluses were not like a sailor's. His wrists were lean, and his whole body seemed loosely held together. She reached out her own hand and he took it, gripped it briefly, then let it drop. "I'm Solen. Been lookin' forward to meetin' you."

She nodded. "Well, I haven't heard much about you, but I was sure happy to see you come riding in this morning."

"Glad to be of any help I can. Don't get along with those Farmers too good myself." He stepped forward, raising his eyebrows for permission, and gave her horse and its burden the same attention he had given his own. He pulled and tugged, shifted a few things, and one time ran his hand up under the packs.

"Well, I hope you didn't pay too much for it. Solid workmanship though. Who made it?"

"One of our Sailmakers, and it was a gift."

He grinned again. "Well, if you didn't pay nothin' for it, it's sure worth the price."

She gave him a stare that told him it was time to stop joking.

"Looks pretty good, though. No rub points. There needs to be somethin' thicker along the horse's back and sides, though, to keep hard corners from diggin' in."

"I packed it very carefully."

"You did, that."

"Did I put in too much?"

He regarded the horse critically, then reached down and lifted one foot. Ebb Tide allowed it without argument. Then he moved around to her head and pulled her lower lip down, peering at her teeth. He nodded and slapped the horse's neck hard enough that dust rose.

"Well, she's in good shape for an old girl. She'll carry you all day with this, long as you walk. She the one that was runnin' with the wild bunch? Scars down the near side?" His hand rested on the canvas over the horse's port shoulder.

"That's right."

He nodded. "Thought so. She got attacked by a puma last year, but she fought him off and run away. Got caught up with the wild ones before her owner could find her. Doubt if he tried too hard, her bein' wounded and old. Mebbe he made a mistake." He slapped the scruffy leg, bringing another cloud of dust. "This little lady's got spunk!"

"Is there a chance the real owner will want her back?"

He shrugged. "I dunno about the laws those Farmers have. I doubt it, but you never know. Might be a rule about salvage, like you Ship people have. Might not. I wouldn't go into town alone with her."

She grinned. "Considering the situation, I don't think a trip to town would be wise in any case."

He snorted. "Huh! Those Farmers'r all het up right now, but if you was to leave them alone for a year or so, then come back with a smaller party and goods they need, like real superior horses, they wouldn't be so unwelcomin'. They'll trade."

"Do you think so?"

"They trade with me, and I ain't exactly the swain you want your daughter comin' home with."

She and Pers shared his laugh.

"I've eaten, but there's still plenty. Come along." Sarasha turned and started back.

"Mebbe better if you stay here to tend the horses. We'll go get some grub. Will you do that?"

93

She reappraised this rough-sounding man. She doubted if the horses needed her to watch them. It galled her to accept his charity, but she knew she had to husband her strength for the trail. She sank down on a nearby rock, held Ebb Tide's halter lines and massaged her foot as well as she could with the bandage still on.

Soon, the two were back, wiping their mouths with their sleeves. Pers nodded to her. "We have to keep moving. We can make two trips a day, even loaded as heavy as we are."

The two men swung up onto their horses.

It seems so easy when Solen does it. The way I used to swing up the rigging.

He whistled and started his mount moving around the camp and up the trail. Pers waited while the other horses formed up of their own accord. He moved his horse to shoulder against one of the slow ones, grinning down at Sarasha.

"This is the lazy one. I have to stay back here to keep her moving."

Sarasha waited until they were out of sight, then swung up on her mount in her own way and followed at her own speed.

The Crew did not rest long at the noon mess, but shouldered their various packs and bundles and moved on. Sarasha again pushed to the lead, but stayed within talking distance of the leader, an older scout named Jogata. He carried a large pack but seemed unfazed by the load.

"Oh, I've carried more, lotsa times. I took a turn out of the Fleet when I was young. Worked the riverboats, 'way upstream. We hadta portage the goods around the falls 'n' rapids. In a hurry, too, with the Master shoutin' that we was wastin' our time and his money every beat we rested."

She smiled down at him. "So we're going pretty slow, are we?"

"Oh, yeah. I could walk twice this fast for mebbe a glass or two 'fore I'd need a rest."

"Why did you come back to the Fleet?"

"I allus intended to. I wanted to see what the rest of the world was like, y'know."

"And did you see it?"

He grinned. "Not much. I went from one kinda boat to another, and then I come home."

"Well, you're not on a boat, now."

"Nope. Din't figger I'd ever be Landlocked."

"Does that bother you?"

"Nope. I figger the Captain done the right thing. We're tough folks. We'll make out all right."

She smiled and moved ahead as the trail narrowed. It was good to find there were others who felt that way. She nodded to herself. *We are a tough people. We'll take this under our keel and make a go of it.*

In the middle of the afternoon, Pers and Solen trotted back through with empty packs, waving as they passed. The horses didn't seem tired, from what she could see. They jogged along with their ears and heads up. She nudged Ebb Tide ahead cheerfully.

By the time her horse stumbled into the night's camp, Sarasha didn't feel so tough. Her bottom was so sore that only the roughness of the trail had kept her from getting off and depending on her crutch.

She slid off Ebb Tide's back and almost crumpled to the ground as her good knee gave her a stab of pain. But it settled as she stretched it out, and soon she was moving at her usual hobble. She led her horse to water a good distance downstream of the camp, then tethered her on a long rope to crop the grass off and on all night and hopefully still get enough sleep to be ready to move on in the morning. One more thing she wished she had asked Solen.

Sarasha again made herself useful to the mess cooks, who were pleased to see her and gave her a similar job to the last time.

As dark settled over the plains, everyone was fed and bedded down in the deep grass. It was strange, lying in a soft spot that did not move, studying the same stars she had stared at, night after night, on watch. She began naming the constellations to distract her from her pains. At least the pain of her bad foot had receded into the surrounding agonies of the day's journey. She was concerned that the horses had not returned, but assumed that Solen was competent enough to keep them out of trouble.

* * *

Sunrise came all too soon, but she roused herself gamely, tending to her horse before going for her own breakfast. Because she travelled faster than most, she had volunteered to stay to clean up once everyone had left.

During the meal, her father strode into camp. He moved smoothly, but she noted darkness under his eyes. He mounted a trunk and raised his hands for silence.

When he had everyone's attention, he lowered his hands. "The news is good, Families and Crew. The Farmers' army has decided to follow the Crew of the *Osprey*, because their camp was closest. But they wasted half the day roaming up and down the beach. That gave the *Osprey*s time to get ahead. All our Raiders are moving over to protect that Crew.

"Our means of communication seem superior to the enemy's. While they have more equipment and heavier arms, we can use our mirror flashes, fires and signal flags to position ourselves where we can do the most damage.

"We would be destroyed if we confronted them in a pitched battle, but the Sea People do not fight like that. We have been attacking and running, and if they are stupid enough to chase us, we turn and encircle the followers once they are away from their main force. This slows them down, because every time we attack, they stop to take up defensive positions."

Her father turned to sweep his whole Crew with his smile. "So, despite their superior speed, they are still a whole day behind the *Osprey* and nowhere near us."

"Does that mean we can stop?"

The Captain shook his head. "The other Crews are all moving on parallel courses to ours. We are staying separate so we don't use up the limited resources of the Prairie: water especially. Any Crew that stops could become the next target. We must maintain our course and get as far away as we can. The *Eagle*'s Raiders must feel that our people are safe, so they can concentrate on protecting the *Osprey*'s Crew."

He turned a frown on his Crew. "One thing we must never forget. We must always help each other. If we were to leave the *Osprey* alone, the mercenaries would take them down easily, then move to the next Crew and destroy us, one by one. The Fleet sticks together."

There was a series of positive murmurs.

"So, my Families and Crew, we must shoulder our burdens for another day."

He turned, jumped down from the crate and strode out of camp, ignoring anyone who spoke to him.

A shout came from the Crew behind him. "Die like the *Eagle*!"

Another voice took up the call, then more. Soon, the whole Crew was cheering. The Captain slowed and turned, a smile crossing his face. When the chant had died, he nodded three times and turned to stride away, more spring in his step.

Sarasha watched him go. Perhaps the *Eagle*'s Crew was as safe as he said. Captain Tourn did not lie to his people. *But I'm sure there are other facts he has not told us.* She thought again of her friends, on foot in the Prairie grass, fighting heavily-armed mercenaries.

Masking her worries, she turned to lade her horse, cheerfully calling to people as they moved out on the trail.

At mid-morning, the horse train passed again. This time, Pers slowed to ride alongside her for a while, but she had no time to ask him anything he had learned about horses. It was more important to hear the news.

"What's going on back there?"

He shrugged. "We took a wide sweep around so we didn't run into any Farmers and went back to the *Eagle*'s beach point to make sure there was nothing left. We had cached some heavy stuff, planks and tables and that, and it hasn't been touched. We'll go back for that with the wagon once this is all over. Right now, we drop this load at tonight's camp, then come back and move the cooks ahead of you after lunch."

"How about the fighting?"

"I've only talked to a few scouts we met along the trail. Things seem to be going as planned. The mercenaries haven't caught up with the *Osprey* yet, and our men are keeping them occupied. That slows them down enough that they aren't even travelling as fast as we are. Solen and I will go over tomorrow to help the *Ospreys* move faster because they will be in danger soon. We don't want a pitched battle if we can avoid it. Speed is our best asset, and these horses represent speed."

The last carrying horse was disappearing up the trail, and Pers gave her an apologetic grin. "Nice to rest, but I've got to keep moving."

"Sore?"

He straightened his legs to lift his rear off the seat pad. "Don't know which is worse, my legs or my butt." He grinned again and pushed his horse into a trot up the trail.

They made good time again that day, and once more camp was set up and waiting for them, with the cooks already at their tasks in the mess. Pers and Solen came in just after sundown, and their horses seemed almost as tired as Pers did. Sarasha stumbled over to watch and help where she could as they fussed over the horses. Solen took especial care with them, checking every horse from nose to tail, especially their hooves. He talked as he worked, and both Sarasha and Pers took in every word.

"Look here. This soft part of the hoof's called the frog. No idea why; that's just what it is. There's a cut here, not too deep. I'll put some of this salve on it to protect it and keep it from gettin' infected. If it ain't better in the mornin', I'll leave her with you, Sarasha. If you keep her on a lead tied to Ebb Tide's pack, she'll follow with no problem."

He slapped the horse's shoulder as he put her hoof down. "She'll be happy to get a day with no work!"

"How did the packing go today?"

Pers grimaced. "Not as well as we would have liked. We went over to move the *Ospreys* and got one load, but when we went back, they were in the middle of a fight. Solen won't take his horses into danger. That isn't the deal we made, and it wouldn't have done any good, anyway. So we left without knowing much and went to help the *Raptors* with one move. They're the next closest to the Farmers' army."

"Could the mercenaries have caught up with the *Osprey*'s Crew?"

"I don't see how. Maybe a lightly armed troop ran on ahead or something."

They continued to work with the horses, learning the proper names for the animals and their equipment, and trying to find out how to treat these important new creatures.

11. Captains Meet

Once again, Captain Tourn did not sleep in camp, if he slept at all. He seemed even more tired as he appeared at the breakfast mess again.

There was a muted rumble to meet him, but no cheer. Word had gone around the camp about the fight yesterday, and everyone was worried.

He took a stand on a crate and regarded his people. "We have had our first battle with the Farmers." He raised his head. "They won't be so quick to tangle with us next time."

Voices rose in question.

"It wasn't the mercenaries. They are all on foot. It was twenty or so of the Farmers themselves, on those big, slow horses they use. They rode ahead alone to attack. They have sturdy saddles, so their horses can carry men in armour with long, heavy swords."

He paused dramatically, then grinned. "Not as long as pike poles, though. They came charging into the *Osprey*'s people, thinking they could dash through and cut them down. But Captain Tory knew they were coming. He issued his men with pikes. We formed up as if to resist the charge, but when the Farmers approached, our line broke up and let the riders through. As the horses ran past, we used the pikes to hook the riders to the ground. We grabbed them before they could even get up and killed them.

"More than twenty Farmers attacked. Half were killed in the first charge. The rest took off running back for the safety of their lines. Our scouts have discovered that several men can run down a horse if they take it in turns. So we had relays of men lining the trail back to the main mercenary army, and they wore out three more horses and took their riders off as well.

"So now the *Osprey*s have thirteen big pack horses to carry their goods. They will be moving much faster now, and their chances of keeping ahead are that much better."

They cheered at that, and Captain Tourn took the opportunity to step down. This time, he came to sit with his wife and daughter, sharing a cup of tea at the end of one of the tables. The Crew respected his privacy.

"Have you slept?"

Arlijn smiled sadly at his wife. "What? No cheers for the victorious leader?"

Verlene reached out and rubbed her hand across the back of his. "You didn't say anything about our losses."

He nodded. "There have been a few. The *Eagle* Crew is always in the thick of any skirmish. We had two wounded in the horse charge. That's a fearsome thing, a charge of big animals like that. It's the land equivalent to a Mastership, I suppose."

"And you were there to savour this experience."

He turned his palms up. "It was my idea. Who else should lead?"

His wife nodded and glanced at Sarasha, who shook her head. "Sounds like my father, all right."

"What do you need?"

His shoulders dropped a fraction. "Besides a good night's sleep? A drink of that tea." He reached across to take his wife's cup, downed it at a gulp without checking to see if it was too hot, and reached for Sarasha's.

When he had finished that one, more slowly, he placed one hand gently on his wife's shoulder and rose. "Duty first."

The two women watched him as he walked away.

"He's doing fine."

Her mother stared at her. "Why do you say that?"

"He used to go through this every storm. He could manage three or four days with little sleep, at the wheel hour after hour, when only his touch or Chan's could keep her from broaching in the following seas. It's hard on him, but it fires him up at the same time."

Verlene nodded. "If he couldn't do this, he'd be figuring out something else."

They shared a grin. "And now I suppose I could get us more tea."

"You could, but I'd better saddle up."

"Saddle up?"

"Yes. The saddle is what you strap on the horse to sit on. I have a modified packsaddle on Ebb Tide. The bridle is what you steer her with. It has a metal piece called the bit that goes in the horse's mouth. Solen gave me one. The halter I used before is for leading and tying her up. The reins are the lines you use to steer her."

Her mother laughed. "You've learned quite a bit."

"I have to." That came out grimmer than Sarasha had meant, and she softened it with a grin. "I also have to learn to ride at a trot. That's the bouncy part. He gave me some tips, but I have to practice. So here I go."

She swung out on her crutch and moved across the camp to her horse.

It would have been a slow process to pack the saddle up, but there seemed to be someone there every time she was loading or unloading. Today, it was Cheynou Chan.

"So you're the one sent out to help the cripple, are you?"

He said nothing, just stared at her.

"I'm sorry, CheyChan, I'm grouchy in the morning. Do you want to learn how to pack her?"

His relieved smile made her feel better, and she took the time to explain everything to him. "When we get a moment, I'll teach you to ride her."

His face lit up. "Really?"

"Sure. You're not too big, like the rest of them."

"Great. So then, should I come and help you every day, so I can learn all I need to know." He paused and gave her a sideways glance. "Without getting my head bitten off?"

She raised her hands in surrender.

He nodded. "Does it always hurt?"

"Why do you say that?"

He shrugged helplessly. "Sorry."

"No, that's all right. I try not to burden everyone."

102

"Yeah, well, I don't guess everyone knows. But I do."

"Don't spread it around. Nobody needs any more trouble than their own right now."

His back straightened. "Don't worry. It'll heal up. Joints take longer."

She smiled and ruffled his hair. "I sure hope you're right. See you tonight."

She did a creditable job of swinging up onto her horse's back and looked down at him. He patted Ebb Tide's shoulder twice, then Sarasha's knee once, and turned away.

She pulled the horse's head around towards the trail, remembering to be much gentler because of the metal bit in her mouth. She was gratified with how much better the animal responded. They pulled out onto the trail, the rising sun stretching their shadow out to the left. They were headed north, towards the Prairie.

The trek continued. Sarasha was hardening up to riding, although the progress of the whole battle, as judged by her father's increasing weariness, was not so optimistic. The terrain remained the same, with swales and long, gradual rises breaking the flatness. And always the sight ahead was the same: waving grass and tall, wide-spreading patches of cloud. It looked so much like the sea, but down on the hard ground, one slogging step at a time, it felt so different.

Finally, on the evening of the fourth day, her father jogged into camp and came straight over to her. "Captains' Conclave one glass before sundown. I'll need a Scribe."

He hurried away before she had time to answer.

Five Captains came into camp that evening, including Tory of the *Osprey* on a huge black horse with white hooves. The beast snorted disdainfully at Ebb Tide yet allowed himself to be tied next to her. To Sarasha's surprise, Orrick Bren also came in mounted. His horse was smaller than the big farm horse, but still much taller than Ebb Tide.

"Where did you get this beauty?"

He smiled. "She's pretty, isn't she? I stole her myself."

She frowned. "You have time to go horse raiding?"

He shook his head, tossing his long forelock away from his eyes. "I should have known better than to admit such a thing to Sarasha the Scathing."

"Who?"

"I can't really think of someone like you with only one name. It seems you need something...more powerful."

She glared up at him. Despite his bulk, he was almost as tall as Yong. "You sound like my father. He can get away with it."

He laughed. "I get the message. I will be more formal in the future. But you can't stop what I call you in my head."

She was beginning to flounder. She wasn't used to hearing another Captain talk like this, joking and laughing. His face, usually set in harsh lines, became almost handsome when he relaxed. Her only option was to attack.

"So what has happened to make you so lighthearted in the middle of this mess?"

Her tone had its intended effect, and he sobered. "I'm sorry. I should be more serious. I don't get much chance to relax."

She was immediately contrite. *It must be hard on him – a single man with all that responsibility and no one to let down with.* There was a pause while she strove for a way to help him.

"Well, if you want to talk horses with anyone, I'm learning as fast as I can."

"So am I." His big shoulders dropped in what she could only see as relief. "I really did steal this one myself, but I didn't run off to hunt for her. I was out doing reconnaissance, and I came around this corner and there she was, swimming in the stream."

"A horse? Swimming in a stream?"

"No, not the horse. The horse's owner."

"A woman? Out here?"

"I said I was on reconnaissance. At least two leagues to the east of the *Osprey*'s path. There are scattered farms over there. Big ones with fortified houses. I suppose this girl was out riding from one of them."

"Girl?"

"Yes. Younger than you, I would guess."

She began to smile. "A young girl swimming in the stream, and there you come, around the corner. What did she do?"

"What do you expect?" He grinned as well. "She screamed and scrambled for her clothes."

"And what did you do?" A sudden thought sobered her. "You didn't..."

His hands came up in a defensive gesture. "No, no, of course not. Please don't look at me like that. I didn't lay a hand on her, I swear to you. I'm sure she is very relieved, but perhaps a bit miffed. I stole her horse instead."

She burst into laughter. "You stole her horse!"

"Yes. I jumped on and kicked my heels into its sides. It took off running like mad, me grabbing on for all I was worth. If I remember correctly, she really did start screaming then. I wouldn't know. I was too busy trying to hang on."

She winced in sympathy. "How did you get her to stop?"

"What, the screaming?"

"Not the screaming." She glared at this weak attempt at humour. "The horse."

"After a while, she slowed down. I figured out that by pulling the lines port and starboard I could steer her, and I made my way back into the *Petrel* camp. That was yesterday morning. I've learned quickly since."

"The lines are called reins."

"Are they? What's this called?" As he laid his hand on the leather, she saw that his knuckles were scarred like a mast'n's.

I heard that he worked his way to the top. Guess he did. She considered the strap that circled the horse's neck, wide on the chest and down between its forelegs.

"Never seen one before. The strap that holds the saddle on, the one it goes through around her ribs? That's called the cinch. Always tighten that twice, or you'll end up riding under the horse. That other strap must be there to keep the saddle from slipping aft. I mean back. My pack harness has something the

105

same. I call it the chest strap. Solen will know. I'll ask him when he comes in. If he comes in."

"True. I'm not sure what will happen, there."

"Well, I suppose we could go to the Conclave and find out."

"Trust you to put me back on duty. Would you like to show me where we will meet?"

"Are you sure you want to be seen walking in with Sarasha the Scathing?"

"I like to be on the winning side. I might as well be there from the beginning."

She stopped, and he turned to face her. "I wish you and Father would quit doing that."

"Doing what?"

"Don't be obtuse. Stop making jokes about me. Yes, it made it easier for the other Captains to accept what I say, but I don't like it. It makes me sound like I'm ambitious, and that is the farthest thing from my mind right now."

"Ambitious?"

"Yes. You Captains are trying to break from the thought patterns of the Priest-Admiral, but you still see everything from that point of view. My father does, too."

"What do you mean?"

"You have been very successful at working your way up through the power structure that created the Priest-Admiral. You can't help but see everything in terms of that power structure."

"I suppose. How does that cause you a problem?"

"Because by the rules of that power structure, I would be very dangerous. A young person with a strong following of top fighters, outspoken and ambitious, would be someone to get rid of immediately in a situation like this. It is very dangerous for me to open my mouth."

"I see."

"Do you?"

"Yes. I do. And your father's jokes are meant to undermine that threat."

"Yes. It's his way. You can help me by following his lead in public, but please don't draw any more attention to me. If I think I must speak in the Conclave, I will speak, but only for the good of the Crew."

"I understand. In the old Fleet, you would have been Beached the day after you spoke up at the Captains' Conclave, and it would have had little to do with your foot."

"Exactly."

His mouth twisted in distaste, and they turned towards the Captain's tent.

Her father and Captain Tory were deep in discussion and barely registered their entrance. She covered her emotions by concentrating on laying out her writing instruments. She was taken aback by Orrick Bren's treatment of her. *He talked with me in a friendly fashion, like no Captain ever speaks to his Crew.*

That was the point. She wasn't his Crew. She peered up from under her hair to get another glimpse of the young Captain in the well-lit tent. Yes, he had the same dark circles under his eyes, the same gaunt mien as her father. Tory seemed worse. These were the men upon whom the onus fell. These were the ones responsible for bringing their people to this trial and through it.

If Captain Bren needed someone to talk to, someone he could relax with, well, that would explain it. She grinned to herself. *And someone who understands his boasting about his horse. I know how that feels.*

The other Captains arrived soon after and the meeting began. It was less formal than any Captains' Conclave she had ever attended. In fact, the only thing that made it seem a Conclave was the scratching of her pen.

For example, she had never seen a Captain put his face in his hands and mumble through his fingers like Captain Frey of the *Falcon* was doing. "What in the name of all the demons from Hell can we do?"

He raised his head. "My people are worn out. They cannot keep going. I have so many wounded. We lost three more yesterday. One was dropped because his bearers were so tired that they stumbled. His wound, already infected, broke open, and he bled to death right there on the trail..." His voice wound down, as if he was reliving the scene.

Arva Sax of the *Night Hawk* shook his head. "My Families are not in much better shape. We have finished the fresh food and are running on ship's biscuit. Kletsh isn't here because his people need him."

Tory nodded. "It's getting tight. The mercenaries will catch up to my Crew some time in the next three days, depending on how may of our Raiders we are willing to spend to hold the army back."

"Something must be done!"

"We need to make a stand." Sax slammed his fist on the table.

Captain Tourn raised his head. "A stand?"

Frey nodded. "Yes. That's it. A stand. We need to show them we are serious."

Sax jumped in. "Right. Show them we are willing to fight."

"Show them what it will cost to follow us."

Bren shook his head. "I'm not sure. The Farmers won't follow us forever. If we could somehow persuade them it's not worth the effort..."

"Exactly!" Frey's voice cracked with enthusiasm. "We need to show them we are the Sea People, and nobody pushes the Sea People around!"

Sarasha turned incredulous eyes to her father. Finally, he spoke. "I agree that things seem difficult. However, we have always agreed that we would not do well in a straight-up battle with these mercenaries. They are better armed, with heavy shields. If we attack them, we will not do well."

Tory raised a hand. "But..." He appeared to be thinking. "...if we could choose the ground, make them attack us..."

Her father nodded. "That is another thought. Perhaps we could entice them into a trap or..."

She could see where this was going. They desperately needed something to do. They would persuade each other that all their wisdom from before was wrong. Finally, she could take no more. She waited for the right moment, then dropped her hands to the table.

"No."

Her soft voice, dropped like a cold splash into their enthusiastic discussion, brought them up short.

"You don't want to do anything of the sort."

They were so astounded that no one stopped her.

"Instead of showing them you are serious, you will do exactly the opposite."

Bren recovered first. After all, he had been warned. "And why is that?"

"Because a desperation attack is exactly that: desperation. It will show them they are close to winning. The best you can hope for is a draw. You cannot beat them. After the fight, the situation will be the same as it is now: them with an advantage in numbers and armament and us with the mobility and communication.

"The only difference is that then they will know we are desperate, and they will push ahead even faster."

For one long moment, they thought about that. She took heart. At least they were thinking.

"The Farmers want the threat removed. Even if we defeat them, they will only go and get a bigger army and try again. Our only solution is to disappear into the Prairie and increase their uncertainty about where we are or how large our force is. Then they will give up and go away."

Sax slammed his hands on the table again. "Fine. And how does an unschooled girl know so much more about warfare than us?"

"Not so unschooled, Captain Sax."

"And has your schooling given you a solution to our problem?"

"Yes."

They stared at her in amazement.

"I'm sure you all know the story of Panay and the Raiders."

Several nods.

"Right. Remember his technique?"

Bren nodded. "He enticed his enemy farther and farther south, into the Ice Ocean, and a storm came and wiped them out while his smaller Ships sheltered in the lee of huge floes, moored to anchors driven into the ice."

Tory snorted in derision. "And are you going to call up a storm?"

"I am giving you examples. Perhaps the Saga of Mender is a better example."

"The Saga of Mender?" Sax leaned back. "That's a myth. You can't seriously believe we will take our battle plan from a poem!"

She did not flinch from the Captain's stare. "And when we are listening to poetry, we turn off our brains?"

His hands corded on the tabletop. "That happened before our people even took to the Sea, you silly girl!"

"So perhaps it means more to us now that we are no longer on the Sea, Captain. Have you listened to the Saga of Mender? He did the same thing as Panay, but on land. He enticed his enemy to follow him farther and farther. Then..."

Two fists hit the table as Orrick Bren started forward. "He cut their supply lines!"

All eyes turned to him.

"Supply lines! That's what she's getting at. The difference between land and water is that on water, the Ships carry months' worth of supplies. These soldiers don't carry all their armour and weapons and all their supplies as well. That's why they are catching up to us. We have to carry everything.

"They have a heavily-armed wagon train. It came through yesterday from the farm towns. Bringing them food and weapons, taking back the wounded. The farther they get from the town, the harder it will get for them. We should hit those trains, cutting the mercenaries off from their base of supplies."

Captain Tourn nodded. "That's what will persuade them to go back. If they think we're going to keep running away and their job will become more and more difficult, soon they will quit."

"But what of my people? We will be overrun very soon, even with the horses."

Bren leaned forward. "We have to revise our courses. We need to pull the other Crews farther to the east, away from their army. Then we don't need to move as far. We can give you all the horses, more men from every Crew to carry your goods."

Frey nodded. "If my people only had to travel half as far, we could free up at least...say, twenty men to help the *Ospreys*."

Tourn leaned forward. "No, you keep your men, Frey. You're the next closest. We'll get the men from the safer Crews. Tory, you'll still be the bait. You realize that."

Captain Tory straightened. "We have been from the beginning. If we get extra help, and if the Farmers get slowed down, then we can do it."

Sarasha's pen flew as they tossed numbers back and forth, pored over maps, planned routes. In the back of the tent, Leide sat under the Captain's hammock and made copies as fast as she could.

The meeting broke up on a strong positive note. When Sarasha passed each Captain a copy of what they had all agreed, none seemed surprised. With optimistic gestures of respect, the Captains parted, each walking straighter than he had when he came.

"Will you walk with me to my horse, Sarasha the Diplomat?"

"Hmm." She took a moment to consider Bren's face, to let him know she was sizing up his humour. "I suppose it would be the diplomatic thing to do."

He strolled beside her, and in the short grass near the trail she moved at an acceptable pace.

"Thanks to you for bailing me out back there."

She could make out his headshake in the half-darkness. "I didn't do anything except listen harder. They would have all got it sooner or later."

"True, but it was better when it came from you."

"I agree. Much more diplomatic."

"So my reputation changes?"

"I doubt it. Not after you told Captain Sax his brain was shut down."

"I did no such thing!"

"Yes, you did. And you were right. It had. Lack of sleep, stress. All our brains had shut down. To think we were in the middle of planning an all-out attack on those mercenaries."

"Oh, that would have worked, too."

"What?" He spun to face her, his hand freezing her crutch arm in place.

"There are several examples in the literature. It would have required about half of our available Raiders to take a suicide stand in a safe place. If they chose their terrain well enough, they could stand off an army about five times their numbers for several days. Long enough for the rest of us to get away. Some of them might have been able to escape after that, but it would be very costly. We will need our young men, come winter."

He stood and stared at her.

"It's true. I can show you the book."

"Oh, I believe you. I'm just standing here wondering how an unschooled girl knows so much more about warfare than five experienced Captains."

When she did not respond, he threw up his hands. "Oh, yes. You have schooling. But still..."

"This is land warfare. The Fleet has never fought ashore for more than one day before retreating to the Ships with its booty. These Captains have been fighting sea battles for a long, long time."

He passed a hand over his face as they continued walking. "Don't I know it. Some of them are so old it's like they have barnacles on their brains."

He stopped. "Except for your father, of course."

She continued to walk, laughing. "You had to say that."

"Well, yes I did, but it's true."

"That's because I don't let him get away with any thinking like that. If he gets any barnacles, they get scraped off quick-like."

"Sarasha the Acerbic."

"Whatever it takes. He's my father."

"And he has to live up to what you envision."

"Right!" She was about to laugh when his next comment stopped her.

"What kind of man will ever be brave enough to marry you?"

There was a long silence. They reached the horses, and he began to saddle his mount. She helped him without speaking.

Finally, as he was about to mount, he turned to her. "I guess I'll never be known as Bren the Diplomat."

She glanced up at him. "No, that's all right. It was a good question. I'm sorry. I've just been thinking."

"About whom you're going to marry?"

"About what kind of man I would want to marry." She shook her head as if to clear it. "Not something a Captain wants to chat about."

He shrugged, leaned against the saddle. "Why not? I don't chat with anyone about anything."

She laid a hand on his arm. "Don't you? Isn't there somebody? A friend, an older relative?"

He shook his head. "No time for that sort of thing. I wanted to be Captain, and I went after that goal. I got it. No complaints."

"But now you want something else. That's natural."

"Right."

"I can understand your problem. It's difficult, being the friend of the Captain."

He chuckled. "Almost as hard as being married to Sarasha the Scathing would be."

"Well, there you have it."

"We each have a problem to solve."

She tossed her head. "Oh, that's easy."

"It is?"

"Sure. You marry me. You get someone you can chat with, and I get someone who can put up with my tongue."

"I hadn't thought of that."

"Well, don't think of it. A Captain doesn't marry a cripple. Not in these times."

"What has your foot got to do with this?"

"A lot. Besides the fact that it makes me grouchy, as I usually am. It's what I said. The Captain doesn't marry a cripple. It's bad enough for my father. What if, when this is all over, we go through the old rules and decide the Beaching rule is one we need to keep?

"It is, you know. For times like this. If each Crew had left even five of their wounded behind, we would all be about one league farther inland right now. No, don't argue with that. It's true. So think. What happens when we decide to apply that law, and my name comes up? Oh no, not her. She's the Captain's daughter. Not her, she's the Captain's wife.

"So the law only applies to certain people, and we're back in the Priest-Admiral's hierarchy. No thank you. Not that you asked, but you have to see it's impossible."

He stared at her a moment, then turned to mount his horse. Then he looked down at her. "You are certainly something to take my mind off my troubles. Can I come back and learn about horses with you?"

She shrugged. "The Prairie is notably free of doors."

"I'll keep it in mind. Good night, Sarasha the Impossible."

"Good night, Orrick Bren the Former Captain."

He reined his horse around and walked her out of camp. Sarasha found a rock to sit on. There was a lot to consider.

12. Night Battle

"Can you imagine how mad they must be?"

Sarasha looked up from the foot of the horse she was tending. "Why?"

Pers stopped grooming. "Well, they knew they had lost a supply train. Three loaded wagons. Then Solen and I took the wagons roundabout and used them to move the *Osprey* camp. Can you imagine how angry those mercenaries will be when they see the wheel-tracks in front of them tomorrow? We've had Yong and his team all along, but with four wagons, we can move the whole Crew almost twice as fast."

Sarasha didn't respond for a moment, staring at the side of the horse in front of her.

"What's wrong? Aren't you happy?"

"I was just thinking. I'd better talk to Father."

"What? Why?" He slid the corral rails shut and hurried to catch up with her.

"Because of what you said. There's going to be a change."

"Oh. Yes. I guess so."

She found her father talking to Tory, who had ridden in to report their success. Both men were smiling, but sobered when they saw her expression.

"What's wrong, Sarasha?"

"Pers says the Farmers will be angry."

"Oh, I'm sure they are."

"Because they will realize that they are not going to catch the *Ospreys*."

Her father nodded, puzzled.

She stared at him a moment. "Well?"

"Well, what?"

"What will they do?"

He held up open hands. "Maybe quit."

"And maybe not."

"Ah." She could see that expression come over her father's face. He turned to Pers. "Do you have a horse that can move?"

"Mine's not too tired."

"Get over to the *Ospreys* as fast as your horse can get you there and still have energy for a ride. Backtrack and check for a raiding party."

He spun to Tory. "Get back to your people. Move them again. Right now. Go all night if you have to. Send your guards out and be ready for anything."

The two men ran to their horses.

Her father started pacing. "What else?"

"The *Falcon*."

"Right. They're the next closest. Who can I send?"

"Pers has to saddle up. If you can catch him, he can go past the *Falcons* on his way."

"Even better." He strode away and she hobbled after him, cursing her incapacity.

Cheynou Chan had been attracted to the commotion, and she called him over. "My father needs some message runners. Find five men and bring them to his tent."

The boy nodded and sprinted away. She slogged after her father and met him just as she heard the thudding of hoofbeats leaving camp.

"I have to inform the others."

"Cheynou is bringing five runners to your tent."

"Are the *Night Hawks* in danger?"

"They've been moving farther west, but I'd send the first, fastest runner to them."

He slowed his pace to match hers. "Can you think of anything else?"

She smiled up at him in the fading light. "Not at the moment. You go ahead. I'll think while I trudge."

"See you at the tent." He strode away. He thought better when he was moving faster. Unlike somebody she could name. She had been on the verge of volunteering to ride to the *Night Hawks*, but knew it would be stupid. *I have to learn to ride faster than a walk.*

Her only thought, when she caught up with her father at their tent, was an obvious one.

"What about us?"

He smiled. "Don't worry, I thought of that, too. We're fifth over, so we should be far enough away. I've pushed the night watches out twice as far and doubled them."

"You need to triple them."

"Why?"

"You doubled the radius, that more than doubles the perimeter. Also, you probably should have a few in between, in case somebody gets past the first line."

"To think I'm being taught simple navigational geometry by an unschooled girl!" He slapped his forehead and was away again, calling out names as he went.

* * *

It was a long, tense night in which absolutely nothing happened. Sarasha tried to sleep because she knew that tomorrow they would be on the move again, but she kept rolling over and bumping her foot, so her rest was intermittent. So she was immediately alert when she heard footsteps trotting towards the tent. Struggling up, she was right behind her father as he greeted the messenger.

"Signal fire, sir. 'All is well,' and 'Enemy dispatched'. From the *Osprey.*"

The Captain poured a drink for the lad, who was perspiring even in the pre-dawn chill. "Good. They must have tried something, and we repulsed them or fooled them." He turned to Sarasha. "What will they do now?"

"Sorry, Captain, sir. I have forgotten to bring my fortune-telling shells with me today."

He grinned. "I had to try. You did well last time."

"Thank you, sir. I hope that fact will be entered in the Log."

"Hmm, yes. I'll try to remember to inform the Captain's Scribe."

"You do that, sir."

They relaxed onto the stools around the table and chatted with the messenger. He could tell them little. He had stood his watch where he could see the signals of several Crews. There had been nothing to note all night, and nothing from the other fires.

"A lack of news is good news, as far as I can tell." The Captain leaned back against the tent pole, and Sarasha could see how tired he was.

"Do you think we dare take a rest day?"

He shook his head. "Not yet. We'll wait until we get an eyewitness report, then we'll decide. We can communicate better with the mirrors after sunrise, anyway. Maybe leave later and not go quite as far."

Verlene was moving slowly about outside by the fire, and after a long while she came in with breakfast. They ate with relish, savouring the food and the moment of calm.

When hoofbeats clattered over the stones of the creek, they were on their feet, the quiet forgotten.

Pers trotted his horse through the sleeping camp and right up to the tent. The animal was lathered, stumbling as it slowed to a walk. Then it stopped, its sides heaving, white froth dripping from its muzzle to fleck its chest.

But Pers was smiling. "We caught them!" He slid out of his saddle in his economical way.

Loosening the girth, he pulled the frothy bit from the horse's mouth before leading the two women into the tent, where he sat down and immediately began his story.

"You were right, Sarasha. They force-marched a two-pronged raid against the *Osprey* camp. Less than half their men, lightly armed. If I had gone that way, I would have ridden right down the trail between them and missed both. But I was coming in from the *Night Hawks*, so I saw the westerly party. I got ahead of them and warned the *Ospreys*. They packed up double-quick, but they left a few tents standing and some fires burning. Then a bunch of us slipped out into the hills around.

"The mercenaries tried to pull the old 'dawn raid' trick. No creativity at all. They encircled the camp and settled down to wait for dawn. And to rest. They were worn out from the fast pace they had set. Our sentries were posted out in the open to

118

make it look good, and we even had some people moving around in the camp, but the tents were full of Raiders.

"We gave them time to get relaxed but not rested, then hit them from outside, quiet as we could. Just when they realized we were attacking and turned to face us, the men in the tents poured out and took them from behind.

"It was still almost dark, so I doubt if anybody did a whole lot of damage to anybody else, but soon they were running back down the trail to their camp. Once they were on the move, it was easier. They were already exhausted, and we ran each one down as he dropped out of the pack.

"About halfway back they made a stand, so we left them. They certainly won't come after us again tonight, and our people are all moved out of range, anyway."

The Captain nodded. "Any sign of another party attacking anyone else?"

"Not that I've heard of."

Verlene shook her head. "There have been no other signal fires."

Captain Tourn stood and stretched. "The sun's coming up. Mirror signals in soon. Do you want breakfast?"

"Soon as I've seen to Patches. He did a lot of running tonight. Solen told me not to water him when he's been running, so I'm waiting for him to cool down."

He moved to his horse, still standing outside the tent. "You know, I have to learn to fight on horseback. It's an amazing feeling, having all that power under you." He caressed the hilt of his sabre, sticking up to the left of the pommel of the saddle.

"Will Solen be angry that you used his horse in battle?"

"No. I've already talked about buying the horse. If Patches had been wounded, it would have been my problem. That's one thing Solen does. He catches wild horses, trains them and sells them."

"So the horse was effective in battle?"

Pers grinned. "I would say so. At one point, I was chasing three of them, and they turned to fight. I took one side so they all couldn't get at me. I got the centre man with my sabre, but the outside man had a spear. He poked it at us, and Patches went right up in the air with his front feet like the stallions do when they fight. He caught the man with both forehooves and flattened him. I was hard put to stay aboard, let me tell you. I dropped my sword, grabbing for the saddle." He reached up and rubbed the pommel. "These handles are useful, at times."

"You dropped your sword?"

"I had the lanyard around my wrist. But it didn't matter. Two were down and the third was running. I wonder if you can teach a horse to do that on command? I'll have to ask Solen."

While they were talking, one of the boys from the lookout point arrived, followed immediately by another.

"Message from the *Night Hawk*, sir. No action."

"Message from the *Falcon*, sir. No action."

Captain Tourn nodded. "Message return: 'keep watch, more to follow.' One of you come down in one glass to collect messages."

They saluted crisply and jogged back out of camp, proud of their small but important part in the battle.

Sarasha's father glanced over at her, then around the circle of Officers and Family Heads gathered to hear the news.

"I'm suggesting we wait one glass. If there is no news, we will start two glasses late and go half the normal distance today, angling a little more east again. Any suggestions?"

Second Officer Palawan stepped forward. "I scouted that area yesterday, sir. There is a small ravine with good water, easily defended, a bit more than half a day away. I was thinking of it for noon, but it was too far."

"Sounds good. Will you take care of the advance party?"

"Yes, sir." Palawan saluted and scurried off.

"How are the Families doing, First Officer Kaya?"

The older man nodded his head sagely. "It will be good to have the short day. We are suffering the absence of the men we sent to help *Osprey*."

"How are the wounded?"

The Surgeon stepped closer to his Captain and spoke in a lowered voice. "Three would have been Beached long ago, Captain. One more yesterday. The others are recovering."

"How are the first three doing?" His voice did not drop, and everyone heard him.

"Very well, sir. Given time, they will all recover to some extent. Talismo will probably recover completely in a month or so."

"Good thing we didn't Beach him, isn't it? What happened to the fourth yesterday?"

The Surgeon shook his head. "I don't know, sir. He seemed to be in a stable situation, but halfway through the morning he lapsed into unconsciousness, and has been in and out of it since."

"Head wound?"

They all nodded in understanding. Head wounds were unpredictable.

"Keep him as quiet as you can. I trust you to do your best, Surgeon. You always do."

The doctor gave a satisfied nod and turned away.

The Captain surveyed the rest of the informal Conclave, but no one spoke.

"An optimistic start to the day, gentlemen. Let us get to our posts."

13. RECONNAISSANCE

They broke up, strolling slowly for the enjoyment of it. Sarasha nodded to her father. "We needed this lift."

"Yes. Where would I find Solen?"

"He'll be with the horses. He always sees to them before he eats."

They made their way to the corral, to find Solen just returning from his charges.

"I have a question, Horseman."

"Yes, Captain?"

"If we are only moving half distance today and the *Osprey* Crew don't need you, can you free up one of your horses for a job?"

"Certainly. What job?"

"I want to send out a scouting party. Pers and Sarasha and one other."

"Pers has already gone ahead with the advance party and three pack horses."

"They can pick him up at the new camp. Him, Sarasha and one other from here."

"Two others."

Her father turned to her. "Why two?"

"Because three men make a reconnaissance party."

"That's what I said. Pers, you, one other."

She shook her head. "I don't count. I'm more likely to be a problem." She could see him about to protest. "Besides which, no one in the Crew knows how to ride. Whoever you send won't be a great help either."

"Doesn't anybody ride?"

"Cheynou Chan has been on Ebb Tide a few times. No one else has come forward."

"I'll get word around. Is that all right, Solen? Pers plus two horses that beginners can ride?"

The wrangler grinned. "They won't be young and they won't be fast, but they'll be gentle."

"Just what we need."

"They also won't have saddles. Send your riders around for a lesson after breakfast."

With that, they moved back into camp. The moment they were alone, Sarasha glanced up at her father.

"Why are you sending me out on this duty?"

"Because I trust your eye and your knowledge. You don't think strategy like a seaman. You're learning land warfare faster than any of us. We need a semi-permanent place to stay. Consider it like a Landbound fortress, but without too much work on our part."

She glanced up at him sideways. *I wonder if that's all it is.*

Half a glass later, Cheynou and an older deckhand were standing, staring dubiously up at the backs of two horses.

"All right. You, the little one. You've ridden some?"

"Twice. My name is Cheynou."

"All right, Cheynou. Do you know how to mount?"

"I can do it the way Sarasha does on Ebb Tide. I'm not sure about this taller horse."

"Have a go. You have to be able to do it. Out there," the wrangler swung an arm to the horizon, "it's pretty flat. You might not find a rock to stand on."

Cheynou made it after three attempts.

"Good enough, Cheynou. If you had a skittish horse, you'd have more trouble, but with Marlu here, you'll do fine. Jest walk 'er around for practice."

He turned to the other man. "Your name is?"

"Feist, sir."

"My name is Solen. Nobody calls me sir. Not out here on the plains, anyways."

"All right, Solen, sir."

"All right, Feist. You ridden before?"

"When I was a kid, Solen, sir. I was brought up on a farm."

"Huh! A Farmer in with all these fishermen?"

Feist returned the grin. "I had a romantic notion back then. I thought the life of a Farmer was tough. So I went to sea."

"And life was tough there?"

"Right. And now I'm back on land, and it's still tough. What a surprise."

These two had something in common, and Sarasha hoped it would help keep the wrangler near them. He was the most important person in all the Crews, if he only knew it.

"So let's get ahorse, and we'll see how you do."

The deckhand grabbed both hands full of mane and lifted himself up by main strength to the level of the horse's back. Then he pushed himself farther up, leaned over to the other side, and swung his leg around.

Solen nodded. "Workable, if not efficient. Can you ride a trot?"

"Sure. That is, I could once."

"Cheynou, come over here and listen to this. You move with the horse like a Ship moves with the sea. If you try to sit still, you'll slide all over, and when he trots, you'll start to bounce. You have to be a part of the horse. Like the horse's front legs are your own.

"So when he walks, you walk. Learn to shift your weight with the step of the horse. When he starts to trot it's real quick, and you have to shift your weight right in time. If it helps, move your legs with the horse's, as if it was you walkin'. That's about all I can tell you. The rest is practice.

"One thing. These horses are all trained to rein-drop. That means if you drop the reins, they stop and stay there. I don't guarantee they'll do it at full gallop. Might not notice. But you don't have to tie them if it's for a short time.

"You leave them alone, you take the bit out of the mouth and tie the rope on the hackamore to a tree or bush. Got it?"

They all nodded.

"Pers knows a lot about what's goin' on. He'll take care of you."

Sarasha turned to her horse. "Should I have my packsaddle?"

He regarded her. "In normal circumstances I'd say no, but it wouldn't be a valuable lesson for you to fall off." He grinned, exposing well-spaced brown teeth. "Besides, you can pack the grub."

The horseman had one more piece of advice. "She can pack the grub and extra water. But all of you pack your own canteen. You can survive to walk a long way if you have water. I figure the chance of one of you havin' to walk home is about fifty-fifty."

"What if we lose one of your horses?"

"Oh, he'll follow the others, but not close enough that you can catch him. If he takes off, I'll have to go track him down. That'll take me away from helpin' you lot, so I suggest you try not to do that."

They all nodded again, very serious now. They went to get ready, but Sarasha lagged back with Solen to ask for his opinion of the ground ahead of them.

"Your father already asked me. The spot you're talkin' about is the edge of the First Drop. The plains slope south to the sea, but every once in a while they seem to break, like. Above the First Drop, there's a long stretch of flat. I doubt if you're gonna find any place to stop out there. You'd have to go four long days to the Second Drop.

"There are shallow canyons out there with water holes in them. Keep an eye out for raptors. They nest on the canyon rims, and you sometimes see them spiral down. I doubt you'll find the water otherwise."

She thanked him and went to get her own travel gear and the food.

When they were rigged out with the right gear and Ebb Tide had her packsaddle on, they mounted. The Captain came over to the corral to see them off.

"There's been no bad news, so we're sticking with the plan. Follow Solen's tracks to the next camp. Sarasha is in charge until you contact Pers. Then you listen to him. From there, go what you think would be a long day on foot, straight north this time. Search for a place to cache important things, like books and equipment. Somewhere easy to find, with a lot of rough terrain to make it possible to hide large bundles.

"Also search for a place to stay for longer. Good water, defendable, space for tents and stock. We'll see you this evening in the new camp."

"Solen thinks we won't find anything."

"We have to make our best try."

That was all he said, but Sarasha knew what he was thinking. *We might be staying at tonight's camp for a while, and it's too close to the Farmers' army. If there's a safer spot nearby, he wants to know.*

They all saluted: it seemed appropriate. He returned the salute, and they reined their horses out onto the trail.

They just walked along for the first glass or so, to give the new riders a chance to get used to the movement of the horses. Soon, Cheynou pushed his horse up beside Sarasha.

"Should we try a little trot?"

Sarasha shook her head. "I'd like to get at least as far as the new camp and have Pers around before I risk disaster. Sorry."

"That's fine. Gives me time to get used to the horse."

The other rider had paused behind them. She turned. "How's it going, Feist?"

The older man nodded twice. "It's comin' back. I never did ride that much. Not for fun or that sort. We always used wagons to ride in. But I bin on a horse plenty, now I think about it. I'll be fine."

"Great." She turned her horse and moved on.

As the morning went along, they moved out of the flat Prairie into an area where the earth was broken, with bare rock sticking out in ridges and individual boulders. Three times they crossed small watercourses that wound their way along the bottom of shallow, steep-sided valleys to join the larger stream.

Then they reached a spot where the main valley had been broken by an upheaval of the earth, and a section of it hung out above the rest. The water flowed out of the valley mouth in a series of small waterfalls. Willow clumps and grass meadows fanned out below this point, a good place for stock.

Farther up, the rocks crowned in two small peaks, separated by the stream. Either one looked defencible, and Pers and the advance party were unloading their packs at the base of the smaller, more westerly one. Sarasha's party stopped for a brief chat with Palawan, who indicated their best route north.

"I didn't go much farther, but if you follow up this stream, the country flattens out again on a higher level. You can ride easily, I'd say, and pick your own course."

"Good enough. See you tonight."

It felt better to have Pers in the lead, up on his tall horse with the saddle. It didn't hurt to see the hilt of his sabre handy either. She had salvaged a bow and a few arrows, and they hung beside her crutch.

The little party threaded its way through the ledges and broken rock fronting the waterfalls and moved upstream. Soon, the walls of rock sank under the Prairie sod, and they came out into the open. As one, they stopped, staring in amazement. Before them stretched a veritable sea, flat and even, fading off into the distance without a feature. Far to the north, there was a line of blue, perhaps with white caps, but it was hard to tell in the haze.

Pers turned to Sarasha. "I somehow feel our mission won't be much use."

She agreed. "The odds of finding a place to live out there seem pretty slim to me at the moment."

"Better chances over there."

They gazed out where Cheynou was pointing. To the east and west, the ridge they had just left behind seemed to extend, sometimes higher, sometimes lower. Eastward, the terrain was much more broken.

"The Captain said to go north, and north we go. There's no point in checking out places that the other Crews will soon get to."

They started their horses ahead in tacit agreement.

After a short while, Cheynou moved up beside Sarasha.

"Shall we trot, now?"

127

She grinned over at the smaller lad. "In a hurry to feel pain, are you?"

"It's coming sooner or later." He shrugged. "Might as well get it over with."

"All right. You stop here and wait while we go ahead. Then you try to trot up to us."

He did as she instructed. Pers, noticing their pause, had stopped some distance ahead. He grinned as she rode up. "First try?"

She nodded.

"Hope he does better than you did."

"Believe me, so do I."

Feist merely grinned, and they all watched.

Sarasha had a sudden thought. "Pers, we'll be occupied with our horses for a while. You keep an eye out, will you? I don't trust this prairie to be as flat as it looks."

He nodded and scanned the immediate area before turning his attention to where the other two looked.

Cheynou kicked his horse, and she started to walk faster. He kicked her again and shouted. She shuffled into a trot, and Sarasha knew how Cheynou felt, with his legs flopping and his head bouncing back and forth. He grabbed for the mane with both hands and hung on grimly. As he approached them, he seemed to settle a bit, but he still wasn't happy.

When the horse reached her companions, she slowed automatically.

"Did it feel as bad as it looked?"

The boy paused a moment to regain his breath. "It was bad at first. But I did better near the end."

Pers nodded. "There's no rush. We've got all day. Do you want to try, Feist?"

"Sure."

The old deckhand lifted the reins and made a clucking sound with his tongue. His horse's ears came up, and she moved out faster. He clucked again and kicked her gently. She lifted to a trot, but the results weren't the same as with Cheynou. Feist's head bounced, but he stayed centred on the

128

horse's back. Soon, he pulled her to a halt and turned to wait for them.

When they reached him, he was red-faced but pleased.

"That didn't seem too bad."

He reached back to touch his rear gingerly. "It'll take practice, all right, but I remembered most of it."

Pers nodded, turned to Sarasha. "You ready for a try?"

"I couldn't very well not be, could I? I like the way CheyChan's horse stopped when she got to the others. Go ahead."

They glanced at her grim face and made no jokes as they moved away.

She let them get quite a distance before she started, waving them on when they stopped the first time. *This is going to take some getting used to.* Lifting the reins one handed, she imitated the clucking sound Feist had used. To her surprise, Ebb Tide immediately moved into a trot.

Sarasha bounced a few times, but she already had her hand entwined in the strap of her saddle. She moved her legs with the horse's, and for a moment she could feel the bouncing lessen. Then she got behind in the cadence and started to bounce again. Gritting her teeth against the pain, she forced her sore foot to move with the horse's leg, and the ride smoothed again. Then Ebb Tide slowed as they caught up with the others.

"Hey, that went pretty good for a while there!"

"I don't know what it looked like. It certainly feels like I need a lot of practice."

Pers leaned down, his face concerned. "But you did have the hang of it for a while, didn't you?"

"I suppose I did. Let's wait awhile, then try again. Now I remember what it's like, I want to ride at a walk for a bit."

"Good idea."

14. THE GREAT PRAIRIE

For the rest of the morning, they rode along the bank above the stream, following the edge of the shallow valley. Occasionally, one of them would try to trot, then slow for the others to catch up. Feist was soon handling it well, and Sarasha cautioned him to take it easy.

"I've been riding for days, and I'm getting sore. You haven't been on a horse for years. You're doing fine. In an emergency, if we have to run, you'll stay on. I wouldn't try for any more than that."

She turned and regarded the younger lad. "CheyChan, you're lucky you're so light. You need more practice."

He grinned ruefully. "That's for sure. I think I have it, and then I lose the rhythm."

"In case of emergencies, you don't want to trot. You have to run." Pers leaned over to peer at the ground.

"Oh no! Is that worse?"

He grinned. "I guess we'll just have to find out. The terrain along here is smooth and the grass is short. Let's have a go. Try to get your horse up to a gallop as quickly as you can."

With that, he clucked to his horse and stood forward in the stirrups. In a moment he was gone, thundering away with Feist close behind him. Sarasha held back for a moment, but there was no other way. It was in over her head, swim or drown. Sharing a grimace with Cheynou, she lifted her hands and kicked as hard as her good foot could manage.

Ebb Tide snorted at this indignity and trotted forward. Sarasha risked losing the rhythm and kicked again, shouting.

The horse surged forward, her gait changing completely. Sarasha felt as if her legs were being thrust forward. Only her hand, grabbing the strap in front of her, kept her from lying head-backwards on the horse's rump. She pulled herself upright and tried to balance.

The movement was smooth and surging, like a quick following sea. They charged on, clods of dirt flying up. She glanced over to see CheyChan beside her, a huge grin on his face.

She grinned back, urging Ebb Tide for more speed, and the head and neck of the other horse slid slowly behind her. Then Cheynou shouted, and his horse began to catch up.

Before they could finish the race, they came up to where Pers and Feist sat their horses, laughing.

"Liked that, didn't you?"

"I've never moved so fast in my life. It was wonderful!"

Pers nodded. "I've calculated it. That's almost twice as fast as the fleetest Messenger Sloop can do on a broad reach with a following sea."

"And it's smooth!"

"Better than trotting."

Feist dropped his grin. "But that doesn't mean you run the horse all the time. They can't do that for long before they wear out."

Sarasha glanced to Pers for confirmation. He nodded. "That's what Solen says. A horse can walk at a fast pace all day and not be tired. They can trot for quite a few glasses. A horse in good shape can gallop for a glass, but then you better give him a breather, or he'll just fall down."

"Don't they stop when they're tired?"

"Not if they're trained. If you push them, they'll keep going until they die."

She looked down at her mount with new regard. "I knew these animals were a serious responsibility. I'm just beginning to realize how grave it is."

They nooned beside the stream and picketed the horses out to graze by the water while they ate. When Cheynou suggested they sit up on the edge of the bank, Sarasha shook her head. "We don't want to make ourselves obvious to anyone else. Not while we're off our horses, with their bits out of their mouths. We'll sit here with our eyes at the rim, so we can keep watch in all directions."

However, their lunch of hardtack and ship's beer passed without incident, and they lay back in the sparse grass to let the warmth of the sun soak into them.

"Why isn't it hot?"

"What do you mean?"

"Well, there's little wind blowing, especially down here in this gully. If it was this warm in a calm at sea, we'd be sweating and hiding in the shade."

Pers compressed his lips as he often did when he was thinking. "Something to do with the lack of dampness in the air, maybe."

"Maybe. Your sweat cools you better when it's dry."

They lay back again. Then Sarasha noticed the older Crewman staring at something.

"What is it, Feist?"

He pointed to the opposite bank. "Over there." He got up, crossed the current on a couple of boulders and mounted the far side. He stooped down, dug around with his fingers, then stood, his hand raised in triumph. "I thought so. Onions."

"Onions?"

"Yes. Wild onions. They're growing all along here."

Interested, the others crossed the stream, Sarasha following more carefully. Once they knew what to search for, it was easy to pick the onions, which had a sweeter and gentler flavour than their domestic brothers. Sarasha began to gather them.

"What will the cooks say if we show up with fresh greens!"

The others began to harvest the plants more seriously, and soon they had one of Ebb Tide's pouches bulging. As they rode out to the north again, Sarasha gazed around. "I wonder what else is out here. It's not as flat as it looks. It seems barren, but there is water and soil. Maybe we'll find all sorts of other good things."

Feist nodded. "There's bushes along the stream. Some will have berries. We have to figure out which ones are good eating."

"And here we have a Farmer to help us."

"Been a long time since I was a Farmer."

"Is that why you didn't come forward to help us with the horses?"

The man shrugged. "I had my appointed tasks. I didn't want to shirk my duty."

Sarasha caught Pers' glance. This was something they would have to work on.

"Feist, we all have to stop thinking like that. If we plan to survive in this new situation, everybody has to start finding new things he or she can do to help. I bet you know more about horses than anyone in the Crew, except perhaps the Captain. You will help the Crew and the Families much more with your farming knowledge than you could by carrying the box you were assigned."

He lifted one side of his mouth and frowned. "You mean, I should find someone else to take my load and come and work with you?"

"I mean that the Ladingmaster will assign someone else to take your load. You'll be assigned to the horses the moment the Captain hears about your background. Think what you could save the camp if you were to notice something wrong with a horse and remember what it is, when no one else knew anything about it?"

He shrugged again. "I don't remember that much."

"You remembered those onions quick enough!"

"Oh, I remember onions. We used to pick them every spring. These are getting old. Losing flavour."

"Well, nobody who is eating hardtack and salt pork will ever complain about that. Let's hope your time with the horses will jog more of those valuable memories. Unless the cooks grab you for foraging."

"Whatever you say, ma'am."

She glanced over, expecting a smile, but he seemed quite serious. "I'm not an officer. Never likely to be."

"Whatever you say, Sarasha."

"Now why does that not sound a whole lot different?"

This time, he did smile.

They turned back in the middle of the afternoon, having found nothing of interest. The stream came in from the east at that point, a good place to identify their route. It was the only landmark they could use on that flat expanse.

"What do you say, Helmsman? How would you find this place again if you had to?"

Cheynou gazed around. "Well, you see that peak over there?"

Sure enough, there was one blue hump higher than the others, off to the northeast.

"Well, I'd take a line on that peak and cross it with a bearing on the higher rock back at the new camp, which I can just barely see on the horizon to the south. When I crossed those two courses," he pointed triumphantly to the ground, "I'd be here."

"How accurate could you be?"

"Depends on how good my transit was. If I had *Eagle*'s main anguler, I could probably come within a few chains. Of course, this bend in the stream helps. If I go, say, ten chains up the stream to make sure there aren't two bends, then I'll be certain."

"But you don't have the *Eagle*'s main whatever-it-is."

"No Navigator is ever without his anguler!"

"So do your job, Navigator."

The boy raised his eyebrows, then slid off his horse. He took a brass mechanism and a small set of folding rulers from a bag on a string inside his shirt and laid them on a flat stone. He then produced a tiny book and proceeded to record several numbers. Satisfied, he put his paraphernalia away and remounted.

"I took three readings. More accurate."

"Good. Make sure your father sees those readings in camp tonight."

"He'll also be able to say how far we went, using my readings and the readings at camp. As long as he can see the same landmarks. Otherwise, we'd have to wait for night and use the stars."

Pers swung his horse around. "I, for one, am not in favour of standing around waiting for the stars to come out. Onions would make a poor supper."

Sarasha scanned the empty prairie. "Let's go CheyChan's ten chains up the stream, then head south from there. No sense retracing our steps."

Pers gestured towards the west. "Why not take a bigger swing?"

"We'd get into terrain the *Sparrowhawk* will soon be covering. No sense. Let's go ten chains."

They kicked their horses into a brief trot, then settled in for the long afternoon trek back to camp.

They found nothing on the way back except another stream, which soon parted company with them, flowing west towards the *Night Hawk's* course.

As the long day wore on, they trotted their horses less and less, and Sarasha could see her companions shifting their weight more and more often, as she did herself.

"Doing all right, Cheynou?"

He grimaced. "I've been more comfortable."

"You could get off and walk."

"And lose my horse and have Solen laugh at me?"

He fastened his gaze on the horizon, and they rode on.

They reached the dropoff just at suppertime and discovered a bustle of activity they had not noted in earlier camps. There was a lightness in people's steps and a cant to their heads that told Sarasha volumes about the morale of her Crew.

The horse'n had to thread their way down the stream because of the tents pitched on every level spot. In the meadows below the waterfall, poles for the temporary corral were already up, using two long ledges that met at an angle to increase the area of grazing. They gratefully slipped off their mounts and stripped them of their equipment. All the horses immediately trotted out into the pasture to roll with great enthusiasm.

"They're just as glad as we are to be finished!"

135

Pers tossed his saddle on a fence rail. "We were only walking them, so there's no need to keep them from water."

"Why do you need to keep them from water?"

"Horses just aren't that smart. If they're thirsty from a long gallop, they'll drink their fill. If the water's too cold, they founder. Whatever that is. I gather it's painful, and they can die."

They looked to Feist, but he shook his head. "No call to gallop farm horses. Never seen water kill one. I'm willing to take the horse'n's word for it, though."

They shared a grin. "Yeah, he seems to know a little about the beasts."

Sarasha regarded the new riders. "How are you two feeling?"

"Like I sunburned my transom and stuck it in salt water."

"Well, get to your tents and check for blisters. If you break blisters, get some salve from the Surgeon, or you won't be back on a horse for a few days. Feist, maybe you could drop the onions off at the mess. They were your find, after all."

They both nodded and hobbled off, bow-legged, about their business. She and Pers headed for the Captain's tent, easy to spot up against the rock.

Verlene brought them a drink of cool beer while they waited for the Captain to finish his discussion with the Watch Officers. Sarasha had always had a soft spot for the bearded First Officer, Dwayo Kaya. He was so dignified and treated everyone with respect, receiving it in return from one and all. He had done a marvelous job in his calm, competent way of keeping the Crew moving steadily, despite the problems caused by loss of the Raiders and Stevedores to the other Crews.

Now, he saluted his Captain and turned away in a businesslike fashion, but not before acknowledging Sarasha and Pers with a brief, sharp nod of his greying head. They half-saluted in return, and he marched off.

"So, how was the ride?"

"Boring."

"Oh. I take it that's the gist of your report?"

"Pretty much." She detailed their day, not forgetting to mention Feist and his abilities.

"That's a problem, isn't it? I'm sure we have others who have Landbound experience and for whatever reason haven't come forward. I'll talk to the Family Heads about it."

15. Victory...

After supper, Pers strolled over, and they invited him in for tea. The three of them sat at the table chatting while Verlene cleared up. The Captain glanced out the tent door to check the bustling camp. "So, this will be our home for a while."

Sarasha shrugged. "If only the Farmers go back to theirs."

"I'm not counting on a complete withdrawal."

"What do you think they'll do next?" Pers sat straighter, ready for discussion.

"They'll try to move ahead for a day or more. What do you two figure?"

Sarasha nodded. "The mercenary leader won't give up too easily. Not good for his reputation."

"The next supply train will be heavily guarded."

She turned to Pers. "That's true. But we have to take it."

"They'll have horses."

"True. They know how we fight: hit hard, then run. They'll be expecting us to try the same thing, and they'll have horsemen along to catch us if we do."

"So we can't do the same thing. We have to do something entirely different."

The Captain's voice cut in. "How can we do something different? Different from what?"

They both turned to him. Sarasha had been unaware he wasn't following their train of thought.

"Different from what the Sea People do. We have been following the same plan for centuries, as far as I can figure out. We come ashore, we attack, we take whatever we can carry back to our Ships."

"But how can we do anything different here? We want those supplies. We have to attack and take them."

"No, we don't. You're still thinking like a Raider."

"What?"

Pers broke in. "She's right. We don't want those supplies. We don't even want the wagons, although it would be nice to have them."

"Aha! We want the mercenaries not to get them."

"Right. If we stop the train from getting through, it doesn't matter if we get the supplies."

"We could burn them where they sat."

"I hate to be so wasteful."

"We'll leave that for a last resort."

From that moment, their three voices intertwined, and it was difficult later to remember which idea had come from whom.

"Right. If we have to, they'll burn like the *Eagle*."

"But we only have to stop them for two days?"

"More like three..."

"...depending on how far away we hit them."

"Right. If we got in close to the town, we would have more time to come back later and get them."

"But if we're too close to town, they'll come out and get them."

"...obvious point is near halfway."

"But how do we get our Raiders halfway? The mercenaries tried to make up one day and they were too tired to fight when they got there because they had to double-pace all day."

"Wagons."

"Wagons?"

"Right. We aren't using the wagons to move the *Osprey*..."

"...so we put our men on the wagons. They ride all day and they go farther than marching men. Then, when the horses are tired, the men march farther."

"Then, if the mercenaries send out a rescue party from their camp..."

"We sit and wait for them, resting up..."

"And go back to raid and run when they're too tired to chase us!"

There was a pause in the conversation, and they all looked at each other.

"Well, wasn't that fun?"

They started at Verlene's voice and turned questioning eyes to her.

"Fun. I've never seen three people having so much fun in my life."

They grinned at each other sheepishly.

"Oh, don't be so guilty. There's nothing wrong with it. It sounds like a good plan." She spoke over her shoulder. "Did you get it all?"

Leide was sitting at the counter behind them, pen in hand.

"Yes. They missed a few details, but they've got the rough plan pretty much worked out." She consulted the parchment in front of her. "We need a middle plan, somewhere between complete success and burning it all. We need to work out the exact position of the attack, taking into account that a rider will try to take the news to the town. I assume we can keep a messenger from getting through to the Farmers' army until after dark. But what you have will do." She smiled as she would at a child who had done a good job at some household task.

Sarasha growled. "Where did you come from?"

Leide's smile turned to a gesture of surprise. "I walked into the tent and your mother shoved a pen in my hand. I've been writing ever since."

"Hmph. Let's see it."

Now there were four heads around the table, several hands pushing the paper back and forth. When it was in front of them in writing, there seemed to be many things they hadn't thought of.

At the next lull in the discussion, Verlene again interrupted. "Will you be going on all night or do you have time for some food?"

Her husband answered her. "We have done enough. The other Captains will want to chew at it before they agree. But we have an excellent plan, here. This will be a pleasure."

He gestured to the parchment. "Sarasha and Leide, could you make a copy for each Captain?" He rose, stretching. "I'm going to talk to Dwayo about the resources we have available if we aren't moving. This battle will be pivotal, and I'm willing to give it a lot more of our support."

He turned in the doorway. "Don't change it too much while I'm gone."

The two girls grinned at each other and went for more writing supplies while Pers wandered out in search of the mess kitchen.

The euphoria soon died; Sarasha spent the night worrying. There were so many things they hadn't thought of. *What if the Farmers are able to field a fleet of fast, lightly armed horses that can chase down the big wagon-pullers?*

No, Solen said there were no horses like his in the area. No, he said few horses like his. What if he's wrong?

What if...? Her head spun. She got down from her hammock and hopped over to the table, kicking a chair with her sore foot in the darkness.

The pain brought her wide awake, and she sat at the table, her head in her hands, ideas sloshing back and forth like foul water in the bilge. What if the mercenaries started acting like Sea Raiders, breaking up into little groups of ravaging power, roaming the Prairie, attacking at will?

No, they wouldn't dare do that. The Sea People had superior mobility and communications.

"What is it, Sarasha?"

She started up from her mother's touch. "Nothing. Can't sleep."

"Foot sore?"

"No more than usual."

"Is it the battle?"

The realization struck her, and she clenched her fists on the table. "I want to be there!"

"But 'Rasha, you can't..."

"I know I can't. That doesn't help any. I want to be there. It won't go the way we planned, I'm sure of it. What if it goes wrong?"

"This isn't a win-or-lose battle. Whatever they do to slow the supply train is good for our people."

"But what if...?"

Her mother's hand gently covered her mouth. "You can what-if yourself crazy, Sarasha. Every woman who sees her man go off to battle learns that. You happen to have sent more than one man off. They're big boys. They can take care of themselves."

"I wish I was sure of that."

"Listen to you!"

"What?"

"After all your spouting of philosophy, you don't really believe it."

"What philosophy? What does that have to do with...?" She shook her head in frustration.

"You say one person shouldn't have control of everyone. You say many people should help decide what happens. But now, when the sails are sheeted in hard and the coast is closing to leeward, you think you're the only one to helm the Ship."

"Oh."

"You have to trust the others, dear."

She thought about that for a moment. Then she peered up at her mother's silhouette against the dim grey of the canvas. "You don't call me 'dear' very often."

Verlene touched her hand. "It doesn't seem appropriate most of the time."

"Only in the night when I need you?"

"Do you?"

"Seems like I do."

'That's all right, then."

"It is."

"So now you listen to me. Go to sleep and don't think about it. They won't be attacking until late tomorrow. If you come up with something crucial in the morning, you can flash a message."

"I didn't think of that."

"You're not thinking. You're stewing."

"I think you're right."

"There. That's thinking."

142

She chuckled. "All right, Mother. You've made your point. Don't try to be witty in the middle of the night. I'm going back to bed."

"So am I, though I don't know why. Between your father's thrashing around and you kicking the furniture, I'm not getting much sleep myself."

"I'll endeavour to kick the furniture more softly next time."

"Thank you, dear. Good night."

She stood and gave her mother a quick, strong hug. "Thank you, Mother."

Her mother disappeared in the darkness, and she made her way back to her hammock. Soon, sleep came.

Not for long. When the first daylight greyed the canvas over her head, the sound of footsteps approaching the tent brought her awake. Her father brushed by as she swung her legs down, and she flinched her foot out of his way.

Following as quickly as she could, she was in time to hear the message. It wasn't much. Just agreement from Captain Cawbur that *Sparrowhawk* had ten more men on the trail behind the messenger. It would take them most of the day to reach the point where the wagons could pick them up. There was no use in the two farthest Crews sending men. They were now more than a day's march to the east of the *Ospreys* and the pursuing army.

As the camp slowly roused itself for the day, more messengers came in. All was going as planned. Once the sun hit the rocks above them, the messengers stopped and the flashes from the mirrors took over. News from farther away filtered through.

Her father did not wait for more than the first confirmations. He had borrowed one of Solen's riding horses, and he was mounted and away at a gallop just as the first rays of the sun probed down into the camp.

Sarasha and her mother watched him out of camp.

"I never asked. Where did he learn so much about horses?"

Her mother smiled. "Many of the Fleet take time to have a misspent youth."

143

"You're joking. Father never misspent a moment in his life."

"Then let's call it off-ship training of an unusual sort. It didn't make him popular in certain high places, but it made him the man he is."

"It seems to have made him a very good rider."

"Among other things."

She smiled over at her mother. "Sounds like the part of the conversation where the daughter doesn't need to hear any more."

"Oh." Verlene smiled. "That, too."

They turned back to their tent.

The best message came in soon after. "Army stopped."

"The mercenaries didn't break camp this morning!"

"They've decided to wait for their supplies."

"That takes pressure off the *Osprey*."

"Also pressure off us. We won't be moving today for sure. Dwayo Kaya needs to hear this."

Her mother nodded. "I'll go myself."

"Great. My mother is now running errands for me." She thwacked her crutch against a rock, then winced and checked the spot for splinters. *Stupid, taking out my anger on the one thing that makes me close to normal.*

She wondered if she would ever be able to put any weight on that foot. The Surgeon had told her that a joint injury often froze up during the healing process, but that exercise would loosen it again. He also mentioned that the exercise involved a lot of pain. However, he didn't want her to start until the general pain decreased. He had reminded her the last time he checked it that the injury was less than a month old. Healing takes time.

Well, so far the pain wasn't decreasing. The broken bones must be pushing against a tender spot because it often hurt even when she didn't move. It also hurt if she left it in one position for any length of time.

Hurt when I move, hurt when I don't move. A wide set of options.

144

A sudden thought hit her. *If the mercenaries are waiting for the wagons, they might send out a party to meet them. What if...*

She snorted at herself in disgust. As if her father and the Captains with him wouldn't consider something like that. *I'm stewing again.*

She shook her head and went to find something else to do.

Breakfast. She swivelled over to the fire and blew on last night's coals. She and her mother usually ate at the mess for lunch and dinner, but Verlene liked to wake up slowly, and they took their time at breakfast when possible.

By the time her mother returned, the water was hot. They wrapped their hands around tea mugs and stared into the fire for a while.

"It's good to be allowed to stay in one place."

Sarasha nodded.

Her mother gave her a longer stare. "Of course, if you plan to sit and stew all day..."

"Sorry."

"Why don't you do something?"

"That's the problem! I can't do anything!"

Verlene snorted: a soft sound of derision. "My daughter, the smart one. Can't even figure out what she should be doing to help her Crew."

"What do you mean?"

"I mean that even a relative simpleton like me can see when someone is wasting her time. Your mind is completely swamped with this one small skirmish. We have several days' battle ahead of us."

"And everyone else is fighting."

"Right. They're too busy to make any plans."

"Mother! You are a genius!"

"No, Sarasha. I've just learned that you geniuses need someone to steer your minds in the right direction."

She regarded her mother for a moment. "Why do you always set yourself lower like that?"

Verlene smiled gently. "I don't set myself anywhere. I know very well where I fit in. Your father is a brilliant man. No surprise there. I'm pretty sharp myself, but not in his rank. Nobody is sure where you fit, but there's no doubt you're very bright. Perhaps not the pure mental power that Pers has, but something else. You're not even very good at some things, but then you make these mental jumps that no one else can. It's sort of fun to watch. Especially when you get going with the other two, like last night."

"And you don't mind?"

"Why would I? I have a place."

"Yes, you said. Keeping me on topic."

"Or on to the next topic, if required."

"To remind me I'm supposed to get rolling on my next duty."

"And what is that going to be?"

"Making plans for what happens next."

"How will you do that?"

"I'm not sure. Things tend to come to me when I'm talking to other people, but Father and Pers are gone."

"Which leaves...besides your dear mother, of course..."

"Leide."

"And..."

"And?"

"You might consider consulting your older friends."

"Who?"

"The much older ones."

"Oh! Books. Mother, you really are a genius!"

For the second time in the past few glasses, she threw her arms around her mother. Then she grabbed her crutch and headed for the doorway.

As she turned to close the flap, she glanced back. Her mother was sitting there, a strange smile on her face. Sarasha leaned back in, her eyebrows raised. Her mother shook her head and smiled a bit wider.

Sarasha spun out the door, her crutch churning the soil.

It was long after dark before the first message arrived. The boy from the signal perch on the top of the highest rock came sliding down the trail. The whole camp could hear the rocks rolling, and a large group gathered to hear his message.

"Fire signal from the *Raptor*. 'Mission successful' and 'messengers afoot'. That's all."

A great sigh of relief gusted through the Crew. There was little conversation. There was nothing to say until the runner got there. Sarasha sympathized with the poor messenger, running through the night on unknown trails. The messengers were members of the Chan family and could navigate by the stars. That was still no guarantee against stepping into a hole or slipping off a loose rock.

* * *

The messenger, one of Cheynou's cousins, arrived near the end of the Middle watch, before the sky began to lighten in the east. He was dead tired and had barely the breath to gasp out his message.

"We did it!"

"Sit down." Verlene steadied the lad and moved him to a stool. "There's no rush now, is there?"

He shook his head, gasping for breath.

"No sense telling the story twice."

People began to arrive. Sarasha and her mother hadn't been the only sleepless ones. Dwayo Kaya was fully dressed. Kyso Yonghal was in his night robe, but had his boots on.

By the time the Officers and Heads had gathered, the messenger had regained his breath.

Verlene slapped his shoulder lightly. "All right, lad. Let's have the official message first."

He sat up straighter and his lips moved for a moment, his eyes staring upward. "Captain Tourn's greetings to his Crew and Families. The mission has achieved its objectives. The supplies have been stopped. Two wagons, twelve horses taken. Two wagons burned. We lost twenty-three dead, sixteen serious wounds. Hukou Ren of the Sailmakers and Brnau Treth

147

of the Deck Crew died in the battle. Sympathy and great honour to their Families."

There was a stifled sob from the growing crowd, and Sarasha winced. Yong and Pers had lost an older cousin, a good man who left a wife and three small children to mourn him. She wasn't so well acquainted with the Sailmaker, but she felt a pang for Tonu and her family.

The messenger cleared his throat and went on. "Other wounded *Eagles* will recover. Same anchorage for one day unless other circumstances arise. Message ends."

There were sombre nods around the circle. The losses to the combined Crews were heavy, but if this was the final blow, it was an acceptable sacrifice. The deaths of only two *Eagles* was much better than Sarasha had expected, because of her father's penchant for finding the danger spots and his men's determination to protect him. She wondered how he had fared in the battle.

The circle closed, but Verlene held up her hand. "No sense in crowding the lad. Please take whatever seats you can, and we'll see what he knows."

The messenger took the mug that Leide offered him and sipped. Then he raised his head to smile at his audience. He had taken the whole of the run to prepare what he would say now, and he was about to enjoy the fruit of his toil.

"It went pretty well the way we had it planned. We mined the trail with a ditch and stopped them, then closed the path behind. They were all ready for us. There were four wagons this time, two horses each, and ten mounted men. Big farm horses, but the men were well armed. Six soldiers plus the driver on each wagon. Good shields, but no bowmen.

"So they got all ready for us to attack." The boy grinned. "But we didn't. We just sat there under cover and waited. And waited."

The messenger let this pause go on for dramatic effect. "After a while, they started to move around. As soon as they did, we started lobbing arrows at them. So they got down behind their shields again.

"Once more, we waited. Captain Tourn was very firm. We weren't in any hurry. Unless the army sent relief, all we had to do was keep the wagons pinned down. We were sure that no messenger had got away to find help.

"So after a while, they started moving around again, but this time we didn't shoot. So they started getting braver, thought maybe they'd get the lead wagon free of the ditch. Once they were all out in the open, we shot again. We really got a lot of them that time.

"The Captain's opinion was that they thought we were afraid to attack, and all they had to do was wait for help. We kept giving them that impression while we picked away at them.

"Finally, the horsemen got anxious. Those horses don't have much protection, and one was already down. If we hadn't wanted the horses so much, we could have killed them all. The horsemen got organized for a charge, so the Captain sent a skirmish at them.

"That was just exactly what the horsemen wanted: a target. So they charged. Exactly where we wanted them to go. That was scary, believe me. When those big horses come thundering down at you, you don't even consider standing firm.

"We broke and ran, just as planned. The horses charged right up behind us and ran into a complete wall of arrows. It was a real mess, let me tell you. Horses really scream when they're hurt." For a moment, the boy lost the thread of his story as the reality of what he had just experienced hit him. He gulped, raised his head again, and continued.

"Then the rest of us rushed out behind, to keep the horsemen from getting back to the wagons. Used the pikes and boathooks on them. Pulled them off whenever we could. The soldiers on the wagon thought they'd come out and help, but our archers persuaded them not to. Two horsemen made it back to the wagon, and two broke out. One headed back towards the Farmers' town, and we let him go. Sent a troop to make sure he didn't turn back. The other one headed north, and the Captain and Pers went out after him. Their horses were much faster, and they ran him to a standstill. They didn't even fight, just herded him back.

"By the time they got back, we were ready for the final attack. But Captain Tourn stopped us. He said there was no sense in anybody else getting killed.

"He went and talked to the one on the horse they had herded back. Told him we'd let them go if they walked away south. Made him drop his weapons and his shield, then let him ride back down to the wagons.

"They talked for a while, then they made up their minds. There were only three horsemen and fifteen soldiers left. They didn't want to trust us, so we let them keep their weapons until they were a good distance down the trail. If they thought they could keep them, Captain Bren was there to remind them it would be foolish. He just sat there on that beautiful horse of his and stared down at them. They dropped their weapons and walked off. We let them take food and water with them. It's a couple days walk back into town.

"Now, here's the strange part. There were two soldiers and a driver who were too injured to walk. The Captain had our Surgeons fix them up as soon as they had finished with our wounded. Then he propped them up in the shade, left them water and food. When one of the men questioned it, he said, 'We aren't savages,' and that was it.

"By that time, we knew from the flashes that the mercenary army had sent out a large party to meet the wagons, and we didn't want to tangle with them. We were able to get two wagons loose and all the horses that were left. We loaded up with everything we could carry from the other two wagons and burned the rest.

"Let me tell you, it felt good to see that smoke go up. A bunch of us were standing around yelling, 'Burn like the *Eagle*.' The others were shouting their Ship names, too. We felt strong.

"Then the Captain said we had to get hull down on the horizon before those soldiers showed up, and we took off. That's when he sent me ahead, so I don't know any more.

They're heading for the *Raptor's* camp with the wounded, going to distribute the supplies when they can. I'm not sure about the deployment from there."

People started calling out questions, and the boy sipped the water and answered as best he could. He hadn't seen the Sailmaker die. Brnau Treth had gone down under a charge, making a stand to keep the horsemen from getting back to the wagons. "He took down one of those big horses with his sabre, so I guess he died pretty well." The boy gulped, a tear creeping down his cheek.

Verlene stood. "All right. The man needs rest. He fought a battle and ran all night. When he wakes up, you can ask him more questions."

The assembled Crew got up slowly and left. Two of the Chans appeared to take the runner to his tent. His fatigue got to him as he tried to rise, and they had to help him across the grass.

Verlene regarded her daughter as the last people left. "That was a good idea of your father's."

"What? Negotiating?"

"Yes."

Sarasha smiled. "Trust you to think of that, Mother. Something that saves lives."

"More than that."

"Yes. I caught what he said. Up to now, the Farmers didn't know we aren't savages. If they think we're open to parley, maybe they won't be so afraid of us."

"They also know we can be trusted to keep our word, once we give it."

"And show mercy to the fallen."

Her mother nodded. "We haven't made such a good start with our new neighbours, but that wasn't our fault. We will have to live with these people somewhere nearby. If we have to fight our way to the beach every time we want to trade and steal everything we need, we will turn into savages."

"Will we ever have a normal trading relationship with these people?"

"There's no reason not to."

"But we just had a war with them!"

"People get over that quickly if the trade is profitable. Actually, we didn't have a war with them."

"True, only some mercenaries they hired."

"That will make a difference."

"It might make for hard trading."

"How so?"

"This must have cost them a great deal. They'll be trying to get their money back from us for years."

Her mother laughed. "It's time for bed. We can solve our future problems in the morning."

It was good to get into her hammock and feel its gentle swing every time she moved. Soon, she drifted off into the first real sleep she had managed in a long while.

16. ...AND AFTER

A triumphant and sombre *Eagle* Crew returned with the bodies of their fallen at sundown the next day. News was good on all sides. The Mercenary camp remained in place. *Ospreys* were an easy day farther out of range. *Raptors* had moved as well, and the other Crews had rested for the day.

Arlijn Tourn did not return on Solen's pack horse. The Captain trotted into camp on a huge black stallion that looked ready to start the battle all over again. He snorted in disdain at the people who circled a safe distance away from him and pawed the ground when another horse came too close.

Just as they were approaching camp, the big horse jerked to a halt. He raised his head and whinnied a high, reaching challenge. An answering call echoed from the pasture. Sarasha thought that no experienced rider ever grabbed for the saddle, but her father did just that. He wrapped the reins around one wrist and gripped the saddle firmly with the other hand.

None too soon.

The Black swung his head and started a spin towards the pasture, his huge hooves churning the sod. But he was too slow. The Captain yarded back on the reins, and the horse's head dropped, his chin pulled close to his chest.

"Whoa, there, boy. You aren't here to play courting games. You will do what you're told, and only what you're told. Have you got that?" The final question was punctuated by a further tug on the reins, sitting the poor horse back on his haunches.

There was a moment's silence, then Arlijn slowly began to release the reins. At one point, the horse took a hesitant step forward, only to be brought up short by the return of pressure. They continued the play, with the reins slackening more each time, until the horse finally stood, quivering, his head still raised, his nostrils wide, staring towards where Solen's stallion paced the length of the corral. The Black whinnied again, and the smaller horse returned the call.

Arlijn waited a moment longer, then slowly pulled his mount's head around. Reluctantly, the huge horse turned, his eyes still fixed in the direction of his rival, but turn he did, and they walked sedately towards the *Eagles*' camp.

Sarasha and Verlene met them where the first tents started. There was no formal homecoming, just Families greeting their returning Raiders in joy or sorrow.

Sarasha moved forward. "Nice horse."

"Be careful, Sarasha."

"Oh, he isn't worried about me. I smell right."

Sure enough, the huge muzzle brushed across her fist, the warm breath snuffling at her.

She grinned up at her father. "He smells my mare. Even a tenderbutt like me can figure that out."

She reached under the stallion's chin and scratched. "That's what you wanted, isn't it, boy?"

There was a scream from the pasture, but before the stallion could raise his head she grabbed the reins under his chin and hauled down sharply. "Don't you try that. You'll get a chance for introductions when we're good and ready, not before."

The stallion shook his head as if trying to dislodge a fly, but she twisted the bit sideways, and soon he stopped. She regarded the horse's mouth with interest. A trickle of blood seeped through the skim of foam on his lip.

"What kind of bit is that, Father?"

The Captain grinned down at her. "A bit that allows a hundredweight like you to handle him."

"But he's bleeding!"

Her father's grin disappeared. "He hasn't been properly trained. Those Farmers don't have much experience fighting with horses."

He swung down from the saddle as he spoke and moved forward to check the horse's mouth.

Sarasha grinned. "Since they've been defeated by men afoot each time, that's a safe bet."

"There is other evidence, and this horse is some of it. He's not much use. He's way too fierce to be a plow horse, but way too slow to be a warhorse. I don't know why they bred up a horse like this or why they kept him, except that he sure is beautiful."

She stood back and surveyed the animal. "Well, that's a good reason to keep anything, I suppose."

"But not to ride him into battle, untrained."

"Our good luck. Is this the one you ran down?"

"Yes. He was no match for Solen's pack horse, which is a good horse, but no racer."

She glanced at her father. "So why did you take him? We have no need of another pretty face around here."

Tourn chuckled. "He's not just another pretty face. He's the sire of our herd."

"You want more like him?"

"No. I've already talked to Orrick about breeding the Black to that mare of his. Now, she is a runner. No good in battle, of course. Too light. But can you imagine the offspring of these two?"

Sarasha glanced across at her mother. "And we thought we were planning ahead!"

Her mother's gesture towards her father said it all.

"So where do we keep him?"

"I've been thinking about that. We can't pasture him with the others. Any ideas?"

Sarasha considered. "There's a spot at the other end of camp that has rocks on three sides and a bit of grass in the bottom. If he can be picketed out for tonight, we might put in some posts and rails tomorrow.

"That is, if we're staying..."

"I have no doubt we're staying for a while. The Mercenaries aren't going anywhere without supplies, and we aren't in any position to do anything about them while they're sitting there. We seem to be at a stalemate."

"I wish we knew what they were thinking."

Her father slanted his head to one side. "I can make several guesses."

"No. I don't mean the army. I mean the Farmers who are hiring them."

"That's more difficult."

"Not if we had some up-to-date information."

"And how do we get that?"

She grinned. "We have the solution to two problems. We need to get Solen's stallion out of camp, and we need information from someone who can get into the Farmers' town without arousing suspicion."

"Good idea. I'll ask him."

"I already have. He was ready to leave tomorrow. In view of the change of situation," she slapped the muscular shoulder beside her, "he might find a more pleasant welcome with the *Night Hawks* tonight."

Solen already had his stallion and three pack horses saddled when they returned from picketing the Black.

"I'll make it look like I'm just comin' in for some supplies, maybe sell a horse or two."

Captain Tourn nodded. "Sarasha has briefed you."

"Very thoroughly. I'll get as much as I can without arousin' suspicion."

"As far as we know, nobody will connect you with us."

"Nobody that's back in town, anyway. If they do, too bad. I'm a free rider, and I work for whoever I choose."

"I doubt the Farmers would see it that way. Mind yourself."

The taller man grinned and swung up on his horse. "I've survived a lifetime out here in the Prairie by bein' very careful of myself."

He clucked to his mount and headed out into the night.

For the next three days, the stalemate continued. No more supply wagons came out from the town, and no messengers, spies or foragers were allowed to cross the blockade that the Crews tightened around the Mercenary camp.

It was a good time for the Families and Crews. Smiles began to appear, and steps to lighten. Laughter and music drifted through the tents.

Feist was out on the Prairie every day with one of the mess cooks, searching for any forage he recognized or even thought looked good. Raiders were rotated back to visit with their Families, and Pers, Cheynou and another trainee rider went farther north to see what was beyond. They returned on the evening of the third day with little to report. They did, however, have two small antelope slung behind their saddles.

"It's an amazing sight. The Prairie just goes on and on, but it isn't really flat. It slopes gradually up to the north, with ups and downs here and there. To the west there's a larger river, which has cut quite a good valley. Down inside, there are stands of trees and bushes with lots of wildlife. I imagine the river valley would be a good place to winter: protection from the wind and wood for fires."

The Captain grinned. "You will discover that there isn't enough wood for fires anywhere here."

"So what do we burn?"

"Whatever is available."

Sarasha snorted. "There's plenty of fuel. We'll be producing it every day."

"What?"

"Dung."

"You're joking."

She shook her head. "There's plenty of mention of it in the old, old stories. It dries out in the sun, and you burn it."

"Won't that be smelly?"

She shrugged. "We don't notice it, but to a Landlocked, the sea is smelly. Their homes are smelly to us. We'll get used to it. Believe me, when that winter wind comes in off the Southern Ocean, you'll burn whatever your flint can put a spark to and be thankful."

Her father nodded. "I'm not surprised to hear this from the Ancients. My experience ashore matches it."

Cheynou sighed. "Oh well, at least we can keep dry."

Leide, who had appeared as soon as Pers rode into camp, slapped his shoulder. "It'll be much easier to keep parchment dry, that's for sure."

"And plenty of parchment available. Just walking around."

Sarasha's face grew serious. "That's another thing I've been looking into. We have been setting our sights on horses because they are so wonderful. But horses aren't the best herd animals. We'll need meat animals and those that give milk. Horse hide makes very poor parchment, as well."

"So we've got to become sheep and goat herders?"

"Perhaps. Maybe cows. Whatever works."

"We could use stock of that kind right now. Our hunters are already eating into the game reserves here."

"We need this settled before winter. That will be expensive, building up a herd so fast. "

"Not right now."

They turned to look at Pers.

"Well, we're at war with the Farmers, aren't we? And they started it?"

Sarasha exchanged glances with her father. Each knew what the other was thinking. "I don't see it as a problem."

He thought a moment. "No, it might help."

"If they thought we were going to continue..."

"...it might be added persuasion."

"Could a few of us mortals be allowed to understand where this elevated conversation is heading?"

Sarasha deferred to her father.

"We could pick up a few head of stock here and there: sheep, goats, cattle. Sarasha and I agree it will make an added incentive to the Farmers to settle. If they believe we will stop once peace is established..."

"Then we had better get moving. Once peace descends, we'll be honour bound to abide by the terms."

"Right. You don't have too long. Once Solen gets back, we'll figure out what to do next."

"And those soldiers out there will be getting hungry."

Her father smiled, shook his head. "No mercenary heads into the field without a reasonable amount of food. It's just the kind of food."

"Sort of like hardtack and ship's beer."

The Captain raised his eyebrows. "I rather like ship's beer."

"Sure, a cool mug on a hot day. Not warm from moving the kegs in the sun, watered down to make it last, three meals a day."

"So the mercenaries aren't in that bad shape?"

"No. The reason they've stopped is to force the Farmers to get them more supplies. If we continue to show the ability to cut them off, they aren't likely to go any farther. If we got them a week out into those plains, they'd never get back."

"But doesn't the same apply to us?"

"We don't plan to come back."

There were nods all around. Another reminder that the decision had been made a long time ago. There was little doubt that the Crews and Families now accepted the inevitability of the Prairie.

Solen made it to camp in the middle of the fourth afternoon. His one remaining packhorse was loaded heavily, and a smaller bundle was slung behind his saddle. Reassured that the Black was securely penned, he went straight to the corral and unloaded his animals. Most of the supplies were for himself, but he tossed one small package to Sarasha.

"That's for the kids."

She opened it to discover a bag full of mixed nuts and candies.

"Oh, thank you, Solen. They'll love these!"

"Yeah, well, the poor little buggers have been through a tough time. They deserve a treat."

She grinned at him. "I hope the news you have for us is as sweet."

"Oh, I'd say so. You get those candies spread around, and I'll see you up at the Captain's tent. I imagine he'll want to do it all official."

159

She nodded and hurried off to the mess tent to let the cooks handle the distribution of the treats.

They waited at the Captain's tent for a select few Family Heads and Officers to arrive to receive Solen's report. As the Captain suggested, it wasn't exactly news that Solen had been with them during the fighting, but no sense in spreading his spying around among the general Crew.

Once the leaders had arrived and a horde of grateful, sticky-fingered children had been shooed away, Tourn motioned to Solen. "So, rider. What's it like in town?"

Solen grinned. "You won't believe this, folks. They're dead scared."

There was a general exclamation.

He nodded, satisfied with the reaction. "That's right. They were always scared of the Sea Raiders, and when eight Ships' worth came ashore after a battle, they didn't know what to think.

"So they decided to act and got up this mercenary army. And now things are not goin' at all the way they want. They're scared out of their wits by this incredible Warlord the Raiders have. The man who outsmarts their mercenaries at every move, who wins every battle. Yessir, they figure this Warlord is some kinda evil genius, and they're terrified. They're already usin' him to scare their kids into bein' good."

There was a murmur of surprise. "And just who is this Warlord they're so afraid of?"

Captain Tourn laughed. "There isn't one, Dwayo."

"Then who..."

"It's us!"

"What do you mean, 'us', Captain?"

"I've been calling the main strategy, but most of the ideas have come from Sarasha and Pers and their friends. The other Captains aren't slow, either."

The grins spread around the circle. "So the Farmers are afraid of someone who doesn't exist."

"That's right." The Captain's face grew serious. "But that's the problem. People who are afraid do stupid things. Like

160

sending this army after us. They have no idea that there was a more than even chance we would simply pack up and disappear to the north without bothering them."

He turned to Solen. "Anything else?"

The horse trader shook his head. "Nothin' logical. There's so much gossip and fear goin' around, they don't have anythin' straight. I don't believe the leaders are doin' much better. They're really stuck since you've been cuttin' off the supply trains. Half of them want to pull the mercenaries back to a defensive perimeter to protect themselves when the Warlord attacks. Of course, that's the townsmen. The Farmers with big spreads know they wouldn't be protected and they want to keep up the battle. Those are the ones you've been seein' out on their clumsy plow horses, tryin' to run you down."

The Captain glanced over at Sarasha. An unlucky development.

Pers shifted in his chair. "My herd-gathering raids will only reinforce the Farmers' worries."

Tourn shrugged. "Too late to do anything about it."

"And that lamb you brought in was just too good." Sarasha smacked her lips. "Hard to pass up the chance for more."

"How are their supplies?"

"Oh, there's no worry for them. Business is goin' on as usual. I sold two horses, no trouble. You haven't touched their farmland, of course."

"You have our thanks, Solen. When this is all over, we will make sure you are appropriately rewarded."

The man grinned. "Just the look on those kids' faces when they came to thank me for the candy was pretty much enough."

Sarasha explained for those who had missed it. "Solen brought back nuts and candy for the children."

Eyes turned to the horseman with new respect.

The Captain stood. "So, now we have the information we need. I will be in touch with the other Captains. Unless anyone has questions?"

There was no response, and the Captain invited Solen into the tent for a drink that was "better than ship's beer."

The rider grinned and jumped to his feet. "Been a hard, hot ride, Captain."

Once they were seated around the small table in the Captain's tent, Arlijn sipped at the glass of deep red wine in his hand. "I certainly hope we can continue to trade enough to keep up my supply of this!"

The horseman sipped at his. "Yes, a man could develop a taste, all right."

Sarasha said nothing, just enjoyed the chance to drink something so smooth and rich.

"Now that it's only us, how afraid are those Farmers? The leaders, I mean. Crazy afraid? Unreasonable, do you think?"

Solen shook his head. "No. They're business afraid. So far, few Farmers have been killed, and no townsmen. Their own territory has not been invaded. There were rumours of stock goin' missin', but nothin' confirmed. The general population is antsy, but the leaders haven't reached the panic stage yet. I'd say at the moment they're just at the stupid stage."

"Excellent. What do you say, Sarasha, Pers? Any clever ideas for our next attack?"

"The best battle is the one you don't have to fight."

"Pardon me?"

Sarasha shrugged. "You heard me."

"All right. I heard you. How can we win the next battle if we don't fight it?"

"Well..."

He glared at her. She was playing his own games with him. She smiled pleasantly and waited.

"I'm sorry. I'm fresh out of inspiration."

There was an edge to his voice; she remembered the stress of the past month and took pity on him. "All right. What is our aim in this war?"

He thought a moment. "To be left alone to do what we want."

"Correct. So if, at this moment, we could get the Farmers to leave *us* alone?"

"Then we win the battle and the war."

162

"Exactly. I calculate that an attack has a fifty-fifty chance of losing us that objective even if we win."

"Continue, please."

"She's right." Pers leaned forward enthusiastically. "You heard what Solen said. They're just frightened, not in panic. If we have too great a victory, maybe kill too many soldiers and some of the Farmers with them, it could push them over that line. Once they start fielding their own men, it will be a whole different war."

"I agree with you. Are you suggesting it's time to negotiate?"

"You've always taught me to bargain when you are strongest. Right now, they're pretty worried about the Warlord and his genius. If he were to lose a battle, they would gain heart."

"We don't want that to happen."

"So we negotiate."

Her father nodded slowly. "Might be a good idea."

"Might be a great idea. Remember, we are the injured party. Poor refugees on the beach, under assault from their greatest enemy: the Sea Raiders. And then the Farmers went and attacked us! We have done nothing but defend ourselves. We might exact a fairly large reparation as a price for going away and not bothering them."

Solen nodded. "Remember, these are Farmers, but also Merchants. They understand bargainin'. They'd be happier to bargain than fight."

Arlijn grinned, but his teeth showed just a little too much. "They won't enjoy this bargaining."

A chuckle ran around the table. The Warlord of the Raiders was about to change his style.

Pers frowned. "What about my herd-gathering?"

Sarasha held up one finger. "That touches on something else. Solen, how well do the Farmers and the townsmen get along?"

He moved his head from side to side. "Pretty well. They're two sides of the same coin: the producers and the sellers."

"But their objectives don't always coincide."

"Perhaps not. I don't see it in this case, though."

She nodded. "I'm not sure, either, but it's worth thinking about. You said that, in town, the rumours of herds being raided didn't matter much. I would suspect that out on the farms, the story is somewhat different."

"Wouldn't be surprised."

"So the Farmers will want something different out of these negotiations."

"Yeah. Security from us!" Everyone looked at Pers and laughed.

"Right. The Merchants will want safety for their town, but that will change when they realize we are ready to go away. If we let on that we plan to be peaceful, distant neighbours, then they'll start asking for trading advantages."

"But the Farmers won't be so happy."

"If I were a Farmer, I wouldn't be. Up until now, the Raiders have always come from the sea. The town took the brunt of the attack because their warehouses are richer."

Her father chuckled. "And now the Farmers will be the worried ones, because we might continue the raiding."

"Which means I can keep on picking up stock?"

"Don't be so eager, Pers." Sarasha cuffed him on the shoulder. "Some of those animals you brought in were pretty poor stuff. We need food, yes, but we need breeding stock as well."

"They don't leave good breeding stock just wandering out by the far fences."

"Right. And we don't want any battles. We want them worried, not angry. It makes your job tougher, but that's the best thing. Try to get us some good breeding stock, but don't kill any Farmers in the process."

The Captain nodded. "Pers, you have five days. Take what supplies you need. Go to the blockade camp and pick up a few of the best stalkers you can find. We don't have many, but try to have representatives from every Crew. Take a big swing out around and sweep back, bringing your new herd with you. That way, you'll get here just about the time that news of your activities arrives. Keep in touch as best you can with the mirrors. If you see any really big signal flames at night, they will be for you. It will mean that the negotiations have reached an important point, and you need to either stop or push them harder. Once we get the herd back here, we can divide it up evenly. Keep track of which prime animal is taken by which Crew, because they should have first choice of their own booty."

He surveyed the table. "Did I miss anything?"

"We should send herders out in a few days to take care of the stock as the herd grows."

"Right. Sarasha, will you and Leide make up copies of our suggestions, so Pers can give them to each Captain he sees, or to the Crew in charge of each Ship's contingent at the camp, for the ones he doesn't? We don't want a bunch going off freelancing, because they'll just hit the nearest farms hard, and that will be counter to our strategy."

Pers nodded and stood. "I'll be off first thing in the morning. Solen, can I take one of the pack animals for supplies?"

"Sure. Luce would be best, but I want to check her over first." The two men stepped to the door, talking, and disappeared into the night.

"And who'll play the main role in this performance?"

Sarasha grinned at her father. "Why, you, of course, on your huge black fighting horse."

"Some fighting horse."

"He's still fighting you pretty well. Don't worry, we can make him look a whole lot better. The armourers have light plate they can work on. From what the Raiders tell us, the chest and flanks of the horse need protecting. Perhaps a skirt like Ebb Tide wears, but with overlapping metal plates?"

"And you trust me with the delicate negotiations?"

"Oh, no. At least two other Captains. And me."

"You? How can I take you along?"

"The Warlord's crippled Scribe? No trouble at all."

"I don't like exposing you to that kind of danger."

She stared at him a moment. "I'll pretend I was listening upwind when you said that."

"Hmm. Sorry. I would like you there. I hope you won't stop the proceedings as you usually do."

"Oh no, Captain. I will be ever so quiet and obedient. Just make sure I get to sit near enough to you that you can see what I'm writing."

"We always have the rigging signals."

She shook her head. "I'm wary about using those when others are watching. In the first place, it's rude. In the second, it doesn't engender trust."

"But you and Leide use them during Conclaves."

"That's just workers communicating silently so as not to bother the important people. When a Captain uses them, it's different."

"I suppose." Then his mind moved on. "If we're negotiating, we need a Captains' Conclave first."

"I'll write that in the message to go with Pers."

"Where?"

"Might as well have it at the blockade camp."

"That's where the talks with the Farmers will have to be."

"Fair enough."

"When?"

"That depends on the contact with the Farmers. If they are willing, we could do it right away. If they don't react favourably, we might have trouble just getting them to listen to our offer."

"So we need to meet as soon as every Captain can get there."

"Right. And if we can make contact before then, no harm done."

"We'll leave in one day. That gives me time to get the Black used to his new trappings, and you time for some more research in your books."

She laughed. "Yes, I have to learn about diplomacy, don't I?"

17. Diplomacy at its Worst

The Farmers' army didn't seem anxious to talk. When the second messenger had been repulsed by several arrows that came too close to be accidental, the three Captains who had arrived at the parley point glanced at each other.

"What's wrong with these barbarians?" Captain Kletsh sniffed. "Don't they recognize a parley signal when they see one?"

Captain Tory laughed a brief, bitter bark. "We haven't shown them one in the last two hundred years."

"I guess my gesture of honour with their wounded went unnoticed."

Tourn glanced at Sarasha and raised his eyebrows towards Solen, who was standing nearby.

She nodded. "We need a different sort of messenger."

The rider met their stare. "Who would that be?"

"Someone they're familiar with. Who isn't one of us."

Solen grinned. "The cost of my services just went way up. Riskin' an arrow wasn't part of the original deal."

Tory slapped the rider on the shoulder. "Man, you help us end this war and you'll have a place in our Families for the rest of your life."

The plainsman's head came up, a glint in his eye. "Do you mean that?"

The Captain hesitated, aware of what he had just offered. Captain Tourn came to his rescue. "I hate to undermine our bargaining position, Solen, but there has never been any question of that. Not after the first two days."

Solen nodded. "Thank you. I'd like to help but I don't see that I'll have any more luck than your other messengers did. The moment I ride in from your camp, they'll figure me for one of yours."

Sarasha stepped up behind him. "Is that an old shirt you're wearing?"

He half-turned. "What? Yeah, it's an old shirt."

"Good." She drew her rigging knife in a long, shallow slash across his shoulder blade.

He yelled in surprise and pain. "What?" He spun to face her. "What...?"

She regarded his face, then measured him a good right fist, high on the cheekbone where it would bruise nicely. The force of the blow rocked him back, but he did not lose his balance. His fists came up, but she smiled at him.

"Now they'll accept you."

"What...?"

"Don't just stand there saying 'What?' Go get some cloth from your own pack and patch yourself up. Nobody else touch him. Then we put him on his horse bareback and chase him into their camp. They won't be able to refuse a refugee."

Solen craned his head, trying to see the cut on his back. "How'm I goin' to patch that?"

"Poorly, I hope. You want to seem as pitiful as possible."

Solen turned to glare at her, then looked to Arlijn. "Captain, I must congratulate you. Your daughter is one of the nastiest people I have had the pleasure to meet." He glanced at her once again. "And one of the smartest."

He stalked off towards his horse, muttering, leaving her to face the stares of the rest of the party. "Well, what did you plan to do? Stand there and talk about the best place to stick a knife in him?"

Tory shook his head and said nothing. She glanced over at Kletsh and caught a grin, quickly hidden in the bristling beard.

"We'd better have something in writing for him to carry. Makes us appear more official, and less like barbarians."

"Which some of us are, more than others."

"Don't worry, Captain Tory," she grinned over at him. "I don't have you planned for any off-ship duty."

"I fervently pray not." He turned and strode away.

Her father stood staring at her a moment. "He meant that."

She shrugged. "I couldn't keep up the joking forever. Sooner or later, he was going to figure it out."

For once, Kletsh laughed. "I've had you figured from the moment you opened your mouth in Captains' Conclave. All I've been trying to figure is whether you're more help or more danger to us."

As he, too, departed, her father shook his head. "I think he was serious, too."

"He was. I would feel like that in his situation."

"We'll just have to make sure he keeps thinking you're a help."

"And the other Captains as well."

Solen appeared, a cloth tied around his shoulder, his unsaddled horse on a lead. "Am I tattered and bashed enough for you, Sarasha?"

She pretended to regard him critically. "I suppose we could tear your shirt a bit more. How about a split lip?"

He glowered at her. "Some day, you'll pay for this. I'm not sure how, but I'll figure something out."

"Just think of all the laughs you got, watching me try to learn to ride a horse."

"Huh! I never even got to see that, and now you're too good at it for any laughs. You spoil all my best entertainment."

"Don't worry. I'll mess up another time, just for you."

"I'm all aquiver with anticipation." He turned to the Captain. "What's my story?"

"We caught you on your way out from town. We forced you to be our messenger, beat you up when you refused."

He glared at Sarasha. "That's close enough to the truth. What do you want from them?"

"Just a meeting. Both the Farmers and the mercenary officers. We'll meet on neutral ground; let's say out on that little open patch of rock twenty chains from their camp. They can bring ten people. We'll bring ten. The rest of their men stay in camp. They can be lined up at the edge in full armour if they like, but one man sets one foot outside, and somebody dies. Do you think you can persuade them we're serious?"

The rider tossed a brief grin to Sarasha. "I imagine." Then he frowned. "Your reputation will pretty much do that for me. What do you offer in return?"

"The same. Our ten will be alone. There won't be a Crew member visible from start to finish."

Solen grinned wider. "Which isn't the same thing. I know about that dry wash t'other side of the stony patch, about half the distance their camp is."

"Maybe they know, maybe they don't. We've been keeping them pretty well contained."

"What do I tell them you want to talk about?"

"Not your job, especially if you're a reluctant messenger."

"I'd agree with that. Makes it easier for me."

"Anything you can come up with, Sarasha?"

"No. The Surgeon's Assistant wants to talk to you, though." She gestured to the man, who had been hovering nearby.

He came forward, all business. "That's a shallow cut with a clean knife, so I don't think you'll have any trouble with it. The mercenaries ought to have a good surgeon with them. Make sure he washes the wound out well before he binds it up. If he doesn't, I'll have to do it over when you get back, and you don't want it messed with twice."

Solen grinned. "Thanks for your concern."

The Assistant stared at him. "When you go into the surgery, make a close inspection. If his place isn't clean, if his tools and swabs aren't spotless, don't let him touch you. You understand that?"

The rider regarded the Surgeon's Assistant with surprise. "Yeah. Yeah, infection. I'll keep an eye open."

The Assistant nodded, satisfied. With a polite inclination of his head to Arlijn and Sarasha, he slipped away.

"Well? Are we ready?"

Sarasha glanced up from where she was writing. "Let's get the timing figured out. We sent the messengers; they were rebuffed. We saw Solen, grabbed him. He got the wound when we grabbed him. He got the bruise when we persuaded him to be our messenger. So it should be a fresh bruise, and there's no sense waiting any longer." She stared at them, thinking.

"We need a mob of Raiders to drive him down into their camp. They can't be chasing him like they want to catch him. They're making him go. Solen, you've got to turn around a couple of times like you want to come back. If our men have to start shooting arrows at you, then turn and head straight into the mercenary camp. From that point, you do what the Farmers say."

"Yeah. That's the key moment, ain't it? What if they shoot me?"

"Well, if they start lobbing arrows near you, don't come back to us. Head out down the valley, and we'll pick you up out of sight around that small hill there."

"And if they do shoot me?"

"Same thing. If you can stay on your horse, do it. If you fall off, then we can forget the game and come get you."

He shook his head. "I'm not sure why I'm doing this."

She allowed her smile to soften. "I do."

He regarded her a moment. "If I come back, you'll have to tell me."

She slapped his good shoulder. "You'll be back."

"I'm beginning to have faith in your plans, Sarasha."

"Thank you, I guess."

"You know what I mean, don't you?"

She did. *It's my plan. If it goes wrong, the guilt is on my head.*

He mounted, she passed him up the parchment of their demands, and the Raiders closed in around him, one grabbing his bridle. The Captain repeated Sarasha's instructions to the Raiders, and they strode off.

Keeping low on the skyline, everyone except the sentries moved to watch Solen's approach to the enemy camp.

As instructed, the Raiders led the rider, surrounded, to just out of bowshot of the camp. Then they opened up and urged him forward, yelling. One of them slapped the rump of his horse with the flat of his sabre, and the horse skittered forward a few steps. Solen yelled in anger and hauled the horse to a stop. There were threatening moves from the Raiders, and he turned back to begin a slow progress towards the mercenary camp. He stopped once, and made as if to turn back, but the Raiders shouted again, one of them half-drawing his bow, and Solen turned with reluctance towards the Farmers' camp again.

A line of soldiers formed up in good order as he approached, their heavy shields overlapping. Other soldiers stood in ranks inside the camp. The mercenaries were taking no chances.

When Solen had proceeded about halfway to the soldiers' lines, there was a shout to halt, reinforced by an arrow that landed very close to his horse's feet. He pulled up.

Sarasha and her companions could hear, faintly, the conversation.

"What do you want?"

"What the feck do you think I want? Let me in or they'll kill me."

"How do we know that?"

Solen threw up his hands. "I could just turn and ride back and you'll find out real fast."

There was a slight pause. Then the voice came again. "What do they want?"

"They want to talk. I want medical attention. I want away from these barbarians."

The soldiers consulted. Sarasha picked out an officer in a bronze chest plate and two men in the half-armour of the Farmers who rode the horses. Finally, the shout came again.

"Dismount and move forward slowly."

"Thank you." The rider complied. Soon, he was surrounded by soldiers and herded inside the camp. No one in the ranks so much as glanced to the side. *Well-disciplined men.*

There was a long pause, and nothing happened.

"They need a little nudge."

Her father nodded. "Time for the Warlord to put in an appearance?"

She grinned. "Can't wait to appear in public in that getup?"

"I admit, it is rather impressive." He started back to camp, and she grabbed her crutch and followed.

Once Arlijn was posed beside the Black, she had to agree. He wore his full Captain's regalia, and the Armourers had added a crest to his helm. Kyso Yonghal had explained it to them. "In battle ashore, soldiers must be able to see their leader as a rallying point. A crest like this, which would just get fouled on rigging on a Ship, is very important on land." He gave a slow smile. "It also makes the wearer seem taller."

The plated skirting for the horse was also impressive, she thought, even to someone who recognized the material as a jib from the night canvas of one of the raiding sloops. The bronze plates glowed nicely on the black background and would protect the horse from most lance and sword thrusts from ground level.

They had also added, at her father's request, an extension to the back and front of the saddle. This was no longer a rider's saddle, with a horn for attaching a rope in front. It was now a high fighting saddle, enclosing the rider, keeping him from being dragged from his horse. The Raiders had learned a lot about fighting men on horseback.

The Captain swung aboard the Black without help, but she could see it took an effort with all his paraphernalia slung about him and his breastplate weighing him down. He settled into the saddle, and the black horse calmed under his master's now-familiar hand on the reins.

There was a notable reaction in the enemy camp when the Captain appeared at the top of the small ridge and halted his horse, peering down. A group of Raiders and Officers stood at a respectful distance, but Sarasha decided to start her own role. She hobbled forward on her crutch and stood beside the Black, her hand on its shoulder, staring down at the camp as well. Let them make of that what they would.

"He won't stand still for long."

"I never expected either of you would. Go ahead. Pace up and down. If they think you're impatient, they may hurry. I'll just stand here."

173

The plume nodded towards her, but her father winked as well. He turned the horse and walked him majestically along the ridge. Sarasha stared down at the camp. *Might as well make good use of my time. These soldiers have a centuries-old tradition of living under canvas for long periods. We could learn from them.*

The camp was laid out in a square, with the tents in an orderly row around the perimeter. In the days while the mercenaries had been static, they had dug a ditch around the whole camp half a chain outside the tents, throwing the dirt inwards to create a small dyke. In case of attack, troops could cross the distance from their tents to this defensive fortification in moments. The officers' tent and the mess fronted a wide, clear area near the centre, where ranks of extra soldiers mustered at the moment.

She counted the men she could see, and her number tallied with previous estimates. An open area like a street led from the main entrance straight to the officers' quarters, with the stream that led through the camp controlled in a ditch beside the street. Latrines and what might be a bath-tent sat on the downstream end of the camp, just far enough away to keep the stream unfouled. On the other side of the main street from the latrines was a more haphazard set of tents, which must be for the Farmers and their mounts and footmen.

She filed all this away in her memory, both for future use by the Crews, and also in case of the need for attack. It seemed that the weakest spot was the part of the dyke just opposite the Farmers' tents, because there were no soldiers quartered right there, and the Farmers would take the longest to get up on their horses and ready to fight. She wondered what the mercenary officer had done to solve that problem, but could see no evidence that he had.

Her father paced his steed back and forth along the ridge, quite enjoying his little play. The horse was getting restless and once, when they turned at the end of his beat, he rose partially on his hind legs. She knew it was no accident. Her father had been training the Black to fight with his front hooves, as Solen had told them stallions did when they vied for dominance of the herd.

Solen. He had not come out of the surgeon's tent yet. There had been a bustle soon after they all entered the officers' tent, and then someone with a bag and a basin of water had gone in. Probably the surgeon. After a while, Solen and the surgeon and the mercenary officer had moved to a smaller tent nearby.

The surgery door was swept aside, and Solen and the officer appeared, apparently in an argument. She grinned. Solen's gestures were obvious. "You want me to go back to those barbarians? You must be crazy."

The officer, however, was adamant. Finally, one of the Farmers stepped forward and raised his hand as if to strike Solen. The officer deftly maneuvered himself between them, urging Solen towards his horse. She filed that away to tell her father. The mercenary would be easier to deal with than the Farmers. Understandable. He was a professional; their lives and families were threatened.

Her father had seen the action as well, and rode down the back of the hill to approach the camp from below. He pushed his horse well within bowshot of the camp, a troop of Raiders spreading out in front of him, and waited.

Soon Solen appeared, riding his horse, his arm encased in a sling. Pacing beside him was the mercenary officer. When they reached easy talking distance from Captain Arlijn, the officer spoke. After a moment, the plume on her father's helm nodded once, curtly. Only then did the officer let go of Solen's bridle and motion him forward.

More and more interesting.

Captain Tourn waited while his Raiders again surrounded Solen and led his horse out of sight around the corner of the hill. The Raider Warlord sat his horse, gazing at the enemy camp. The officer stood gazing back. Finally, Arlijn nodded again, wheeled his horse and moved back to camp at a dignified pace.

By the time Sarasha made it down the hill, Solen was seated comfortably on an officer's camp stool, and the

Surgeon's Assistant was prying at the bandages on his shoulder.

"How was his surgery?"

"Cleaner than your mess kitchen."

"I should hope so. I've talked to the cooks time and again about keeping the work surfaces clean. Did he sponge out the wound?"

"Aye, he did that. Hurt like hell."

"Probably alcohol. Not deep enough for a hot iron."

Solen spotted Sarasha. "Are you listening to this?"

"I guess I did it just right."

He glowered at her. "Well, for your information, I am now under the diplomatic protection of Commander Haskel of Haskel's Mercenary Force. So you'd better watch yourself from now on. It's true. Ask the Captain."

Captain Tourn nodded. "True enough. The Commander wouldn't let him go until I guaranteed his safety."

Captain Sax raised his eyebrows. "You've done well for yourself, young man. No matter what the outcome of this war, you have been guaranteed the protection of the winning side."

"You could say I paid a price."

"You did."

Captain Tourn pulled off his helm. "So, what did they say?"

"Well, they hemmed and harrumphed a bit, but they'll be there, as you asked."

"Just that, no arguments, no quibbles?"

"The Farmers were gettin' ready with all sorts of objections, but the Commander told them the plan sounded reasonable, that was the way things were usually done, an' it was a good sign. The Farmers backed down. There's no doubt Haskel's in charge in his own camp."

"Did he suggest a time?"

"Tomorrow mornin', two of their hours after sunup."

Arlijn calculated. "That's near the start of the Third watch."

"We'll know when they start forming up to move out." Sax put his thumbs in his belt and drummed his fingers on his upper thighs, a gesture Sarasha had seen him use before when he was satisfied. "So, who do we send?"

"All the Captains who can be here by that time, plus a couple of First Officers. One or two Family Heads; it doesn't matter from which Crews. We want them to see the different colours, show our solidarity with each other. Sarasha will go as Scribe."

Sax nodded, as did the other two Captains.

"So we will have a Captains' Conclave later this evening, in case some of the others get here later on. Anything else, gentlemen?"

They all shook their heads.

"Then I would like to officially thank Solen for his service to the Fleet today and remind us all of the promise that was made."

The Captains all inclined their heads to the rider, who was struggling to keep his pleased smile under control. Then the group broke up, leaving Sarasha and her father with the hero of the hour.

"Unless you'd rather go back to the Farmers?"

Solen grinned at the Captain, tossed a thumb towards Sarasha. "I might be safer there."

"The thought had occurred to me."

"No, Captain. I will be seen by one and all, very clearly leadin' my one remainin' pack horse up over that hill and away from the camp, obviously free."

"Good idea. No sense in giving anything away."

"Correct. I'll be headin' back to the *Eagle* camp to pick up the other two horses I've got there. Do you have anythin' you need done?"

Sarasha laughed. "How are you at herding?"

"Herdin' what? Cows, sheep, goats? No experience, no desire to learn. Why do you think I took up with horses?"

"Too bad. Pers would enjoy the help, and you could take his Crew some supplies. I'm sure they need more, with the new herders out to supplement his Raiders."

"I'll cut past the *Osprey* camp, then. They're supplyin' him."

Captain Tourn stopped the rider as he was about to leave. "The Fleet owes you a lot, Solen. And Sarasha owes you an apology."

"For what? It was considerable easier than gettin' stuck with a coupla arrows. She did what she had to do, and I can't figure any way that woulda been cleaner. Your daughter ain't easy, Captain, but she's too often right."

"That about sums her up."

The rider pointed a finger at Sarasha, grinning. "But I'm still gonna collect. I'm just gonna wait a while and let you stew, worryin' about how and when it's gonna happen."

She smiled sweetly at him. "I'm all atremble, Solen."

"Good. I like my women like that." He strode towards his horse.

She lifted her crutch, but he was already too far away to reach, so she dropped the end back to the ground in disgust.

"You do impress the men, don't you?"

"My methods are unorthodox, but they work. If I wanted a husband, I'd be doing all right."

"You don't?"

"No."

"Why not?"

"At the moment, I'm too busy being a part of the Raider Warlord. After that, I'll be too busy with getting this Fleet properly settled on the Beach. After that, when I'm no use any more, I'll think about what to do about it."

"I can't see a time when you're of no use, Sarasha."

She shrugged. "When it comes, I'll figure it out."

He regarded her strangely. "Your foot must be sore today, with all that running up and down the hill."

She rounded on him, anger washing through her. "Will you forget about my foot being sore? I never use that for an excuse, and I wish you would stop making it for me. Whether my foot is sore or not, I'm doing what I have to do. Just like I did with Solen today."

He nodded. "All right, Sarasha. I won't mention it again unless you do."

178

They turned together towards the tent they were sharing. "And don't wait for me. I'm sure you have things to do."

He said nothing, but stepped out, leaving her stumbling along at her own awkward pace. *Why did I take my frustration out on one of the two people I love most in this world?*

18. Diplomacy Works

At the Captains' Conclave that evening, they thrashed out a plan the Farmers might agree to. All the Captains attended, except for Soren of the *Pelican*. He had remained with his Crew because of some dispute that required his mediation, and he didn't think he could get to the blockade camp in time. He had sent his First, a lanky redhead with a limp: an old wound that did not keep him from showing up, dusty and tired, in time for the meeting.

It didn't take Captain Tourn long to persuade them, as Sarasha had suggested, that the truth was the best line to take.

"It is in their best interests to be good to us, and we must make the point that it would have been better if they had done so from the start. We would simply like to move into the Prairie and make a new life for ourselves there. If we are successful, we could become trading partners. If we are not successful, it will be necessary to supplement our lives in the way our people usually have.

"The better they treat us, the better chance we have of succeeding and the better chance we have of becoming acceptable, peaceful, neighbours."

Kletsh frowned. "And what if they don't choose to believe this?"

"Then we will have no choice but to drop the peaceful attempts and continue straight on with the battle."

They all nodded, including Kletsh. "What are we asking for?"

"We haven't decided. That's why I have brought Baetor Huin, my Quartermaster Family Head. This is all about trading. I wouldn't dream of bargaining without his advice."

The Quartermaster moved forward at his ponderous gait, and Sarasha sighed inwardly. She could never learn to like the man, but when it came to getting the best deal for his Ship, no trader could top him.

The other Captains knew him by reputation and were willing to let an expert guide them in their choices.

Sarasha wrote the plan in detail: what to ask for at first, what was padded in as giveaways, what was important.

The gist of it went in two directions: reparation in the form of supplies and breeding stock; future concessions in trading. The first part was necessary to aid their immediate survival. The second would assist them in establishing future prosperity.

Baetor Huin was having trouble persuading the Captains that the trading concessions were of more importance. Captain Sax was about to state for the third time how important it was to have good sheep, because of the value of wool, when Sarasha decided she had heard enough.

"Hmh."

The Captain paused and regarded her, eyebrows raised.

"Baetor Huin is right. It isn't just the small amount of extra money we will make from the trading concessions. It's the interdependence that will slowly increase as trading progresses. The Farmers don't know it yet, but the town will benefit from our presence. Once our herds are up to size and we start producing more horses, hides and wool than the locals can buy, we will start shipping our goods to other ports along the Southern Shore. Where better to ship them from than a port where we already have an established presence? The Seafarers are a sturdy people. We can survive without anyone's help. If we trade with these Farmers, our power and wealth will increase much faster. As will theirs."

Sax nodded. "Good thoughts, Sarasha. Please go on, Baetor Huin." Then he turned to Captain Cawbur, who was sitting next to him, and spoke in a conversational tone. "When the famous Baetor Huin is supported by Sarasha the Wise, who would dare to argue?"

A chuckle ran around the table, and the Quartermaster's gaze touched upon her. He was too wily a bargainer to let on, but he would see her differently from now on. That was probably to the good.

The Conclave was able to conclude on a note of enthusiastic Concurrence, and Baetor Huin was invited to take one of the ten places at the bargaining the next day. He sat with his Captain and Sarasha in their tent later discussing the finer points of the bargaining.

Sarasha reminded the two older men of the main point to consider. "We are dealing with two forces here. The Farmers are the ones we are supposed to be bargaining with. However, the mercenaries will have some say in the outcome. From what we have gathered, the mercenary Commander, a man named Haskel, is held in high esteem by the Farmers. He is the professional, and they are used to hiring people and letting them do their job.

"I read him as an honourable man, a true professional, and he will advise his clients as to what is best for them. He may or may not remind them of the costs involved in keeping his army in the field if they do not achieve peace. I would guess that whatever reparations they pay us, they will not be more than the fees for the mercenaries for...what, Captain, another ten days?"

Her father shrugged. "I've not been in the habit of hiring mercenaries lately, but in essence you are right. The sooner they end the war, the less money they spend. They will be aware of this."

Baetor nodded. "So we can keep that uppermost in their minds as we bargain."

"There is one more factor we have discussed, Captain. Do we have any idea if there are representatives of the townspeople in the camp?"

Baetor's eyes lit up. He turned to Sarasha with interest. "Is there a division?"

"Possibly. The townspeople are merchants, and they want to protect their commerce. They will be most receptive to your trading ideas. The Farmers want security from raids. They will not agree on some points, and will not care about others."

Arlijn nodded. "In fact, the Farmers may see us as potential rivals in the production of wool and hides. They might stick on some of the trading points we make."

Baetor nodded thoughtfully and sat drumming his fingers on the table. Then his head rose and he stared at Sarasha, then at her father, then back at her again.

"It's you, isn't it?"

They waited.

He nodded. "I see it now. When you spoke out of turn at that first Conclave, I thought you had too many brains for your own good. But I was wrong, wasn't I? It's you who's been feeding the Captain all these new ideas. I'm willing to give three-to-one you've been reading those books you insisted on saving and finding all sorts of help from the Ancients."

Captain Tourn chuckled. "You are a clever man, Baetor, but you missed it by a hair. It isn't her. Well, it isn't just her. It's her, and it's me, and it's Pers Treth, and even Leide Tourn and little Cheynou Chan."

Sarasha smiled too. "And to be fair, it's sometimes also other Captains like Tory of the *Osprey*, who has done more than his share during this war. And Solen the horseman, who has taught us and helped us more than he ever was hired to do."

She paused a moment. "And now it's also you."

After a moment, the Quartermaster burst into laughter. "Captain, I have to hand it to you. You always were one to listen to others, and I often said it made it easy for me to do my job. But this is taking it further than I ever expected. Oh yes, everybody said, 'things are going to be different, things are going to change,' but I never expected anything like this."

He wiped his eyes, and his face sobered. "I'll tell you one thing, Captain. I don't care if it's you, or Sarasha, or the whole lot of you. There's a genius running this Crew and this Fleet, and I'm beginning to think we might make a go, here on the land. Trading wool, stock, and hides all over the Southern Ocean, are we? I'm ready for that!"

Sarasha glanced slyly at the heavy-set man. "You know, Baetor, the Crews will need an agent in the Farmers' town.

183

We'll also need warehouses and a big mansion, to impress the townsfolk and our trading partners who come in on ships."

He stared at her, then raised a thick forefinger. "Don't you go trying your wiles on me, young lady. I'm on to you now. I've had that in mind for a long time, ever since I saw the smoke from the old *Eagle*'s pyre, and realized I had no home. That's difficult for a man my age."

He dropped his hand. "But for a while I have to go where my Crew and my Family go. I have to learn to ride one of those horses, because that's what the *Eagles* do now, and I'm an *Eagle*, and I'll never be anything else.

"Now, I'm ready to turn in. Tomorrow will be an historic day in the annals of the Fleet, and I hope you get my role written down right, young lady!"

He turned to the Captain. "I'm grateful you have offered to share your tent, sir. I wasn't looking forward to sleeping on the ground."

Sarasha wasn't looking forward to it either, but she had immediately offered her hammock when she heard the elderly man was coming. She gathered her things together and slipped out into the night to bed down in the long grass where Ebb Tide was picketed. The slow munch of the horse's feeding lulled her, and she slept.

* * *

Rising tension filled the camp the next morning. The Crew was talking louder, walking faster, their backs straight. The lull in warfare had given people time to rest, those small, debilitating wounds and blisters time to heal. Everyone anticipated the results of the coming Conclave.

Sarasha had a quick bite at the mess tent, then found a couple of young Raiders to help her load Ebb Tide's packsaddle with a small folding table, three deck chairs and all her writing implements.

Once again, her father appeared in his Warlord regalia: his horse calmer now he was used to the extra weight and

184

movement of the armour. When a scout jogged in with word that there was action from the Farmers, the Captains formed up.

Sarasha mounted Ebb Tide and slipped out to the Conclave site. She unloaded her horse and picketed her some distance away. Then she set up the three chairs, two facing the third, and put her table and stool close to the solo chair. The message would not be lost on the assembly. One person spoke for the Fleet. The others could make their own choices.

She stood by her stool as the Captains and Family Heads filed out of camp. Her father did not ride his horse, but a young Raider, chosen from the *Pelican* for his size and strength, led the animal a few paces behind.

The party from the Farmers' camp appeared soon after. Commander Haskel walked between two civilians: a Farmer dressed in armour and a smaller man wearing an ornately embroidered coat. This would be the townsman. Two other Farmers in armour followed. The rest of the party consisted of soldiers in full infantry armour, swords sheathed, pikes held aloft. These parked themselves in a line behind their clients as the men figured out who should sit. Without a blink, the Commander solved the problem, taking a position behind and between the chairs.

Then Captain Tourn took off his helm and sat. His Captains took one step forward and adopted a 'rest easy' pose. The Farmers also sat, and Haskel assumed a similar pose to that of the Captains. Sarasha took to her stool and lifted her pen.

Captain Tourn spoke first, maintaining his leadership of the Conclave. "I am Arlijn Tourn. I lead one group of my people. I was formerly a Captain of a Ship, but those terms are meaningless on land. My fellow former Captains are..." and he named the Captains in order of their precedence. When he had finished, he gazed politely at the men opposite.

After a short pause and a glance at his companion, the one in the embroidered coat spoke. "I am Noveyn, a merchant in the town of Ternata. My friend is Struven of Vrengata, a local

185

landowner. Byaren of Nangata and Erlin of Mawgata are also local nobility. Commander Haskel leads our troops."

He paused a moment. "I was under the impression that we were to bring only ten to this meeting. I count eleven in your party."

Tourn allowed his glance to slip right, then left, pointedly ignoring Sarasha. "I count ten."

The Merchant thought about that, then decided to let it go. "You asked for this meeting, ex-Captain Tourn. What do you want?"

Tourn held out his hands in an apologetic gesture. "I should first state my regret that I did not extend the invitation sooner. If we had had this meeting a month ago, I would be happily headed out for the Northern Prairie and you would be sitting at home in your warehouse, counting your profits.

"As it is, here we are out in this uncomfortable place, throwing sticks at each other, and for no reason I can fathom."

There was a brief pause. The two Farmer emissaries glanced at each other. Obviously, they had not expected such a statement.

This time, the Farmer spoke. "I suppose we must accept your apology. It seems the only polite thing to do."

One of the pair behind him – the burly individual in brown and gold armour and a full beard – muttered something to his partner. Sarasha remembered him because he rode the most beautiful horse in the camp, a huge red mare.

The first Farmer ignored this aside. "And now we must ask your intentions. You have invaded our land once again, and we have legitimate concerns for our safety."

"I have stated our intentions. Before your mercenaries attacked us, we had planned to move to the north, seeking to make our life on the open Prairie, as we formerly roamed the open Ocean."

The man with the beard stepped forward a pace. "To be precise, ex-Captain, we did not attack you. We sent our forces out to protect ourselves. It was your men who attacked us."

186

Sarasha was impressed that her father could summon such a heartfelt chuckle in the tension of this debate, but chuckle he did.

"Come, Byaren of Nangata. Do you expect this assembly of intelligent men to believe that a camp full of women and children, marched on by an army of hostile soldiers, is going to sit there and welcome them with open arms?"

"If your intentions are as peaceful as you say, yes, I do."

Captain Tourn stared at the burly Farmer. Then he spoke as if the distraction had not happened. "We sympathize with the townspeople and Farmers hereabouts. When a fleet of Ships carries out a full-scale battle on your doorstep, so to speak, and the aggressor and larger portion of that fleet has treated you badly in the past, you have reason to be worried.

"However, when the attacking fleet departs and we, their victims, run aground on your shoreline, we do not understand your reaction. Surely the enemies of your enemies have potential to be your allies, perhaps your friends?"

"A Raider is a Raider, ex-Captain, or whatever you are." The red beard jutted forward. "Why should we trust you?"

Again, the Captain took a moment to stare straight at the other. "Trust is something you earn. When there has been warfare, trust is a difficult thing to develop. But if two parties demonstrate a willingness to solve a dispute, that is the first and longest step towards developing trust.

"The second factor that allows us to settle this is if we can find common objectives. Let us consider the situation as it sits right now. I do not believe either side wanted this fight. You don't want us on your doorstep. We don't want to be here. Is that not a common goal we can agree on?"

"We can agree that we will be very happy when you lot are pushed back into the ocean you were drug up from."

Sarasha continued scribbling with her pen. Without raising her head, she spoke in a conversational tone, but loud enough to be heard by all. "If the blockhead with the beard could control his mouth as well as he controls that beautiful red horse of his, I bet we could solve this mess in half the time."

There was a moment of complete silence, and she continued to write. Then, she looked up expectantly, as if waiting for more. The other side were staring at her, uncertain how to react.

"You bring up a good point, Byaren of Nangata. It is important for trust that there is honesty between the parties." Tourn's total lack of reaction to Sarasha's interjection made it difficult for anyone to respond to her insult. After a confused moment, they focused on his words.

"While we understand the antipathy you may have for us, you must be aware that it is not possible for us to return to the Ocean. That is one reason we burned our Ships. As you could no doubt see, we have had a falling out with the Priest-Admiral and his folk. Doubtless, also, you could see that we lost."

Sarasha reached out and wrote in large letters on a new piece of parchment. "Fleet Coming."

"So you are stuck with us. We cannot go back. We are here, for good or for ill. Shall we battle until you have killed us, to the last woman, the last child? We are not an easy people; I admit it. The cost to you will be high.

"And there is one other factor you may not have considered, because you do not realize the state of affairs in the Fleet of the Priest-Admiral. When we left the Fleet, we caused him much grief, more than the loss of eight Ships to a storm would have. We were a symbol of widespread disaffection. His power is waning. He used that failing power to crush our Ships, but he dared not, at that moment, try to finish us off.

"So, he will go away, consolidate his power, and then come back for us."

Sarasha caught the surprised glance shared between the two opposing leaders. *Aha! They never considered this.*

"So," the Captain spread his hands, "as I said at the first. No matter who started what problem, these are the facts. We are here. The Fleet is out there, coming back. If we continue to fight, we weaken ourselves. Our people will flee into the Prairie unprepared, to perish in the winter storms. Your people will sit with a reduced army in the path of the vengeful Fleet.

"No, I do not believe it is in anyone's best interest to continue the fight. Do you wish to discuss this?"

The Merchant waved a hand in front of his face. "We will not try to hide it. The facts are as you have stated. We did not want you here, and we were willing to sacrifice much to ensure our safety.

"But the situation has changed. Our safety is not ensured. If the Raiders are coming back, and if, as you say, you really do wish to leave and not harm us, then I can see good reason to end the fighting."

"But..." The bearded one was silenced by his companion's firm hand on his arm.

The seated Farmer spoke. "What offer are you willing to make in order that we should stop this pursuit?"

"As the injured party in this situation, I wanted to ask you the same question, Struven of Vrengata."

"Injured party?"

"How many of your people have died? How much of your goods have been destroyed or lost? How many of your Families have been driven, day after day, upon a strange trail, their only possessions what they can carry on their backs?"

"And the backs of our horses."

Nobody saw fit to silence that outburst. In fact, there were a few grins showing on the faces of the Captains.

The Merchant raised one finger. "What about our wagonloads of goods, our horses?"

"I believe your Commander will tell you that materiel lost as a consequence of failed strategy is a spoil of war, and not usually considered for reparation."

They glanced back, and Haskel nodded gravely.

The eyes of the Merchant and the Farmer met for a moment. Then the Merchant spoke.

"What do you request?"

19. The View from Shore

"First, that you pull your soldiers from their pursuit. Under normal circumstances, we would ask that you disband them or send them away. As the situation lies, I suggest you keep them nearby. If I may give you an unasked-for piece of advice, you should use them to train up your local militias as quickly as possible. The Fleet cannot stay in these waters past mid-summer because it follows the fishing runs. It is a pattern centuries in the making, and the present Priest-Admiral is not the man to change so important a tradition. So the attack must come within the next two months if it is to come at all.

"We are also short of perishable supplies such as vegetables, fruits, and flour. We could agree on an appropriate amount of those goods to help us survive until we can grow or buy our own.

"We assume the only way to make a living on the Prairie is by herding. If the land were good enough for farming, you would be expanding in that direction."

The seated Farmer nodded. "The Prairie seems to grow crops well, but the good leaches out of the soil in five years or so. Once the sod is gone, the winter winds dry out the topsoil and blow it away."

Tourn nodded. "So we need to develop our herds quickly. A good number of your hardiest breeding stock would be very helpful. Horses, cows, sheep, goats. Any others you would suggest. Not your fattest and heaviest: your hardiest."

The Merchant glanced at his Farmer partner. You could see what both were thinking. If the Farmers provided the animals and the Merchants gave the goods, the load might be spread evenly.

"I believe we can help you. What amounts of these items do your people require?"

The Captain leaned back in his chair, which creaked under the weight of his armour. "Do you require time to communicate with your people? If we have agreed that the warfare will stop, there is time to finalize the details."

The Merchant nodded. "Perhaps if you could give us an idea of the quantities you require, we could give our people a better idea of the cost of this calamity which has been dropped, willy-nilly, on our heads."

"I understand. This situation has been slow in developing for our people, and still it has taken us a long time to become resigned to it. We do not expect you to react any more quickly.

"I can estimate our needs." He held out a hand, and Sarasha placed the papers in it. "There is also the matter of trading."

She could almost see the Merchant's ears perk up. "What trading?"

"We need goods we cannot produce out on the Prairie. We will develop our own products to trade so we can purchase these things. Once we can produce more than your people can use, we will be selling to other ports. If we have been induced to trade with you, then your port will be our shipping point."

"You are suggesting that we make it convenient for you to trade with us, because this could develop into a profitable situation for both parties."

"You state it so clearly."

The Merchant smiled and nodded briefly at the compliment. Again, he glanced at his Farmer companion, but it was a more calculating look than before.

Again, Sarasha wrote in large letters. "Give the Farmer something."

"In turn, we will undertake to cease any actions we might be planning against citizens of the area. We would even be willing to help deal with any bandit problems you may have. Lawless peoples are a concern for us as well."

The Farmer relaxed.

Sarasha hid her smile. *We have dealt with both sides of the equation.*

The Captain arose and stretched mightily.

"Let us meet tomorrow and see what fruits our discussions bear."

The Farmer and the Merchant rose to depart, and Tourn was just turning away when Haskel's crisp voice stopped him. "I assume you will allow our messengers through?"

"Of course. Parties of less than four men may leave your camp in any direction. Fully laden soldiers withdrawing towards the coast may leave in groups of twenty. We will pull our pickets back and leave only observers. If you don't mind, we will stay at this camp. It is convenient for discussions, and we would feel more comfortable, even in this new peace, with our forces near."

Haskel nodded. "Suits me. What about resupply?"

"That depends on how long the talks last. I would suggest that since you are no longer attacking us, you only need a similar number of soldiers in your camp to what we have in ours. If you were to send a good number of your soldiers back to the town, we would be happy to let the others have resupply."

Sarasha spoke aside in an undertone. "Us too."

He ignored her, but she knew he had heard her.

The soldier considered. "I will discuss this with my clients."

"Perhaps your resupply could include the same for our people."

Tourn inclined his head to his fellow Captain. "A good idea, Orrick Bren. What do you say, Commander Haskel?"

"Again, I must ask my principals. It sounds reasonable to me."

"You are a reasonable man, Commander Haskel."

"I try to be. It is an unreasonable world, most of the time."

"As this month's events clearly demonstrate."

They all turned and walked away, leaving Sarasha in sole possession of the conference ground. She packed her things unaided and brought Ebb Tide over, loaded her and swung aboard for the short ride back to camp. It felt strange to be alone in the middle of such momentous events. Of course, her people's sentries were watching over her. Round the corner of the hill, two of them saluted her from their posts as she went by. She grinned and saluted in return.

The Captains were already sitting in front of the *Eagle* tent when she arrived, but didn't seem to be talking business yet. They all regarded her expectantly. *They are waiting for me!* She swung off her horse and busied herself with getting out her papers to cover her red face.

As she sat in the empty chair beside her father, Orrick Bren laughed out loud. "Sarasha, you had them completely flummoxed."

There was an appreciative chuckle.

Kletsh slapped his knee. "That poor Landbound clod. He had no idea what to do, seriously insulted by a person who didn't seem to exist."

"He was spoiling any chance we had for agreement. I wonder why he was there?"

"Probably because he demanded to be there. He seems the type."

Sarasha regarded Captain Kletsh a moment. "Don't judge him completely on what you saw today. He is a superb horseman. One of the few who handled himself well in battle, according to reports."

The older Captain nodded. "I take your point, Sarasha. He could be more than a dangerous loudmouth. Perhaps he was placed in the group with specific instructions."

"Or he could be a fine man with good reason to hate the Raiders. We'll never find out as long as we stay enemies."

Captain Sax punched one palm with the other fist. "I have to admit, things I heard today worry me. Tourn, are you certain the Priest-Admiral will return?"

"Does anyone here have any doubt?"

Head shakes around the circle.

Sax pursed his lips. "So we should stay and fight?"

Captain Tourn held up his hands. "I made no suggestion. I placed facts before the Farmers that I felt they should know."

"We could pack up and leave."

"We could. In fact, we are far enough inland already that the Priest-Admiral wouldn't risk coming after us. His shore parties do not have the resources or experience to wage that sort of campaign. Not like Haskel's men have. We could sit here and laugh at him."

Orrick Bren shook his head. "I'm not sure I like that."

Menendan Cawbur, who rarely spoke, frowned. "Why not, Captain Bren? I thought this was your advice. We pack up, head inland, disappear. Forget the Fleet and the Priest-Admiral, and let them forget us."

"I have had more time to think. More time to see the lay of the land here."

Cawbur raised his eyebrows. "You mean you want to stay here at the coast, now?"

"No. I was wondering what would happen if the Priest-Admiral came here prepared for war and found us gone. What would he do then?"

Ulric Soren of the *Pelican* barked a laugh. "He'd solve our present problem for us."

"That's what I'm afraid of."

"You're afraid of our two enemies wiping each other out?"

Bren passed a hand over his forehead. "Ulric, I have to admit that half a month ago I would have agreed with you. It's different now."

"How is it different?" Lukin Frey of the *Falcon* leaned forward, eyebrows raised. "Now that you've fought with these Farmers, you see them as people?"

"That's a good point, Lukin, and partly true. However, I was thinking more of the future. We are Landlocked now. The line has been drawn, and it is the high tide line. We are on the uphill side of that line. Our lives are tied up with the Farmers, like it or not. If the Priest-Admiral destroys these people, then we will have no one to trade with in the future."

Seber Tory laughed. "The youngest of us has the most interest in the future. He has time to see more of it."

They all chuckled.

"But he has a good point." The *Osprey* Captain held up one finger. "We all know how Raiders think. If a place is soft and rich, they return often. If the Fleet has good Raiding here, with the added incentive of finding us, they will return, again and again, until these Farmers are destroyed, and we will not dare to show our faces. This coast, and the trading possibilities it gives us, will be cut off."

Bren grinned. "On the other hand, if we join up with these Farmers..."

"...and give the Priest-Admiral a severe drubbing..."

"...he won't dare come back..."

"...and we'll have given these Farmers less reason to hate us."

"Wait, wait."

They all turned to Sarasha.

"What? What's wrong?"

"Nothing's wrong," she frowned. "You're all talking too fast. I can't get it all down!"

"So you think it's a good idea?"

She held her free hand up. "Now you expect me to write at double speed and think, too! Whatever happened to proper procedure for a Captains' Conclave?"

They laughed again, and Orrick Bren regarded her. "So, Sarasha the Scribe. What have you written down?"

"Lacking a vote, I still predict concurrence. We are better off throwing in our lot with these Farmers and giving the Priest-Admiral a kick in the butt which will discourage him from visiting in the future."

"A kick in the butt? That sounds highly informal for the official Log."

She grinned at her father. "Sorry, sir. I just got carried away by the enthusiasm of the Conclave."

Hamon Kletsh slapped the table. "I call the vote, then. Do we stay and fight?"

Eight nods.

"Then I suggest the Scribe write that in the official Log in appropriate and formal language and have copies sent to us all.

This is a serious decision, gentlemen, one that will affect our futures. I hope all of our Crews and Families see it as we do when they are asked once again to send their Raiders out into danger."

The nods of agreement were even more sombre.

"But, dammit, I would like one more chance to kick the Priest-Admiral's butt!"

20. RED BEARD

Sarasha pulled her horse to a stop and listened. Yes, there were definitely hoofbeats behind her. Heavy, slow ones. It could only be one of the Farmers. She kneed Ebb Tide off the trail and down into the creek bed behind a thicket of willows. Only one Farmer was stupid or brave enough to follow her, so close to her own camp and the peace talks.

Sure enough, the horse coming around the corner was large. Huge, in fact. And red. The bearded rider went past her, then stopped. He gazed around, puzzled, fingering the hilt of his broadsword.

She gave him a moment longer, then reined Ebb Tide quietly out of the willows behind him. Only the rustling of the leaves warned him, and he craned his head around, half-drawing his sword. Belatedly, he pulled the mare's head as well, and she clumsily turned to face Sarasha.

"Well, if it isn't our little crippled friend."

"I doubt if 'friend' covers it, but since I prevented you from making an even bigger fool of yourself, I suppose you could call me that."

"You prevented what?"

"I allowed you to save a small amount of face, which you seemed determined to throw away."

The big mare shuffled uncertainly under his tight rein, and he settled her absent-mindedly as he spoke. "What do you mean?"

"I mean that now you can say that you did your duty, making sure the nasty pirates knew that someone wasn't afraid of them. Of course, you were also completely messing up the peace talks. If they had gone wrong, everyone would have blamed you. The other problem would have been if your own side had finally got angry enough to tell you to shut up. Then you would have been embarrassed in front of both your friends and your enemies. Yes, I probably did you a big favour." She nodded once, as if to herself.

"You won't be surprised if I disagree with you?"

"Not at the moment. If you live long enough, which I doubt, you might gain the wisdom later."

"At the moment, it's you who should be worried about living any longer." Again, he fingered his sword hilt.

She laughed out loud, then stopped. "You are joking, aren't you?"

"Why would I joke?"

"Because I can't believe anyone who handles a horse the way you do is really that stupid."

"You have an amazing talent for making an insult hard to object to. It won't save you, of course."

"Save me from what? Do you really think you could lay a finger on me without suffering the consequences?"

"Who is going to stop me?"

"You are, of course, assuming that your big, clumsy horse could catch me."

"This is a war horse!"

"No, it isn't. It's an overgrown plow horse."

"It's a war horse. I have ridden over lines of infantry, who scatter in front of me like chaff before the wind."

"So there was infantry who were stupid enough to try a stand against you. What success have you had against my people?"

"Against cowards afraid to stand and fight?" His head came up, and a sneer wrinkled his lip.

She smiled. "Against a coward who would attack women and children?"

"I have attacked no women and children!"

"Your mercenaries have chased us for ten days. We had sick and wounded before you came. Do you think they all survived?"

"You are the Sea Raiders. We had every right to defend ourselves."

"Like you are planning to do now? Against me?"

"I could."

"I wouldn't, if I were you."

"Who will stop me?"

"Oh. You're back to that again." She raised her voice. "Raiders!"

An answer came from the willows: very close. "Yes, Sarasha?"

"No matter what happens, you will not kill this man. You will tie him up and sling him on his stomach across that fancy, useless saddle of his, march him back to his own people and tell them that he has broken the truce. Let them deal with him. No matter what happens to me. Is that clear?"

"Yes, Sarasha. Very clear. Killing him would be fun, but we like your idea better."

"Thank you for your understanding." She turned her attention back to the Farmer confronting her. "Did you really think you could leave your camp without being followed?"

He had the grace to look abashed.

"I'll tell you what, Byaren. Let's pretend you're not angry. Let's pretend that you have calmed down enough that you aren't acting stupid any more. I don't know what has made you so afraid of the Sea People, but whatever it was, it is in the past. The situation has changed, and you need to settle that ghost for yourself."

"I'm not afraid of you!"

"Of course you are. Otherwise, why are you so angry?"

He sat back on his horse and thought about that for a moment.

"M-hm. I detect the glimmer of intelligence breaking through."

He stared at her, then leaned forward, resting his forearms on the saddle in front of him. "Are you always this hard to get along with?"

"Only to my friends. And to my enemies, of course."

"Ah. So the rest of the world is safe, then."

"I'm pleased at your concern for the rest of the world."

"And if I'm not angry any more, what will we pretend next?"

"We will pretend that you are angry at me, and we will see if you can catch me on that beautiful red lump of granite you are riding."

"You mean have a race? Me against you?"

"Not a race. A chase."

"And if I catch you?"

"Then you will have proved your point, and I expect you to be gentleman enough to leave your sword sheathed."

"And if I don't catch you?"

"Then I will have proved my point, and I will be polite enough not to make too much fun of you." She pretended to ponder. "That is, until I have decided whether you are a friend or an enemy. After that, the rules get looser."

"I can live with that. How much of a head start do you want?"

"Head start? I don't..." In the middle of her sentence, she heeled Ebb Tide back into the bushes, down through the creek and up the other side. There was a level spot beyond, and the little horse lifted willingly into her smooth gallop. Sarasha glanced back to see the head and shoulders of the red mare burst through the willows, huge front hooves flailing at the loose boulders of the bank. Then the war horse was out on the flat, beginning to pick up speed. Sarasha stayed on the open prairie long enough to determine that the larger horse was gaining on her. Then she cut around a pile of rocks and headed up a short, gravelly slope.

Once she got to the top, she turned for a breather and looked down. The red horse was gamely clawing her way up the hill, her rider standing in the stirrups and urging her on.

Sarasha waited, watching his technique. *No whip. Didn't think he would.* When he was halfway up to her, she took Ebb Tide in a controlled slide down the other side and back into the creek bed. She splashed up the stream until the rocks closed in and she could barely squeeze her horse between them. Then she cut out of the creek and circled back, standing Ebb Tide quietly above the bank behind a clump of willows.

Soon, the red mare appeared, blowing hard, the water spraying three times her height into the air around her. As the rocks closed in, her progress slowed until the big horse's gait was held to a slow scramble. Sarasha paced alongside them until the bearded man glanced up and saw her. He reined in and sat there, both he and his horse breathing heavily.

"You can outrun me on the flat."

"I can?"

"You were catching up. That's why I went up the hill. You didn't do so well there."

"That dratted rock rolled around under her feet."

"You tried to go at it too fast."

"Too fast?"

"If you walk her up something like that, she'll get to the top faster and in better shape. I thought you'd know that. You've been riding a long time, I can tell."

"I haven't exactly tried chasing someone up a gravel bank before."

She smiled. "Then you may thank me for the lesson."

He glared up at her, about to retort. Then he stopped, and that expression came into his eyes again. He raised his voice. "Raiders!"

"Yes." The voice that came from the other side of the creek sounded a bit breathless.

"I think I'm in trouble. Can you protect me?"

"In what way, Farmer?"

"Sarasha has decided that I am a friend or an enemy. What do I do now?"

There was a snicker. "Cover your ears and run."

"Can't do that. I'm stuck in a creek that only goes upstream."

There was a slithering in the willows and a face appeared, staring down at him. "I'm sorry, Farmer, but if you're up against someone who can make streams run uphill, you'll be dealing with it yourself. We just try to stay out of her way."

201

"Thanks for the advice. It's a little late."

Sarasha moved her horse forward. "Would you have taken it, earlier?"

He grinned, and she could see that under the bristling beard he was younger than she had supposed. About as young as he had been acting, in fact. "Probably not. I'm not known for taking advice."

"Not something to be proud of, is it?"

He shrugged. "Maybe not."

"We will give you a hand to get that horse out of the creek, if Sarasha says so."

Sarasha shook her head. "He just has to scrape between those two boulders and there's an easy path. I wouldn't put the horse in danger." She turned to the rider. "I noticed that neither would you."

He slapped the sweating shoulder in front of him. "I certainly wouldn't. Not on a stupid race."

"Oh. Only if you're stupid mad."

He looked abashed at that. "I wasn't..."

"Then why are you out on this battlefield?"

His back stiffened. "Because..." Then he stopped. "You're laughing at me."

"M-hm."

"Great. Now she's decided. Sarasha, may I bring my horse out of the water and go back to my camp?"

"Certainly. I have business to take care of. It was a pleasure playing with you."

"I caught that."

"Maybe you have more brains than I thought." She sobered. "When you get back to your camp, it's important that you tell Captain Haskel and your other horseman friends what happened out here today. If the Priest-Admiral sends his Raiders ashore, you're going to get even more nasty lessons about fighting against foot soldiers. The only reason we hooked those riders off their horses was because we wanted the horses. We have long spears, and we could have killed them all."

He nodded somberly. "Thanks, Sarasha. I'll do that." He pulled his horse ahead and eased her out of the creek.

"Tell me, Sarasha, why did you stop and talk to me?"

She gave him a level stare. "Because if you're worth it, I want you as a friend. If you weren't worth it, we would have dealt with you here and now."

He stared at her, then over at the three Raiders who were standing on the bank, watching. "She means that, doesn't she?"

They all nodded seriously.

He also nodded, thoughtfully. Then, with an open-handed salute, he reined his horse back down the trail.

She saluted the Raiders in her own way and continued in the other direction.

She grinned to herself as she rode. *Byaren seems bright enough, and if he isn't, Haskel will sift through his story and pick up a lot more than the fact that a small pony can escape a big horse in hilly country.*

21. The Eye of the Storm

The jangle of voices outside her tent brought Sarasha fuming from her books. Finally, some time to herself because the negotiators had taken a day to consult their supporters, and now this...

But as she listened, her anger faded. A new voice, high and clear, with the accent of the Farmers. *And not practiced at hearing the word 'no.'* Sarasha hid a grin as she stepped out the door.

"Is the Captain here?" The sentry glanced around, his brow wrinkled.

"He went to the *Night Hawk* camp this morning. Is there a problem?"

The lad glanced over his shoulder. "She wouldn't stop, Sarasha. Just kept riding into camp. It wouldn't be right to put an arrow in her back, what with the war being over, so I did what she asked and brought her here."

"Is someone covering for you?"

"Yes, ma'am."

"Then you did about right. You can go back to your watch. Thank you for showing the lady here."

After a last admiring glance at the woman on the tall roan horse, he hurried back towards the west side of camp.

Sarasha turned to the woman. "Would you like to come in out of the sun?"

The stranger stared down at Sarasha and did not move. "I'm looking for the man who stole my horse. Where can I find him?"

"The man who stole your horse." Sarasha let the woman wait while she considered. "Would that be a leggy, light brown mare with darker mane and tail? Runs like the wind is pushing her?" Sarasha shook her head. "I don't think you'll be getting her back."

"Who said I was looking for the horse?"

Sarasha's gaze snapped to the other woman's face. There was a smile lurking in those full lips. Young lips. This girl was no older than Sarasha herself.

"So you want Captain Bren, do you?"

"A Captain, is he? All the better. I'm not sure I want him, but I'm looking for him. They sent me here."

"You aren't quite there yet. His camp is still the better part of a day's ride. Are you sure you wouldn't like to come in for a cool drink?" She glanced at the horse, peered again, puzzled. "We can take care of your horse, too."

The stranger swung down in businesslike fashion. As she stepped away from the horse, it seemed as if she was wearing a dress, but the garment must part in the middle because the woman had been riding astride.

Sarasha glanced at the horse again before they entered the tent. "If you don't mind my asking, your horse, well...he's a male, isn't he?"

"Pardon me? Oh no. He's a gelding."

"Gelding?"

"Yes. Oh, of course, you people don't know about horses, do you? If a male horse isn't the best breeding quality, we geld him when he's very young. You can't have that many stallions running around. Think of the problems it would cause. Plus, it tones them down, makes them better riding horses."

Sarasha nodded. "We have a lot to learn about horses."

The woman scanned the tent as she seated herself. "You have this set up quite cozily."

Sarasha grinned. "Now that the war's over, we have time to get out the few nice things we could save."

"Sorry. I didn't mean to bring that up."

"You didn't bring it up. I did, and now you mention it, that was a poor way to repay a compliment. Thank you."

The girl smiled and held out a hand. "I'm Kendra. My father has Kirigata, the nearest estate over west of here."

"I'm Sarasha Tourn. Orrick told me about you. You're the one in the creek. That screamed."

"Screamed? I did not scream!"

"That's not what he said."

"Well, let me tell you, Sarasha, that your friend Orrick, Captain Bren, or whoever he is, if he told you I screamed, then he's a better storyteller than he is a horse thief!"

Sarasha placed mugs in front of them both and sat. "I can't wait to hear your side of the tale. You were swimming?"

"Oh, I was swimming, all right. I bathe in the Little River quite often when the weather's hot. It's the same one that goes through here, and it passes some distance south of our manor. I had no idea there was anybody within a day's ride. My father had been keeping track of the war, and he said they were nowhere near us yet."

"I gather Orrick was on reconnaissance."

"Well, he reconnoitered more than he expected, let me tell you."

"Hmm."

"Yes. There I was, swimming happily in the cool water, when suddenly there's this man standing on the side of the creek, holding out my dress and telling me I have to get into it."

"Your dress? He never mentioned the dress."

"So I told him to turn his back, and he said no, he couldn't, because there was a war going on and I was technically his enemy. So I said fine, and I came out, dried myself off and got dressed with him standing all stiff and staring straight ahead, just off to the side so I was sure he wasn't staring at me. I tell you, it could have been funny if I hadn't been so scared.

"So then, once I was dressed, he asked me some questions, like where I was from, and how far was that, and how long would it take to walk there. When he asked me if my boots were good for walking as well as riding, I got suspicious. Then he said, 'I'm sorry, ma'am, but I have to take your horse.' Well, I can tell you, I wasn't too happy about that.

"But he insisted. He said his people needed the horse more than I did, and when the war was over, I could come and see about it."

The girl took a sip of her beer. A humorous look came into her eyes. "And then he jumped on my horse. I'll bet he'd never been on a horse before."

"He hadn't."

"I only remembered that later. At the time, I was too busy telling him exactly what I thought of him and his horse-thieving people, his heritage, his progeny and several less pleasant things."

"In a fairly loud voice?"

"Oh, yes. He heard me, all right. Even as he was riding away in that amateurish, floppy way."

"So that explains the screaming part."

Kendra peered into her mug. "I suppose it might. Say, what is this drink?"

"Ship's beer. Sorry, we have nothing better in the hold right now. We don't have a hold to keep it in, as you may have noticed."

"No, that's fine. I like it."

"You haven't been drinking it for weeks like we have."

"Well, if you want something else, come over to our farm. We have our own beer and cider."

"I doubt if you want two or three hundred thirsty Ship people descending on your farm on a hot day."

"Let's make it a personal invitation."

"In that case, I might take you up on it. But first we have to get you to Captain Bren's camp. They're over to the east about a day's walk on foot."

Kendra thought a moment. "I wouldn't get there and back by nightfall."

"Not if your horse has already come from Kirigata today. Does your father expect you back tonight?"

A slow grin slipped onto the girl's face. "My father has learned not to expect."

"So you could stay out, and there wouldn't be fifty Farmers with hoes and pitchforks storming after you?"

"No. We don't have that many hands. It would be at least two days before they'd even start to worry."

"Isn't that dangerous?"

"You're starting to sound like my father. I suppose it is, but a girl has to pay for her independence. I've paid. In many ways."

There's a story there, if I ever get the chance to ask. "Then we have two choices. I can take you over to Orrick's camp now, and we'd arrive about dark. Or you can stay here overnight, and we can go across in the morning, get there at a decent time. The advantage of the second plan is that I can send a message to find out if he's there."

"You can?"

"Certainly. I'll use the mirror system. It's no secret by now. We're not supposed to use it for social calls, so I'll just ask if he's in camp."

"That would be convenient. Thank you."

"Just wait here a moment." Sarasha scribbled a quick note, picked up her crutch, and swiveled out the door. Nabbing the first child she saw, she pressed the paper into her hand and told her to take it up to the signal post and wait for a reply. Pleased to be of service, the girl scampered off.

Sarasha turned to see her guest standing in the tent doorway.

"How does that work?"

"I just asked Kendie to take the message up to the signal post in the rocks, there." Sarasha gestured upwards.

"Kendie?"

"Her real name's Kendra, just like yours. They can see quite a long way from that peak. They'll flash a message over to the *Sparrowhawk* camp to relay to the *Storm Petrels*. Orrick can answer the same way. It's easier to send in the middle of the day. Once the sun gets low in the afternoon, it's hard to send signals east. Easy to come west, though."

"So how long will it take?"

"It depends on whether there are other messages and if the watchers are paying attention. A glass or two." They returned to the shade of the tent.

"How long is a glass?"

Sarasha picked up the small glass on the shelf and turned it over. "Twice as long as it takes this to run through. It's a half-glass."

"How interesting."

"How do you tell time?"

"Mostly by sundials."

"We don't have dials because they lose accuracy if you try to use them in different places."

"I see. You know, I think I'll take you up on your offer." She turned back into the tent. "I like this place. You certainly have nice textiles."

Sarasha couldn't help but lift her head. "Traded from all over the Southern Ocean."

"I suppose. Where do you sleep?"

Sarasha swung aside the drape. "That's Mother and Father's room. I'm over here."

"Oh my. Hammocks! Will it upset anyone if I don't sleep in a hammock?"

"Then where would you sleep?"

"On the floor. If that's all right. Is that all right?"

"Of course. The ground's pretty hard, though. We set the tent where there was no grass."

"I have my bedroll with me. I didn't expect to be going home tonight." She moved towards the doorway. "And my horse is cooled down enough. He'll be thirsty."

"Sure. Let's take him down to the pastures. If he's gelded, he won't have any trouble with my father's stallion, then?"

"No. He's very easy to get along with." She picked up the reins and trailed Sarasha down through the tents. The horse followed much more easily than Ebb Tide.

When they approached the paddock, the Black's head came up, his nostrils checking the breeze. Sarasha called out to him, and his head swung towards her, ears forward.

"That's your father's horse?"

"M-hm. You know enough about horses that I don't have to tell you to be careful."

"Oh, do I ever. That's Jassen's big stallion, the one he never could handle. Nasty beast, from what I've heard."

"My father handles him all right. He just wasn't trained properly."

"Your father handles him. Of course he does. I've just figured it all out. He's the Warlord, isn't he? Your father's the Raider Warlord!"

"That's him, all right." Sarasha chuckled. "The Raider Warlord."

"Oh." The girl paused. "I wasn't thinking the Warlord might have a family and a tent and everything. Oh, I feel so stupid. Why wouldn't he?"

She stopped, her hand covering her mouth. "Will he mind me staying in his tent?"

"I've already asked you. Why would he mind?"

"Well, if you're the Raider Warlord, you don't just have girls staying over because they almost invite themselves. I can go somewhere else."

"Don't be silly. This Raider Warlord stuff is mostly in the imagination of your own people. He's my father and he's a gentleman. He'll be happy to have you as a guest."

"Oh. All right, then. I tell you, won't my friends be thrilled when they find out I stayed overnight with the Raider Warlord!"

"I wouldn't make such a big issue of it. We're just offering you accommodation, like we would to any traveller who had business with the Fleet."

"I'm sorry. You people are strange to us, you know. We find it hard to see you as real, ordinary people at all."

"I can see. That's why I thought it important to invite you to stay."

"So I can discover that the Raider Warlord is an ordinary family man with a wife and a very nice daughter with a crippled foot." She stopped, her hand to her mouth again. "Oh, I'm sorry. Should I have mentioned that?"

"It's there. I don't try to hide it."

"Right. Was it that way...you know. From birth?"

"No, the maintopmast came down and crushed it. In the sea battle."

"Oh! It's recent then! Does it hurt a lot?"

"Most of the time."

"Oh, I'm so sorry. But it's healing?"

"The Surgeon tells me it's too early to tell. I think he's just trying to make me feel better; heaven knows why. The foot was pretty mashed."

Kendra winced sympathetically, and for once did not respond. She began stripping the saddle from her horse, but Sarasha could tell she was thinking. After a moment, she stopped.

"Wait a minute. The crippled foot. The girl with the crippled foot. Are you the Lame Scribe?"

"I'm the Captain's Scribe, yes."

"And you were at the peace talks?"

"There must be a Scribe to record all Conclaves."

The girl laughed out loud and leaned against her horse, her finger pointing at Sarasha. "Then you're the one who stepped all over Byaren's toes and stuffed his beard down his throat!"

"I did nothing of the sort! Where did you hear that silliness?"

"From Byaren himself. I know you didn't actually do those things, but you might as well have. Oh, he was angry. He was stomping up and down and shouting about what he would do to that...well, let's just say he made some very uncomplimentary comparisons."

Kendra was now laughing so hard that she had to gasp for air. "And now I meet you, and you're this nice, pretty little thing. Oh, I can't wait to see him again."

Sarasha couldn't help but smile at the other girl's infectious laughter. "Thanks for the 'pretty' part. When you get to know me better, you probably won't find me quite so nice."

"Oh, I don't imagine I will. But still..." She went off into more laughter, and the black horse, finally sure that there was no danger around, came over to investigate.

The approach of the huge animal sobered the girls, and they watched the Black assure himself that the new horse was no threat. Then he turned to Sarasha. She dug in her pocket and held out her hand, palm flat. The horse snuffled at it, then cleaned up his treat with one sweep of his upper lip.

"He likes wild onions. Good thing. It's the only fresh vegetable we have a lot of."

"He is a beauty, isn't he?" Kendra reached up to stroke the glossy shoulder. The stallion glanced at her, accepting the homage.

"He is, and he's taming down, now. Not with other horses, but I don't think that will ever happen. He has to be the Captain of the herd."

"Well, he is the biggest and strongest horse ever bred in this area. He wins all the pulling contests."

"Pulling contests?"

"Yes. Oh. I suppose you think of him as a war horse. He's a farm horse, and he earns his keep just like all the rest of us. His teammate is almost as big as he is, a gelding, of course, and between them, they can out-pull any three other horses. They've proved it a few times."

Kendra turned and gazed at Sarasha. "I don't want to sound like a merchant or anything, but are your people short of vegetables?"

"Yes. Usually we have a lot of pickled and preserved things, but we couldn't carry all our provisions, and we left behind a lot of the heavy stuff."

"And do you have...well, do you have money?"

"We have some money. We were traders, after all. Each Ship has a strongbox."

"So if you come over to my father's farm, he can sell you a limited range of vegetables. It's the wrong time of year for most of them, but the new onions are up, and lettuce, chard and maybe some spinach. When we thin the beets and the carrots, we eat the little ones we pull out. Tasty with butter on them!"

"You're making me hungry. Come and talk to my father about this."

The two girls made their way back to the Captain's tent, chatting about this and that.

"So why do you want to see Orrick? I wasn't joking about the horse. He's already got the breeding plan worked out."

"I didn't really think he would give her back."

"You plan to steal her?"

"The thought did pass my mind, but..."

"So what are you planning?"

The taller girl shrugged. "I got restless. Everyone's talking about you Sea People, and I thought I'd like to find out what your life is like. The only way to do that is to come and visit. So here I am. I figured on imposing on my horse thief. I knew he was a gentleman, and I thought he'd feel guilty so he'd have to welcome me."

"You called that right. He would have. We'll go over there tomorrow and give him more trouble than he's ever had in his life."

"But he's a Captain!"

"And I'm a Captain's daughter. So what? He reacts to teasing just like any other man."

"You seem to know a lot about him. Is he a friend of yours?" The other girl stopped. "Wait a minute. He isn't a special friend or something, is he? I'm not pushing in on you or anything?"

Sarasha laughed. "Don't worry, Kendra. He is a special friend. Special enough so we have an agreement he won't marry me. The field is clear. Go in there and sweep him off his feet, carry him away and marry him before his head clears." She took a searching look at the taller girl. "Do you realize what it would be like to be the wife of a Captain?"

Kendra shrugged. "Not much different from being married to one of the local nobility, which is what will happen sooner or later if I don't do something different."

"Don't go marrying Orrick just to do something different. He's worth more than that."

213

"Sarasha, I will not hurt your friend. Don't worry about that." She grinned. "But you don't mind if I look him over, check out his teeth, that sort of thing?"

"I'm not sure of the courtship rituals you Farmers have, but I'd keep my fingers out of his mouth on a first meeting."

"Second meeting."

22. A Visitor

They laughed again and swung through the door of the tent, right into Sarasha's father, who was just leaving. Sarasha's foot hit the ground painfully, and she stifled a moan. Too late. He immediately stopped and held her arms, lifting her almost off the floor. "I'm so sorry, Sarasha. Are you all right?"

She squirmed free. "Yes, I'm all right. Don't worry so much. Father, I'd like you to meet Kendra of Kirigata, daughter of one of the Farmers. She's come over to sell us some vegetables and steal her horse back from Orrick Bren. Kendra, this is my father, Captain Arlijn Tourn."

The girl dropped in a formal curtsey, her hand swishing the skirt of her riding dress gracefully. "It is an honour to meet you, Captain Tourn. I have heard so much about you."

"And my mother, Verlene."

"And you, too, my Lady. Your daughter has been so gracious to me, her parents must be wonderful people." She paused and stared at them. "Did I say something wrong?"

"No, no, not at all. In fact, that was said very prettily."

"Thank you, I'm sure, Lady Tourn."

"I'm not usually referred to as 'Lady', Miss Kendra."

"Of course not. What is the proper title I should use?"

"Verlene."

Sarasha watched for her mother's wry smile. The Farmer girl noticed it, too.

"I see. You don't use titles like that at all."

Arlijn shook his head. "Oh, we do. Or at least, we did. Back in the Fleet, everyone knew his title and his entitlement. Especially on the Masterships."

"Are those the huge ones? I never saw one of them up close. They're frightening, even from a distance."

"Those are the ones. I gather you have heard our story?"

"I'm just beginning to understand. You rebelled against all that power and formality, so you have dropped all the forced civility and fake politeness. Oh, I love it!"

"You do?"

"Of course. I had to learn all that stuff as well. We're on the other end, I'm afraid, just starting up. A hundred years ago we were only a bunch of farmers, moving into the wilderness so we could take title to our own land. Now look at us. We call ourselves lords and ladies and behave in the manner you have just rejected. You will consider us so snobbish!"

"I'm sure we will make allowances, my dear."

"Thank you, Verlene. I hope my people will make allowances for you, in whatever way we need to. It's very important to make allowances for the differences in others, don't you think?"

Sarasha snorted. "Have you just dropped back into your 'polite speech' form?"

Kendra cocked her head to one side. "No, I mean that. I've always been a little different from everybody, so I'm sensitive to that sort of thing. You must understand, Sarasha."

Sarasha glanced at her foot. "I only got this in the battle."

"Not the foot. Being the Captain's daughter and his Scribe."

"Oh. Yes. I know about that."

The Farmer girl smiled. "So, now we've met each other, what do we do next?"

Verlene returned the smile. "I go about getting supper ready, which will be a very special meal, just for you, of boiled salt pork with wild onion garnish and roasted potatoes, which, because of the occasion, we will cook in olive oil."

Kendra thought a moment, then gave the older woman a level stare. "You're making fun of me, aren't you?"

"Not about the olive oil. That is something we save for special treats. The salt pork is, unfortunately, our staple diet these days. The supplies that we are supposed to receive as part of the peace settlement are very slow in coming. We would dearly love to find a source of fresh vegetables."

"If you listen to Sarasha, that's what I came here to talk about."

"And did you?"

"I never thought to. But now that the opportunity presents itself..."

Sarasha laughed. "For once, your father will be pleased with you."

"He might. It might almost make up for losing the horse."

"Did he say you lost it?"

"I did take her out where she could get stolen. She's my horse, but she's a prime breeding mare."

"We could figure that out. Father wants to breed her with the Black."

The girl turned on the Captain in horror. "That huge thing? You couldn't do that! Her offspring would be so slow, she'd be too embarrassed to raise her head! She's a racing horse!"

"Is that what she is?"

"She's bred to run. You can see how long her legs are."

"Perfect."

"What do you mean?"

"I mean my beautiful Black out there is a marvellous specimen of a plow horse, but he runs like one. Sarasha's pony can beat him in anything but a straight, flat race. I want to breed some speed into his line. Can you imagine the fighting power of a horse just a little lighter than he is, but with her love of running?"

"Fighting power?"

"Yes, of course. We will produce the finest war horses ever bred."

"What do you want war horses for?"

"To ride, to fight, to sell."

"To fight whom?"

"The Priest-Admiral and anyone else who might want to steal our freedom."

"Oh."

Sarasha pulled her new friend down onto a stool. "Kendra, we have just escaped from terrible tyranny. Our freedom was bought at a huge price. The ability to defend that freedom means a lot to us."

"I can understand that. So you think my Owena's running ability combined with the Black's strength will give you that?"

Arlijn laughed. "Well, if he could turn in his own length like Sarasha's Ebb Tide can, I wouldn't complain."

"Then you need mountain pony stock."

"Mountain pony." Her father's voice lost its jocularity. "What are mountain ponies?"

"We don't see them very often. They're built something like Ebb Tide but taller and heavier. They're too big to be considered ponies, but they move so quickly and have such good balance they seem smaller. Some mountain pony blood might counteract the clumsiness of those big plow horses."

"How do you know so much about breeding?"

She glanced at Sarasha, grinning. "I'm a farm girl, remember? Breeding is an important part of my life."

"Then why do you breed such large, clums...wait a minute. I can answer that for myself. You breed the horses you need. It's only when you take them out of their proper purpose and turn them into war horses that they look bad."

"Exactly. And they aren't that clumsy, either. I've seen a plow horse at full gallop vault a puppy that dashed in its way, put one foot on either side of the dog and miss it completely. It wasn't luck."

"It was luck for the dog!"

Laughter rang from the tent, and footsteps sounded outside. "What's all the commotion?"

Sarasha rose. "Come in, Pers. I'd like you to meet one of the local people."

He entered, stopping in the doorway when he saw the visitor. Leide, following behind him, gave him a playful shove, then froze as well.

"Pers, Leide, this is Kendra of Kirigata, a member of the town's nobility."

Pers stiffened and gave his best salute. Leide, even more flustered than usual, bowed her head, then stuck out her hand.

Kendra smiled graciously and shook hands with both of them in the Farmers' way. Sarasha smiled privately as Pers

218

fumbled the handshake, but Leide handled it as if she knew what was going on. She had been keeping her eyes open.

Sarasha found more mugs for beer, and they sat around the table talking mostly horses, with Pers and the Farmer girl monopolizing the conversation. It turned out that Pers was familiar with the mountain ponies as well because Solen had a high regard for them.

He had plans for catching some, but Kendra had stories of how wily, fast and difficult to catch they were.

Sarasha realized, after a while, that Leide wasn't saying anything. Just as she turned to her cousin, the younger girl sprang to her feet.

"Excuse me. There's a...there's something I have to..." and she was through the tent flap and gone, her face ashen.

"Will you excuse me a moment? There is something I forgot to tell Leide." She exited the tent, calling the girl's name softly. She had not gone far. Her sobs gave her away.

"What was that all about?"

Leide made a flapping motion with her hand. "Oh, nothing. Nothing, really."

"Right. You disappear from a normal social gathering, taking the risk of giving offense to an important visitor, and all for nothing."

Leide's head came up. "Did I?"

"Yes."

"Offend her?"

"Of course not. She was just puzzled, that's all. As were the rest of us."

"Well, she can stay puzzled, then."

Sarasha reached out, turned Leide by the shoulder. "What are you talking about? What has that girl done to you?"

Leide's head came up. "Oh, you didn't notice? You, the famous Sarasha, had that going on under your nose and you didn't even notice?"

Sarasha suppressed a smile. "Well, if it was going on under my nose and I didn't notice, I guess that means I have no idea what you're talking about."

"Didn't you see the way he was staring at her?"

"The way who...oh."

"Aha! You did see!"

"The way Pers was looking at Kendra?"

"Yes, the way he was staring at her. And she's so b...beautiful..." The sobs threatened again.

Sarasha sighed. "Leide..."

"Oh, I know what you're going to say. You're going to tell me I'm a silly girl, and I should stop being so stupid. I told myself that."

"Thank you for saving us that bit of embarrassment."

"But then I saw him, and he had that dumb expression on his face that the boys get...and then I knew."

"Then you knew he had fallen topgallant to keel in love with her, and he never would look at you again."

"You saw it too?" The tearstained face came up, piteously.

"Leide. Look at me." She put one hand on either cheek and held her there. "This is my face, Leide. This is the face of someone trying desperately not to burst out laughing. I have never," she slapped a cheek gently, "heard," the other cheek, "such bilge," another slap, "in," slap, "my," slap, "life!" At the end, she released her hold, but left her hands, fingers splayed outwards in an expression of total helplessness.

"Then you don't think..."

"No, I don't think...! And neither are you. Thinking. You're reacting like a silly goose, and I'm ashamed of you."

"Oh. I'm sorry, 'Rasha, but..."

"Yes, and you should be. But don't worry about it. Everybody goes through this sort of stupidity at one time or another."

"But you don't."

A moment of silence. "I guess I've been lucky so far."

"So what should I do?"

"Don't ask me, Leide. Have you two ever talked? Have you made any kind of understanding?"

"Understanding about what?"

"All right. That's it. That's the end of my patience and the end of my big sister act. From now on, if you insist on acting like a silly girl, you'll have to accept the consequences. Sit down here, and I'll go and get Pers. After that, it's up to you."

"But don't tell him…?"

"…what a twit he's fallen in love with? I wouldn't dream of it. It would be beneath the dignity of our Family to admit we raised such a person."

Without waiting for a response, she spun on her crutch and stumped back to the tent.

She slipped in silently and waited for a lull in the conversation.

"I know it's proper manners to give your guest all your attention, but not all of us get to ignore the little problems of daily life."

"Oh, that is quite all right. Your parents have been filling in for you admirably."

Sarasha exchanged a grin with her mother. "I'm glad of that. I tried so hard to bring them up well."

She pointed a finger at Pers. "I have a little job for you, sailor." She twisted her hand and crooked the finger. "Better if it didn't wait."

She let him make a polite farewell, then followed him out into the darkness. When they were far enough from the tent that their voices wouldn't carry, she grabbed his arm and spun him to face her.

"Can you imagine, Pers, why Leide might be just a little upset?"

"What? Leide is upset? What happened? What's wrong?"

"What do you suppose, Pers? Since you're the cause of it, I thought you might have an inkling."

"Me? But what…? What did I do? I… I hardly even talked to her."

"Hmm. Might have something to do with it."

"What?"

"And sitting there with your jaw gaping open and your tongue hanging out, staring at another girl."

"I was not..." He stopped. "What are you talking about?"

"What am I talking about?" She mimicked his tone. "What do you think?"

"That Leide is upset because she thinks I was interested in that Farmer girl?"

"What do you think?"

"But that's ridiculous. Leide knows better than that."

"Does she?"

"Of course she does. I'm not interested in anyone else."

"Told her that, did you?"

"But...she knows. Leide always understands..."

"Pers." Her upheld palm stopped him. "There are things that nobody just 'understands.' There are things that you have to spell out for them, no matter how smart they are."

He stood in front of her, a puzzled expression on his face, and her patience snapped.

"Look, you hammerhead. You figure because she's smart, she should be watching you all the time and understanding you. Did you ever figure that, because she can come up with all those ideas, she can also come up with all sorts of reasons why you don't really care about her?"

"But I do care!"

"Have you ever said so?"

"Well..."

"In other words, no. Why should it always be her that has to figure out what's going on in your head? She's the one who's out there, crying. You figure out what's wrong. You're supposed to be so smart."

"She's what?"

"She's out there crying. Didn't you notice what a hurry she was in when she left the tent? No, don't even answer. You didn't."

"But what do I...?"

"In the names of every deity we no longer believe in! You're the smart one! Figure it out for yourself!"

She stared into that puzzled face, so different from his usual sharp manner, and struggled against the urge to slap some sense into him.

After a moment, the anger left her, and she sighed. "A hint?"

"Please, Sarasha."

"If you don't know what to do, there's one person who does."

"Great. Who?"

This time, her fist rose of its own accord.

"Oh...oh!" A grin began to spread. "Oh, I see. Thanks, Sarasha. Which way did she go?"

Sarasha flapped an exasperated hand in the appropriate direction and returned to her tent, shaking her head.

Kendra was sharing a chuckle with her hosts. She raised her head as Sarasha entered. "I don't want to intrude, Sarasha, but was that what I thought it was?"

"Oh, probably."

"And did you solve it?"

Sarasha sighed. "You deal with horses all the time, right? Did it ever occur to you how strange it is that horses are so big and powerful, and yet you have to be so careful with them because one little thing can ruin them, make them completely ineffective, or even kill them?"

"I noticed."

"I find people very much the same."

Until the peals of laughter rang out, she didn't realize that she had said something funny.

23. Peace

Sarasha was beginning to feel out of place. It wasn't just the size of her horse that caused Kendra and Orrick to speak to each other over her head; there were other things going on that worked the same way.

She reined in, and they noticed after a pace or two and stopped as well, looking back at her.

"All right, you two. I should be getting back to the *Eagle* camp."

They seemed surprised and perhaps a little disappointed.

"Why? What's wrong?"

"Nothing's wrong. You remember that problem I was dealing with the other night, Kendra?"

"Yes." The girl grinned.

"M-hm. Well, I do that kind of thing as seldom as I possibly can."

"Oh."

"Right. So I'd better get back and deal with a bunch of more important things."

Orrick glanced from one to the other, aware that there was a subtext to this conversation, but too polite to ask.

"Nice seeing you again, Orrick. Thank you for taking us in for the night and putting up with us all morning. That was an excellent lunch. I'll tell the galley about those berries your people found."

Orrick pushed his horse closer. "Sarasha, you are not usually this polite. What's going on?"

She laughed and shot the taller girl a wicked glance. "She can fill you in if she likes. It's better if I go now. Drop in for the night on your way back, Kendra. You're always welcome."

She started to rein her horse away, then turned back. "And let your father know where you are. Orrick can push a flash message through as far as the *Ospreys*, and maybe they can figure a way to deliver it to Kirigata without getting stuck full of arrows."

With that, she saluted them casually and kicked Ebb Tide into a trot. As she left, she could hear Kendra's response to the Captain's look. "Just a minor Crew problem she was helping her father with. She seems to take on a lot of that…"

And then she could hear no more. She chuckled, wondering how much of that drivel Orrick would take before he called her on it.

By the time she reached the *Eagle* camp, she was tired and sore, and it was too late to catch supper, either at her parents' tent or the general mess.

"At least you get fed." She grabbed a currying brush and began to work her horse over as Solen had taught her. The horse had no comment to give, munching happily at the handful of oats that was all the Ship could afford.

Once Ebb Tide was clean, fed and watered, Sarasha took up her crutch to hobble back to her tent. As she was sliding home the corral rails, she heard voices. Soft voices, just over the edge of the rock in front of her. Curious, she clambered down.

There, sitting close together, were Pers and Leide. Sitting very close together. In fact, each had an arm about the other. Sarasha turned hastily away, but her crutch knocked loose a stone, and they both turned. Pers started away, but Leide firmed her grip on his waist.

"You're back already?"

"Seems like it. I gather you two have settled your little problem?"

Leide grinned. "I guess sometimes a person just needs some sense slapped into her."

Pers turned to her, astounded. "She didn't really…?"

"Oh yes, she did. Very gently, mind you."

He shook his head. "I'm glad it wasn't me."

"You should be. I wouldn't have been so gentle."

"I don't suppose."

"Does this mean that both of you can now work at full power instead of three-quarters? I expect you to be worth more than two people if you put your heads together."

225

They both nodded. "Don't worry, 'Rasha. We'll be ready. Say the word."

Pers was about to rise. "What's happening now?"

"Nothing I need you for." She held out a restraining hand. "I'm too late coming in to get supper at the mess, so I'll see what I can scratch up at home."

"Let me get something for you!"

"No, thank you, Leide. You two sit here and enjoy the evening. You deserve it."

"No, that's all right, Sarasha. Leide and I can..." Pers began to scramble to his feet.

She reached out with her crutch and, not so gently, pushed him back down. "I said no, and I meant it. The last thing I need is you two mooning over me in pathetic gratitude for doing something you should have done for yourselves a month ago."

He subsided, and Leide shook her head. "You certainly have a way with words, Sarasha."

"Why does everyone expect me to be any different? I'll make you a bargain, Leide. You go around being nice to everyone, and I'll go around being myself, and sooner or later, it will all even out. All right?"

Her cousin glanced up at her, then nodded. "All right, Sarasha, whatever you say."

She stood there, not sure what that meant. The girl was ducking a fight, and Sarasha was exasperated that she had been about to start one. She found a smile.

"Glad we got that straight. I mean it. You two have been working as hard as anyone, and you deserve time to yourselves. Take it."

They smiled at her, smiled at each other, and she was gone before they noticed.

She stumped up the path, a vague disquiet in her breast. She should be happy for these people. She was. She just wasn't happy. Was she jealous? Not specifically. She had never been interested in Pers that way, and she had told Orrick that she wouldn't marry him. No, she was just jealous in a general way, that they could be so happy, the lot of them.

She wondered why she wasn't happy. *I just helped win a war; I just manipulated two couples into happy situations. I should be very pleased with myself.*

Now that she thought of it, she was pleased with herself.

She just wasn't happy.

* * *

As the days went on and the peace talks progressed, the feeling increased. While everyone else seemed happier and happier, she felt worse and worse. True, she was too busy to think about it most of the time. The duty of Scribing the Conclave had become hers by default. The Scribes from the other Ships, though much more experienced, showed no interest in taking her place so she stayed on. Two Junior Scribes from the *Storm Petrel* and the *Sparrowhawk* appeared to help Leide with the copying, and between the four of them they covered everything required for the talks.

Conferences took place in the mornings at the same open space where they had started. Afternoons were set aside for the individual negotiators to hold Conclave with their own people. Then, in the evening, a private meeting took place in Captain Tourn's tent, where he, Baetor Huin and sometimes Orrick Bren joined Sarasha, Pers and some of their other friends in the deliberations.

Captain Tourn had established himself as the head of the Sea People's negotiators, and no one saw any need to make a change. He was always careful to include the other Captains or their representatives in all decisions.

Late one evening, after a particularly fruitless session, Leide lifted the growing mass of parchment she had been paging through and slammed it back on the table. "Why is this taking so long? Look at all the writing. It's a waste of parchment as well as time. Wouldn't those people all be better off preparing for the Priest-Admiral's return?"

227

Pers nodded. "The people sitting at this table could thrash out a reasonable agreement in five glasses. Why does everybody talk so much?"

Captain Tourn smiled at them. "It takes a lot of talking. That's how treaties have to be made. If I were to sit down with Noveyn and Erlin, we could come up with a solution quickly. But none of the other people involved would feel they had anything to do with the solution, so they would not feel especially bound by it.

"As it is, everyone who says their say feels they have been part of the agreement. Thus the agreement will represent everyone's interests, and will be more easily accepted."

Sarasha's grin was evil. "Of course, we could always keep fighting until somebody won. Then the winner could dictate the terms to the loser and spend the next fifty years worrying about when the loser would have another try at him."

Leide sighed. "You're right. I just can't stand the waste of time."

Captain Tourn nodded. "You are right in that sense."

"Then why don't we do something about it?"

"What do you suggest, Sarasha?"

"Leide says we should be preparing for war. Why don't we?"

Her father regarded her. "And how do you see that happening?"

"While the rest of us are wading through this morass, somebody goes over and has a chat with Byaren, gets him to contact Commander Haskel and start figuring out what to do when the Priest-Admiral shows up with thirty Ships and five thousand Raiders."

"Where did you get those numbers?"

"I made them up. That's something else we need to work on. We know the Fleet. We can figure out what resources he's likely to have."

"And who are we assigning to this?"

She grimaced. "It can't be me. I've allowed myself to get caught up in this wonderful game. Why don't we send Pers?"

Eyes turned to the young sailor. He shrugged. "Better than sitting around here listening to Leide complain." He paused to receive a kick on the shin, which he manfully ignored. "I've noticed Solen wandering around looking bored, too."

Captain Bren had been sitting in the shadow and now leaned forward. "It's not something we can do officially. Not at this stage of the negotiations."

Sarasha raised her hands in horror. "All the deities forfend we should do anything to upset anyone. This has to be just a few people sitting down and chatting. We couldn't even do any training together in case there was an incident."

The two Captains exchanged glances. "Captain Bren and I have business elsewhere."

Everyone was silent as the two men left, giving them time to get out of earshot before starting.

Pers rubbed his hands together. "This sounds like my type of assignment." He looked up to see Leide and Sarasha both glaring at him. "Well, it is!"

"That's right, and we don't get to go, so don't be quite so pleased."

"Oh. Sarasha. I'm sorry. How do we contact these people?"

"By going over to Kirigata and managing to get admitted without being shot. Ask for Kendra and tell her what you want. She'll arrange everything."

"She will?"

"That's right."

"Can we trust her?"

"With what? You just want to talk to Byaren. Don't worry, she's on our side. At least, she soon will be."

"What do you mean?"

"Don't worry about it." She waited, but he did not respond. "I said not to worry about it. Have I ever led you wrong?"

Pers gazed innocently upwards. "This from Sarasha, who always demands honesty from everyone."

"It's private, and it's not my place to tell you. I would if I could. Now stop looking so virtuous and go find Solen. He needs to hear about this."

229

With a cheerful swing to his step, Pers strode out the door. The two left stared glumly at each other. Leide picked up a pen. "So much for fun."

"Doing your duty for your Family and Crew brings the greatest fulfillment."

"Can I quote you on that?" Leide reached for parchment.

"Don't you dare."

The next day, after another endless round of ploy and counter-ploy, Sarasha sat rubbing her hand idly over the familiar patina of the *Eagle*'s Chart Table while she waited for everyone to finish their interminable rites of departure. Yong, whom she had not seen lately, had appeared with the Table on his wagon the day before. When pressed for details, he only shrugged. "Some things are worth keeping."

He was so proud of himself that it didn't take much prying. They had hidden the Table a few chains inland from the original camp, in a cleft of rock covered with a pile of broken planks. Once hostilities had ceased, he had gone back for it.

"But it's still dangerous out there. Many of the Farmers wouldn't hesitate to take those horses back if they caught you alone."

"I wasn't exactly alone."

"You weren't?"

"No. That big bearded fellow? Byaren?"

"We have met. Several times."

"He does ride around a lot."

She grinned. "He says his horse needs exercise."

"I came across him the other day and we got talking. He agreed to come for a ride with me. Said he was bored with the peace talks. Too peaceful."

"So Byaren came with you to get the Table?"

"That's right. Why are you so surprised?"

"The more I learn about him, the more he surprises me. What did you think?"

"I could take a long trip in a small boat with him."

"High praise."

"And if there were horses involved, I'd let him be Captain."

"He is very good with that horse of his."

"And with other horses as well. He taught me a lot as we went along. He knows more about farming than fighting, I'll bet."

"Well, that will make one of our plans a lot easier." She suppressed a grin. "You need to talk to Pers."

"I guess I'll go and talk to Pers, then."

"Why, Yong," she favoured him with her sweetest smile, "what a good idea!"

As he turned away, she could have sworn she heard him chuckle.

They had set the Table in the centre of the meeting place, now covered by a wide awning to keep off the noon sun and the evening dew. That morning, the Farmers had commented on its workmanship, but she doubted if they understood the significance of its presence at the centre of negotiations.

She mused on these thoughts as she waited for everyone to leave. So Byaren had offered to spend some time with a Raider. *Hmm. Maybe just one more nudge...*

She schooled her expression. There was enough mistrust in the air. Her sitting there at the Chart Table smiling at nothing wouldn't help. The Farmers watched her because her infrequent comments were always sharp and to the point.

Finally, the opposite party gathered themselves and left the meeting place. As usual, the mercenary Commander waited until his clients were well away before turning his back on the enemy.

"So, Commander Haskel. You are in a very interesting situation here."

"How so?"

"Being hired for a defensive war."

"Why do you find that interesting?"

She glanced at him, noting his incisive curiosity. *If this is a test, so be it.* "Fighting a defensive war must pull you in two different directions. You have been hired by people who don't want a war. That means the sooner you win the war, the sooner you're out of a job."

"That's the same for all mercenary work."

"Not if you hire out to someone who is expanding his holdings. If you win, it's a sure thing he will expand again, human nature being what it is. Also, the people who start wars don't need your advice so much."

"And don't tend to listen to it." He was smiling, now.

"The people who don't want a war are not fighters, so your advice is important to them. A less principled man might be tempted to keep the war going so as to stay employed."

He sat opposite her. "Many fledgling commanders make that mistake at the beginning. They only consider the present battle and keeping their troops fighting. They fail to realize that a mercenary's reputation keeps him fed. Finishing any conflict with dispatch is the surest way to get hired again. My troops get most of their wages from former satisfied patrons. The next most comes from people who have heard about us from satisfied patrons. Once in a long while, we pick up work because we happen to be close by. Not often. You don't survive as a mercenary if you depend too much on luck."

"Either physically or commercially."

He laughed out loud.

"So tell me, Commander Haskel. Where does a mercenary commander learn all the things you know? Is there a school? A book somewhere?"

"A book? That tells you how to be a mercenary? You must be joking."

"Why not? I get many of my ideas from books. Scrolls, ancient writings, the lot."

He smiled. "No, Sarasha, you can't learn to be a mercenary officer from a book."

Her hand slapped the table. "Don't be patronizing. That's not what I meant. Of course you learn from experience. But you just said many officers make certain mistakes. Most mercenaries get to become officers by being good in battle. Correct?"

"That is our trade."

"M-hm. How many days a year do your men actually fight?"

He shrugged. "It varies. Not that many, if that's what you're getting at."

"Therefore, your main qualifications for the job matter a great deal for some of the time, and probably get in the way for most of the rest of the time."

"I would have to agree." He leaned his elbows on the table, his pale blue eyes regarding her with interest over his steepled fingers.

"So what counts outside the battle is what you could learn from a book. Supplies, transport, that sort of thing."

"I suppose. Why is this important to you?"

"My people are going into a war, Commander Haskel."

"I thought the war was over. Everyone else seems to agree."

"This was just an opening skirmish. We are heading into the battle of our lives against the toughest opponent there is: Nature. We are going out into that Prairie with little knowledge and fewer resources. This first skirmish has taught us a lot. What it has taught me is what I don't know.

"If I could open a book and say, 'Two hundred and thirty people, a distance of ninety leagues. Dry weather. Commander Haskel says we need so many wagons of dry foods, so many sacks of flour, these many horses, this much feed for the horses...' you understand?"

"For the inexperienced, I can see that would be helpful."

"So, just write it up for us, will you? We'll pay."

"You are joking."

"When have you ever heard me joke?"

"All the time, it seems to me."

She gave him her best smile. "You haven't been listening."

"Ah."

"So think about it. It would be a shame for all that knowledge to disappear because of one lucky sword-thrust."

"Nice of you to think of me that way."

"I'm not usually thought of as 'nice,' Commander Haskel."

He sniffed. "It's an overrated character trait."

"So will you do it?"

He considered. "We are, at the moment, technically still enemies. This is hardly time for such a decision."

"Fair enough."

He rose to leave.

"There is another thing."

He turned back.

"I don't expect you to reveal your dealings with your clients, especially since, as you say, we are still enemies, but I think it safe to assume that they have retained you in case we are correct, and the Priest-Admiral returns."

"And if they have?"

"There is a good chance that we will soon be fighting on the same side. My people have demonstrated convincingly that the Farmers need some strategy lessons on the topic of fighting Sea Raiders."

"I wouldn't be violating any trust if I agreed with you."

"And perhaps, since that attack could be sooner rather than later, it would be to everyone's advantage to have some kind of battle plans already formed and some time to drill."

"A great advantage."

"So if one of the Farmers were to come to you and invite you to meet with some friends of his to discuss this possibility, you wouldn't refuse?"

"As long as it didn't interfere with my duties to my clients."

"Fair enough. I think the use of the Farmers' heavy horses would be a place to start."

"Yes. They can be very effective. If they had been under my command..." he stopped, shook his head.

"I'm sure you have plenty of ideas. Thank you, Commander Haskel. We will talk on these matters later."

"I would be pleased."

He turned once more and walked alone towards the mercenary camp. She pulled the canvas over the Chart Table, patted its firm bulk just once, swung up on her horse and rode at a dignified pace back to her camp.

24. From an Exposed Anchorage to a Lee Shore

By the time the peace talks wound to their eventual close, Sarasha was so tired of the whole thing she hardly noticed it was over. She had continued to fulfill her duties, but had long since run out of things to say.

Then, once the talks were over, she discovered she was even more bored.

She had expected that once the bargaining was done, everyone would sign a paper and they could get on with their lives. Such was not the case. Each side had to take the plan to their people and go over it in minute detail so it could be officially approved by everyone. Only then would the signing ceremony take place.

So in between, they waited.

She had almost waited long enough, and was beginning to wonder if it was worth waiting for anything, anyway, when a voice intruded.

"Busy?"

She opened her eyes. "CheyChan. What do *you* want?"

He regarded her a moment. "Why are you so grouchy?"

That brought her upright on the bench. "Where do you get the nerve to call me grouchy?"

"Point proven. You're grouchy. Now tell me why."

"Listen, shrimp. I don't have to tell you anything. Now disappear!"

She rose and took a threatening step towards him. It was the only one she could take because her crutch had fallen over and was out of reach.

"I'm not afraid of you." He picked up the crutch, handing it to her.

"You're not afraid of me? What a strange thing to say."

"Everybody else is."

"Thanks a lot, kid." She used the crutch to stumble back to the chair. "Just what a girl wants to hear."

"Well, that's good, anyway."

"Hmm?" She glanced at him.

"If it bothers you, that's good. If you don't want people to be afraid of you, that's good."

"I see."

He grinned. "And I'm not, so that's also good."

"Hmph."

"So, why are you so grouchy?"

She turned to give him her best stare. "You don't give up, do you?"

"I thought we were making progress."

"Towards where?"

"Wherever we want to go."

"Cheynou, what, exactly, did you come here for?"

"To see you."

"Fine. You've seen me. You can go away happy."

"And to find out why you're so grouchy."

"I'd settle for you going away. The 'happy' is optional."

"I guess you don't want to tell me." He nodded slowly.

"You're the one who says I'm grouchy. Did it occur to you I might be thinking and I don't take to being disturbed?"

His eyebrows went up. "What are you thinking about?"

She paused. "You really want to know?"

He shrugged. "It's better than asking about the grouchy. At least I'm getting answers this time."

The size of her sigh was only slightly exaggerated. "All right. You've made yourself a deal. Pull up a chair."

When he did so, she gave him another stare. "You're sure you want to hear this?"

"Of course. Do you want to tell me?"

"I don't mind. I'm thinking. About a lot of things."

"You have a lot to think about. You have a lot of responsibilities."

"Yes, but this is different. You see, when you're young, you take a lot of things for granted. Your Ship, your Crew, your Family, your body."

"Ah."

236

"Right. And now I've lost a lot of that. So I have to use my brain. I have to rearrange my view of the world, and my place in it, to take all these things into account."

"That sounds right."

"So I consider what to do with my life, and what is expected of me, and whether I can do those things, whether I will be useful enough. Whether I can match up to what is expected of me, to what I expect of myself."

"I see."

She regarded him a moment, then shook her head. He didn't see. He just thought he did. "Do you remember Rosart Tourn?"

"No. I heard about him, though. He fell overboard when I was little."

"He didn't fall. He jumped."

"Jumped?"

"Not even jumped. More like flew. I saw it happen. He took the end of a rope, timed it exactly for the roll of the Ship, and swung out to the end and let go. For a moment, I thought he was really flying, but he went out and out, and down and down, and then he hit the water and was gone."

"I see."

"Do you?"

"Sure. He suicided, and you watched. That's a hard thing to get over. Did you like him?"

"I didn't know him that well. I was too young. He had everything, you know? He was handsome, graceful, he was an excellent mast'n, everybody liked him..."

"...but you didn't know him very well."

"I didn't get the chance."

"So why do you bring him up?"

"He made a decision. It was either through a sudden insight or through hours of agonizing, but he figured out that the world he was living in was not the one he wanted to live in. So he left it."

"So how does your new reality match up with what you want? Have you decided to leave it? Considering suicide?"

"Doesn't everybody?"

"No. At least, if they do, they don't tell me."

"And if they don't tell you, Mister Persistence, then I guess it doesn't happen."

"In that case, no, everybody doesn't think about it. And you do?"

She shrugged. "I always consider all the options. It's a talent I have."

"Aye, well, use those great talents of yours to look around you. This is a world where a lot of people need you."

"It is?"

"Don't act stupid. Of course it is. And it's pretty selfish of you to consider ducking out on us."

"I'm not ducking out on you!"

"Yes, you are. You know, suicide is the most selfish thing a person can do."

"It is?"

"It means you've decided that your little problems are more important than anyone else's, and your difficulty in dealing with them is worse than anyone else's. It means you put yourself and your needs and problems up above everybody else and their problems."

"Does it."

"You're smart. Figure it another way. Explain it to me."

"Well..."

"You see? You can't. So don't you even think about things like that, because it just isn't fair!"

He rose to stand over her, his fists balled at his sides. All at once, he spun and sprinted out of the tent.

"Hey, Cheynou, how's...?" The tent door swept aside and Yong stood there. "What was that all about?"

She shook her head, then rested it in her hands. "I think I've just had another burden added to my load."

He grinned. "Heavy though it is."

"Yes."

"And what burden is that? If I may ask."

She sighed. "I don't know. Something Cheynou has cooked up."

He regarded her a moment. "You're serious, aren't you?"

"Couldn't be more."

"What has that kid done to upset you?"

"You've got it backwards. It's what I've done to upset him."

"Oh. And what's that?"

"I'm grouchy."

"Hah! You've always been grouchy. Never bothered any of us."

"Yeah, but he had to know why. So I told him."

"Oh. Why?"

"I'm not telling you! I don't need another one running out of my tent."

"Now I'm getting interested."

"Well, I'm not. Yong, I don't want to be rude, but I didn't sleep well last night and I'm really tired. I've had about enough of this kind of talk today. Did you come over for a specific reason?"

"No, I just dropped in to visit. I haven't been around much. There's always freighting to be done."

"Aye, well, thanks for dropping in, but...as I said, I'm really tired."

"Sure. I'll go visit Leide and Pers, then. You seen them around?"

"No, but if you find one, you'll find the other."

"I noticed. Great, isn't it?"

"About time."

"Yes, it was. I wonder what finally got them to notice each other?"

"Ask them. I'm sure you'll hear a great story."

He regarded her a moment, then nodded. "I might do that. I'll drop in again later. You have a rest and maybe you'll feel more like having visitors."

"I might."

He slapped her shoulder gently and left the tent.

She sat a moment, her arms crossed on the table in front of her. Then she got up and hopped over to her hammock. With her usual practiced motion, she swung herself into the netting, hooked her crutch with a now-habitual gesture over the tie-rope, and lay back, staring at her foot.

She wondered if the pain was maybe a little less, or whether she was just getting used to it. She began the exercises the Surgeon had given her. It was difficult to figure out how hard to try. She had long ago satisfied herself that she had the mental strength to push through pain to the point of doing damage to her body. The difficulty here was to separate the pain of the stretching ligaments from the pain of the injuries and from the pain of the damage that might become permanent if she pushed it too far.

Not that it made much difference. She pushed and stretched the offending foot as far as she could bear, and it still didn't move very far. The swelling seemed to have gone down a little; it was hard to tell. If she exercised too much, it would come back.

She leaned over and poked the exposed skin. It responded sluggishly, as if there was fluid underneath. She assumed that wasn't good. Healthy joints didn't have fluid puffing out the skin around them. She reached out, took her toes in both hands, and pulled them towards her.

She stopped, a muttered oath on her lips. That sharp, burning pain was nothing natural. She pulled again, gentler. There was a certain point where the discomfort changed from the slow, aching stretch to the sharp, biting pain. That seemed to be the limit of what she could do in that direction.

She tried working side to side. Pushing outward didn't seem too bad, but when she rolled the ankle inward, she once more got the sharp pain. She worked the ankle within the limits presented by that pain.

Next, she tried putting weight on it. First, she tried the ball of her foot, but once it flexed to the point where the sharp pain started, she knew that was of little use. She moved to a rock that stuck up through the sod that lined the floor and put her heel on it. That was better. She could put quite a bit of weight on her heel without the sharp pain. Maybe some day she could have a special shoe made that kept the weight on her heel, and left the useless front of her foot clear of the ground and protected.

With an exclamation of disgust, she flopped back in her hammock and stared at the canvas above her. What difference did it make? The pain never went away. It was less or more, depending on what she did.

She thought again of her cousin, Rosart. What kind of pain had he been feeling that would cause him to end his life? Maybe he truly believed the next world was a better place, so he went there. She had no idea. The doubts raised by their rebellion against their religion put everything in jeopardy. If the threat of Damnation was only a club invented by the hierarchy to keep people obedient, then the promise of Paradise was only an enticement to do the same thing.

Where did that leave her? Stuck in this world, perhaps, since the next one wasn't anywhere near a sure thing.

As Cheynou had reminded her, there were a lot of things she still had to do in this world. As far as she could figure, the only real reason for leaving was if the act of going would have some use. Anything other than that was, as Cheynou had said, selfish. A waste of resources the Crew needed. As of the moment, things would have to get a whole lot worse for her to bet on the next world over this one.

Unless the speeches at the ceremony were really bad.

* * *

As she should have expected, the principals in the peace process, those who had done most of the actual bargaining, were exceptionally pleased with themselves and required a public display to honour their work.

For this auspicious occasion, the proceedings moved to the Town Hall, which was big enough to accommodate everyone. Well, everyone important. Sarasha sighed as she rummaged

241

through her pack. "What am I supposed to wear for this whatever-it-is?"

"Your official Scribe's Tabard, of course."

"Oh, that. I don't see it here. Maybe I left it back at the Peace Talks Camp."

Her mother glanced over at her, then away. "Then go find another one."

"Where do I find a Scribe's Tabard?"

"I'm sure you have a better idea than I do, Sarasha. Stop moping around and get moving. We only have about a glass before it starts."

"All right." She sat on a bench and stared at her hands. At least they hadn't changed. Her crutch and her horse saw to that. She clenched two tight fists, held them for a moment, then gave up the effort.

She still had the strength of her hands. That had always been a source of pride for her; heaven knew why. She could swing from the rigging for hours, moving gracefully, looping from stay to spar to halyard, always taking the shortest route, far above the deck. When the Ship rolled in a beam sea, she could look down and see the frothing water below her, and sometimes she would dream of swinging out on a line and then letting go, to fly farther and farther away from the Ship and all aboard her.

Then she remembered Rosart. Until the conversation with Cheynou, she had forgotten about him. He had been one of the best mast'n on the Ship. When she was younger, she had watched him move about the rigging and had modelled her movements on his. Despite her idolatry, he had remained aloof, moody.

The chill ran through her again as she remembered the day. Something about his poise as he stood on the upper tops'l yard, a loose line in his hand. In spite of the sway of the Ship, the masts arcing port to starboard across the sky, he had stood, gracefully bending with the rhythm of the sea. She had watched in awe as his balance showed the perfect coupling of man, Ship, and Ocean. Then, as the Ship made a greater sway to port, he had leaned off the spar and swung in a perfect arc on the line, down, down, then out, out, and up. She had revelled in his glorious swoop, not realizing until the last, fatal moment that he had released the line and was flying free in a falling curve that ended in a tiny splash on the crest of a wave, far from the Ship.

She had stood, dumb with shock, her childhood training forcing her eyes to fix on the spot where the man had gone down, but he never surfaced. Now she remembered her dreams when she was younger, that he had simply swooped from air to water and arced away below the surface, gliding through the Ocean as he had through the air.

What would it be like to swoop and glide and soar like a dolphin, like an albatross, free of the restrictions of gravity and the three dimensions of reality?

"Sarasha, are you ready?"

"Pardon?"

"Are you ready? Did you find a tabard?"

"A tabard? Oh. No, I didn't."

"What have you been doing for the last glass? I thought you went to find a tabard."

"No...I...I've been...thinking."

"Do your thinking at a time when we aren't expected at a formal occasion."

"Mother, do I have to go?"

Verlene stopped in the middle of her path across the room. "Sarasha?" She turned and stared at her daughter, concern spreading across her face. "What's wrong?"

She cringed under her mother's regard, under the realization dawning in her mother's eyes.

"Sarasha, I thought we had solved this problem."

"It doesn't seem like it, Mother. I guess we only pushed it aside for a few years."

At that moment, her mother's pain hurt more than her foot. "I'm sorry, Mother. I'll deal with it. I'll get a tabard." She struggled upright. "I'll find Leide. She'll have a spare." The smile was weak, but she held it on. "You know Leide. She always has a spare of everything."

She clamped her teeth against the pain of her foot when she heedlessly thumped it against the stool as she rose. Taking a firmer hold of her temper and her crutch, she forced herself to exit the tent instead of flinging the infuriating stick through the canvas.

The force of the summer sun, moderated by the sea breeze, brought her back to reality as she stumped across the campsite to Leide's tent. Buoyed by her anger, she found it easier to force cheerfulness into her voice.

"Anyone home?"

"Of course I'm home. Are you ready?"

Sarasha waited until Leide opened the tent and regarded her. "Do I look ready?"

"Sarasha! Where's your tabard? What happened to your hair?"

"My hair?"

"Yes, your hair! You aren't going to an important Conclave like this with your hair all blowing in the wind like Restday on the afterdeck!"

Sarasha pawed at her hair that, in truth, was blowing around her face. "I hadn't thought about it. Who says this is so important?"

Leide's face got that pained expression that showed how much the ineptitude of the general population disappointed her. "Everyone says it's important, Sarasha. We've only stopped a war and been working on the peace negotiations for eleven days. You come in here and I'll do your hair. Where's your Scribe's Tabard?"

Sarasha took refuge in the spark of anger that burned beneath the surface. "I left it in camp. May I borrow your spare?"

"It's only my Apprentice Tabard. It's pretty threadbare."

"Nonsense. You were an Apprentice shorter than anyone. You hardly wore it."

"But what will it look like if the Chief Scribe of the peace talks shows up in an Apprentice Tabard?"

Now the irritation was helpful. "Don't be so picky, Leide. Nobody but you and me can tell the difference. If it makes you feel better, I'll shift my Chief Scribe's rosette to cover the Apprentice badge. After all, the main people we want to impress are these Farmers, and they have no idea what any of this means."

"I suppose."

"I more than suppose. I know. So haul out this threadbare tabard, and let's get organized."

Leide started to turn away, then stopped. "Glad you're back to normal, Sarasha."

"What kind of nonsense are you talking about?"

Leide grinned. "Exactly," and spun into the tent.

"Hmph." Sarasha followed.

25. Fleet in the Offing

Sarasha only felt a small twinge of guilt at her joyful reaction when the proceedings were interrupted.

Just as she had reached the point of nausea with the speeches, the corner of her eye caught a small disturbance at the side of the crowded hall. Bored with the ceremonies, she seized on this useful point of interest. Someone had burst into the side doorway and been immediately shushed by those nearby.

This person, whoever he was, made his way with frustrating slowness to the side of the dais, where he came up against one of the town Marshals, who officiously, though quietly, started to move him aside.

Sarasha got a glimpse of the offender: a young man, his shirt drenched with sweat, anxious tension twisting his whole body. A small surge of interest burbled in her breast.

Finally, the urgency of the message got through. The Marshal turned abruptly and pushed his way around the back, followed by the messenger.

It didn't take long after that. She watched the bad news ripple across the platform until it reached Byaren, where propriety ended. The burly Farmer jumped to his feet, interrupting the smooth flow of the speech of the Merchant who currently held the floor.

"Fleet on the horizon!"

There was an instant buzz of concern. *More for the indignity of Byaren's interruption than the import of his message. These people will soon get a rude awakening.*

To bolster his argument, Byaren hauled the messenger up beside him. "What is it, man?"

"Ships, sir. On the horizon."

"How many?"

"Hard to tell, sir. At least twenty."

Now the concern became real.

"Twenty ships on the horizon?"

246

"At least twenty, Lord Byaren. Maybe more. Too far away to tell."

Pandemonium burst out in the crowded room. Sarasha was able to monitor the movement from her position on the side of the dais. In the midst of chaos, only two other men acted. Haskel leaned over to her father and murmured something. The Captain nodded, and Haskel rose and departed. Her father approached Byaren, spoke in his ear. The bearded Farmer nodded, and her father disappeared out the back door as well.

The stocky Farmer held up his hand for silence, to no avail. His face reddened, and he took a deep breath.

Sarasha was the only one in the room prepared for the roar. "Silence!"

She took advantage of the sudden stillness to worm her way off the platform and follow her father. As she left, she heard Byaren snapping out orders. She nodded to herself. *That lad is coming along nicely.* She only hoped the shock of the threat would keep the usual authorities off balance long enough for the younger leader to establish himself.

She found Captain Tourn putting the bit in his horse's mouth, and did the same with her mount. "What's his plan?" She stared at the dunes obscuring the Priest-Admiral's Fleet.

Her father swung up on the Black, shaking his head. "Hard to say. We took his wind, despite the fact that he won the battle. One thing's sure; this won't be a sneak raid. He will come in with all flags flying to make sure everybody knows he dealt with us for good."

She swung up and Ebb Tide paced beside the Black. "Any chance he's arranged a special shoreside attack?"

"That's one thing we can count on. He'll do what the Raiders have always done. He'll sail up, anchor, and send in the boats. Straight in, up the beach and destroy everything they can."

"So we have to stop them."

"That's the plan."

"He came back earlier than we expected. What does that mean?"

"One of two things. Either he regained his control faster than we expected and is now ready for us…"

"…or he didn't regain his control as well as he'd like and he's decided to use us as an example."

Her father grinned over at her. "Of course, he could have realized the error of his ways and has come back to offer us a return to the fold."

She rode a moment, considering. "Don't be too sure you're funny."

"What do you mean?"

"Can you see the Priest-Admiral making a magnanimous gesture, rehabilitating any of the heretics who want to recant and be enfolded in the arms of the Fleet? Before he stomps the rest?"

Her father raised his eyebrows. "That would be like him."

"The question is, which possibility is the true one, and how do we find out?"

"The number of bottoms he brings will tell us something. It's the height of the tuna run, and most Ships will want to be fishing. If he has regained his full power, he will bring them all as a demonstration of his control."

"So if the Fleet fills the harbour, we're in trouble."

"Sarasha, if we reach the shore and there are more than fifty Ships out there, we go back and start evacuating the townsfolk."

"Any way we could put up a token resistance and draw their main force away from the town?"

"Good thought. However, I doubt if it will be necessary."

She glanced up to see her father staring ahead, grinning.

"What do you see from way up there on your charger?"

"Just a moment. I'm counting. Twenty, twenty-one…twenty-four. He only brought twenty-four Ships!"

"How many Masterships?"

"Twelve. That's expected. They're the most loyal ones. There are only twenty-seven Masterships in total. About eight

248

are with the Eastern Fleet, leaving nineteen. If he left a half-dozen to shepherd the rest of the Fleet while they fish the tuna, he'd have about twelve to come and slap our wrists."

Sarasha kicked Ebb Tide into a trot and soon burst onto the flat sand of the beach. There they were in the offing, a fine sight in any other circumstances. The Fleet travelled in Battle Formation, with the usual three phalanxes of Masterships leading and flanking the Priest-Admiral's Flagship. Twelve smaller Familyships spread out to either side, all sail straining to keep in formation with their larger sisters.

The two *Eagles* sat their horses, regarding this display.

"How soon will they attack?"

"It would be stupid of them to do anything but attack immediately."

"The Priest-Admiral didn't get to be where he is by being stupid."

"No. Only rigid, uncreative, and cruel."

"All right. It will take them several glasses, though. They still have to sound all the way in because they don't know the bottom. After that, they'll anchor, form up on deck, load the boats, then row in. We have that time to prepare for them."

A large rowing barge was dragging the chain across the mouth of the anchorage, and the harbour walls bristled with townsfolk and mercenaries.

Captain Tourn sat his horse for a moment, then nodded. "They've been through this before. Let's go see what Haskel and Byaren have arranged."

At the Town Hall, the celebratory bunting flapped desolately in the hot wind. They left their horses in front and climbed the short flight of steps to the main door. As they entered, Pers, Yong, and Sarasha's other supporters moved in behind them.

The room was mostly empty. Only Byaren, Haskel, and several other leaders and Captains sat at a table on the dais, hands flying, voices raised. They stopped when the Captain entered.

"What word, Captain Tourn?"

"Twelve Masterships. Only twenty-four Ships in total!"

Byaren gazed at the faces of the Captains. "What does that mean?"

"It means the Priest-Admiral could not achieve complete control of the Fleet. He has come back here to try to regain his status by cleaning us out."

Haskel nodded. "Numbers?"

Captain Tourn met the eyes of the other Captains. "A Familyship can muster about fifty Raiders. That's six hundred. The Masterships: twice that many. Another twelve hundred. Less than two thousand, for sure. What can we put up against them?"

Haskel did not hesitate. "I have seven hundred. The Town Guard is another fifty. How many men can the local landowners muster?"

Byaren grinned. "More than they came up with when your lot got beached. Even then there was argument whether to fight you, make peace, or sit still and hope you went away. We can get five hundred footmen and about a hundred horse. Only forty of those fully armed, though. Captains, how many men can we count on from you?"

Captain Tourn deferred to Hamon Kletsh. The older man considered. "We can only field about three hundred. All are seasoned fighters, but only half of those will get here in time for the first attack. After that, if we pull most of our Raiders in, we can give the full number."

In the brief silence that followed, Sarasha realized what was happening. *Everyone is waiting for Father to speak.* She suppressed a giggle. The Raider Warlord had to perform his magic in the light of day with everyone watching. She gazed at him and raised her eyebrows.

His mouth lifted at one corner, acknowledging her message. He surveyed the assembled leaders. "Who's in charge?"

The town leaders exchanged glances. There were no shrugs, but the message was clear. They had no one.

Captain Tourn glanced at the three Farmers, but they shook their heads. Eyes turned to Commander Haskel. The greying mercenary shook his head too. "It is much better to have a leader from your ranks, if anyone qualifies. I can coordinate with him."

"Fine. As long as we have that clear. The Sea People will lead the defense in our usual manner. We have the most experience with Raiders. We need a quick strategy meeting. Byaren, you'll be leading the group you have been drilling with?"

Puzzled looks shot around the Farmers as the bearded youth nodded. "We're ready, sir."

"Good. Let's sit down with you and Commander Haskel, the leader of the Town Guard, whoever is in charge of the local levies, and some of my people. The rest of you, please see to the evacuation of anyone who wants to leave and the organization of any weapons and materials you can find. The townspeople will be responsible for fire containment and medical aid if they attack here."

Relieved to be told what to do, the rest filed out. The Captains moved to take their places at the table. Sarasha glanced over her shoulder and tossed her head once. Leide and Yong moved to stand in spaces between the chairs. Pers and Solen flanked Byaren. She commandeered the chair beside her father and swung her pouch onto the table, setting up to write. When she looked up, pen in hand, her father nodded.

"All right. Many of you have raided. Consider it from the opposite point. What concerned you most? What made victory difficult?"

The suggestions flew so fast it was hard to keep track of them all:

"...the tide line is the place."

"...always hated that."

"...aye, you feel really vulnerable."

"Remember, we used to have one boat stand off to cover the others with our archers."

"...the Priest-Admiral called it cowardice."

251

"...had to stop."

"...stupid."

"...arrows. I was always afraid they'd pop up out of the dunes with twenty bowmen and skewer us all."

"...never did, though."

"...stupid, too."

"...good thing."

She raised her voice. "All right, all right. Slow down. I can't write as fast as five of you. Am I getting it straight that when you raided ashore you were always afraid of an attack just as you hit the beach?"

"Aye. When we were still grouped in the boats."

"With arrows."

"When it was too early to jump out and disperse, but too late to turn back."

"That's right. We always go in...went in with the wind behind us, but that meant higher surf. Once you get on that last wave, there's no going back."

"So if we wait in the dunes and hit them with a squad of archers just as they're coming ashore..."

"That would work. Guaranteed."

"There are no guarantees. Anything else?"

"What about the horses?" That was the first Farmer accent she had heard so far.

"What do you mean?"

Byaren peered around under the force of everyone's attention. "Well, we found out about fighting from horseback against men on foot. If they can break and run, spread out, we aren't so effective. What if we went in just as the boats came ashore...?"

"...right after the arrow barrage!"

"...that's right. We do a charge down the beach and clobber them before they have a chance to get out of the water. My horse can gallop in water knee-deep on a man."

Eyes turned to Sarasha. It sounded good to her, but she knew nothing about close-in fighting. She turned her attention to her father.

"I can see it working. The arrows will impede their disembarkation. The boats are very shallow draught. Our big horses could jump them. I see one charge from the west, with our sword arms to the sea. Then we keep going. The archers keep shooting until the raiders start spreading out, then they withdraw. We don't want a battle right there; we haven't the men."

"What if their Raiders overrun our archers?"

Captain Tourn grinned. "Archers are good at running. The ones that fight on land, anyway."

"Horses."

"What?"

"Couldn't the horses pick up the archers?"

"How?"

Sarasha spread her hands. "I'm not sure. There's something I read once about a cavalry unit that dropped their archers on a hill then charged into battle. I always thought that meant the archers marched with the cavalry and stopped at the hill, but it never sounded right. Maybe they rode on the horses as well."

Pers leaned forward with enthusiasm. "I saw a picture I never could figure out. They don't ride the horses. They run alongside. I bet they have a strap to grab. They swing their weight on it and away they go."

"Are you willing to try?"

Pers grinned. "As long as I'm the one riding the horse."

"It would take practice."

"We have time for that."

"About a glass. Can we borrow a squad of archers, Commander Haskel?"

"I'll ask for volunteers. What you said about bowmen is correct, Captain. They are always complaining about being targeted by cavalry or heavy foot and having no choice but to run away. They'll be happy to try anything that will help them escape."

"Fine. That solves the initial attack. Then what?"

"Once the Raiders are on the beach, we don't want to attack them. One-to-one is too costly."

Haskel nodded. "Can we draw them into a trap?"

Captain Tourn frowned in thought. "What did you have in mind?"

"We need to induce them to split their forces, then get them to a place where we can attack them at our advantage. We are more mobile because of the horses."

"We also have the wagons."

"Wagons?"

Pers grinned. "We can deliver soldiers to a different point on the field faster than they can run, and they arrive rested."

Yong held up a hand. "Not completely rested. In rough terrain and at high speed, the wagons are not comfortable."

"How many men can you transport?"

Pers and Yong exchanged a few words with Solen. "We can move fifty men. If there are any Farmers who will provide wagons...as many more as they have wagons."

Captain Tourn shook his head. "Let's not count on farm wagons. Most of them were commandeered for evacuation."

"So we need to entice the Raiders to split up. What's the best bait?"

"We are."

Eyes turned to Sarasha. She shrugged. "That's the easiest one. Who is the Priest-Admiral after? Us. The moment any of our Crews show up, they'll be after us at a run."

"Good enough. We'll do it that way then." Byaren shot an enquiring glance at Captain Tourn, received an encouraging nod. "Small parties of your men go in and entice groups of Raiders into the dunes. We'll have larger forces waiting for them. The dunes will help," he leaned over the table, "like this."

He laid two scraps of parchment beside each other. "Two dunes. Lead them in between. Then the archers open up from the top of the dunes on either side. When they try to attack, the mercenaries hold them from above. Then the horses make a charge when they're jammed together."

Haskel nodded, pleased. "And when we've wiped them out, you pull up behind with the wagons, load my men and whip them down the beach to the next spot. How will we know where the next spot is?"

"Mirrors. Our people already have their assignments."

"Any other ideas?"

"Attack."

Questioning looks shot Sarasha's way.

She tossed up her hands. "The Masterships have never been attacked while their men are ashore. The Priest-Admiral desperately needs to win this battle. He will be less cautious than usual. He will put too much power on the beach, leaving the Ships undermanned."

Hamon Kletsh seemed uncertain. "Who do we send? We need all our forces here. We couldn't mount an effective attack on the Ships, too. What boats would we use?"

Orrick Bren shook his head. "We don't need an effective attack, just enough to scare them into bringing their forces back to the Ships. What about sailors to man the boats?"

"We have lots of sailors available and a fleet to move them."

It was the first time Leide had spoken at any such Conclave, and her cheeks were fiery red, but her head stayed up.

"Who?"

"The women. All the sloops, gigs and lighters we salvaged and hid in that small cove to the north along the beach. We brought them back down as soon as the fighting stopped so we could fish. Give me a fighting force of fifty men and we'll attack five different Familyships. The women can take them there, pull back and wait for them. Take them off if things go wrong or come on board and help sail the Ship if they overcome one."

"Don't attack five Ships." This came from Lukin Frey. "Attack one. Take it, batten the crew below, then run it down on the anchored fleet. Try to ram a Mastership. That'll bring them running back!"

Captain Tourn's hand slapped the table. "Take all the *Eagle* Crew you can find," a quick nod from Orrick Bren, "and any *Storm Petrels*. We don't have time for other plans. Everyone get about your business. Commander Haskel and I will be on the town wall where we can see the ground. Once the battle starts, I'll be..." He slowed when he realized Sarasha was staring at him, shaking her head.

He sighed. "I'll be on the wall with Commander Haskel."

She winked at him as she gathered up her papers. Then she slung her scrip over her shoulder and turned to Leide. "We have boats to organize. Can you get a horse?"

The girl grinned. "I can find one."

There was a crowd at the door, and Sarasha had learned to avoid situations where her foot might be jostled. She found herself standing beside Commander Haskel as she waited.

"So that's how it's done."

She grinned at him. "Just had your first chance to work with the Raider Warlord?"

"Yes, I did. I think I have something to learn from him. Or her."

"More likely 'us'. After all, you're part of it, now."

"I suppose. I can't see running a mercenary troop like that, but no question it works for you people."

"Us people."

"Yes, it works for us."

The crowd thinned, and she followed the soldier outside. As she mounted Ebb Tide, Leide rode up on a little pony with a fancy rig.

"Where did you get that beauty?"

"Friend of Kendra's loaned it to me. She's so happy to be helping in the battle."

"Good enough. Tide's high." She kicked her horse from a standing start into a full gallop, and they stormed down the street, scattering citizens and soldiers alike.

They split up at the east gate, Sarasha heading to the temporary camp outside the walls to get a crew, Leide up the beach to arrange the boats. Once she had put the word out, Sarasha headed down to the beach as well.

Soon, their forces began to arrive: some Sarasha knew, some she didn't. Many of the women showed up armed. There would be enough cutlasses and pikes to put up a spirited defense of the little armada, even once the Raiders were gone.

Once the positions had been assigned, Sarasha gathered the Crews together. "All right. Leide's in charge. She's got the only boat with a big enough mast for a Signals halyard. Head upwind along the shore. They won't pay you any attention. You're only the fishing fleet heading for safety. You're not quite on a lee shore, and the sloops point up well, so you can tow the gigs. If the wind comes around on you, they can row and pull the sloops," she grinned, "so be polite to each other."

She turned to Leide, speaking so the others could hear. "Wait until the attack has started shoreward, then head for the smallest Familyship that's farthest upwind. Run down on her and swarm her from all sides. Batten the Crew and Families below and get the anchor up. Tow the little boats so you can get away if you need to. Keep a skeleton crew in the boats at all times. That's an order." She swung to face them all. "We don't need everyone to be heroes. We need people who will obey orders and do their duties." She let that sink in.

"You are the final tactic that will win this battle. You are about to strike a huge blow against the Priest-Admiral."

They all cheered.

"And if you just happen to run a ram into the middle of a Mastership..."

Under the renewed cheering, she took Leide aside. "Don't go for the Flagship. It'll be too hard to get away from the middle of the Fleet. You're on your own, Leide. You'll do fine."

The younger girl swallowed, squared her shoulders. "I'll do it, Sarasha. I won't fail you."

"Don't worry about failing anyone, Leide. Make enough fuss that they think they're in danger. Anything you can come up with."

She slapped her cousin's shoulder and turned away, to come face to face with three breathless mercenaries, each loaded down with what seemed to be water skins.

"You're Sarasha, right?"

"Yes."

"Captain Haskel sent these." The soldier offered her a bag. It sloshed like water, but it smelled strange.

"Oil. Like lamp oil, but it burns faster. See the rag?"

She held up a hand. "Leide, you need to hear this."

The other girl approached, and the man continued. "Take a flint and steel and hit this rag with a spark. It burns fast. Once the fuse is lit, throw it. The bag bursts when it hits, and all the oil burns."

Leide grinned and reached for the bag, hefting it with a nod. "Anyone got a flint?"

Several hands reached, offering. "Put them away. Take several bags each. Put them in the fastest sloops. Thanks, soldier."

She turned away, and Sarasha stood beside the panting mercenaries, watching the little fleet put to sea and scoot away on the breeze.

Sarasha turned to the soldiers. "I'd like to offer you a ride back to the town, but my horse is rather small."

They chuckled, and the sergeant tossed his head towards the approaching Fleet. "Don't worry, Sarasha. I know enough about boats to figure that it's gonna take a lot of candles to get ready for an attack."

"Don't be too sure. The boats will be over the side before the anchor catches. Those Masterships are superbly handled."

"Well, we won't stop for a beer on the way back, then."

"Fair enough." She stumped over and mounted. "Give Commander Haskel my thanks if I don't see him first. I have no idea what Leide has in mind for those oil bombs, but I imagine it will be spectacular." She turned Ebb Tide and started back along the beach.

The man walked alongside, regarding her quizzically. "You mean that young thing was the officer? She's in charge?"

258

"She isn't an officer, but she is in charge. The whole raid was her idea, and she's going to see it through."

"Will they take her orders?"

She laughed. "You have to understand the Sea People, soldier. When a signal goes up the mast of her Ship, they will all obey. A signal flag doesn't care who puts it on the halyard."

"Hmm." He shook his head once and plodded along beside her. "Interesting. You people are all interesting. Any of you might join up?"

"With Haskel's? I hadn't thought of it."

"Haskel is always recruiting. Don't often get them already trained."

"Our people are free to go where they will. Some might take work to earn money to support the rest of the Crew."

"Well, there you go, then."

"Fine. Thanks for the idea. I'll pull ahead."

He waved a hand in permission, and she trotted forward.

At the town gate, a messenger awaited her. "The Captain says you're to join him on the wall."

She grinned to herself. Should have expected that. She nodded. "Message received. I'll come with you."

The two of them mounted the short staircase to the top of the wall. It wasn't a high wall, but it afforded a view far down the beach to where the sails of Leide's little fleet were disappearing in the haze. If that was the view the Masterships had, well enough. Out of sight, out of mind.

She joined the group on the wall, affording her father a decent whack across the backs of his legs with her crutch. A few townsmen reacted with horror, but the Captain just grinned. "I need a Scribe. Prepare to write the history of the battle as it happens. A rare opportunity."

She laid her parchment on the top of the wall in front of her, weighed down by the rest of her implements. "I'll start the timing from the moment the Flagship drops her anchor."

"Good thought." He turned to the Signaller beside him. "Flash to all posts. Time from the Flagship's anchor drop."

Sarasha began to write.

259

26. Battle on the Beach

Record of the Battle on the Beach of Port Ternata
Recording Scribe: Sarasha Tourn, (formerly) Sea
Eagle.
Commanding:
  – Captain Arlijn Tourn, Sea Eagle
  – Commander Haskel, Haskel's Mercenary Troop

Forces:
>Haskel's Mercenary Troop: Foot: 700
>Ternata City Guard: Foot: 50
>Farmers' Levies: Foot: 500 Horse: 100
>Sea People's Crews: 150
>Small Boat Fleet: 100 Raiders and crew
>Total forces: 1600

Enemy Forces

Priest-Admiral Ballajero and the Raider Fleet:
~~2000~~ 2500

(Crews and Families aboard: unnumbered)

Hostilities began with the dropping of the anchor
of the Priest-Admiral's Flagship a quarter-glass
after the fifth bell.

First Glass:

The Raider boats got away in good order
immediately the anchors were down. Each Mastership
sent four lighters and one longboat, carrying about
125 Raiders. Each Familyship sent two lighters and
one longboat, with about 80 Raiders, for a total of 96
boats. Upon observing the embarkation, Captain

Tourn upped his estimate of Raider numbers from 2000 to 2500

Comments overheard:

Commander Haskel: "Do they know how many men we have?"

Captain Tourn: "Apparently not."

Haskel: "Do they know about the horse?"

Tourn: "Most likely not."

Haskel: "Not very smart."

Tourn: "They do what they have always done. Intelligence does not enter into it."

Landside Forces Deployment

- Haskel's Mercenaries in several pockets in the sand dunes east of town, about one chain back from the beach.

- All available archers in a loose line along the first dune inshore from the beach.

- The Horse in a single group behind the largest dune outside the town wall.

- The small-boat attack flotilla had already disappeared along the coast to the east.

- The local foot levies were dispersed with Haskel's men.

- The Sea People's Raiders were dispersed with Haskel's men.

- The Town Guard manned the town walls, bolstered by many of the town women and older boys, all with metallic objects about their persons to simulate men in armour. The purpose of this was to persuade the Priest-Admiral that the townspeople had locked themselves up in their town and that he had free range of the beach, as usually happens in these raids.

The Raider flotilla rowed from the anchored Ships to the beach. True to Fleet Procedures, all boats waited outside the surf line until the total force was assembled. Then they all surfed to the beach, many taking the same wave. Thus the Raider boats arrived on the beach in perfect formation, almost all at the same time.

During the final run in, the archers ashore had gathered opposite the beaching points.

Second Glass

With admirable restraint, the archers waited until all boats were ashore and Raiders were starting to disembark. Then the archers stood and rained arrows on the intruders. After five volleys, the Horse began their charge.

The Horse galloped the full length of the beach in one angled line. The leaders were in the water. They stampeded over the boats, a risky manouver that fortunately resulted in no accidents. Most of them, as ordered, did not stop, but continued to attack each boat as they reached it. The Horse following took the Raiders who had already achieved the beach, driving them away from the boats, running many of them down.

The archers continued shooting until the Horse arrived, and resumed their barrage as soon as the Horse had passed.

The Horse finished their charge and wheeled behind the first dune, to retrace their steps two chains inland, picking up archers as they came. In this way the beach, in a matter of a half a glass, was completely cleared of Landbound forces.

The Raiders were left in charge of their objective, at an estimated loss of 30% of their men. The opposing forces were now approximately equal in size. The Landsmen had lost five horsemen, two horses, and one archer who had the bad luck to lose his footing and tumble down the face of the dune into the Raiders fleeing the Horse charge.

Before the Horse had finished picking up the archers, the first of the Sea People attacked at the far eastern end. Twenty brave Raptors charged the Raiders, engaged briefly, then retreated, drawing approximately one hundred enemy after them. This force was lured three dunes inland then decimated by the combined weight of Haskel's troops and the local levies.

The Landbound forces then climbed into waiting farm wagons, to gallop at full speed westward to reinforce the second Landbound force, which had just engaged approximately 150 Raiders who had followed a group of Falcons inland. Again, the defenders were completely successful and destroyed their attackers with small loss to themselves.

Third Glass

By the time the third group of decoys, a combination of Pelicans and Night Hawks, made their attack, the Raiders had reformed. A force of at least three hundred followed the lure, and the ambush in the dunes had not sufficient forces to make a successful attack. This stalemate continued until the Horse, having deposited the archers in safety, returned to make their charge, and destroyed the formation of Raiders that had held until that point.

At this time, the Raiders on the beach had formed completely under one command. The next unfortunate decoys, a mixed group of Sea People, were met with aggressive attack, and the whole Raider force moved after them at a slow pace in good order.

Landbound forces responded by drawing all foot soldiers together, and a pitched battle would have ensued had not the Landbound Warlord sent flashes from the town walls for all Landbound troops to withdraw to the town.

Because of the discipline demonstrated by the Raider troops, this withdrawal could have been costly to the Landbound forces, but at this point the Raider forces stopped their attack.

Signals were raised on the Flagship, and all attention was drawn to the Ocean.

At the windward end of the anchored Fleet, the smallest of the attackers, the *Erne*, had raised anchor and was making sail. She was accompanied by a fleet of smaller sails and rowing gigs. She pulled in alongside the next Ship, the *Plover*, and a fierce but brief battle ensued. Then she broke away, and the

Plover, too, made sail, running down upon the anchored Ships.

As these two Ships lined themselves on ramming course with the first two Masterships, the Grizzly and the Tiger, the smaller fleet dispersed, aiming for other Ships of the anchored Fleet.

Grizzly made a valiant attempt to raise her anchor and flee, but succeeded only in presenting her side to the approaching Plover. The Plover's ram took her amidships, and the two, locked together, drifted downwind towards the beach west of Port Ternata. The Tiger was less seamanlike and thus had more luck. The Erne struck her abaft the foremast chainplate, and the two Ships swung to the Tiger's anchor, linked together. The other small Ships deployed themselves through the Fleet, lobbing fire onto the decks of the anchored Ships, and left a chain of smoking vessels behind them.

Fourth Glass

Following the burst of signals from the Flagship, the Raider fighters swarmed back to their boats, leaving their wounded on the beach, and fought back through the surf to pull for their Ships. The Grizzly freed herself from the Plover, and both got anchors down before they ran aground.

As the attackers left the beach, the Landbound's fleet of smaller sails retrieved their boarding parties and raced away downwind, the sailboats towing the gigs, to land just to the west of the port.

265

At this point, the Landbound command declared the battle completed successfully.

Estimated results

Landbound:

Haskel's Mercenaries: Dead: 3. Wounded: 12

Local Levies   Dead: 7. Wounded: 32

Local Horse   Dead: 6. Wounded: 16

Sea People   Dead: 5. Wounded: 7

City Guard   Dead: 0. Wounded: 1 (Broken wrist from fall)

Total Lost   Dead: 21. Wounded: 68
                Prisoners: 0

Raiders:

Dead: (left on beach) 700

Wounded: (left on beach) 45

Wounded or died afloat: Unknown.

Prisoners: 236

Conclusion

Landbound Command considered this an almost-decisive battle. The Priest-Admiral retrieved near 1500 able men off the beach, and probably still has 500 to 1000 more, although not experienced Raiders, left on board his Ships. The damage to the Priest-Admiral's prestige and the morale of his forces is much more important.

All agreed that further action would be necessary to persuade the Priest-Admiral to leave the area and not return.

27. GHOSTS

Sarasha stood looking at the old man who huddled near the fire, the flickering light warming the creases on his cheeks.

"So, Gats. I hear you have a tale to tell me."

"Ah. You are Sarasha of the *Sea Eagle.*"

"M-hm."

"I do have a tale for you, Sarasha of the *Eagle.*"

She looked down at the hunched figure, his eyes glowing back at her through bushy brows. "And what kind of story would help us get rid of the Priest-Admiral and his lot?"

"Got no idea, Young Sarasha. Captain Bren says, 'Tell her about the Death of Ships, Gats.' So I tell you about the Death of Ships. What you do with the story is up to you."

"All right." She sat on the log beside him. "Tell the story."

"Well, now, Young Sarasha, this isn't rightly a story. It's more of a legend."

"I'm listening, whatever it is."

He grinned, a few teeth showing over his thin lips. "Always in a hurry, Young Sarasha. Wait a few moments for an old man."

She stifled a sigh. *Orrick says this man has something for me. The less I talk, the sooner he will get to it.*

"This isn't one of my stories, and I can't say why Captain Bren wants me to tell you, but he said to explain it, so explain it I will."

In spite of herself, she was intrigued. "Explain what?"

"What happens when a Ship dies."

"Oh. What happens? I don't understand. To the Ship or to the Crew?"

"Ah! She doesn't know! The Captain was right."

"So tell me!"

"It goes like this, Young Sarasha. When a Ship dies, just like a person, her soul leaves the hull and floats away. It floats on the rising wind up to the Heavenly Skies, just like our souls do. Did you know that?"

"I have heard people say something like that, but I never...understood it, exactly."

"Well, now you can understand. Oh, you won't hear the Priest-Admiral speaking about it in his sermons on the Mastership. But us old folks keep more of the lore alive than the Priest-Admiral and his Scribes."

"Don't you speak ill of Scribes to me, Old Gats."

"Hah! Still got plenty of spunk, haven't you, Young Sarasha? Good for you. Good for you." He paused as if to remember where he was.

"So, the soul of the Ship floats up to the Heavenly Skies and begins to sail the Heavenly Seas. But she doesn't sail alone. She sails with all the other Ships that have died before her. In the one Great Heavenly Fleet."

"I see."

"But that isn't what's important."

"Oh? And what's important?"

"What's important is who rules in that Heavenly Fleet. Which Ship gives way to which other: who runs up the signal flags and who has to obey those flags."

He peered up at her. "Did you ever think of what happens if she was a bad Ship? If she lived in evil and revelled in godless deeds? What if she turned cravenly away from battle and died in disgrace?" He nodded judiciously. "And what if she was a good Ship and fought brave and true and bore her Crew through the worst storms, sank all their enemies to the depths?"

"I never thought of that. What happens?"

"Well, the good Ships are Saved and go to the Heavenly Fleet. And the bad Ships are Doomed and go to the Fleet of Damnation."

"That sounds right."

"But that's not the good part." He chuckled, a deep sound from that thin old chest. "That's not the good part at all. You know what the good part is?"

She waited as he paused dramatically.

"They're the same Fleet!"

"The same?"

"You heard me right, Young Sarasha. The Ships are all in the same Fleet. And the Saved Ships are the leaders, and the Doomed Ships have to give way and do what they're told."

"I see."

"Maybe not." He leaned farther forward, his voice dropping. "You see, the Crews of the Doomed Ships become the slaves of the Crews of the Saved Ships."

"I see."

"And the best part of all? You know what the best part of all is?"

"No, I don't. What's the best part of all?"

His head turned to her, and she wondered whether she had overdone it.

"Don't you be too smart, Young Sarasha. You listen to this. The Ships that have to serve any particular Ship are the Ships," a hardened forefinger tapped her arm with each word, "That. She. Sank."

Sarasha took a moment to absorb this. "So you mean the old *Condor* is up there, cruising in the Heavenly Fleet with two Masterships sailing in attendance on her, obeying her every signal?"

"That's right!" The old man rocked in silent laughter. "And it gets even better!"

Now Sarasha was interested. "What?"

"The Captain! You know what happens to him? The Captain has to serve on the Saved Ship. He has to take a position as the lowest bilge cleaner on the Ship. Below every single member of the Crew. For Eternity!"

Sarasha grinned. "Now, I like that, Gats. I like that a whole lot."

"Now do you see why the Captain wanted me to tell you this?"

She considered. "Let's suppose that a Ship was burned and had already gone to her Heavenly Reward, but somehow the Crew of that Ship was able to sink another Ship. Might that last Ship have to follow the Ship of the Crew that sank her?"

269

"Don't see why not."

"Aha. And maybe on that Ship, up there on the Heavenly Ocean, those members of the Crew that died with her, they might be looking back to our Ocean? Maybe even coming back to ride the winds?"

"Especially if there was unfinished business."

"Riding the wind, screaming for vengeance."

"I like that, Young Sarasha. Screaming for vengeance sounds like a good story."

"Oh, it's a good story, all right. It just hasn't happened yet."

The old eyes stared up at her, and the wrinkled face split in a wide grin. "I get the feeling I'm going to get a chance to tell it, Young Sarasha."

"I'll go and do my best, Gats. Thanks to you for a great idea." She stood up, then turned back to him. "Why do you call me 'Young Sarasha' all the time?"

He chuckled again. "Because I knew Old Sarasha."

"Old Sarasha? My great-grandmother."

"Oh, yes, I knew her."

"I never did. She died before I was born. I guess she was quite a character. Nobody talks about her much."

"Huh! A character she was. Tried to have her Beached a handful of times, they did. But she was always too smart for them. They could never bring anything against her. She could talk the wind all the way around the compass, Sarasha could. Plus, everybody knew she was the brains that ran the *Eagle*. Priest-Admiral would have chewed a hole in his golden mainsail if he knew a woman was running a Ship. But the old Captain, he kept it quiet, and Old Sarasha couldn't have cared less who got credit for anything as long as the Ship prospered."

"Good for her."

"And I say 'Amen' to that, in spite of there bein' no Priest and no Religion on these Ships any more."

"And no Ships, either."

"Aye, that too, Young Sarasha. That too."

"Anyway, thanks for the information. I'll come back and tell you a story some day."

"You do that. And I'll tell you some stories about your great-grandmother."

"It's a deal." She bowed in formal agreement and turned away from the fire. She had work to do.

* * *

It was just after dawn when Orrick Bren met Sarasha and the crew of his gig, wind-blown and wet, staggering with fatigue, stumbling over the sand towards camp.

"Nice day for a morning walk."

She leveled him a glance. "Bracing."

"There were a lot of lights and noises on the *Cheetah* last night."

She turned to regard the Mastership, riding high in the morning light. She shrugged. "New wind. Probably heard ghosts in the rigging."

"Ghosts?"

"Sailors." She sniffed. "Superstitious lot."

"Yes. She seems to have sustained no damage from those ghosts, has she?"

"Seems not. Rising wind. Will they be checking their lines?"

"Standard practice."

"With a little wind like this they might, say, haul in a few turns of anchor rode? Check the first couple of fathoms that were under water?"

"I doubt it. It isn't in the Standards for this much wind. I'd say only a very imaginative Captain would do that."

"Too bad. It's amazing what floats down on your anchor rode, just lying there innocently in the water."

"So should we keep an eye on the *Cheetah* this morning?"

"Might be entertaining. I'm off to bed." She faced the gig's bosun. "Thanks for the ride, boys. Lotsa fun."

He saluted. "Any time, ma'am. And I mean that."

He turned with his men, and they trudged along the beach to where the *Petrels* were quartered.

Orrick Bren settled himself in to wait, but it did not take long.

"Sarasha!"

She turned back, following his gaze. The *Cheetah* was moving ever so slowly backwards, her bow falling off the wind.

"Seems her anchor rode went."

"Hmph. Poor seamanship."

"I wonder what he'll do now?"

She peered out over the water. "Probably put on sail and move out of there. What would you do?"

"I'd try to get back to where I was anchored, get the divers down. Anchors are expensive."

"A bit of upwind work, then. You a betting man, Orrick? What tack do you figure?"

"Too late to bet. He won't tack towards shore. He's already got his helm over, pushing the stern to port. It'll be port tack."

"I like port tack."

"You do?"

"M-hm. Today, anyway. Let's see how he does."

The big Ship began to pivot slowly as the rudder held the stern, and the wind pushed the bow around to starboard. Foresails blossomed above the bowsprit and staysails between the masts. Soon, the Mastership was fore-and-aft rigged, a configuration that allowed her to move slowly a few degrees to windward.

Sarasha eyed Captain Bren. "They did that right smartly, don't you think?"

"Say what you might about the Masterships. They have sharp crews, well trained."

"Trained under the lash."

"That's true." He shrugged." Still, they got those sails on right quickly."

"She's pointing well, isn't she?"

"For a boat that was designed for speed downwind, she's doing well."

"Put a lot of strain on the port stays, though. Rising wind, waves building." Sarasha scratched her chin in thought. "A lot of sideways force, I'd say."

"Nothing they weren't built to handle."

"If they were new."

He turned to stare at her. "New?"

"Wear and tear, rats, that sort of thing."

"Rats?"

"Rats chew things."

His face began to open, from a grin to a full smile. "And the rats were bad last night, were they?"

"Almost as bad as the ghosts."

"Now I really want to watch."

The two stood, shoulder-to-shoulder, along with a growing crowd. Any unusual action on the part of the Fleet brought people to see. So there was a good-sized audience to watch disaster fall.

The foretopmast went first, toppling slowly, it seemed, down towards the water on the lee side. The lower foremast followed, pulling the whole of the main over with it. Like a set of matchsticks falling, the rest went as well: the middlemast, then the mizzen, then the spankermast last of all. It broke halfway up, and the huge fore-and-aft sail folded, then tore across, flogging to ribbons in the wind as it fell.

A great cheer rose from the crowd on the beach.

"Now we'll see what level of seamen they are. How long till they've got an anchor down?"

She considered. "Not long. They must have been readying the spare while they sailed, and the masts went aft when they fell, because the foremast started. They'll be starting it down now, and it'll catch any moment."

He nodded. "I wouldn't bet against that. As I said, you can't fault their crews."

Sure enough, soon the bow of the boat began to point to windward, the stern to slide away from the wind. There she lay, the half of the spankermast the only spar that rose above the sterncastle.

"So did the ghosts tell them anything about this, last night?"

"I doubt it. But there might have been something about avenging the *Eagle*."

"Oh. Very good." He turned back to watch the spectacle with the other cheering, hooting, crews.

28. Bitter Triumph

The dunes were alive with people. There were groups of Raiders from the rebel Ships and patrols of mercenaries, interspersed with mounted Farmers in pairs and threes. But there were also unarmed townsfolk, women, even children, all shouting and waving as if it were a festival.

"We'd better get these folks back to their homes."

"Is there any danger?" Byaren peered down at her from his big red horse, a grin on his face.

"Well, if the Priest-Admiral had sent a party roundabout to catch us from behind, this would be a good time for them to show up."

His head snapped up and he scanned the area. Then he calmed. "Nobody in sight. The sentries are still at their posts."

She nodded. "Haskel's men know their business, all right."

"But we still better get these people back to town." He turned his horse and rode toward the nearest group of celebrants.

Soon, he had help, and the mounted horsemen gradually herded the laughing, chattering crowd back towards town. Seeing them safe, Sarasha turned her attention elsewhere.

She found her father in much the same mood, sitting his huge black horse, staring out at the anchored Ships.

"How did you do that?" He indicated the crowd streaming landward.

"Told them the boogeyman might come along the beach."

"So what will he do now?"

"My question exactly."

"Will he give up and go away?"

"He's left it rather late in the season." Sarasha mused a moment. "He might try one last trick. Bad luck, his top supporter having his Ship fall apart like that."

"His bad luck started the day he banished the *Eagle* from the Fleet."

"Not all luck."

"So it was you."

"M-hm."

"I thought so. When I heard about the cackling and the screaming, I was pretty sure."

"Screaming?"

"Like a banshee on the wind, I heard."

She shook her head. "I may have chuckled a couple of times."

"Well, if they heard banshees on the wind, then that's what they heard."

"That was sort of the idea."

He nodded, and seemed about to rein his horse around, but then he turned back to her. "Who took you out?"

"Why does it matter?"

"I'd like to thank him for bringing you back."

She grinned. "Thank him for more than that. Cutting the anchor rode was his idea."

"Hmm. So...are you going to tell me?"

"Orrick loaned me the crew of his gig."

"Good choice. Ship's best Oarsmen."

"A proud crew. The bosun's a good man."

"I'm sure you'll let Bren know."

"He already does."

"Why not ours?"

"Better this way. Spread the glory around."

"Good thought."

They turned as one, the small horse and the big one, and walked back towards the town. As they rode, Sarasha realized that her father's horse wasn't keeping pace. She slowed Ebb Tide to let him catch up. "What are you thinking?"

"What you told me."

"What I told you when?"

"About how you got the crowd to go back."

"Oh. You mean there really might be?"

"That's right."

"But Haskel had patrols out."

"And he pulled them in when the attack came and there was no one in range to be dangerous. Let's cast an eye to the east. That's most likely, since no one lives out there. Next horsemen we see, we'll send them west."

"But we would have seen them come ashore."

"At night? Two nights ago? Three?"

"He sent a party ahead, before he even got here? That sounds too creative for the Priest-Admiral."

"What if he finally listened to one of his brighter Captains?"

She nodded reluctantly. "It wouldn't hurt to check."

They sent two other horsemen galloping away in the opposite direction and loped their horses out along the beach.

"They wouldn't be coming along the beach, would they?"

"No, they would be too easy to spot."

"So they're in the dunes."

"I imagine so. No way to find them unless we ride right on top of them."

"That might be interesting."

"Well, let's head inland a chain or two. Spread out and cover more territory."

As they walked their horses through the sand, Sarasha's mind was whirling. If there had been a shore party, they should have been there to attack when the main party beached. That meant something had held them up. Perhaps fear of being spotted. Or the soft sand. That meant they had to be close to the town. *If we don't come on them in another few chains…*

A shout that wasn't her father's brought her head up. She heard the soft pounding of the Black's hooves, and her father shot into sight around the dune ahead of her at full gallop.

By the time he reached her, she was already moving. She glanced back over her shoulder as a row of heads popped up over the dune: bowmen. She laid herself low over Ebb Tide's neck and urged her on.

Her father came up on her right side, his stallion towering over her, just as the first arrows fell.

"Hold formation. I'm bigger and I'm armoured."

277

She knew her horse was faster than his, but the logic of his plan was undeniable. They raced on for a moment, the shower of arrows falling around them as the bowmen got their range. There was a clatter, then another, as arrows struck his backplate or the skirting around the horse's sides. Then there was a scraping and a thud, and her father let out a sudden breath, more a grunt.

"Got me."

She craned her neck backwards. "Where?"

"High in the shoulder. Through the arm hole. Keep riding."

The arrows fell away as they reached the limit of the bows, and she slowed.

"No, no, keep riding. You have to warn them. I'll make it."

"Can you stay in the saddle?"

"Yes, but it doesn't matter. You have the fastest horse. Go!"

With a despairing glance over her shoulder, she kicked her good heel hard against Ebb Tide's side, and the little horse spurted ahead. Sarasha concentrated on the ground in front, looking for obstacles that might trip the horse or throw them. When the terrain allowed, she cut towards the beach where the sand was harder. Soon, the slipping and sliding stopped, and they thundered straight down the tide line. She spared a glance back, to see her father lumbering along behind, his horse gasping, the rider weaving but clinging to the saddle.

She hit the first sentries and called a warning as she galloped by. One sentry ran to the top of the dune. Mirror flashes would soon overtake her, but still she galloped.

She hauled her sweating pony to a sliding stop in front of a surprised group of officers. "Raiders in the dunes." She pointed back. "East!"

There was instant action and shouts as the officers rallied their men. "How many?"

"Didn't see them. Father's coming behind."

She turned to see the Black stampede up to them, slewing to a stop, his eyes wild. Her father tumbled out of the saddle, staggered, righted himself.

"Quite a bunch. Hundred or more. Bowmen and swords. Half a glass."

He reeled as one of the officers reached him, sliding an arm under his good shoulder.

"Watch the Ships. New attack."

Then his eyes rolled up and he sagged. In her hurry to reach him, she left her crutch on her saddle, and she winced as her sore foot touched down.

Orders were snapped, and she was vaguely aware of a battle forming around her, but all her attention was on her father. He lay on his good side, the arrow protruding from the armhole of his cuirass. His breath was uneven as if every intake hurt him. A small froth of bright red blood appeared at the lower corner of his mouth. *Lungs.*

She knew then that he would never make it. It was impossible to remove a barbed war arrow from a lung, and the usual trick of breaking the shaft off and pushing it through would only tear him up more.

A stretcher arrived, and he was gently lifted aboard and hustled away from the growing battle. She remounted her horse and followed, ignoring the bustle around her: the soldiers, Farmers and their own Raiders heading east to meet the threat.

At the Surgeon's tent, the door was blocked. "You can't come in, Sarasha. There's nothing you can do, and he'll be drugged to dull the pain. You'll have to wait."

She stared in the Assistant Surgeon's face, uncomprehending. He took her arm and led her to a bench. "Sit there. We'll call you if there's anything to report."

She was about to sit when a sudden thought brought her upright. "Mother!"

"Your mother has been sent for. Mirrors. She got the message, but she's back at the *Eagle* camp, so it will take a couple of days for her to get here."

She regarded him. "He won't last that long, will he."

The Assistant thought a moment and read her expression more carefully, considering whom he was talking to. "No, he won't. It's a lung, and he's bleeding inside. It's a matter of glasses, not days."

"Then I should be with him."

"I'll check."

He ducked back into the tent and returned almost immediately. "He wants you."

Her father was half-lying, propped up so that his right shoulder was higher, his head supported by pillows and blankets and his eyes half-closed.

"He refused the potion. Says he has to talk to you first."

Her father's eyes opened, and she could see the brightness in them, the tears of pain. She dropped her crutch and knelt to his level.

"It's the lung, Sarasha."

"They said."

"I need to talk to you."

"If you can."

"Sarasha, you have to listen to me. Just this once."

"I always listen to you, Father."

"No, you don't. But this one's important."

"All right. I'm listening."

"Get one thing straight. This wasn't your fault."

"What do you mean?"

He managed a ghost of a grin. "That's right. I want you to argue with me face to face so you can hear how stupid you sound." He coughed, and the pain washed across his countenance.

"I know you. Some day you'll have it all figured out how it was your fault and how you should have prevented it. And it will all be complete bilge. Against everything you believe in. You are not my mother, my guardian, nor my Captain. I made a mistake, and you know what you always say about mistakes."

"Two. It's two mistakes that kill you."

"Well, you'll have to rewrite it. One mistake and a shot of bad luck seems to be enough. I wasn't careful, and I got too close to them. How's the battle going?"

"I have no idea."

"Go and find out and report back to me. You have my message?"

"Yes, Father. I was not to blame, and if I ever start to blame myself, I'm to remember you looking at me with your most severe stare and telling me firmly that it's all bilge."

"Good girl." He winced once more. "Now, about your mother."

"She's coming."

"Not fast enough...you know what to tell her. She doesn't need to hear it out loud. Just say I...was thinking of her. No regrets, no apologies...she'll understand."

The tears began to flow, and she buried her head in the blankets. After a moment, his hand gently lifted her up.

"Now go check on the war. I'm going to...let them give me something...for the pain."

"Oh. Yes. Right." She stood, swaying, then regained the use of her crutch. "I'll go find out."

"Don't forget to take your sword." Again that shadow of a smile.

"I won't. It's right on my saddle."

"Away you go."

She turned in the tent door to look back at him. He knew. Then she turned out the door with a sob, threw herself on her horse and headed east.

29. Further Ahead

As she left the camp, she found a group of horsemen milling about. She stormed up to them and slid Ebb Tide to a halt in front of the big red charger. "We have a job to do. Let's go. I'm not waiting for you."

She pushed her horse ahead, despite the fact that the red mare was directly in front of her. Cued by the uncertain tug of Byaren's hand, the huge horse shied awkwardly aside, then turned to follow. Sarasha lifted her pony to a gallop and headed out on the sand.

There was fierce fighting up the beach. The Raiders from the Ships had ensconced themselves between two tall dunes and were holding a firm wall at either end of the small valley they held. Their archers held the dune tops: a precarious perch that so far they had kept. The shore forces milled around against the solid front, making little progress.

The soldiers from the town had little warning and fell back in panic as Sarasha burst among them. Then she was on the Raider line, her sword swinging, her horse shouldering men in all directions. A spear thrust forward, grazing Ebb Tide's shoulder, and the horse reared, screaming, her hooves churning in front of her. She fell forward, pawing the spearman to the earth, and lunged on.

As Sarasha swung her sword, she heard pandemonium behind her as the line of big farm horses ploughed in her wake. She grinned to herself. This was what Byaren meant. A tight formation of men, unable to get away, could be trampled into the sand by a charge of heavy horse.

The smile became a chuckle, and by the time she reached the rear of the other enemy line, it flowered into hysterical laughter. She cut down and down, reaching forward to hew a path for her horse, fending off the ineffectual thrusts of spears that couldn't be turned towards her quickly enough in the press of men.

In a brief, frenzied moment, she was clear and pulling her horse to a twisting halt. She came face-to-face with Byaren on the big red.

"Don't go back in there, Sarasha. It's too dangerous!"

"Dangerous? This is a war, you idiot. It's supposed to be dangerous!" Laughing at her own wit, she ducked her horse around him and began her second charge. It went even smoother this time, as the two Raider lines had collapsed against each other. Again, she headed the spear-thrust of the heavy charge, and even sooner this time was free again and turning for the next attack.

This time, the red horse pushed closer. "Sarasha. It's too dangerous in there."

"So what?"

"Look. You may want to kill yourself, but every time you go into that melee, we have to follow. We've lost two already, and there will be more if we go in again. They're completely messed up now, and the soldiers could get in and attack if they weren't so worried about getting run down by their own horse."

"Oh." The bubble of excitement wavered, shrank.

"Let's reform here and see where we're needed next."

"I suppose." There was something weighing on her, something she didn't want to remember.

Then she remembered. The thought hit her harder this time. *He's dying back there in the tent. He wants me to stay away, to be out here helping my Family and Crew. That's my duty.*

Gamely, she struggled to make her mind work. *What did he say? Right.* "Has anyone checked for other attacks?"

"Let's find out."

They rode together over to the mercenary standard where Commander Haskel was giving orders. He stopped talking and glanced up at the two riders. "Nice charge. Exactly what we needed. The second one was perhaps an elaboration, but convenient."

Byaren nodded. "Has there been any word on other attacks?"

The mercenary shook his head. "There was a flurry of activity aboard several Ships, but no boats pulled away. We sent extra riders to the west, but have had no reports of enemy activity there."

Sarasha regarded Byaren, then turned back to Haskel. "Should we go somewhere more central or stay here in case of need?"

The Commander glanced over to where the Raider lines were being pushed closer and closer together by mercenaries with interlocking shields, methodically hewing their way against their lightly armed opponents. "This battle has been over for some time. They just don't know it yet. The only thing that could make a difference is another attack from somewhere else, so central is your best position. As you choose."

She nodded briskly and raised her eyebrows to the bearded horseman beside her. He signalled his agreement by reining the red horse towards the town.

After a while, she realized that he was glancing over at her.

"What?"

"That was some charge."

"It seemed to work."

"It certainly did. Another time, though..." He paused uncertainly.

"Right. Don't get so far ahead."

"By the time we got to the battle, they were starting to close around you. Another moment, they'd have had you off that little horse. We're most vulnerable to the rear."

"I suppose."

"Yes, you should. Dammit, Sarasha, you can't just do irresponsible things like that!"

"And who's telling me not to be irresponsible?"

"Exactly. If I tell you you're irresponsible, then you have gone way out."

"I suppose. It just seemed the right thing to do."

"Haven't I said the same thing, time after time! And you know what they always say to me?"

"Something about thinking with your brain, not your balls?"

He blinked, set back by her rough expression. Then he nodded. "Sometimes even worse."

She sighed. "I suppose they're right." Then she looked up at him. "But it was a fine charge, wasn't it?"

"Oh yes, it was."

"Don't hate me any more?"

"Why would I hate you?"

"I talked to Kendra."

He laughed. "That would explain it. When I told her, the incident was rather fresh in my mind. I may have been a bit fervent."

"I recall that 'rabid' was one of the words she used."

"You did insult me in front of everyone. And there was nothing I could do about it."

"You were making a fool of yourself in front of everyone. There was something you could do about that. And you did. What's the problem?"

"When I calmed down, I realized that."

"They usually do."

"Who?"

"The people I insult. I don't do it for fun. There's always a reason."

"Well, as long as one of them doesn't get at you before he's calmed down, then you're all right."

"So far, so good."

He laughed at that, glancing over at her. "What? Not even a smile?"

She sighed, staring straight ahead. "By the time we get back to camp, I expect my father to be dead. He took an arrow when we discovered the enemy."

"What!"

"M-hm."

"Oh." He rode in silence for a while. "So that explains it."

"What?"

"The charge."

"I guess so."

"It was still a fine charge. Won the battle. Any chance he'll get through it?"

"Lung."

"Oh."

"My mother's back up on the Prairie. She'll never make it in time."

"Rough on her."

"She's never ridden a horse."

"Really?"

"Aye. She'll learn quick. But it will all be for nothing." Once again, hot tears ran down her face. She said no more, merely pushed her horse ahead. He took her meaning and rode silently behind her.

By the time they reached the camp, the signals had passed them. The battle was over, the enemy Raiders mostly dead, a few taken prisoner.

Byaren glanced over at Sarasha. "I guess you're free to go check on your father, then."

The weight settled heavier inside her. "I suppose."

She steered Ebb Tide over to the Surgeon's tent and, with a nod of permission from the sentry outside, pushed through the doorway.

Her father lay where she had left him, but she knew at a glance that he was no longer there. That strong lift of the head, the set of shoulders that shouted 'Captain' was gone. She knelt beside the bed, gazing at his face. It was blank. The slight twitch of a smile that was always hovering at the corner of his mouth was gone. The furrows that often crossed his brow were smooth.

She sat back on the dirt floor of the tent, her mind as blank as his face. There was nothing, now. She did not touch his hand. There would be nothing there.

She raised her eyes to the Assistant Surgeon, standing quietly nearby. "Did he say anything else?"

"Yes, he did, Sarasha. Especially for you. Once he had taken the medicine, he was in less pain, but his mind was wandering; you know how it is. He became quite fixed on one thing he had not told you."

"What was that?"

"He kept talking about his mistake. He wanted you to understand his mistake."

"And what was that?"

"He said that, riding the horse, he was moving so fast, he didn't look far enough ahead. He said you must look farther ahead, Sarasha."

The Assistant regarded her quizzically. He had delivered a message, but he wasn't sure what he had delivered.

"Oh. I understand. We were searching for the Raiders, and he was moving too fast. He's not used to being on a horse. He got too close to them. That's why he got shot. If he'd been paying attention farther ahead, he might have seen them sooner."

"Oh. I wondered why he was so insistent on it, though. He kept saying, 'Look farther ahead, Sarasha, look farther ahead.' Like it meant something more."

"That explains it, then."

"I suppose. People get funny notions when they've been given a lot of that pain potion."

She rose slowly. "Have the other Captains been informed?"

"Yes."

"Then everything is taken care of until my mother gets here?"

"Nothing else to be done."

"Then I have something I have to do."

He nodded and turned away. She stayed a moment, studying her father's dead, blank, face. She understood very well. Finally, she moved to the door. There, she turned back for one last moment. "I'm going to be a bad leader for a little while, Father. Just a little while."

As she left the tent, she met three Captains hurrying towards her. "Sarasha, we just heard. We are so sorry..."

"Believe me, so am I. Captain Kletsh, you read the weather as well as any man in the Fleet. Do those high clouds mean what I think they mean?"

He stopped, uncertain, but her firm gaze focused him. "I...uh...Yes. Wind dropping. A new system passing through later."

"Storm?"

He stared at the sky. "At this time of year? Doubt it. Fresher winds, though. Why do you ask?"

"A calm evening?"

"Yes, until around midnight."

"Then?"

He gazed at the sky again. "The new system will move slow, I'd say. Winds will start filling in about midnight. Southeast, I'd guess."

"Good. Thank you, Captain Kletsh." She regarded them all. "Thank you for the kind words regarding my father. Please take care of my mother if she arrives and I'm not available."

They nodded and stood, uncertain whether to go or stay.

"Orrick, where's your gig crew?"

"They moved up the beach when the attack came. Just this side of the town dock. Going for a ride?"

"The sea air clears my thoughts."

"I'm sure." He turned to follow the other Captains, and she mounted and rode towards the docks.

Over the evening, the wind dropped to almost nothing. At the turn of the tide, the attacking fleet hung on slack anchor rodes, their sterns swinging in all directions. At dark, the tide changed, and they all streamed out again.

Sarasha raised herself in the bow of the little boat, steadying her weight on one foot. The black wall of the Mastership slid past her, weedy and rank in the dim light. They moved forward, past the bow, to where the anchor rode plunged down into the black water. She reached up, got a good grip on the line, and tugged. There was no give. The weight of the huge Ship, pressed by the tide, held it firm. She slung her good leg over the damp line and hauled herself upward. It was good to be moving freely again, her arms pulling, leg pushing. The weight of the oil sacks strung about her body swung in rhythm to her movements, and in no time at all she had swarmed up to the prow of the Ship and lofted herself into the nets along the bowsprit. She froze there, listening. There was no sound. She peered back down, but the little gig had disappeared into the night below.

Calculating the throw of the deck lanterns, she slid out below the bowsprit to where it disappeared in the darkness. Then, slowly, ever so slowly, she inched up onto the forestay, easing over the jib furled there in its cover. Then up the stay itself, hand over hand into deeper darkness. Ship's lights were designed to illuminate the area around the Ship and were shielded to prevent reflection off the rigging into the eyes of those on watch. It would work against the Priest-Admiral tonight.

As she approached the crow's-nest, she slowed. There would be someone on watch there. She slid upward, peering ahead in the darkness. Yes, there he was, a darker shadow against the stars over on the port side. She edged forward, holding her breath until she gained the outside of the rail. There she crouched, resting.

After a long while, the figure above her stretched and moved towards her. She reached up and scratched lightly with one fingernail on the wood of the rail. The figure paused. Just as he began to move, she scratched again. This time, he came towards her. She froze. He came forward—curious, not alarmed—and put his hands on the rail above her head to lean out.

The moment his head cleared the rail, she swung out and up, one hand grabbing his hair, jerking him forward.

He cleared the rail neatly, and she let him drop, somersaulting with a despairing wail to the deck far below. His body caught twice on lines as he went down, jolting each time, then hit with a shuddering splat.

She swung up into the crow's-nest and froze, flat on the planks, her eye against a crack.

There was immediate reaction on deck. Lights flared, figures ran, then stopped and stood in a circle, unwilling to touch the body. Predictably, they all looked down, then up. She waited. When they looked down again, she chuckled. Not loudly, but on and on without stopping. They looked up again, then at each other, puzzled.

She stopped.

She could hear the concerned murmur rising, groaning, as more and more men gathered below her. Then an officer burst from the companionway, striding with purpose towards the group of stunned sailors, a sharp question ringing out. Just as they turned to heed him, she laughed, a high, ringing cackle, cut off abruptly. She poured the contents of one leather bottle onto the mast and any furled sails she could reach. She placed the fuse material where it would catch, lit it with a quick flash of her flint, and took to the mast, climbing upwards on the dark side. Reaching the next stay, she slid quietly aft to the mainmast, coming in above the sentry posted there. The the flames below helped her, now, attracting the sentry's attention and blinding him to the danger sliding out of the darkness above. He dropped like a sack under her weight, although she almost cried aloud from the pain when her foot hit his shoulder.

This one fell silently and cleanly, but the sound he made when he hit the deck brought everyone running. She had to work fast, now. She poured the next bag, lit the shorter fuse, and reached down to a lower inner stay, sliding aft to the centremast, below the sentry there. This time she poured the volatile oil down the mast and didn't bother with a fuse. With a single click of her flint on the steel, the small rag in her hand lit, and she poked it towards the oily mast.

She was rewarded with a sudden rush of blue flame, which burst from her position and roared upward. She grabbed a stay and slid away as the fire crept down the mast, its light showing the amazed face of the sentry, leaning out to see what was happening.

From her next post on the mizzenmast, she lit the bags as the soldier had shown her, lobbing them from her central position as far as she could in all directions. She saved one for her final coup.

Moving lower and lower in the rigging as she came aft, she peered down in the darkness. Then she saw it. Rather, they showed her. Several men appeared on deck, lanterns in their hands, revealing the dark maw of a companionway. She lobbed the last bag, now burning brightly, down that hole and saw the blossom of light as it burst one deck below, flames shooting in all directions.

During this action the two forward masts had become an inferno, and there was enough light for her to be concerned for her own safety. She slid aft and down, judging her last swing to land her on the rail of the sterncastle. From there it was easy enough to cut loose a length of rope, trail it over the rail and let herself down into the darkness.

She could see the glistening water below her, but as she approached that level, a shadow disengaged itself from the gloom under the stern, and firm hands guided her aboard. She felt a hand grope for her sore foot, then seize the leg above and hold it steady as she dropped.

Then she was sitting on the forward thwart, and the rowers pulled lustily away.

"Quiet yet, lads. They might still hear us."

"Not likely. Not with that goin' on."

She had not examined her handiwork, preferring to save her night sight for the task at hand, but now she raised her eyes.

The foremast was burning from crow's-nest to tip, the flames working rapidly out through the sails furled along the spars. The mainmast was burning, too. The centremast hadn't really caught well, but the flames had moved farther down, sparks and falling drops raining ing on the deck and cabintops. Fire from her dropped bombs on the maindeck aft were reaching up to join their partners aloft.

It was the after companionway that gave her the most pleasure. Flames were already shooting aloft from the draft. She could see the glow of the fire through several portholes, spreading rapidly through the innards of the Ship. Sparks, smoke, and flaming debris lifted away on the rising wind.

As she sat in rapt attention, a voice startled her. "I got an idea."

"What?" She turned to see the bosun's grin gleaming in the red light.

"They're all gonna be watchin' the show, right?" His sweeping hand indicated the anchored fleet.

"True. What are they not going to see?"

"Us goin' upwind, cuttin' a coupla anchor rodes. Can you imagine if one of them drifted right down onto her? In a rising wind?"

"You are diabolical, dishonourable and no true seaman to take pleasure in such a filthy deed."

"That's right, ma'am. I'm not a seaman at all. I'm one of those Plainsmen everybody's talkin' about these days."

"Well, Plainsman, let's go cut some ropes, then."

They shared a grin in the light of the doomed Ship, and he turned to give orders to the men at the oars.

When three Ships were drifting ponderously towards their dying sister, the final one bright with three remaining oil bombs lobbed on deck for interest, they pulled for shore. There was no sense overdoing it and getting in trouble because the oarsmen were too tired to escape.

Sarasha reached down and hauled out the short oar for the forward thwart, pulling away cheerfully. Her arms were sorer than she had hoped, but that was to be expected after two months of inactivity. They rowed silently, the glow of the burning Ships lighting their faces.

Then the last wave lifted them, and the rush of the surf raced them to shore in silent jubilation. The sailors jumped out and hauled the little skiff far up the beach, refusing to put it down and let her out. When they were far above the tide line, they relented and obeyed her hissed commands, grinning as they helped her out and put her crutch in her hand. Then two of them swept her up again and they ran up the beach and into the real darkness of the dunes.

A sentry hailed them, and soon they had light. The sailors refused to let her down until they reached the grove of stunted trees where Ebb Tide stood, patiently chomping on the contents of her nosebag. Then they waved her away, their cheers lifting her back towards the town.

In the dawn, a desolate sight cheered the watchers on shore. The Mastership was a dark hulk, settling lower and lower in the water as the swarm of tiny men and small lighters tried desperately to salvage what they could before she sank. They were hampered by the spread of drowned sails, masts and rigging that littered the water in all directions, and the rising wind that thrashed their sails and threw spray over everyone.

To leeward of the dying monster two of the other anchored Ships showed soot and fire damage: one from their lobbed oil bombs, one from a close brush with the burning Ship.

There was a burst of activity on the sinking hulk, with figures appearing from below and rushing in panic to the sides. Soon, all the boats pulled away. With a slow heave, the bow of the Mastership seemed to droop, and the sterncastle began a painful climb. Then, faster and faster, she slid forward, and then all that was left was a pool of oily water, bubbling and frothing in the centre, a ring of flotsam expanding away on the waves.

30. Last Move

A few glasses later, Sarasha stood in front of the leaders of the shoreside army. "Tell your men to stay out of the rigging tonight."

"Why, Sarasha? You have something spectacular planned?"

"And I want all the glory for myself? Think about it. The Priest-Admiral knows those weren't ghosts in the rigging last night. Anybody who steps aboard one of those Ships tonight will get caught."

There were several nods.

"I agree. Whatever the rest of you do, there will be no *Petrels* on the water tonight."

"Wait a moment, Captain Bren. I said in the rigging."

He turned to her, a smile growing. "What do you have in mind?"

"I have nothing. I suggest a meeting with your best Shipwrights. The ones who put these Ships together."

"And can tell us how they come apart?"

She shrugged. "Rigging was my concern. I'm out of ideas."

Bren turned to Captain Kletsh in dismay. "Sarasha the Ingenious admits to being out of ideas. Whatever shall we do?"

The old Captain passed a keen eye over her. "What we used to do when she was too young to interfere. A meeting with a Ship's Carpenter or two might be in order."

"Captain Bren, you should tell them what old Gats said."

"Go ahead."

"It was your idea. Afraid it isn't good enough?"

He held up his hands in mock surrender, and turned to the group. "One of my people reminded me of the legend of the Death of Ships. I'm sure you are familiar with it..." He proceeded to outline what Sarasha had heard the day before.

Seber Tory snorted. "And how will this old man's tale help us?"

"The Priest-Admiral's people are believers. They believe in his gods, and they believe in a lot of other things, including that old folk tale. If they think the ghosts of our Ships are floating around, out to seek vengeance on them, it will demoralize them. Remind any of your Crews that are on the water tonight. Let them be creative."

Once again, there was concurrence.

"So, shall we take a glass or two to find our experts, then meet to discuss how to make the Priest-Admiral's Fleet fall apart?"

"And what should we be doing, while you are out performing your sailor tricks?"

Dwayo Kaya, now Captain of the *Eagles,* spoke up for the first time. "If I were you, Byaren of Nangata, I'd be asking Commander Haskel how to repel a larger attack than we have so far seen."

Alder Jaspen nodded. "Good thought, Captain Kaya. If the Priest-Admiral doesn't do something soon, he will start to lose Ships. They'll just pull up anchor and slip away in the night. Many of them will never come back. He'll be getting desperate, and he'll go for an all-out assault."

Byaren stroked his beard. "Does that mean he'll leave his Ships poorly guarded?"

"Not after Leide's attack."

"But that was just a decoy. We need a serious attack on his Ships, the moment he gets near the shore."

"Very good strategy, for a Landbound."

"Thank you, Captain Bren. It's up to you sailors to figure out how."

Captain Kletsh held up a hand for silence. The only sound was the rising wind, whistling in the eaves of the Town Hall where they met. When puzzled frowns started to appear, he chuckled. "Wind. Raiders like to attack on a wind because they can move in faster. We can take advantage of that. We pick the smallest Ship, the farthest upwind. Just like Leide did in the first attack but with a larger force this time. We move a party of Raiders up the beach tonight with our fastest sloops. Tomorrow, as soon as the landing party gets far enough away from their Ships, we swoop down on that Ship, take her, up anchor, and start for the next. We can take that one, too. By that time, most of the Captains will be ripping up the signal flags to get their fighters back to protect themselves."

"What do we do with the Ships we take?"

"Run them aground and let our boats take us off."

"That would be appropriate."

"What about the Families and Crew?"

"We don't wish them any harm. Maybe we won't run them aground too hard."

"Good idea. Just hard enough that they can decide for themselves whether to go or stay."

Sarasha was watching Lukin Frey. He had a thoughtful expression on his face, and twice he shook his head slightly. After a moment, he met her glance, raised his eyebrows. She responded in kind.

He nodded and turned his attention to the rest. "Sorry, it won't work."

There was a surprised pause.

He shook his head more firmly. "It won't work. It's too much like Leide's attack. The Priest-Admiral isn't creative, but he has a long memory. Did he ever forget a wrong done to him? Did a successful tactic ever work twice against him?"

"Then what do you suggest?"

"I don't suggest anything. I am keeping us from wasting our time."

A series of glum nods, then silence.

"We have been very creative, so far," Orrick Bren mused. "We have come up with a new attack each time. We have done nothing the Raiders ever do. There is one thing we haven't done."

They regarded him with expectation. Sarasha hid a smile.

"Standard Raider practices."

Pers nodded. "The one thing they won't be expecting."

Byaren glanced from one to the other. "What would Raiders do in this situation?"

"Attack before they do."

"Really?"

"Most definitely. We always attacked. We fought when we wanted to, then we disappeared before anyone could bring a stronger force against us."

"So how would you apply that now? You have no Ships to attack a Ship."

Yong leaned into the conversation. "If we could put a serious force on the water, we could take a Ship, even with a good force aboard her. Then we could use that to take another, maybe two or three. Take them for certain, not just to fake an attack. Sail them away."

"Make it seem like they ran?"

"Won't work. We won't take one of those Ships without a real battle."

"Then what do we do?"

"Get them to chase us?"

In the pause, the older Captains began to shake their heads. "Then you're back where we were before. They're faster and stronger. They chase us, they board, and they take the Ships back. We'd be lucky to escape in the little boats. They'd send their small boats after us. Chase us ashore."

"Where we would have the reinforcements to protect our Crews."

Captain Kletsh shrugged. "True, but then we're still back to where we started. Unless we run a few Masterships aground or burn them, we haven't damaged any more than their morale. And we still wouldn't have dealt with the real problem: that they have such a large force of Raiders."

Orrick Bren punched his own fist in frustration. "But there must be a way! What has changed? What do we have that we never had before?"

"Local help."

"Local knowledge."

Pers and Yong spoke at the same time.

Bren's face brightened. "Masterships draw twice the water a Familyship does. If we can get them to chase us somewhere so shallow that a Familyship can go but a Mastership can't, we can run them aground." He swung to Byaren. "Are there any shoals in the bay? Hidden ones that don't show above the water level?"

The Farmer's glance passed the question to Noveyn the Merchant, who frowned thoughtfully.

"Yes, there are dangerous places. The fishermen could tell you."

"Then let's get some fishermen!"

Captain Bren nodded. "Get me your most experienced fishermen. We'll meet tonight and make plans for tomorrow."

"Too late."

Pers stared the table down. "Too late. The Priest-Admiral will be expecting a counter-attack during his attack tomorrow."

Several nods responded.

"So attack now."

Everyone stared at Menendan Cawbur, amazed at this uncharacteristic comment.

"Now?"

The older Captain stood. "You forget that we are the Sea People, and we stand down for no one. Wait for darkness, yes, but then attack!"

Eyes met around the table. More nods.

Orrick Bren stood. "So you are suggesting we put together the strongest force we can, slip out under cover of darkness and take over as many Ships as possible. If we can, we get the Priest-Admiral to chase us onto a reef. If we get away, we take the Ship out of sight around the point downwind. Then what?"

Hamon Kletsh shrugged. "Improvise. If you get away, follow the coastline. Next good spot, run her aground, anchor her, whatever. Deal with the Families and Crew. Offer them the chance to join us. They probably won't. Only the most loyal will have left the fishing to come after us. But try. After that, get yourselves ashore. We'll have a shore party follow you, pick you up. The smaller boats can be hauled inland if we can get horses and wagons close. The larger sloops can tack out over the horizon and come back from upwind, hide in that rocky harbour to the east."

"And don't forget the Shipwrights."

Captain Bren frowned. "You'll have trouble sneaking up on anyone out there tonight. They'll have boats patrolling in the water. I'd bet every Ship will be lit up like Midwinter's Night."

Pers chuckled. "They won't be watching under the water."

"Under!"

"We'll use swimmers. And you folks will provide a real loud distraction, I'm sure."

Byaren shook his head. "These all sound like wonderful ideas. What I don't like is that you're planning them for tonight before they attack. Even if it all works out, the Priest-Admiral will still have enough men to match our forces. Can't we get a plan that kills a whole lot more of them?"

There was a bit of a chuckle at that, but Captain Bren shook his head. "You have to understand the Sea People. This is only part of the Fleet. If they choose to attack us, the Sea People could show up with more than triple our forces here. What we have to do is persuade them to leave us alone. That means it is much more important to make them afraid than it is to kill them."

Byaren nodded, partially convinced. "And what if they attack today?"

Captain Kletsh shook his head. "Not with the Flagship just gone down. But if they do..." he laughed and clapped the Farmer on the shoulder, "...you'll get your chance to kill a few more."

As this conversation continued and the plans firmed up, Sarasha wrote her notes and kept her own counsel. It was painful to see the others assuming the leadership her father had once provided, but it was also good to see that they were able. When the Conclave broke up in Concurrence, she gathered her papers silently.

"Not contributing much today, Sarasha."

She turned to see Orrick in the doorway. "They don't seem to need a Warlord today."

He came back in, regarding her. "That must hurt."

"Not too much, Orrick. We always said it isn't good to give all the power to one person."

"Not all leadership is bad, Sarasha."

"Of course not! What do you mean?"

"You're always going on about how bad it is to let someone lead. Groups of people need leaders."

"I suppose they do. But how do you stop the leaders from taking over?"

"If people are aware of the problem and the leaders are also aware of it, they can avoid trouble of that sort."

"I'm not so sure. These people have spent their lives under a tyrannical system. What they think of as freedom, others might see as dictatorship."

"Then take your own advice, Sarasha."

She frowned at his smile. "What advice is that?"

"Let the people choose for themselves."

"But what if the course they choose is the wrong one?"

"And here we come, full circle again. Do you want to tell people what to do, or don't you?"

She shrugged and trudged away to her hammock, fighting the fatigue and the other pain that dragged every step even more than the sand on her crutch.

31. A COSTLY WIN

Sarasha woke late that afternoon, sensing the heightened tension in the camp. Voices were louder, and there was more movement of people and horses. She yawned and stretched. She was still stiff and sore, but she felt better for the sleep.

Swinging out of her hammock, she grabbed her crutch and moved into the kitchen area, then stopped. Her mother sat there, her head cradled in her arms on the table. There was no movement but the slow rise and fall of her shoulders.

Sarasha slipped as quietly as possible around the sleeping figure and out to the fire. She stoked up the flames, swung a kettle over them, and went to find tea.

As she set the warm, sweet-smelling teapot on the table, her mother's head stirred. A sleepy voice mumbled from the tangle of hair. "Is that tea?"

"Fresh brewed, Mother."

"Oh, good. For a moment there I thought I had dreamed it, and I would wake up to a cold fire and an empty tent."

"How are you feeling?"

Her mother sighed. "How did you feel after your first day on a horse?"

"Like that, hey?"

"No, twice that bad. I spent two days on a horse."

"At least you had a saddle."

"That's supposed to help? I thought the saddle was to protect the horse."

"A bit of both."

Her mother cradled the mug, took a sip. "Ah, that's better. I may decide to join the world after all. I considered sleeping through till night and then keeping right on going."

"With all the bustle around here, I doubt you'd make it."

"I did sort of hear something. What's going on?"

"Oh, there's all sorts of ideas for making the evening unpleasant for the Priest-Admiral and his lot."

Her mother's expression sharpened. "I hope you aren't included in any of them."

"Not really. I had an idea..."

"Whatever it was, you can let it go. You're staying here with me tonight."

"Am I?"

"Yes. I have no authority any more, but I'm putting my foot down on this point."

Sarasha sighed. "All right, Mother. My heart wasn't in it, anyway."

Her mother stared at her. "I'm not at all sure I like the sound of that."

She let a small flicker of resentment flare. "You can't have it both ways! If I wanted to go, I would."

"I suppose you're right."

"But if I don't go, what do I do?"

"Is that an honest question?"

"It is. You once told me that was what you did. You got me going in the right direction. Now the old direction is closed. The Raider Warlord is no more. What do I do now?"

Her mother sat straighter. "You start looking ahead. What problems have to be solved next."

A great pain swelled in Sarasha's chest. Her throat burned and she could feel the tears welling. "That's what Father said. His last message to me, while I was out fighting, was, 'Look farther ahead'."

Her mother nodded, her own lip twisting. "So let's get to it. What is the next problem?"

Sarasha made a great effort and controlled her thoughts. *What next?* She considered out loud. "Let's assume that whatever happens tonight, the Priest-Admiral decides to give up and go away. Where will we be?"

She clapped her hands to her head. "Oh no!"

"What?"

A hysterical giggle burst out. "We'll go back to what we were doing when the Fleet was sighted!"

"What was that?" Her mother regarded her with concern.

"Listening to some of the most boring speeches you ever heard. They'll want to start all over again!"

Her mother smiled, just a bit. "Let's call that an insoluble problem we must suffer through. What else?"

"Well, the prisoners…"

"Prisoners?"

"Quite a few wounded were abandoned on the beach after the first attack. A few of their Raiders surrendered when they were surrounded in the dunes. Many drifted ashore from the wrecks. Some of them will have drifted on purpose; whether as spies or to join us, how can we tell? Almost three hundred in total. If one of the Ships we capture tonight decides to come over to us, we'll have a whole new Crew to fit in."

"What are the chances of that happening?"

"It depends on the conditions. I can't see any Crew who still had their Ship choosing to come on the beach with us. I can see them waiting for the Fleet to sail away to the east, then heading west, never to return. They would have to leave Fleet waters. Any Fleet Ships that found them would sink them as heretics."

"But they might be able to make a life to the west? Does anyone know what's out there?"

"No, but that's only because the Priest-Admirals didn't want anyone getting too far out of their control. According to legend, there is a passage far to the west that will take a Ship all the way to the fabled Inner Sea, where the Ancients live. How much truth is in that tale?"

"And if the captured Crew doesn't choose to join us?"

"We'll have to let them go. We can't kill them. The Ship isn't much use to us for the same reasons. We wouldn't dare use it around here either."

"I suppose you could use them to solve all your problems."

"Put all the other captives and wounded aboard and send them off? I would hate to send anyone back to the Fleet if they didn't want to go." She thought a moment. "But I would never take anyone's Ship away from them. I know too much how that feels."

"But if they ask to stay, how can you trust them?"

"How can the Farmers trust us? They'll have some proving to do. They can't stay here, because the townspeople will always think of them as possible spies.

"No, they'll be well and truly Beached, just like we are. They'll have to come with us, where there's no chance of them doing any damage. We'll divide them up and keep an eye on them."

Verlene smiled a little. "There. Now you've solved one problem. What's the next one?"

They were still tossing ideas back and forth in the growing dusk when Leide joined them, wind-blown and harried.

"What's up, girl? Forgot your comb today?"

Leide patted her hair absently. "I was just down on the beach. The Priest-Admiral has moved his flag."

"We assumed he would."

"Guess which Mastership he chose?"

"That shouldn't be too hard to figure out. It will either be the Ship of his foremost supporter, temporarily, or his weakest supporter, and he's taking it over."

"Good thinking, Sarasha."

"So which one was it?"

"He wouldn't dare take over another Ship. He's gone on board the *Wolverine!*"

Sarasha exchanged glances with her mother. "Exactly what we thought he'd do. It's nice when the enemy is predictable. Doesn't do us much good, though."

"But don't you see? The *Wolverine* is the Mastership that rammed us in the final battle. Now our enemies are together in one place. One blow could destroy them all!" Leide's face was positively glowing with enthusiasm.

Sarasha laughed. "Calm down there, Leide. I'm sure you're right. But that doesn't help us. It's not as if we can take on a Mastership. Especially one with a bunch of the Priest-Admiral's Private Guard to reinforce the regular Crew."

Leide put her hands on her hips. She had not sat down for this conversation, pacing back and forth in the small tent. Now she faced Sarasha aggressively. "Tell me your opinion of the plans they made for tonight."

Sarasha shrugged. "They have a chance of success."

"Huh! What kind of success? To steal a Familyship or two? What kind of success is that? What we need is something to destroy their morale completely, make them leave because they are afraid to stay."

"I agree with you there, but I haven't any ideas. I did what I could, but I can't see anyone going into the rigging of the Flagship tonight."

"All right, not the rigging, then. What about another plan? What have you been working on?"

Sarasha glanced at her mother. "We've been sitting here figuring what will happen once the Fleet sails. That seems to be the most productive thing we could be doing at the moment."

Her cousin nodded. "That's good, Sarasha. You've done your share of the fighting and your family has made the greatest sacrifice. Make good plans so when this war is over, our people can survive. You can trust the rest of us to hold up our end."

Sarasha half-rose, but her cousin was already out the door, her footfalls pounding softly in the sand, fading towards the beach. Sarasha turned to her mother. "I don't like this at all."

Verlene shook her head. "Neither do I."

"What is she going to do?"

"You have a better chance of figuring her out than I do."

"She's going to do something stupid. I can tell. She gets that stare, her eyes all wide and enthusiastic, and her brains just go out the porthole. She's cobbled up a plan for attacking the Flagship."

The older woman raised her eyebrows. "She's a smart girl. Maybe she'll succeed."

"Don't be silly, Mother. What chance does she have of taking out a Mastership?"

She got no response. Her mother simply gazed at her.

"Right. I managed. But that was the first time. That was easy. Now, they're ready for us. She doesn't have a chance."

Verlene shrugged. "Once again, Sarasha, you can't tell people what to do. Maybe she'll come up with an idea; maybe she won't. Maybe she'll be successful; maybe she won't."

"The best I can do is find out what she has planned and help her all I can, then."

"I have to agree, there. Except for one thing."

"I don't go with her."

"Right."

"She wouldn't let me, anyway. You heard what she said."

"True. And you would let her make that decision?"

Sarasha grinned and held out a hand, tipping it one way, then the other. "If I really thought I could help? Maybe."

She grabbed her crutch. "But right now, I'd better find her and see what she has planned. Probably a frontal assault all by herself. Scare them to death."

Two glasses later, as full dark approached, Sarasha once more cursed the luck that had brought the mast crashing down on her foot. She was dead tired from thrashing up and down the beach, but she had not found her cousin anywhere. The only piece of information she could glean was that the crew of Orrick's gig was missing as well. None of their other friends had any idea where Leide was, either.

She found Tonu just before she sailed off with the departing attack armada, but the Sailmaker had little information. "She was at that meeting with the Shipwrights and stayed behind talking to one of the older men. That's all I know."

Pers knew nothing either, being too full of plans for the attack. Sarasha swallowed her frustration as the crews ran their boats into the water and boarded smoothly, leaving her waving at their departure. Unable to find anything to do, she returned to her tent. It would be two or three more glasses before the attack was launched, so there was nothing to do but wait. Her mother was sympathetic but could do nothing for her.

Finally, she decided that the best she could do was to be as close as possible and as ready to help as she could. She saddled

Ebb Tide, slung her bow and a full quiver of arrows in front of her and went to patrol the beach.

As she ambled along, she assessed the enemy. They had not moved their anchorage because that would be too much like running away, and the Priest-Admiral couldn't afford to show weakness, especially now. Sarasha mused on that. *If you achieve power by force, then you are restricted in your tactics by the need to maintain your power. Thus, the Priest-Admiral can't throw his whole attention against the external enemy, because he's too busy keeping his own people in line.*

She peered out over the water to the Fleet. Lights showed on every mast and down every stay. Boats with lanterns held high patrolled around every Ship. The new Flagship was especially well lit, with sentries patrolling the decks in regular beats. That thought prompted her mind to race as she timed the patrols. *Yes, it would be possible, if you were nimble enough, to get aboard.*

If you could get to the Ship without being noticed. If you could climb that mountainous side without being seen by the patrol boats. If you could find a dark spot to hide once you went in over the rail.

32. Final Reckoning

She shook her head. She hoped Leide wasn't...

Cries and lights shot up from a Familyship far out on the water. The attack had begun. She smiled grimly. Good move. They had not taken the windward Ship, assuming it would have more guards posted. They had taken one on the seaward side of the Fleet, but slightly to leeward of the Flagship. She hoped they would be quick, because that meant reinforcements would be coming very quickly, riding the waves down to them.

Sure enough, there was a bustle around the Masterships anchored in the centre of the Fleet, and lights pulled away. She strained her eyes, but could discern nothing of the struggle on the Familyship.

The cries and sounds of battle continued for less than half a glass, then subsided. She found herself holding her breath, listening.

Then the lights started to go out on the embattled Familyship. Soon, it disappeared from sight in the darkness. All she could see was the bobbing lights of the boats full of reinforcements, converging on that black spot in the anchorage.

What does that mean? I hope our people have been successful and are blacking out and sneaking away. She peered into the darkness: waiting, listening.

The darkness was getting less. Her eyes were drawn to the left, where the Flagship was moored. There seemed to be even more lights there. *Is the Priest-Admiral boarding more reinforcements or weighing anchor to follow?* Light was coming from the portholes as well. In fact, every line of the huge Ship was outlined in fiery orange. Screams began to float across the water, and a mob of people milled about on deck.

The first lick of flame rose above the railing and soon every companionway in the midships area was shooting flame and smoke. Now there was panic on the *Wolverine.* Boats were slung over the side, people rushing to jump into them. Screams and splashes showed that one had overturned.

In an incredibly short time the whole midships of the Mastership was blazing. Flames spread for'ard and aft, and the sterncastle seemed filled with red light, streaming out the transom windows.

At this point the deck became too dangerous, and those aboard flung themselves into the sea. Sarasha watched, fascinated, as the whole Ship, from stem to sterncastle, became engulfed in flames, the fiery roar drowning the cries of the victims.

Then her attention was caught by action closer to her. In the light of the burning Mastership a small boat was rowing madly for shore, chased by two boatloads of Raiders. The small boat was pulling away, but the pursuers had archers aboard, and arrows fell all around the quarry. One of the rowers must have been hit, for there was a tangle of oars and the boat slued sideways. This problem was quickly sorted, but they had lost time, and now only three pairs of oars were out.

Sarasha kicked her pony to a gallop down the beach to the point the chase was approaching. She unlimbered her bow and sat her horse impatiently, waiting for the enemy to come within range. She glanced around desperately. There were many people on the beach, and she shouted for help.

"Somebody bring archers. Archers, hurry!"

She continued to call as the uneven race progressed. A cry, and one oar dropped, but the other continued to pull. Shoulder wound. With three oars on one side and two on the other, the little gig still splashed evenly ahead. There was movement in the stern of the gig and the third oar reappeared. The bosun must have changed places with the wounded man. With three pairs of oars and a fresh rower, the little boat surged ahead, and for a moment seemed to be winning the race. The archers had ceased their barrage, only shooting once in a while as their target moved farther and farther from the light of the burning Ship.

Three soldiers came panting up. "What's going on?"

"Someone's trying to get ashore. Any bows?"

"I have mine."

"Go off to the port...to the left there, so you can shoot past our men without hitting them. Loose as soon as the enemy comes anywhere close to range. You other two, head back inland and find us archers."

They scrambled away, and she resumed her watch. The gig was now approaching the shore, and she could reach it with her arrow, but that was no use. More people ran up, and she sent them off to find help as well.

Then a galloping of hooves approached and two horses raced up, two men piling off each as they stopped, slinging their bows to the front. "That's the *Storm Petrel's* gig. Shoot at the boats chasing her."

Soon, the five archers were dropping arrows into the water between hunters and hunted, and one or two stronger arms began to find their range. Shouts of pain and anger turned to fear as more and more arrows started grouping on the pursuing boats.

Laughter and cheers broke out as the two Fleet boats broke off their chase, clashing oars in their hurry to escape the growing rain of arrows. The little gig pulled into the surf and rode ashore, to be grabbed and run up the sand before the rowers could even drop their oars.

Using her horse to advantage, Sarasha pushed her way down to the gig. Her shout quieted the jostling, cheering, mob.

"What happened? Was Leide with you?"

The bosun looked up from where he was tending the wounded rower. "That she was, Sarasha. No longer."

Sarasha piled off her horse, ignoring the pain as her foot hit the ground.

"Where is she?"

He tossed his head towards the flaming Mastership. "She didn't get off that we could see. We hung around as long as we could, Sarasha. That's how we got spotted. She told us not to, but we hung around."

Sarasha was now at the gunwale of the gig. "I need to know, Bosun. What did she do?"

The man tied off the bandage he had put around his sailor's shoulder and grunted with satisfaction. "That'll do you until the Surgeon gets at it. Not too serious." He slapped the man's good shoulder and turned to Sarasha.

"She was talking to the Shipwrights, ma'am. They told her something that gave her a plan. She got us to take her out and she went aboard. She said she was headed for the oil storage. If she didn't come back, we was to get out of there. That's what she said, Sarasha. We hung around as long as we could, then we left when we knew there wasn't any point."

She nodded. "I'm sure you did, Bosun. You almost paid for it. Come on, I'll walk you back to camp, and you can tell me more."

He helped his injured shipmate out of the boat and turned him over to the rest of the Crew. "Take him to the Surgeon's tent and then you can come back and watch the fun. I'm going back to camp to report to the Captain."

Sarasha remounted, and the man stepped out alongside the horse. "That's all? What was her plan?"

He glanced sideways at her. "It was a good plan, Sarasha, or we wouldn't have taken her. One of the Shipwrights had worked on Masterships when he was younger. He told her about the secret passages."

"Secret passages?"

The man grinned. "Sure. Everybody belowdecks has heard of the secret passages. Of course, nobody ever found one, but we all heard about them."

Thinking of the neatly boarded-up companionway outside the Captain's cabin on the *Eagle*, Sarasha nodded.

"It seems they really exist on the Masterships. One of them's a secret way overboard from the Priest-Captain's cabins. Comes out under the stern above the rudder. So Leide has us drop her off outside the circle of patrol boats and swims in, just as the attack is taking everyone's attention. The plan is to climb up on the rudder, open the trap and head for the oil storage.

"She didn't take but a little oil with her, and fuses like Commander Haskel gave you the other day. Kept it dry in a little oiled pouch, and away she went."

He looked over his shoulder at the havoc on the water. "I guess she made it."

"What was the plan to retrieve her?"

"We was to come back when we heard anything, go to a certain spot and wait for her to swim back to us. She never made it."

"Obviously."

They paced in silence for a while.

"She left a message for you."

"She did?"

"Yes. She said to tell you she figured it a good trade."

"Good trade?"

"Yeah. She laughed about that. She said if she didn't make it back, then one girl was a good trade for a Mastership, and the Flagship at that."

A lump grew in Sarasha's throat as she remembered Leide's words that evening.

"Did she even plan on coming back?" Sarasha tried to speak, had to gulp, then continued. "Of course she planned to come back. That oil went up awfully fast, though. She probably got trapped by the fire or the sailors coming to try to put it out."

The man nodded, a blur beside her in the dark. Then his face turned up to her, his anxiety showing, even in the dark. "We did right, didn't we? Taking her out?"

"Of course you did. It was a good plan, and look!" She craned backwards to where the glow of the fire was now fading.

"I just wish she'd got out."

"Maybe she did. There's plenty of people in the water. Maybe she dived overboard."

"It's a long swim to the beach."

"If they picked her up, she can still get away. It's complete chaos out there, and there's too many people for everybody to know everybody, let alone worry about asking questions."

By this time, they had reached the Sea People's camp, and Sarasha picked Captain Bren out of the mob of people milling around. He made his way over to her.

"What's happened, Sarasha?"

She nodded to the bosun. "He's the one to talk to. I have to go back to the beach."

Without another word, she spun her horse and worked her way out of the crowd, heading back to the shoreline.

There was a growing mob of people on the sand, but no further boats pulled out of the surf. It was far too early for anyone to have swum ashore even if they could overcome the long distance and the cold water.

Sarasha stared out into the darkness, trying to remember the positions of the anchored Fleet, wondering if the boarding parties had taken advantage of the distraction to take another Ship or two. They wouldn't know until dawn.

For the rest of the night, she rode up and down the beach, eyes peering at every dark patch of weed, every particular curl of wave that might be a swimmer come ashore. Her task was made harder by the flotsam from the various battles and sinkings that had taken place over the past month.

The eastern sky began to pale, and she could see more and more, but nothing showed. With the turn of the tide, fire-blackened flotsam began drifting in, and the first body washed ashore. Calls from up and down the beach drew attention to more bodies, and she galloped back and forth, but none was Leide's.

With the approaching daylight the anchored Fleet appeared out of the morning mist. By Sarasha's count, there were only two Ships missing. The *Wolverine* had gone down and one Familyship was gone. Flags rattled up and down the halyards on the remaining Masterships, coded so no one ashore could understand them.

Finally, as the sun began to warm the beach, clear signals ran up the mast of the *Wolf*. The Priest-Admiral had chosen his new Flagship. All Ships were to remain at anchor to await further orders. That was all.

Down on the water, boats rowed around, some purposefully, others wandering. Every once in a while one would stop to haul something out of the water, then continue the search.

Patrols on shore also gathered whatever floated in. Some of it was valuable: trunks, boxes, barrels and individual pieces of furniture: mostly fire-blackened, some completely clear.

A wagon came down the beach to collect the bodies and lay them out on a patch of sand within sight of the Fleet. The Captains and the other leaders of the Shoreside forces were out with the patrols, so they were all aware when the Priest-Admiral's longboat pulled away from the *Wolf* and headed for shore, a treaty flag fluttering from its short forward mast.

Sarasha peered out as the longboat approached. The stiff figure in the stern didn't look like the Priest-Admiral and wasn't wearing the ceremonial headdress. She gave a sharp chuckle. *Probably lost it.*

However, when the longboat hit the beach, it was Noremsen, the Captain of the *Wolf*, who jumped to the sand, heedless of the knee-deep water, and waded ashore.

The assembled leaders stood back to allow him room to come to dry land. For a moment he stood there, taking in the disparate group in front of him. Finally, he spoke.

"I am Fleg Noremsen, Captain of the Mastership *Wolf*. I have assumed the Priest-Admiral's position of this Fleet temporarily, as provided in the Regulations, until a new Priest-Admiral can be chosen. Who speaks for the Landbound?"

A series of glances around the semi-circle, and Captain Kletsh stepped forward, together with Noveyn the Merchant and Struven of Vrengata. "We speak for the Landside Forces. You know me well. This is Noveyn of Ternata and Struven of Vrengata. What happened to the Priest-Admiral?"

314

"Priest-Admiral Ballajero went down with the *Wolverine*. Apparently, a boarding party forced its way into his cabins and locked him in. The Crew tried to break down the door, but the fire was too close. He never escaped."

Sarasha's loud laugh turned all heads. "That boarding party was a sixteen-year-old girl. Her name was Leide. She's the one who took the whole Flagship, all by herself."

There was a murmur in the crowd, but no one spoke. The new Priest-Admiral passed a hand over his brow, and Sarasha saw that it shook slightly. "Whatever happened, it has happened. We are willing to treat with you."

Kletsh nodded. "What do you need?"

The Priest-Admiral shrugged. "The bodies of our dead."

Struven nodded. "We will continue to gather them, treating them with due respect. They will be available to your shore parties. As long as your people go nowhere else and come in single boats, they may take them at any time."

Fleg Noremsen inclined his head. "We have one further request. Our Fleet must sail today. We have stayed in these waters overlong and have other matters to deal with. We would prefer that one Ship stay to collect the bodies that appear in the next two or three days. Will you undertake not to attack that Ship, if she anchors in the bay and offers no provocation?"

Noveyn met Noremsen's eye. "You are asking permission to anchor one Ship in our bay for two or three days, in order to collect any bodies that appear?"

"That is correct."

"And in turn, you will do what?"

"Leave."

"That is all?"

"I am not in a position to make decisions for the Fleet. If you wish more, you must deal with the new Priest-Admiral when he is chosen."

Captain Kletsh nodded. "We understand. What about your people who are ashore here?"

"Which people ashore?"

315

"The wounded, the prisoners."

"Oh. Yes, we will take them off if you agree."

"Same terms as the bodies. One boat at a time. And the Ship we took last night?"

The Priest-Admiral raised his hands. "You have taken her. You will do as you choose."

"If we decide to keep the Ship, will you receive her Families and Crew?"

"I suppose we must."

The old Captain nodded. "That is sufficient."

"We are agreed?"

The other two nodded their heads.

"Then the Fleet will sail as soon as we have gathered our people."

"There is one more thing, Priest-Admiral."

Once again, all eyes turned to Sarasha, perched above the crowd on her horse.

The Priest-Admiral regarded her a moment, then turned to the negotiators. "Who is this woman who speaks in Conclave so freely?"

Captain Kletsh grinned. "She is the woman who, of all on this beach, the new Priest-Admiral should listen to, and should be afraid of. Take good advice from an old Captain, Priest-Admiral. When Sarasha the Scribe speaks, listen."

The beaten man shook his head and stared at her, lips pressed together in a line.

She waited until silence descended. "I am Sarasha the Lame and I speak what I know. Hear me well, Priest-Admiral Noremsen, for I do not threaten. I only speak truth, with which you may do as you will. Look about you. Who do you see? You see Merchants and Farmers, mercenaries and former Sea People. Forged into one army, one force, a rock against which the waves of the Fleet break and fall and break again.

"This new alliance has had less than two months to gather itself. The former Sea People have had mere days to teach the horsemen how to fight against Sea Raiders. The horsemen are

316

now learning to breed their horses for fighting, to armour them against footmen.

"By next year, should you return, the forces arrayed against you will be three times the power that confronted you today. In five years, the powers will be ten times what you see now.

"The People of the Land are in ascendancy, Priest-Admiral. The Raiders of the Sea have had their day. The power of the Priest-Admiral is on the wane, Fleg Noremsen, and if I were you, I would consider twice and thrice about seeking the Silver Flag for my Ship. And then I would think again."

The old seaman stared at her without reacting. Then he nodded once, a gesture of respect and acknowledgement. "And that is your advice for me, Sarasha the Lame." A hint of iron returned to his voice. "And what can you tell me that would make me accept this advice? What do you have to bolster your credibility when I speak to my Captains on this topic?"

She sat her horse and stared down at him, waiting.

Finally, Orrick Bren stepped forward. "If I may intrude, Priest-Admiral, I might point out that the Fleet has lost two Flagships in the past three days. The first was destroyed by Sarasha. Alone. The second was taken by her cousin, Leide, who sacrificed herself in order to ensure that the Priest-Admiral was aboard when she sank. Learn as we have learned, Priest-Admiral. Sarasha the Lame speaks truth. Heed her well."

It seemed the last blow to the poor man's reserves of strength. A measure of the stiffness went out of his spine and Sarasha again noted the tremble in his hand.

"If what I see before me is true, then I indeed must listen. If the Priest-Admiral of the Fleet must stand and listen to a youngster a third his age, and a woman to boot, then that is the only fact I need to tell me that my life has truly changed, and I must learn to deal with this new world, whether I like it or not."

He retreated to where his crew had their boat ready for him. There, he turned and confronted them once more. "I will send boats in, one at a time, to retrieve our living and our dead.

317

One Ship will stay for three days to tidy up the mess. My Fleet will take no action against you at this time. More, I cannot guarantee."

There was no need of response, and he entered his boat. His oarsmen whisked him through the breakers, and soon he was rowing back to his Ship. Within three glasses the anchors were rising, sails blossomed on the yards and the Fleet, its usual pomp made tawdry by blackened sails and missing elements, pulled away towards the southeast. One unlucky Familyship stayed at anchor.

As the Fleet left the bay, one small Ship slipped around the headland from the opposite direction and bore away towards the watchers on the beach. The *Snow Goose* pulled in as close to shore as only local knowledge will allow and dropped her anchor off the town. Soon, a flotilla of small craft launched from her sides, and the victorious sailors rowed and sailed ashore to the cheers of their fellows on land. The *Snow Goose*, once more under the command of her proper owners, raised her sails again and hurried off after the retreating Fleet.

Sarasha sat her pony in solitude, dread in her heart, searching for Pers.

When his skiff pulled ashore, she rode down to meet him, using the power of her horse to shoulder through the merry crowd and cut him away.

His smiling face turned up to her, a hint of surprise in his eyes. "Hey, Sarasha. It worked just like we planned. The Fleet's gone! You'll have to tell me all about it. Where's Leide?"

She pressed her lips together and urged Ebb Tide closer, slowly edging him away from the cheering crowd. When they were clear enough that she could be heard, she slipped off her horse and faced him.

"The Fleet didn't leave because you stole the *Snow Goose*, Pers. It left because the *Wolverine* burned and the Priest-Admiral burned with her."

"Yes, we saw the blaze as we were leaving. It saved us. Their reinforcements might have caught us, but as soon as the Flagship went up, they turned and went back. Who did it?"

318

"Leide."

"Leide? She burned the Flagship?"

"That's right. She went aboard, set the oil stores on fire. Then she found the Priest-Admiral, forced him into his cabin and barred the door. They tried to break it down, but the fire moved too fast, and they had to leave."

He stared at her a moment. "But Leide..."

She reached out, placed a hand on his shoulder. "We'll never know, Pers. I guess she stayed to make sure the Priest-Admiral didn't escape."

"What?"

"She went down with the *Wolverine,* Pers. She took down the Flagship and the Priest-Admiral all by herself, but she went down with them."

Sarasha watched in agony as the colour washed out of his face, as the ebullience faded from his body.

"She stayed..."

"That's right, Pers. She stayed. The *Wolverine* went up incredibly fast. Once the oil got burning, the whole Ship sank in little more than a glass."

"Oh."

"You know what she told the bosun of the gig when they dropped her in the water?"

"What?"

"She told him that if she didn't get back, it would be a good trade. One girl for a Flagship. When she found she could take the Priest-Admiral as well, I guess she thought it was a bonus not to be missed. He was an evil man, Pers. It was a good thing she did."

He did not respond, merely stood there, mute. She put her hands on his shoulders, turned him to face her.

"And you will not take anything away from her."

"What?" That got through to him.

"You will not have any negative thoughts about what she did. You will not be angry with her for her sacrifice. That would only be selfish, wouldn't it?"

"What do you mean?" He wasn't really thinking, only asking questions from habit.

"Can you count how many lives she saved by driving them away last night? Can you figure how many men would have died today, if the Fleet had attacked like the Priest-Admiral planned? She saved all those people, Pers. What are her death and your sorrow compared to that?"

Finally, something registered, and expression returned to his face. "What is her death? That's an easy thing for you to say..."

Her hand covered his lips gently. "Pers, do you have any doubt in your mind that her last thought, besides her love of you, was of how proud I would be? I have to live with that for the rest of my life. Don't tell me how easy it is.

"She is a hero, Pers. The greatest hero of this whole war. Nobody has made the sacrifice she has made, nobody has had the success she has had. Cling to that thought, Pers. Keep that in your mind for the next few days. Don't let anything you say, do, or think take away from that.

"And when you feel like crying, Pers, come to me, and we can cry together."

"You? Sarasha? Cry?"

"Pers," she shook her head slowly, "you think I don't cry? With the pain and the knowledge of the pain I have caused? Come and see me, Pers, when the pain is the worst, and I will cry with you. Now, you must go and be a hero."

She pushed his shoulder, turning him toward the crowd. "Play the hero, Pers. Sometimes it takes your thoughts away from the pain."

33. Funeral Fire

Sarasha stood with her arm around her mother's waist. Tears ran down their faces as the Captain's pyre burned. "I can't get used to this."

"Nor I. It's so different from what we have done for centuries."

"It was that or bury him in the ground."

Her mother shuddered. "I can't see him liking that."

"He's dead, Mother. His likes and dislikes are past us now."

"Yes, it's silly superstition. We all decided that," Verlene turned an earnest face to her daughter, "but now that it comes to the real moment, I can't be sure."

Sarasha sighed. "Something in me wants to see the old ceremony, with the sail-wrapped bundle sliding off the plank. But face it, Mother, the water's not deep enough."

Her mother glanced at the small stream that ran through the *Eagle* camp and smothered a hysterical giggle. "Hardly enough for a decent splash."

Sarasha tightened her arm. "Do we stand here until the whole fire burns down?"

Verlene shrugged. "I suppose we're starting a tradition."

"What would be appropriate?"

"We owe his memory at least that time."

"We do."

They stood there, each lost in her own thoughts. The fire crackled louder, and the logs settled under the dark bundle. Verlene began to sob softly. Sarasha reached around and pulled her mother's head to her breast, stroking her hair. After a while the sobs ended, and Verlene straightened again, tossing her hair out of her eyes.

Sarasha looked around, catching the eye of Captain Bren, who came to them straight away.

"My mother and I will stay. It won't help us to have all of you here."

"We wish to pay the deepest respect to your father."

"You already have. There must be things the Captains need to discuss. Take Captain Kaya back to the camp and get him on course with the new plans. He has been focused on the needs of the *Eagle*. It will take him a while to get familiar with the complexities of his new situation."

"There is no hurry."

"Yes, there is. We have spent too much of the summer in unproductive warfare. We need to start our new life. Now."

"Sarasha the Prescient speaks, and we mortals must obey."

She glanced at him, but any smile that hovered on his lips was gone. "Then do so."

He nodded and spun on his heel. Soon, the Captains were filing back to the *Eagle* camp, and gradually the others followed.

When there was only a handful left, Sarasha regarded them. Her special group was there: Pers, Yong, Tonu, and Cheynou. She had caught Yong's signal, sending the rest back to camp. She warmed at the thought of their support. Then she caught Pers' face, and the emptiness returned.

Farther back, Byaren and Kendra stood, unsure of their place or their next move. They had hesitantly asked permission to attend the funeral as representatives of the Farmers.

Commander Haskel had no such reservations. He stood at ease with his honour guard: five of his best men, all practiced in the art of farewell.

With a sweep of her arm, Sarasha gathered them together. "My mother and I will stay until the last ember falls. We are warmed by your support, but you need not stay."

Haskel nodded. "It is appropriate. My men and I will withdraw a distance and allow you space."

"That isn't what I meant..."

"Nonetheless. We would not leave the family of so great a man defenseless at such a time."

"What do you mean? The fighting is over. The Priest-Admiral and his Ships are gone."

Haskel smiled faintly. "First rule in Haskel's Mercenary Handbook. 'It is a convenient enemy who shows up when you expect him.' We will stay."

"It's highly unlikely..."

He shook his head. "There are other enemies. Loneliness, desolation, grief."

She restrained herself from throwing her arms around the old soldier and sobbing on his breast.

He seemed to understand, for he reached out and laid a gentle hand on her shoulder. "Sometimes, all our friends can do is be near. It is up to us to reach out to them if there be need."

She glanced back. Yong and Tonu were standing close behind her, one to either side. Pers stepped into the small circle. "We have fought a terrible enemy and defeated him at great cost to ourselves, our Crews and our Families. The unity that brought us through that battle must continue to sustain us now."

"The war is yet to be won."

Sarasha turned in surprise; the voice was Cheynou Chan's. He reddened, then raised his chin. "With the Captain gone, we must band together even stronger."

"But my father was the kingpin of our unity. He was the leader, the one who brought us together, who gave the orders, made the plans."

"That's not true, Sarasha."

She turned at her mother's quiet voice. "What do you mean?"

"I mean that he was not the leader. He was the front, the Raider Warlord, but that was only for the benefit of the others."

"Then who...?" She stared at them. "What...?"

Yong stepped forward, placing both hands on her shoulders. "Sarasha, back there in camp, the other Captains are performing the ritual of the passing of authority. The old authority, recognized in our former lives."

"Yes."

"Who told them to?"

She felt her brow furrow.

"You did." That fierce affirmation came from Tonu, crowding her elbow.

"I did?"

"Yes, Sarasha. The Captains' Conclaves have changed. I have attended, and I have seen it. They have their discussions, they make their plans, and then they wait to see what you say. The real passing of authority must happen now, here."

"What authority?"

Pers moved closer to her as well. "The real authority, which will drive our people forward from this point. We have all seen it, Sarasha. You and your father were a formidable force. You made the plans, and he made the connection with the other Crews. We supported you, kept you supplied with the best information, the best ideas we could come up with.

"Now that he is gone, our task is more difficult, but not impossible. You are still the Captain's Scribe. Dwayo Kaya will depend on you more than your father ever did."

"But that's not right."

"No, it isn't, but I'm sure you will push him out of the nest quickly."

There were smiles at this comparison.

Her mother's arm was around her waist. "The transfer of authority must happen here, Sarasha, in the time and place of your father's Passing. All here recognize your position. Important representatives of our allies are here as well."

Eyes turned to the three outsiders. Haskel nodded. "I understand."

Byaren opened his mouth but closed it again as Kendra squeezed his arm. "I hope you're not expecting us to swing any influence in the halls of power over there." She tossed her head to the west. "Neither of us exactly represents the attitudes of the local community."

Sarasha found herself smiling. "All the more reason for you to treat with us. You have a much better chance of figuring out what is going on in our heads!"

Byaren laughed outright, caught himself, reddened, spoke anyway. "Some chance!"

324

"You are both a whole lot more like us than you might like to think."

Kendra smiled. "Thank you."

"I'm glad you see it as a compliment."

Sarasha turned to the others. "All right. Now is not the time to equivocate. I will accept the responsibility you have placed on me, at least temporarily. You all know my reluctance to assume any authority, but circumstances force me in that direction. In this place, at the time of my father's Passing, I accept. I will do my best to provide whatever leadership I can. I expect all of you to continue to support me with your ideas and your strength. Yes, I also understand the need for your emotional support.

"And this is a warning; you must watch me carefully. None of you quite realize how my father and I interacted. Yes, I was the creative one, but sometimes my plans were far from possible. It was my father who had the knowledge and the experience to turn my ideas into practical plans. Without him, I am likely to make mistakes. He could always pick up my errors. He was so thoughtful, so practical, and..." The tears ran down her face, and she knew if she said any more she would burst into uncontrollable sobs.

Her mother pulled her in closer, and her friends tightened their circle. She could feel their hands on her, caressing, patting, awkwardly, gently. Finally, she could straighten her shoulders. Her head came up, and they fell back, regarding her, waiting.

She mopped her cheeks with her sleeves: right, then left. "Some leader. All right. I have requests. My mother and I have decided to stay here. Some of you may stay, as you choose. However, the Captains need a Scribe, and Leide is not there. Tonu, will you assure that someone is recording Captain Kaya's Investiture? There must be several Scribes around here somewhere."

The girl sprinted away, and she turned her attention to the others. "CheyChan, we need the Helmsmen to chart our course out into the plains. Talk to your father. Tell him what we need. Unofficially, of course."

When the lad had gone, she gazed at the three friends left, the three strangers who remained. "The rest of us need not stand in silence. Let us talk of my father and celebrate the accomplishments of his life."

They all sat in a line, Sarasha and her mother in the middle, the Farmers on their left, the *Eagles* on their right. The mercenaries stood easy in the timeless patience of soldiers the world over. They well understood the necessity of time spent in grieving, in the sacrifice of comfort as the symbol of a loss.

As the sun set and the logs burned down to ashes, they talked. Since the strangers had not known Arlijn, there was much explanation required, and many stories to support the points made, interspersed with both laughter and tears.

CheyChan returned with his mission completed. He carried a skin of wine, which they passed around as they spoke.

And so Captain Arlijn Tourn made his Passing, mourned by Family and Crew, by good friends and former enemies. If his soul, somewhere in its onward journey, paused to peer back at the small group on the hillside, he would surely profess himself satisfied at such a closing.

34. ROUNDUP

Sarasha wiped a filthy sleeve across her sweating brow and looked down at the herd with satisfaction and a wry grin. This was certainly not the usual departing procedure for a Ship of the Fleet: the anchor weighs, the sails unfurl and she swoops away on wind and wave.

This is much messier.

The last wagons, those with the heavy loads, would not even leave camp for two days. The herd itself would take half the day to get out on the trail. She laughed to herself as she imagined the first of the leggy cattle pulling into the evening campsite just as the herd of pigs were finally driven, squealing their protests, from the old camp.

They had been warned about pigs, but the Galley Chief had insisted, more out of habit than anything else, she thought. If these specific animals made it to the salt barrel for winter, she would be quite surprised.

Pers galloped up, Patches lathered and dusty. "How are we doing?"

"About as well as a bunch of amateurs could expect. Where's Solen?"

"Out leading where he should be. Lucky dog."

"At least the wind's from the east."

"I wouldn't want to be the ones riding astern if it was in our faces."

"It's called 'riding drag,' or something like that."

"Probably. You'd be dragging your butt by the end of the day, that's for sure."

"How long will Solen stay with us?"

He grinned. "A long time."

"I can't figure it. A loner like him?"

Pers shook his head. "He's not a loner, just different from the Farmers. He goes his own way, and that doesn't sit well with them. So he went."

"I see. With us, everything's different, so he can be as different as he likes."

"He wouldn't have done too well in the Fleet."

"Neither did we." She shook her head wryly. "Misfits, the lot of us."

"Not misfits. We fit someplace different."

She gazed out to the Prairie to the north. "Do you think our place is out there?"

"It is now."

"It has to be."

Pers rose in his stirrups, peering back towards camp. "You've got a visitor."

She craned around but could only distinguish dim figures moving through the fine dust. "How can you tell?"

"There aren't too many horses like that one."

Trust Pers to recognize an individual horse. "Oh. I see her now." The tall horse stood out from the rest of the hazy movement. Pers waved his hat and whistled. Kendra spotted him and lifted her gelding to a graceful lope. The two waited for her, taking pleasure in watching the animal move.

In no time at all, the Farmer girl pulled up beside them. She wore her usual divided skirt and a blue silk blouse, her hair loosely held at the back of her head. She replaced her hat, which had swung behind her during the gallop. "How's it going?"

Sarasha swept her hand across the scene. "You can tell better than I can."

Her friend stared out across the combined herds. "Chaos?"

"Hard to tell with all that dust."

"They're moving. Once the cattle are gone, the dust will thin out. The other stock moves more slowly, grazing as they go, so they don't raise half so much."

"I gather that's the idea."

Kendra laughed. "Don't sound so discouraged. This will all become second nature to you in a while."

"I'm looking forward to that."

328

Pers lifted his reins. Patches danced a step or two, instantly ready for action. "I just remembered. I'm supposed to help load the pack horses."

With a nod to the two girls, he was off down the slope to the camp.

"A rather sudden departure."

Sarasha grinned. "His mind works like that."

"He is a rather good-looking lad, isn't he?"

"Huh! Don't even consider it. Only Leide was smart enough to keep up with him."

"What about you? Are you smart enough?"

"Perhaps, but Leide was always the one for him. Besides, I'm not in the market."

"Hah! Every girl our age is in the market."

"Every normal girl."

"Every normal girl? What's wrong with you?"

"What's wrong with me?"

"Your foot? What's that got to do with anything? It's not the part of your anatomy you need, from what I've been told." The other girl grinned down from her tall horse.

Sarasha refused to join in the joke. "That's one part of our lives you don't understand. We don't have the freedom to do what we want to."

"I thought you had all the freedom anybody could want. That's why I'm here."

Sarasha glanced slyly at her friend. "Then why are you here? The *Petrels* are two camps east."

"He doesn't need a distraction right now, so I thought I'd come and bother you. I'll probably drop into his camp tonight when it's too late to turn me away.

"But you're changing the subject. Why wouldn't you get married like anybody else?"

Sarasha shook her head. "I try to explain it, and everybody just nods and treats me like it was my head that was injured, not my foot."

"Try me."

"No, you take it from me. I won't become a burden on my Crew, and that goes twice for a man, especially one I like."

Kendra shook her head. "Stubbornness is both an asset and a detriment to one's character."

"Did your old uncle used to say that?"

"I didn't have an old uncle. I read it in a book."

"So it must be true."

"Which gets you off the topic again."

"Did you just come over here to annoy me?"

Kendra gazed down on her friend again. "If you're getting testy, don't bother. I won't put up with it."

Sarasha considered bristling, then decided not to. It was true. If Kendra didn't like the way the conversation was going, she would just turn her horse around, set heels to him and be gone.

"Then don't pester me about things I can't change. It's not as if I like it."

"Don't you?"

"What does that mean?"

"You can figure it out."

Her father's familiar sentence was what did it. She slapped the ends of the reins against Ebb Tide's shoulder and sent the surprised pony skittering down the hill. She ignored Kendra's surprised shout, losing it in the pounding of her pony's hooves.

Angling away from the herd, she plunged across the Prairie, heedless of gopher holes, snakes and other dangers. As she rode, her mind roiled. Try as she might, she couldn't throw off the darkness that had crept in. The loss of her Ship, so many of her friends, and finally Father and Leide. The responsibility that was continually being forced upon her. The worry of the life ahead of her that stretched, like the Prairie, on and on, frightening and empty, to the hazy horizon. She kicked the horse's side, and they ran on and on to a hazy nowhere.

Finally, Ebb Tide's laboured breathing brought her to her senses, and she leaned back, allowing the little horse to slow to a walk. Sarasha eyed the pony critically. She was sweated up, but she had looked worse in the past and shown no ill effects.

They continued to tramp across the drying grass, a gentle breeze cooling their sweat. Finally, Sarasha tugged gently on the reins, and the horse stopped. They stayed there a moment, gazing outward, then turned back to the dust cloud that signalled the life of the Crew. Off to the east she could see another cloud rising as the *Night Hawks* started their own drive northward. A bend in the dropoff obscured the view to the west, but the great migration was starting out from six other camps as well.

Cutting off to the side, she rode back to the dropoff and dismounted at a point where she could see the camp and the herds winding away. She noted the roan down in the pasture, so Kendra had decided to stay. Another apology due. Lately, it seemed she was always apologizing for something. Before, in the old days, she had never apologized. A little thought wiggled up through her consciousness, telling her that there could be two reasons for that.

Without her father there to temper her impulses, she would have to be doubly careful. What if she made a decision that killed someone? Worse still, what if she led her people into a huge disaster? She shifted her foot, but the deep, throbbing ache did not abate. *It has been long enough now. Healing should be complete. What you have is what you've got, girl. Deal with it if you can.*

She studied the herd, moving along now. The *Eagle* was mobile again. She and her father had pulled them through. That task was finished. *They don't need me anymore, but they haven't realized it yet.*

What worried her was that they didn't seem to want to be free. *They want to make me their leader. I can already see it happening. They are so used to having someone make up their minds for them. As long as there is someone there, they can't free themselves.*

They would be better off making their own decisions. The loss of her father was a blessing in one respect, forcing the Crew and Families to take responsibility for themselves. *I can only take them backwards.*

Sarasha turned to the edge of the escarpment, gazing out over the broken country they had covered so laboriously. Back there was the Great Southern Ocean, rough and dangerous, but all the life she had ever known. A cold emptiness nudged the small of her back: the breath of the wide, barren Prairie, where the wind was never still. She stared down, first at her foot, then over the edge of the cliff in front of her. The bottom was far enough and rocky enough...

Too easy. Too wasteful.

She turned and stared northward, across the wide plains that would become her home. *The Prairie isn't so different from the Ocean. It nurtures and supports you, but one small slip and it kills you. Your greatest friend: your deadliest enemy.* Without a backward glance, she lurched to her horse, mounted smoothly, and rode away to the north.

THE END

About the Author

Brought up in a logging camp with no electricity, Gordon Long learned his storytelling in the traditional way: at his father's knee. He now spends his time editing, publishing, travelling, blogging and writing fantasy and social commentary, although sometimes the boundaries blur.

Gordon lives in Tsawwassen, British Columbia, with his wife, Linda, and their Nova Scotia Duck Tolling Retriever, Josh. When he is not writing and publishing, he works on projects with the Surrey Seniors' Planning Table, and is a staff writer for <indiesunlimited.com>

More from Gordon A Long

Other Titles Available at Smashwords, Amazon and
other outlets

"Zoysana's Choice" Petrellan Saga Book 4
"The Innkeeper's Husband" Petrellan Saga Book 5

"Out of Mischief" World of Change Book 1
"Into Trouble" World of Change Book 2
"Mountains of Mischief" World of Change Book 3
"The Trouble with Tents" World of Change Book 4
"Queen of Mischief" World of Change Book 5

"A Sword Called...Kitten?" Cat with Many Claws Book 1
"The Cat with Many Claws" Book 2
"Cloud Cat" A Cat with Many Claws Tale
"Sword Called Kitten: The Early Years" Short Stories

"Storm over Savournon"
A novel of the French Revolution

"Why Are People So Stupid?" Social Humour with a Point

Look for Gordon's books, selected reviews, poetry and
short stories at <airbornpress.ca>

Gordon's opinions on humanity are at the
"Are People Really That Stupid?" blog

Find his weekly reviews and his ideas on writing at
"Renaissance Writer"

www.ingramcontent.com/pod-product-compliance
Lightning Source LLC
Chambersburg PA
CBHW070534260626
47161CB00002B/386